To Dorothy
with love from Denis
Happy Birthday 2015

The Curse Of Kings

GW00721972

Volun
'The King's Chalice'

Janet K L Seal

Janet K L Seal

www.BretwaldaBooks.com
@Bretwaldabooks
bretwaldabooks.blogspot.co.uk/
Bretwalda Books on Facebook

While most of the events and characters are based on historical incidents and figures, this novel is entirely a work of fiction.

Front cover phot: Krzysztof Mizera
Back cover photo: Jean-Pol GRANDMONT

First Published 2014
Text Copyright © Janet K L Seal 2014
Janet K L Seal asserts her moral rights to be regarded as the author of this book.
All rights reserved. No reproduction of any part of this publication is permitted without the prior written permission of the publisher:
Bretwalda Books
Unit 8, Fir Tree Close, Epsom,
Surrey KT17 3LD
info@BretwaldaBooks.com
www.BretwaldaBooks.com
ISBN 978-1-909698-19-2

Printed and bound in Great Britain
Marston Book Services Ltd, Oxfordshire

DEDICATION
FOR
THE CURSE OF KINGS

For Shirley
Time and time again I have been glad to have a friend like you
– a diamond, a treasure, a friend beyond compare.

Town of Saxon Wymburne

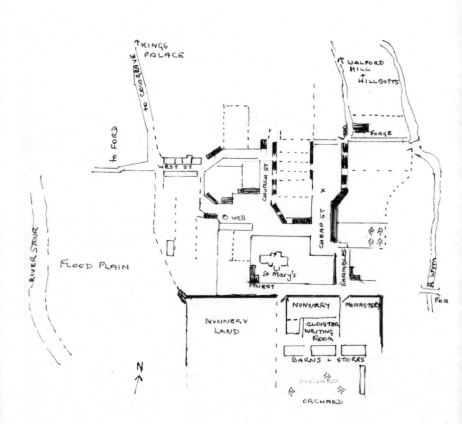

Family Tree

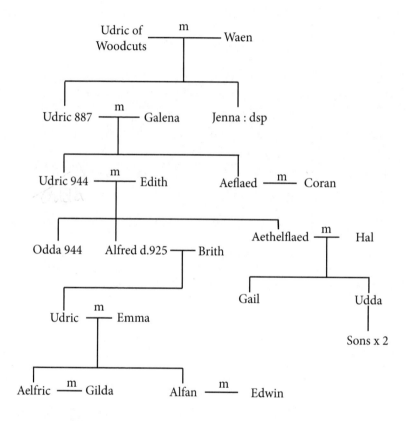

GLOSSARY

caul	birth membrane of lambs
Fyrd	army - 40 days fighting, garrison duty or road repairs
burghs	towns, often with markets.
vill	hamlet
Heliers	roofers
Coffer	Chest, often lockable
Moot	meeting of manor, hundred or shire
nithing	worthless scum
heriot	tax on a death
Reeve	Elected by tenants working under steward
Witan	Council
Wolfshead	homeless outlaw
Haulms	pea plants after harvest
Thegn	knight
Frankpledge	12 men responsible for and to each other
Welhal/welhail	old saxon greeting
Ealdorman	Earl of a shire, often the sheriff
Staller	Man in charge of horses and their stabling when travelling
Sumpter pony	Often native breed loaded with paniers etc
Ersling	Lowest of the low, a disparaging description of someone
Heriot	death tax
Geld	tax money
Pallium	Archbishop's cloak
Villein	farmer of small plot
Martlets	heraldic birds
Lymer dog	Large hairy hunting hound
byre	cow house
posse	Band of men led by sheriff or guard looking for wrong-doer
paillasse	straw stuffed mattress
Cresset light	consisting of a bowl of oil/fat with a wick
cniht	Senior thegn status, a knight
vassals	tenants or bondsmen owing loyalty to a lord
byrnie	chain mail jacket laced - easy to adjust
Seax	Bent-bladed traditional Saxon sword
manchet	flat, hard brown bread
Tithing group	Ten men who were responsible to and for each other and providing produce to church

CONTENTS

Prologue
The Curse of Kings

A small estate was given to Udric's father in AD905 after he had saved the life of the prince, his rise from slavery and living on the land illegally since the death of King Alfred being ignored. Patronage brought its own rewards but also fostered bitter hatred, to the extent of being blamed for murder.

Seemingly unchanged by royal friendships, the family retain their own values and remain loyal, breeding and caring for horses. Udric survives a knife wound and marries well, further ammunition for his enemies.

Heirs squabble, legitimacy being all important whether for the throne or lands, lifetimes being cut short by inherited illness, accident or murder.

A freed Welsh slave becomes steward of the estate, his family directly affected by the fortunes of his lord.

The monastery and king's palace close to the town ensure its prosperity but jealousy can breed baser qualities. Rents have to be paid, mostly in goods. Men are obliged to serve in the King's army, all reasons for unrest.

Service to the King comes in many forms and Udric has to settle a dispute which brings back memories of the founding of his estate many years ago.

When his father and elder brother are both killed in battle, Udric's youngest son Alfred is suddenly a ward of the Bishop and is thrust into the violence of court, the influence of Abbot Dunstan and the increase in crime. Young King Edwy favours the boy and gives him a position under the county sheriff.

In the town accusations of murder must be heard before the body can be buried and disputes must be settled by time honoured, barbaric methods.

Chapter One
AD958

The Trial by Ordeal attracted a crowd. No-one had never witnessed such an event and they were anxious to watch and share the appalling novelty. Since the smith's son had lit the fire in the Church of St. Mary in Wymburne word had quickly spread. The acidic smell of fear spread around the white faced men who watched in horrified fascination. The glowing brazier was dull in comparison to the shimmering bright redness of the iron bar held by the smith in the jaws of his pincers. The three marked out paces which would have to be walked by the accused stood out clearly, the lines like scars in the packed earth.

Nothing in the old King's laws set out a monetary fine for damage to one's honour; they only applied to hurt to the body. Alfred, a man known for fairness from a small estate outside the town, was deputizing for the Sheriff, but neither he nor the Wymburne Town Reeve had been able to dissuade the town sawyer from issuing his challenge. He was certain the carter owed him twelve shillings.

The carter's bare hand was shaking as he reached out for the iron which would burn the flesh and sinew of his hand and perhaps destroy its use for ever. Sweat ran down his face in oily rivulets, his eyes bulged in terror. The onlookers held their breath, anticipation mixed with abhorrence at the barbaric, but time enshrined method of establishing the truth.

The reeve's lips were parted in salacious expectation of another's torture.

Alfred felt his gorge rise and feared he would be sick. He held the bandages, strips of linen which would wrap the carter's hand for three days. At the end of that time, the wound would be examined. If it was healing the carter's honesty would be proven beyond doubt.

'God Almighty let this be over soon', he prayed silently lowering his eyelids to avoid witnessing a man's agony.

"No, stop! I never meant it to get this far." The sawyer's reedy voice was rising with panic, his words strident but broken and ending in a whimper.

The smith dropped the iron bar into a leather bucket of water. Steam rose and bubbles spat as the metal cooled. The collective breath, released in a sudden rush of air caused the candles to waver. Shadows leapt and writhed on the painted walls; the pigeons roosting above lifted as one and flew to another rafter.

The carter's knees buckled slowly. His body folded onto itself, his head resting on the floor by the marked earth. One grey feather floated gently down in the silence.

"Everyone should go home," ordered the Town Reeve whose complexion was only just returning to its normal ruddiness. There was a smell of sweat, ripe and sour as men turned away from the brazier that had warmed their faces but not their hearts.

"Thank you Master Smith. It is to be hoped that such a thing can be avoided in the future. No doubt you will collect your equipment in the morning. I bid you a good night!" Alfred found he was enunciating every word with care as if he had drunk too much ale. His mouth was parched and the sweat drying tightly on his neck.

Outside dusk was falling, pink and purple streaks alternating with the grey clouds. There was a low buzz of conversation as men returned to their homes, sandals slapping on the earth growing fainter as they drew away from the church.

Crossing the stones placed at the ford, Alfred ignored the rows of distorted vines as he strode up towards the heath on Colhill and almost ran down the other side as darkness descended. He knew every tussock of grass, every tree and bush between Wymburne and Uddings. Singing lustily, his shoulders and neck gradually relaxed; the night air, cool and clean filled his lungs as bawdy words rang out in the dim light.

An owl shrieked in the distance and small rodents scuttled for cover as his leather boots trampled grass and leaf-mould. He was unaware of other eyes which watched his progress, watchers who debated his worth, his vulnerability and the risk involved in attacking an armed man in the prime of his life.

Several times over the next few months Alfred made regular visits to see the steward of the King's palace whose pride was slightly hurt when the Sheriff's recent visit to Wymburne to hold an inquest had been reported to him. In early spring sunshine when budding leaves and singing birds herald the promise of summer warmth, Alfred shared a jug of ale in the tiny room allocated as the steward's office.

"You were not called because you were neither witness nor juror. Being a separate jurisdiction to the town they guard their independence fiercely. The widow thought her husband may have been murdered which turned out not to be the case. Lord Alward had the bible from the nunnery brought out for the men to swear their oaths."

"Yes I heard about the Abbess guarding her precious book. Quite a formidable woman by the sounds of things!"

"God's Blood, I would not cross her in a million years! Anyway the town will gossip about that rather than moan about the taxes King Edwy has imposed. He may not attend to all the charters and grants the Council put in front of him but he knows when his coffers are empty! I have been to the Tarrants on behalf of the Sheriff. Even in the smallest hamlet the men are grumbling that the tax is too heavy. A man collecting the King's dues would need a whole garrison of men to guard him.

I suppose you also heard about the ordeal. That it did not actually take place was only because the accuser admitted he was mistaken but not before the smith had the iron in his pincers. There were many who were relieved to return to their homes without witnessing ….."

"Excuse me master," a blond head peered into the small chamber followed by a stocky frame with wide, powerful shoulders. The steward introduced the visitor to Alfred. "This is Hal; he comes from the outlying area and works here because he wants to see how we improve the lighter soil."

"Yes Lord, I want to improve the chalky earth of my father's rented farm. Here at Kingston where there is similar land, it has already been ploughed successfully to produce good crops. Everyone has sheep in our village but few crops are grown so we have to buy expensive cereals, even for bread."

Moving the conversation to more general matters the young man admitted to Alfred that he had already seen and admired Aethelflaed at Wymburne but had made no approach to her. He had an open face with bright blue eyes, sometimes hidden by his long blond hair. His manners were easy, respectful of his elders but not so subservient as to appear obsequious. The fact that the young freeman had submitted himself to a term of bonded employment in order to learn impressed Alfred enormously. As soon as he had gone the steward once again brought up the contentious subject of the broken palings on the boundary between Uddings and the King's hunting forest of Wymborneholt. Alfred denied that any of his cottars had broken through, laughingly adding that there was plenty of wood on his own estate and no-one would have the need to steal from hunting land. Both were thoughtful as he left, the steward anxious to get to the bottom of the mystery and Alfred to question those who lived closest to the affected fence and might have heard something.

He made discreet enquiries as to the lineage of the young man and found that he was partly of Danish birth, his father being the new tenant of Woodcutts Farm beyond Cranburne, under the church to whom it now belonged.

Memories of the stories he had heard of this farm flooded back, confused with the tales of grandfather Udda's narrow escapes.

The chance to find out more arose some weeks later when Lord Alward asked him to mediate in a dispute over spoiled water at Sexpenna. Alfred rode slowly with a clerk towards the village aware of the number of lambs gambolling in the charge of shepherds. A dragonfly with iridescent wings buzzed passed looking for still water. He noticed landmarks which his grandfather had described so long ago. Having been used to riding since he was young, he smiled as he remembered Udda describing the discomfort of being mounted for the first time on Prince Aethelwold's baggage horse on the way to Wymburne, and how the leg shackle had caused the scar which had been visible until his death.

The village of Sexpenna was still a small group of sod walled huts thatched with grass, heather and mud, while the church was bigger than expected, having two small un-glazed windows. Outside, just as described by Udda, was the whipping post where his great grandfather Udric, had stood. It seemed that nothing had changed since Udda had watched the trial of his father in front of Carwulf, the Sheriff of Dorset at that time.

"Good day," the priest greeted him, interrupting Alfred's thoughts. "You must be the King's man?"

Alfred admitted that he was here on behalf of the Sheriff to settle a dispute between two parishioners. "Perhaps you could tell me a bit about the village."

Despite a slight breeze blowing up the hill the two men sat on benches outside the priest's house next door to the church. The clerk busied himself sharpening quills and stirring the ink in a small glass pot. Mugs of poor quality ale were brought out by a raggedly dressed woman who left without saying a word, her misery expressed in stooped shoulders and a downcast expression. The nearby midden steamed unpleasantly in the weak sunshine, flies swarming around the cottage from which a sour smell issued. Inching a little further from the shabby priest with his soiled gown, Alfred's first taste of the beer caused him to shudder. It was sour, with a muddy appearance, very different from the mellow brew made on his own estate. The cleric appeared not to notice, slurping from his mug greedily.

At first the priest was eager to hear the most recent rumour that the Lady Elgifu, having apparently been rescued from bondage in Ireland, had sadly died despite being nursed by monks in Gloucester. She had been King Edwy's wife although many thought her a promiscuous slut.

This apart, the tales of her persecution by the church and subsequent branding as a whore had given rise to a wave of sympathy.

As dusk fell, Alfred reminded the priest of the reason for his visit to the chalk downland area of the two settlements. The sun tinged the edges of the clouds with pink, a promise of fair weather the following day. It cast shadows but also highlighted the dandruff on the cleric's shoulders.

"It is like this sir," began the priest realising that he would get no further news from Alfred. "Richard, son of Guthrum, God rest his tortured soul, soaked hides in the small stream which appears in winter at the edge of his field. He dug a pit which he lined with clay, and filled it with the stream's water. The pit flooded the field of the neighbouring farm, spoiling the land around it. The neighbour's well water is also sour, hardly fit for animals to drink."

"This Guthrum you mention, he died recently?"

"Oh no, he took his own life some time ago." The priest crossed himself quickly before adding, "Some say he could not live with his conscience after his neighbours were accused of murder and were evicted from their farm. It all happened long before my time here, but 'tis the same farm whose water has been spoiled," he added, chewing at a snag on his nail.

"Then Richard is the son, and he still lives next to Woodcutts Farm?"

"Yes, he lives on his own; a most unpopular man, keeps himself to himself. He has no wife or children to help. Of course he is very old now and bad tempered most of the time."

Alfred was thoughtful and made no reply. Richard the son of Guthrum would be older than his grandfather who had died recently. "Who had Woodcutts Farm then, after it was ..," he paused, not wanting the priest to know how much he already knew, "after it was left empty?" he added lamely.

Wiping his mouth on his sleeve, the priest launched into yet another episode of village life which had been related to him by the previous occupant of the church.

"Apparently a distant relative of the people of the farm, one Garth, a younger son of a younger son, got the farm from the King, Eadred I think it was. He came just after Bata the priest here had died quite suddenly. No-one knew the man well. He always dressed in dark, almost black, homespun clothes. He was not endowed with much physical strength and had an ugly face too, his nose being crooked, broken I suppose. Anyway, he had no son but worked hard and bartered for labour and harvest help. It was too much for one man after he injured himself. The wound went bad and he died in great pain."

'The dark man,' thought Alfred, 'the man who tried to kill grandfather'. For a brief moment he considered taking revenge for the evil events of the past but dismissed it somewhat reluctantly as an unworthy thought. The priest continued his tale totally unaware of his listener's personal interest in the matter.

"The farm was empty again so it was given to the church of Wilton, the see of Salisbury you know, which owns much land round here. After all it is close to the county border and God's Kingdom knows no boundaries!" The priest chuckled at his own joke and Alfred smiled politely, seeming to appreciate the churchman's sense of humour.

King Eadred, the ruler of Wessex until three years ago, had been known to give many favours to the church but Alfred had not been aware that the family's old farm had been in the charge of his own sponsor, Wulfric, Bishop of Salisbury. There had been no reason for the matter to be discussed. There is no way that the church would relinquish land so recently acquired, particularly as senior clerics were outraged that Abbot Dunstan had been banished. He knew that many other priests had been removed from their churches to be replaced with men of the King's choice, further adding to his unpopularity.

After a restless night, sharing a pallet with the clerk who snored continuously, and during which he was bitten by numerous insects, Alfred attended the court and listened to the arguments put forward by Richard the tanner, and Vann of Woodcutts.

Richard was indeed an old, disagreeable man, shabbily dressed in clothes which showed many signs of wear and dirt. There was ingrained dirt in every bit of flesh which was exposed; his scrawny neck and loose jowls resembled the folds of an aged game cock. Thin red lines were scattered on his nose and cheeks, his eyes rheumy and embittered. It became obvious that his farm had not prospered for years, and that he had turned to tanning hides as an alternative way of making a living.

"I am forced to work for the demesne farm of the church for two days a week, and three days at harvest time instead of paying rent in money which leaves little time to farm my own land," he grumbled, obviously hating the attention of the men attending the moot.

"Many years failure of my crops has left me ill and penniless. I was literally at my wits end as to how to feed myself, let alone the four remaining farm animals which have had to fend for themselves. Indeed I have been scolded many times for letting them stray. The poisoning of Woodcutts Farm water was not intended." By now the man was looking extremely uncomfortable, frail and feeble. He was blinking rapidly in the bright daylight, wiping his forehead with his dirty sleeve.

Alfred took a moment to consider all the facts which he had garnered. The accused had not tried to defend himself with paltry excuses and seemed resigned to whatever punishment was meted out to him. Trying desperately not to scratch one of the bites on the soft skin of his inner thigh, he cleared his throat before announcing his decision.

"I find in favour of Vann of Woodcutts. I order the accused to stop tanning hides in the stream between the two properties because of the bad effects of rotting tissue," announced Alfred. " However, having made enquiries as to the exact situation of Richard's farm from the jurymen, I recommend that a suitable pit be dug on the far side of his land, on a slope which could catch rainwater but below which there is nothing which would be affected by leakage of tanning liquid. It should be done so that the smell is not offensive to others. Until Richard worked the hides there was no tanner in the village. All hides were carted to Hamtun then after treatment they were brought all the way back for working. It will be useful to have your own tanner in the village, but the water supply must be kept clean for the animals and fields.

The Woodcutts well must be drained with your assistance and left to refill with clean water through the chalk rock. In the meantime Richard must arrange to supply water to Vann to supplement his other well. Fortunately winter is coming and the rains will clean the land and the stream. How say you Vann? Will you be satisfied with this?"

There was silence as he finished speaking. If they had expected immediate dramatic punishment of the guilty man they were disappointed. Alfred had come to the conclusion that a fine was not practical if a man had no money. That Richard had no surplus crop or animals to pay with instead of coins had also become obvious. No doubt he would be forced to part with one of the beasts to pay the increased tax which King Edwy had announced. Assisting with the drainage of Vann's well would take time and effort but hopefully by Christmas the water would be clean again.

Vann stood uncertainly with his eldest son, talking in low tones. Both were fair-haired, stocky and strongly muscled. Judgement had been in his favour but he was unused to justice being meted out in the form of labour by the offender.

"The ox needs two buckets of water a day. I have fenced off the stream so that he cannot drink the foul water. If Richard keeps him watered until my old well is clean then I shall be satisfied." Vann folded his arms and turned to his neighbour.

Alfred turned towards Richard to obtain his submission to the judgement. Looking considerably relieved, the old man bowed his head, acknowledging the court's decision.

Some of the men were talking quietly amongst themselves while the clerk carefully cleaned his pens. Some were surprised by such an eminently sensible judgement which, while condemning Richard, son of Guthrum, for spoiling valuable water, also gave him the opportunity to make amends without undue hardship. More unusually for a man sent by the Sheriff, Alfred had suggested a way in which the offender could contribute to the future needs of the village. They nodded approval, stared at him as if seeking to know what manner of man he was before leaving thoughtfully for their homes.

Accepting a much better brew of ale from the farmer's wife, Alfred could not resist looking around him. He imagined his own grandfather bringing beasts back to the stalls and working on the gently undulating fields which surrounded the small homestead. He admired the neatness of the yard and the good condition of the ox which munched contentedly on a tether. Several sheep grazed in the distance.

"You have kept the farm well, but I am surprised that you can spare a son to work elsewhere."

If Vann was surprised that Alfred already knew of his family then he gave no sign. He smiled proudly showing gaps in his front teeth and put his arm around the shoulder of his well built eldest son drawing him forward.

"Dicon here does the work of two men my lord. He ploughs all day and still has the strength to cut turf or repair the hurdles to keep the sheep safe. Hal on the other hand dreams of growing better crops on this stony ground of ours. At the moment we grow enough only for our own needs. We trade sheep for next year's seed, and hurdles of course, as there are no trees here for firewood or fencing." He waved his arm to emphasise the absence of all but a few stunted thorn bushes.

Alfred nodded, understanding the need to barter for even the most basic necessities. "I have met Hal in Wymburne. He learns good husbandry from the King's own reeve. I see you fold your sheep on the cornfield here, not on the common land. We too dung our own fields before the ploughing begins. Their dung seems to add heart to the earth."

Vann hesitantly brought up the subject of the judgement which Alfred had made at the court hearing admitting that it had been a novel solution. "It is only a small farm, only a living for one family. Dicon will inherit this farm being the eldest. Hal would have ended up working on church lands so he chose to find another lord."

"I can always use a strong young man on my estate," offered Alfred. "We have many trees and heavier soil in most parts, with some clay, but there is plenty of heathland which would suit sheep well. At the present time we only have sufficient goats and sheep for our own needs, pasture for the horses. Much of the land grows corn for the mill."

"I am glad of your offer," Vann replied formally. "He must make his own way in the world. Already he talks of a young woman he wishes to take to wife but he needs to establish himself first. She lives on an estate with her widowed mother close to Wymburne, my lord."

"I was briefly at the King's court and left my widowed mother, Lady Edith and Aethelflaed at Uddings. From the description Hal gave me it would appear that he admires my sister! I called to see the steward of the King's palace and heard good reports of him." Laughing at the coincidence, Alfred's face reflected his pleasure in meeting Hal's family.

He left the farm after assuring Vann that he had no objection to his youngest son courting his sister. The two men parted firm friends, Alfred promising to speak to Hal about his offer when he saw him in church.

He rode back to his own lands the following day in a thoughtful mood. The clerk had gone ahead in order that he could enjoy a relaxed ride across the heathland of Holt on the way home. The deer ran for the cover of Cranburne forest as he approached while startled bustards flew noisily from the shelter of one small bush to the next clump of ground cover. The King's hunting parties had obviously not ridden across the area for some time and the land was well stocked with game.

After dining on mutton flavoured pottage with fruits soaked in honeyed water, Alfred told Aethelflaed that Hal had his permission to speak to her.

"He seems pleasant, respectful and determined. His father and brother now farm Woodcutts at Sexpenna as tenants of the church. There may be Danish blood in the family as every one of them is flaxen haired. I know how disappointed you were when your visit to Winchester was cancelled but this young man might take your fancy!"

She could barely contain her pleasure at the prospect of being courted, her eyes alive with excitement and happiness. Edith enjoyed watching her daughter blossom, but insisted that Aethelflaed still helped to run the household. For once there was no pouting or frowning with displeasure, her burgeoning joy influencing the way she carried out all but the most distasteful chores. Her constant questions about the young man eventually irritated Alfred, adding to the discomfort of some inflamed flea bites.

"Good Lord little one, he is only human not the arch-angel Gabriel! Wait until Sunday and contain yourself in patience. You are spinning round enough to make me giddy!" He smiled to take the sting out of his words, her dimpled smile quickly restored.

His sister's childish behaviour and the itching of his legs was temporarily forgotten when news from the King's court was relayed by a visiting preacher on his way from Hamtun. The florid faced priest was heading for Hortune where he was to find a suitable site for a religious house for the Benedictine monks. Explaining that he had come late to the priesthood, having been a mason, his prior had sent him to explore the area. Over a mug of ale and sweetmeats the priest lowered his voice conspiratorially.

"Lord Edwy's lifestyle has angered many senior churchmen to such an extent that they have persuaded Edgar of Mercia, the King's younger brother, to take control of all the northern and eastern territories! Only Wessex remains under King Edwy. Edgar has styled himself King of Mercia which has angered our lord King so much that he is ill again."

"From childhood Lord Edwy has suffered stomach aches. Since the death of his wife last year, the King can eat little solid food. Possibly it's similar to the disease his uncle, the late lord Eadred, was afflicted with and from what I heard, the curse of Kings before him. It does not surprise me that the business of the court has apparently been left in the hands of minor officials. Surely it is treasonous of his brother to assume Kingship of Mercia? He was appointed deputy, under Edwy, but not in his own right."

"Well, that is what is being talked about," stated the priest as if to justify his comments, scratching his tonsure thoughtfully. "While the King either enjoys a life of continuous pleasure, debauching and wenching which angers the churchmen, he is not even ruling Wessex properly. Last year he demanded heavy taxes but where has the money gone? Most of the ministers have already made their excuses and gone to join Lord Edgar. Now no decisions are being made, nothing is being done. It will be every man for himself shortly." He shrugged then stared into the depths of his mug debating whether to continue repeating the conversation of merchants which he had overheard.

"The eastern Danes already support the younger brother. What worries me is that they could call in their less civilised relatives from the northern lands at any time. Dunstan, our senior Abbot, has sent messages from exile in Flanders. He is calling for the Council to be convened as a matter of urgency," continued the priest over his hastily prepared meal. "We are all in God's hands if the King will not turn from his sinful ways."

Discussing the priest's news with his mother later in her private solar, a room full of memories, loving closeness and the bond between husband and wife in that most sacred of places, the marriage bed, Alfred confirmed that these were not the first rumours of dissension he had heard.

"I took my oath to King Edwy and will remain loyal to him until his death or mine," he stated forcefully. "Even though many will say it is not my place, I think he may have need of my services. Well, my company. We have shared a moment of crisis before and he trusted me then. I witnessed his humiliation at the hands of Dunstan and understand why he dislikes the man. If he is behind this rebellion, then my Lord is in some danger."

Promising to return soon for the feasting, Alfred took the bay stallion from the stable and rode to Winchester with the reports from his court hearings and the judgements firmly attached to his saddle beside his staff of office. A small amount of money raised by fines was secured inside his scrip. Throughout his visits to various towns and villages he had encountered many, high and low born who grumbled at the taxes. He silently thanked God once again that the collection of such dues was not his responsibility.

He saw two wild looking men on the road a little way ahead. While they did not act in a threatening way Alfred took the precaution of sliding his sword gently from its scabbard over his shoulder. The light reflected off the polished blade as he tightened the reins with his left hand. Immediately the stallion became more collected, shorter in its paces, snorting loudly, showing threatening, yellow teeth. The two men looked shame-faced as they stepped onto the grassy ridge beside the road to let him past. Once safely beyond their reach he shouted a greeting, careless as to whether they heard him or not. He did not care if they thought him an incompetent rider, the stallion had reacted in exactly the way he knew it would. He relaxed the pressure on the reins and patted its sleek neck before putting the sword away.

The diadem on his forehead gave him immediate entry through the tall gateway, past slackly lounging guards and through rubbish strewn, stinking streets. The whole atmosphere was one of indiscipline and sloppiness. No one appeared to be alert or conscious of the danger such laxity could bring. Hardly able to contain his anger as one guard indicated he could enter the inner gates by motioning him on with his thumb, Alfred led the stallion briskly to the stables.

Outside the King's private apartments several clerks waited for the opportunity to present pleas or other business. Some said they had waited for days, grumbling that nothing was being done to count the tallies or sign documents. The rushes had obviously not been renewed since his last visit. There was a distinct odour of vomit, of spilt ale and worse. The fires were smoking, little heat coming from the wood which smouldered instead of burning brightly. Curls of smoke hung in the stale atmosphere.

"Is anyone with the King?" he asked abruptly and when answered with an insolent shrug he could feel his irritation change subtly into anger, simmering annoyance barely covered by a veneer of civility.

Taking a deep breath, screwing up his courage, Alfred was aware of fixing a pleasant smile on his face as he strode briskly into the royal apartments, fully aware that his intrusion could bring royal wrath down on his own head. His brief friendship with King Edwy might count for nothing. As he entered everyone turned towards him, their faces showing a mixture of astonishment and haughty resentment.

"My Lord," he announced loudly looking directly at Edwy, "I bring you the judgements from the East Dorset lands which you sent me to supervise. May I advise you of the details?" He made no apology for interrupting a game of dice between the King and his lounging companions.

Initially the King's face showed anger but as Alfred started to spread out the documents he reluctantly dismissed the young men and got up from his bed. Calling for fresh ale he listened to the reports. Pausing only to be sure the server had gone, Aelfric took the opportunity to persuade the King to attend to other urgent matters which awaited his attention. "They say your brother is getting the upper hand. Many of his supporters were yours. Come to the hall now and show everyone that you are still their lord."

For a moment there was hesitation. Alfred feared he had gone too far, overstepped the boundary between friendship and natural concern. A subject does not order his King to attend to business, to do anything. He gulped nervously and tried to hide his nerves.

Alfred selected a fresh surcoat from the chest and helped the King to dress, combing the lank fair hair back from his face.

The royal diadem secure and a bracelet on his upper arm completed the transformation from dissolute young man to a royal King with something approaching dignity. Alfred noted the deep pain lines around his mouth and eyes. Briskly, to hide his concern, he drew back the curtain and announced that the King would attend to all pleas and duties in the great hall.

"No one has bullied me like this before," Edwy joked as the two men made their way past the guards and the poorly trimmed torches to the dais in the hall. "Stay with me while I see to their demands. My stomach rots within me so that I cannot think straight for the pain."

Leaving the King comfortably seated and the fire now ablaze, Alfred called a serving girl to fetch mulled wine and poppy juice for the King. 'Should his counsellors be called? It is not proper for me to advise or witness deeds.' Worries sped through Alfred's mind as he selected the driest logs for the fire. 'Where's his physician? Even the captain of the guards is not present. Oh Lord, as God is my witness, where are his counsellors?'

Word that the King was attending to business spread like wildfire. Within minutes the hall was crowded, men pressing forward, arguing, each claiming precedence. Alfred feared that the mass would overwhelm his lord in his fragile state of health. Ushers hastily arrived and helped to keep order, demanding less noise in the King's presence.

Reports of Edgar's successes in Mercia and of those thegns who now called him King were among the matters that needed his attention. A number asked for time to pay their taxes, a clerk noting the King's response to each of these. Edwy appeared to be unmoved, steadily attending to the business presented to him. After having dealt with the most urgent documents and some more minor pleas, everyone could see that the King was clearly exhausted.

Alfred picked up the reports, explaining that they needed further consideration and persuaded the King to withdraw and rest before the evening meal in the great hall. The poppy juice had dulled the pain, leaving drowsiness its only legacy as the King rose slowly, his hands gripping the arm rests for support.

"Come with me friend, I have need of a companion and a wise head. You have the reports of my brother's conduct?"

Alfred went willingly but was aware that many cast jealous glances in his direction and criticised his apparent pride as the King linked his own arm through his. He only caught a glimpse but was fairly certain that the young Earl of Chester was one of those whose black looks were full of hate and threatened retribution.

'Damn the man! Trust him to be among those hanging back to see which side to back. He hasn't got a trusty thought in his head and few will guard my back after this afternoon.'

As the King and Alfred made their way out of the hall past guards who now at least gave a semblance of alertness, he was aware that the King needed support. Already his lips were pressed together, his pale skin showing through the badly barbered beard as if he had over-imbibed of mead or other strong drink.

Alfred's reaction to the unfriendly looks and scornful comments was indignation. Had he not taken the initial precipitate action none of them would have got the king to deal with their affairs. Others might claim that he was taking too much on himself but not one of them had mustered the courage to intrude upon the king. Mind you, his own invasion of the royal privacy could have ended in a cell if the King had protested!

Once the curtain was drawn the King slumped on his fur covered bed gripping his stomach. "God's Blood but it is on fire in my belly," moaned the King. "I am cursed and must pay for my ungodliness."

Sympathising with his companion's pain, Alfred recommended that the King take another sip of the painkilling draught.

"My brother seeks to take my Kingdom. He is not satisfied with Mercia now and must rule all the land. Dunstan is behind it all, he has opposed me from the night my saintly uncle died. Archbishop Odo and he openly hated my beautiful lady wife. I know he was the instrument of Elfgifu's injuries and death. I banished him to save the old man's skin for there were many who knew he had tried my patience. Does he not realise that he owes his life to me?"

Alfred did not comment as the King rambled on, sometimes rational and then as sleep overtook him, only the odd word was clearly audible. Covering the young man gently with furs, he withdrew and sat quietly, thoughtfully, on a stool outside, his shoulders leaning against the wooden post. He had picked up a small beautifully illustrated book. The gold leaf and brilliant pigments shone from each of the fine parchment pages. Turning each one reverently he became engrossed, stroking the capitals with reverence. The book had been made at Wymburne, by the nuns in that fortress-like building. He felt such pride in their workmanship, craftsmanship which surely must have been inspired by their piety and godliness. He wondered if the Abbess spent time working on something so beautiful. He was in awe of such a woman, a lady who governed both men and the women in the monastery. For a moment he recalled her proud demeanour as she carried the Bible for men to swear on and how few could take their eyes off the huge tome.

A servant approached anxious to know if the King would attend the meal in the great hall.

"The King wishes food to be brought to him as he is studying the newly-arrived reports from the regions," announced Alfred with a flash of inspiration. He did not want to emphasise how sick the King had become. Nor did he wish the servants to know that their lord was currently in a drugged stupor. He closed the little prayer book carefully and stroked the smooth leather fastened with tooled gold.

The servant returned with food which Alfred took from him with thanks. He then pushed aside the curtain, letting it fall back behind him as he apologised to the sleeping King for interrupting him in his work. If anyone outside had been listening they would have come to the conclusion that the King was indeed hard at work and was not to be disturbed.

Alfred ate his own fill from the platters and then wrapped his cloak about him. The King continued to sleep with the aid of the drug, a fact which he was unwilling to share with anyone who might have been supporters of Edgar, the usurper of the King's northern lands.

On waking the King was astonished to find Alfred calmly waiting for him. "My Lord, you must be hungry now but eat slowly to avoid disturbing the peace in your belly."

For several days Alfred was the King's closest companion. He found it necessary to parry the jibes of the senior advisors assuring them that he would be returning to Dorset shortly.

He wanted to distance himself from the jealousy and resentment he could feel increasing every day. He experienced sarcasm, utterly undeserved, but resolved to endure it for the sake of the king's health. His closeness to the King caused considerable envy and unpleasantness among thegns who stressed their much greater standing in the hierarchy of the capital.

As soon as the King felt sufficiently well to take the court on a visit to the western provinces, Alfred left, assuring Edwy of his continued loyalty. "You are strong again. I shall join you on your tour. For now, my own small estate needs me but send for me sooner if I can be of service. The Earl of Chester still plagues me and no doubt has friends and cronies who envy my closeness to you. Lord Alward offers me his protection but he has many duties. We have few men who are practiced in arms at Uddings so the sooner I return there the better."

This was the first time he had actually named the noble whose family took every opportunity to belittle him, often behind his back so that he felt unable to honourably call the man out for his nasty, cruel jibes. "My brother, Odda, is the one skilled with weapons. Me, I prefer the quiet life, the dogs, the horses and learning the law from your justice men."

King Edwy raised an eyebrow but did not comment. He had raised Alfred for his loyalty, friendship and selflessness, all qualities which were rarely present in one man and certainly not in the Earl of Chester. He remained thoughtful as Alfred bowed and left his private room where servants packed his coffers in readiness for the move.

Rumours abounded, which even the king could not ignore. News came from many sources that Abbot Dunstan had advised the King of Mercia to hold a Council of all the kingdom's advisors and thegns. He was confident that there was now sufficient discontent in Wessex for even the most loyal of King Edwy's thegns to be in favour of a change of leader.

As he rode steadily towards Cranburne the irritation gradually lessened until it was replaced by the joy of returning home again. Even the air was cleaner, a spicy aroma of pines mixed with the odour of livestock that lingers round farms and homesteads. The smell of damp earth beneath the horse's hoofs rose at every step.

The horns sounded all over the estate to announce his return, a noise which never failed to thrill. Dogs rushed from every quarter, tails wagging, toothy smiles and hanging tongues. His stallion neighed loudly not to be outdone and his call was answered from the paddocks.

"Sometimes animals are nicer than people. They do not hide their feelings or speak falsely. A dog's loyalty is so obvious, so unashamedly honest and open." Alfred dismounted and stroked each animal in turn. By the time Edith had taken off her apron and patted her hair into some semblance of order Alfred was well licked, laughing at the canine antics performed for his benefit. Her full lipped mouth still made girlish dimples in the cheeks as she smiled, but her hair was now grey, her eyes less bright but still admiring of her younger son.

Chapter Two

Vann's blond haired son arrived to take up Alfred's offer. His cheerful face and willingness to do even the hardest work soon made him popular with the farm workers. Hal's sun-touched skin glowed with health. Aethelflaed watched him working through discreetly lowered eyes, her dark lashes shadowing the interest she was trying to disguise. Deep inside a fluttering of burgeoning love was nurtured by the exchange of glances.

Everyone was helping the swineherd to construct a sturdy home of timber, raised on a small mound to keep the floor dry, similar to the one already built for the sheep-ward on the common grazing land. At midday food was taken to them in baskets, the bread still warm from the oven. Aethelflaed had initially been somewhat annoyed when Edith had suggested she should supervise the filling of these containers, pouting ungraciously.

"T'is time you learned how to run a household my dear. One day you may have your own workers who will appreciate a good meal in the cold weather."

"I shall have servants to do that for me," she retorted sullenly banging the cheese into the basket. "I don't see why Hal is being treated as a labourer."

The muttering continued until Edith finally snapped at her, demanding that for once she should do as she was told before the food became cold.

Wrapping a woollen shawl closely about her shoulders, Aethelflaed walked unwillingly to the common where the workers mixed the muddy compound which would fill the cracks in the walls of the house. Her feet were already filthy and her hands chilled, but as soon as she saw Hal among the men who gathered round she forgot her discomfort. Ignoring his companion's grins, the young man and Aethelflaed were soon engrossed in conversation, his food apparently forgotten.

"I have to learn how to do more than just look after a few sheep. There is not room for me on my father's farm so I mean to become a steward on a big estate, in time of course." Hal's sun-tanned face blushed for he had not intended to boast of his hopes for the future.

"We have two, one for here and one for Uddings which also belongs to my brother. Of course they are not very big. Where you worked in Wymburne was huge wasn't it? Most of the families have been here for ages, well at least since my grandfather's time," she added remembering the stories of the building of the first house there. One day I will tell you how grandfather was given Uddings but now it is time to return. Everyone is watching us and mother will be waiting!"

At Uddings, in the old timber manor house, Owenson's wife, now thoroughly matronly in manner and shape, baked for the cottagers and supervised the store rooms, enjoying her weekly trips to the market in Wymburne where her increase in status had caused very satisfying respect from the townsfolk. Her husband was now in charge of the horses, their son learning from him. 'So far from his father's original situation, arriving fettered and lower than a churl' she thought as she walked along the stalls to compare produce.

"There are some lawless people around," Alfred commented during the evening meal at his Didlington hall one day. "Rumours and stories of our King's wildness have not encouraged men to obey the law or to respect the elders of the shire. It is well to be on our guard at all times," he added thoughtfully. "This manor is more vulnerable being close to the road."

Commenting on his apparent loss of appetite, Edith quietly asked if the meal was not to his liking. Alfred hastily assured her that the food was excellent as usual but that he had matters on his mind.

"I have been thinking that it is time I found myself a wife! My sister is eager to marry Hal but she is too scatter-brained to manage here on her own. If they stayed here, with you to direct her, then I would live at Uddings. After all, the woods provide timber and firewood together with autumn pannage for the pigs. The heath is ideal for the sheep while the meadow sloping down towards the stream provides excellent grazing for the horses. Grandfather's house is stoutly built, and with the recent improvements it withstands most of the elements."

Alfred was referring to the scraped lamb cauls which had been stretched over the north facing window of Uddings to provide even more comfort. 'In the meantime, young Hal might be deemed to be without a lord and should become my man', thought Alfred. 'I must speak to the boy. Harvest is too distant for a stranger's oath; it's not as if his father was already sworn to accept me as lord. Besides, he may have been on the palace steward's list for service in the fyrd but he should now be our man.'

He puzzled over his dilemma, deciding to ask Hal if he would take his oath at dinner one day. He felt sure there would be no shortage of sponsors.

Some weeks later while visiting Cranburne, Alfred was invited to stay the night at the Keeper's house; a solid farmhouse boasting several rooms in addition to the kitchen which was built apart from the hall. He was neatly dressed, the green tunic clean and his cloak brushed, all of which gave him confidence as he took the proffered stool.

Ale was brought quickly by a young woman and poured carefully into carved horn goblets. The Keeper, a tall, ruddy faced man of some thirty years, introduced his daughter Brith, murmuring that his wife was long dead. "My daughter runs my household now and a fine housewife she has become," he boasted with that unique blend of pride and love that only a father's voice can portray.

Alfred had seen the girl from a distance several times before but now he had been properly introduced he could not take his eyes off her. She blushed and left the hall hurriedly, smiling as she turned from him. Aware that his host was still speaking, he tried to concentrate. His heart was already beating faster and he was conscious of his maleness.

"Each year higher taxes are demanded," the keeper complained. The commissioners employ bully-boys. I fear for the safety of the cottagers, especially if their daughters are pretty. There have been accusations of unwarranted advances and even worse," he whispered confidentially. It was with great difficulty that Alfred brought the conversation back to the subject of his daughter. A warmth had spread throughout his body, an uninvited heat in his loins emphasised how physically aroused he was by the sight of this wonderful girl.

At the meal, almost a feast held in his honour, he managed to watch Brith less directly. She smiled modestly when he addressed her, showing good, even teeth. On returning the napkin to the servant who held a basin of water to wash hands in, he heard her thank the young boy kindly before dismissing him to have his own meal.

Alfred hardly noticed his surroundings. Cupid had not just fired one arrow into his heart but released a quiverful; each missile reaching its target. His mind was soaring so that he was hardly concentrating when his host modestly admitted to having recently been appointed to the position of Keeper of the Forest by King Edwy. Apart from now possessing the home farm at Cranburne, he was responsible for collecting fines from those who stole game or wood from the forest, a portion of which was his own to keep.

"I try to be fair," explained the keeper. "The King has not hunted in the forest for four years now but one never knows when he could arrive and expect good sport. Stores are always held against such an eventuality, but meanwhile I supervise the felling of suitable trees, the coppicing of the hazel bushes for hurdle making and issue licences for the grazing of stock at certain times of the year."

"There were no disputes to be heard on the last circuit with the Sheriff's men so you must be doing an excellent job," responded Alfred dutifully. "The King has gone to his Western shires. I shall join him soon. If the occasion arises, only good reports of your office will be given I assure you!"

Before leaving Alfred asked permission to court Brith. "If the girl is willing then I too am willing," was the immediate and hearty response. "She does not go to court with me, staying here to look after the house. Had she been another son she could not have been more valuable."

Alfred's enquiries revealed that the son was serving the King in the Commission for the collection of taxes, an unpopular position at any time but more so when the ruler was thought to be spending those monies unwisely.

It was the first time he had been so strongly attracted to a maiden. His heart was beating furiously so that he had to wipe the sweat discreetly from his neck. "I would take you away with me now," he stated abruptly, his eagerness outweighing any other considerations or polite approach. Having seen men at court make physical overtures to serving girls and other wenches, he instinctively knew that this rough, uncouth method of courtship was not at all suitable for the girl who behaved demurely without a trace of artifice. Brith smoothed the front of her overdress to cover her confusion and give herself time to calm down before raising her eyes to his face again. Looking into her calm brown eyes beneath well kept eyebrows, Alfred knew, with certainty, that he had met his soul mate. His heart beat settled to a rhythmic thump, the small vein in his temple throbbing in unison.

"Nay lord Alfred, I cannot leave my father so suddenly. I am needed to run the estate and the household when he is away."

After apologising for his clumsy approach, he was almost too tongue-tied to talk of trivial matters. His awkward attempts were interrupted when her father noisily approached them.

"I have asked your daughter to be my wife," stated Alfred facing the older man. "My business hereabouts is finished for the quarter. I must return to Uddings very soon as it too has no master at the moment, although it is looked after very well by my steward and his family."

"Stay a while and tell us more of this Uddings," Brith invited her suitor. "Is it near the King's palace?" she waved a moth away from the candle flame and rose gracefully to close the shutters.

Alfred was eager to tell them of his estate, of the King's horses at Uddings, of the sturdy sheep grazing at Didlington and of the crossbred pigs he folded on virgin land before it was put to the plough. "Our oxen are direct descendants of my grandfather's," he added proudly, then realised after he had spoken, that they could not be the slightest bit interested in the breeding of his beasts.

In turn, Brith and her father told Alfred of their small woodland estate, with the small game and honey to be taken every year. "The King allows me to take a wounded buck but there are few of those!" he joked unsure if his future son in law would draw his own conclusions or inform the King of a possible breach of the terms of his office. They chatted over a last mug of ale before the stars punctured the darkness of the night time sky.

Inviting them to visit Uddings in one month's time, declaring that the time could not pass quickly enough as far as he was concerned Alfred blushed furiously. He felt like a small boy offered a treat. He had studied the heavens last night but irreverently felt that Brith's eyes shone more brightly that the sun, stars and moon put together.

"I shall recall my son if he can be spared from his duties. It is time he shared the management of what could be his one day," Brith's father said seriously. "My daughter will not come to you without a dowry but the estate is my son's birthright. She will have silver and fine jewellery, two young oxen and her own servants."

Brith watched Alfred closely as he apparently considered the bride-gifts her father had mentioned. She was relieved to see no sign of a frown on his face. He nodded mutely, totally inexperienced in such matters, never having valued a potential wife before, although he had heard his contemporaries at court boasting of the wealth their wives had brought to them. He already had a household, all he wished for was a wife and now he had found the girl he wanted, not just to be his hand-fast woman, but to make his own for all time.

"You have horses?" he queried.

Mistaking his question as a request for beasts to be included in the dower, Brith's father hastily added that Brith would of course be bringing her own lady's riding horse with her.

Momentarily embarrassed when he realised his blunder, Alfred was reduced to the stammer often experienced when a young boy's voice changed to that of a man.

"Your pardon, I was only enquiring if horses should be brought from Uddings to enable you to visit, not suggesting in the least that the bride price was insufficient." Now his flush was one of confusion but a quick glimpse at the keeper's face assured him that no offence had been taken. A whimsical smile played around his lips as if he understood Alfred's naivety and total lack of practice in courtship.

"I would want to ride my own mare," Brith interrupted. "If father permits me to take her that is," she added, aware that her father was frowning at her forwardness. Putting her arm through her father's, she apologised for her lack of modesty.

"I will accompany my father next month my lord, but now if you give me leave, there is much to attend to in the household."

Brith left the room, quietly drawing the heavy curtain back in place to give her father and Alfred privacy from the curious servants who were taking longer than usual to clear the hall. Some had entered with no more than a bundle of twigs for the fire while others brought ale when there was already a full jug on the table. Brith gently shooed them out ahead of her but could not prevent her sudden happiness spreading to all around her. She skipped a few paces before slowing to a modest walk.

"She is a gentle, biddable child and like you, I suspect, unused to admiration. You have a lifetime ahead in which to enjoy married happiness or, God forbid, to wish you had never set eyes on each other! There are many who marry for position, for gain in wealth or estate; these marriages have even chances of being happy. My dear late wife always wanted Brith to find love," he added nostalgically momentarily lost in his thoughts.

Alfred finally left reluctantly, hoping the month would pass quickly. The July sun had not yet burnt off the morning mist and the air still held remnants of the dampness of night. All the way home he sang the bawdiest songs he could recall, his tenor voice startling shepherds and wildlife alike.

Arriving at his mother's house still in a state of euphoria and grinning broadly, he immediately informed Edith of the invitation he had issued to his betrothed and her father.

"I have longed for this day since your father died," she admitted. "Tell me of her. Is she comely of face? Does she manage a household?"

"One question at once! Yes, yes, and yes!" laughed Alfred hugging Edith in his happiness. When his sister joined them she too was included in her brother's joy. When he later described to her how he had been completely smitten, bowled over and submerged in a sense of unreality, at the speed with which his blood had coursed through his body, she grinned widely, the summer freckles on her nose adding to the cheeky look she gave her brother. "So dear brother, you have fallen in love! I felt the same when my eyes locked with Hal's. A lightning bolt struck both of us at the same time and there we were in church of all places. Surely those around me, mother included, must have felt the sudden heat, the passion between us. All of a sudden I have no interest at all in going to court, not that I could join the Queen's household now that she is dead, God rest her soul."

Both of them crossed themselves quickly, the rumours of the lady Elgiva's tortured death still fresh in everyone's mind.

Over the next few weeks there was a great deal of activity as the floor rushes were changed, trestles scrubbed with sand, curtain hangings shaken and guest mattresses re-stuffed with the finest woollen tags in the store room. Much of the work was unnecessary as Edith and Aethelflaed kept the house welcoming at all times. The importance of such an occasion could not be missed by even the lowest kitchen servant, all of whom had been willingly cajoled into doing extra work.

Excitement spread to the stables and beyond as the date for the visit approached. Harness was oiled yet again, the horses brushed until they shone with health. Even the oxen received attention from the enthusiastic oxherd and his lads. The swineherd selected the fattest pig for slaughter, the shepherd his finest spring lambs, all of which had fattened on good grass since the visit had been announced. Aethelflaed, who had been somewhat secretive recently, proudly presented her brother with a new outer coat she had sewn herself.

"Hal carved the fasteners from sheep's horn," she announced, her voice betraying the great love which had developed between them. "His father has great skill with the knife and taught him to fashion many useful things from the horn of the oxen and the ram," she added. Her long hair was plaited and hung down her back. The sun had lightened the top-most strands so that reddish hues were evident. Small curls which had escaped framed her pretty face which was losing the roundness of childhood and becoming more mature each week.

"I hope your lady likes me," she fretted. She already had a vague impression of this paragon of virtue her brother had fallen in love with.

Wearing the new jerkin over a freshly washed tunic, King Edwy's diadem tied firmly round his combed shoulder length brown hair, Alfred greeted his guests formally in the courtyard. Even the dogs had suffered the attention of a brush and waved their tails slowly, unsure if they were welcome. Not a weed or trace of animal dirt had been permitted to spoil the beaten smoothness of the forecourt for several days as the household readied itself for the arrival of the master's intended bride.

Aware of his tenants' interest in his love life, Alfred did not have the heart to bid those who lingered when the visitors were finally in sight, to be about their duties. Introducing his mother, Edith and his sister Aethelflaed more formally now that everyone was standing at the same level, he ushered the guests inside to sit beside the brightly burning fire which kept the great hall warm. Simple sconces had also been lit to provide light around the walls showing off the woven cloths. At the meal, Edith was impressed by the girl's modesty and pretty thanks for any small service provided for her comfort. Men at the lower tables gawped unashamedly until reminded of their manners by a fierce dig in the ribs from a neighbour's elbow. Whispered words of approval passed between the men and women occupying the benches.

Brith's father hesitantly expressed his admiration for the quality of the stock and the abundance of crops under cultivation which they had passed, not that he had any great knowledge of farming.

"It was not always like this," replied Alfred brightly, "King Aethelstan gave my father the choice of two parcels of land; the one, a fully working homestead in the East or this wild piece by Uddings, my grandfather's land. My father chose this land. Come, I will take you down to the mill. A portion of the flour is sent to the King's hunting lodge as you know!"

Obviously impressed by the wealth of his future son as they walked on the narrow path between meadows where horses grazed contentedly, Brithric brought up the subject of the date of his daughter's wedding.

"Presuming that you are still of the same mind, I know that my daughter has been counting the days to the suggested date, the eve of Christmas night. My son returns very soon, the King excuses him for the time being," he said. "Actually he will not be sorry for it is unpleasant forcing people to pay their dues. Like me, he has compassion unlike some of the ruffians who travel with him. Brithricson abhors unnecessary violence, particularly against women and poor people but some seem to revel in their power and ability to make others suffer. I am glad he is returning home even if it is not for long."

Alfred considered the date, aware that the harvest would soon start followed by the autumn tasks and the annual gathering of the berries and fruits which still formed a vital part of the winter stores.

"I would say it was an ideal time to wed. We will live at Uddings, my grandfather's house. My mother will continue to run these lands here, with the help of Aethelflaed and Hal." Alfred indicated the extent of the Didlington lands as the name was now pronounced.

"She is indeed a lovely girl," approved Edith whispering to Alfred when everyone had gone to their beds. "I am glad you are not chasing after a girl at court with all their airs and graces. Brith is modest yet has wit and humour. Your father, rest his soul, would have been as happy as I am for you both. Her father, Lord Brithric seems pleasant; he will be lonely when she weds." Her voice rose wistfully as she thought of her own loss when her husband Udric and their firstborn son had been killed in battle.

They talked for a few moments more in the darkness before settling down.

The party rode southwards to Uddings past fields where corn was already standing thickly. Owenson and his wife proudly demonstrated the care they had taken of their lord's property in his absence. Brith's father admitted to being impressed before promising furs for their bed. "Also there are bed hangings for the bridal chamber, which were part of my wife's dower when we wed. They shall be yours, daughter."

The horses too received their share of praise, Owenson's son explaining the breeding of the bigger Norman horses so prized by the nobles for use in battles. Brith showed no fear when offering the biggest stallion a small crust. It drew its lips back to display large yellow teeth, a cross between a smile and a grimace which she found amusing. The beast breathed in the scent of her hair then lowered its head for her to stroke. "Remarkable!" commented Brithric, "such a fearsome animal yet he too has fallen under my daughter's spell!" He was so pleased with his own wit that for a moment he was convulsed with giggles like a young child. Alfred and Brith looked at each other, their eyebrows raised in unison above rolling eyes.

As the moment of departure approached Brith tearfully hugged Alfred, her usual calm and dignity deserting her. "I shall count the days; even this month has passed with painful slowness."

He lifted her up onto the pony, holding her hand longer than was absolutely necessary, whispering that he too wished the months to pass quickly so that they could be together. When he finally released her he became aware that his mother and Brithric appeared to be deep in conversation, also apparently parting somewhat reluctantly.

Standing side by side Edith and Alfred they waved their visitors farewell, each aware of highly charged emotions.

"I merely expressed my wish that the harvest is brought in safely and quickly so that the New Year will come the sooner and afterwards... well, the Yule-tide feasting," she explained, smoothing her veil self-consciously as her blushing subsided.

Alfred smiled but made no comment, his mind already whirling with plans to make Uddings ready for his bride.

"If there was money to spare it would be nice to have glass in the windows at Uddings but Lord Alward said that it costs a fortune, a veritable ransom and that only the King can afford it. Well, people wonder where their tax money goes! It would not be a comfort for them to know that it buys fancy glass windows for his palace!" The dog walking silently beside him twitched an ear listening to Alfred. He sat down on the leaf-mould beneath the remnants of the once mighty oak close to the stables. The grey muzzled dog wriggled in ecstasy when he scratched its ragged ears.

"God willing no one will be called to the fyrd now. The King will have made peace with his brother and there are no rumours of raiding parties for once. Well, old one, there is work to do. Yours might be done when dawn comes but mine starts at first light. I know you prowl round the homestead in the darkness so find a sunny spot for your rest." He gave the dog one last pat and stood up to brush off the flecks of last winter's leaves. The dog inched forward to purloin the warm patch on the ground and settled down, its tail curled over its grizzled face. It sighed contentedly as Alfred walked away.

The crops were safely gathered and stacked by everyone who could be spared from other work. The children picked the last grains and stored them to fatten the fowl through the winter months. Flocks of pigeons tried to steal the valuable morsels but were frightened away by the youngest children throwing stones or any other missile they could manage. The shepherd took the opportunity to stun a couple of birds with his sling and shot. He wrung their necks in one efficient movement shoving the still warm bodies into a large bag hanging over his shoulder.

"The more the merrier," he called out cheerfully to the children reminding them to save any round pebbles they found for his collection of shot.

The corn was being winnowed in a good breeze beside the barn when a messenger wearing a red and yellow diadem clattering into the yard demanding to speak to Alfred. His horse's sides were heaving, froth and spume hanging from its mouth. Owenson frowned, stroking the exhausted beast sympathetically.

"I have been sent to the King's ton at Wymburne from King Edgar of Mercia," the courier announced proudly, "to inform the people of Dorsetshire and Hamtun that King Eadwy has died. He will lie in state for..," the messenger paused, counted his fingers, "two more days before burial at Winchester."

"He will be buried on Sunday then, the Lords Day?" queried Alfred, visibly shocked by the news of the young man's death. He could feel the blood draining from his face, a tightening in his chest as he remembered sitting by the King's bed when he had been dosed with poppy juice to relieve his stomach pains.

The messenger frowned and merely repeated the number of days until the burial. Being unable to read he repeated by memory any messages he was charged to carry, adjusting the number of days by the number of nights since leaving the court.

"Messages have been sent to all parts of King Edgar's Kingdom and those of his late brother's territory of Wessex to inform all the people that Edgar is King of the whole land," repeated the servant quickly. He toyed with his baton obviously waiting for Alfred's reaction.

"I will attend the King's burial. Your news has shocked me, for lord Edwy was still young. Do you need food or ale, for a moment my duties as host have been blown from my mind?"

Having refused both on the basis that both his and his horse's needs would be attended to at the King's palace, the messenger re-mounted.

As soon as he had ridden on to Wymburne, Alfred called for his own horse.

"I must leave for court immediately. No doubt others will already be on the road. Hopefully nothing will happen to delay my wedding. Now by God's blood, all I want is to stay at home but I ought to see King Edwy laid to rest. No doubt the sickness of his stomach was the cause. Poor man, he suffered!"

He took his diadem from the coffer in his bed chamber and fastened his sword belt around his waist before setting off.

Edith sighed, hoping that he would be back very soon to oversee the livestock. The sky had been dull all day with few glimpses of the sun from which little heat penetrated the October air. She pulled a shawl closer round her shoulders watching as Alfred's figure became smaller and smaller in the distance. He turned at his boundary and waved.

Chapter Three
AD959

Edgar's officials had obviously been primed to quote the late King's praises and good deeds during his short, four year reign. Despite his own youth, being only sixteen summers old, the King of Mercia had already developed a regal manner, behaving with great dignity as his elder brother, whose body had been brought from his palace at Frome was laid to rest beneath the stone floor of the great church. Many of the nobles from both Wessex and Mercia had gathered for the ceremony. Even during the long burial Mass they spent the time greeting each other and exchanging news. Few seemed to be genuinely sorry that Edwy had died. They recalled his scandalous behaviour with Elfgifu and her mother; the taking of his grandmother's entire estate, jewels and wealth for his own coffers; and the levying of harsh taxes purely to finance what appeared to be a profligate lifestyle. All these sins could be laid at the door of the man whose robed body was buried this day. Alfred noticed how quickly many thegns transferred their attention to Edgar.

The small figure of the new King was surrounded by many of the rich nobles who had eagerly taken his late brother's gifts, the fair head well below that of those who now curried favour with him.

The Council's election of Edgar as King of a united realm was a mere formality. There had been a loud chorus of 'ayes' leaving the seneschal with no reason to conduct a count.

"My Lord, will you set a date for your coronation?" asked the leading councillor formally. "It could be arranged for All Hallows Day if that would please you."

Alfred was doing some quick reckoning in his head and discreetly using his fingers behind his back. A coronation on the First day of November would still leave time for him to supervise the annual cull of his surplus stock and prepare for his own wedding.

The King meanwhile looked as though he was involved in some sort of inner turmoil. He was chewing his lower lip and running his hands through his hair.

"No, I will not have the crown placed on my head until I have proved my worthiness to wear it. I shall wear my father's circlet; for the time being that will be sufficient.

Hear me now all present - all those who have been in office in Wessex under my late brother shall continue in their posts, their loyalty to me being assumed for the time being." For such a small man he had a surprisingly loud and pleasant voice. There had not been a single cough or shuffle as the new King announced his first orders. A warm cloak of royal purple was fastened on his slight shoulders as once again men gathered around hoping to be noticed.

Listening from the back of the hall Alfred heard a collective sigh of relief. He spotted his future father by marriage on the far side of the hall and made his way over to him.

"My Lord, a sad occasion to meet, but I am glad to see you again so soon. How is my lady Brith?"

Upon being assured that she was well, busy with preparations to become his bride and at the same time overseeing many of the household's winter chores, both men turned their attentions to more pressing matters.

One leading Bishop was urging King Edgar to accept the oaths of loyalty from those present to which he agreed. Starting with the leading thegns from his new territory of Wessex, the elderly thegn of Dorset, Wulfric limped forward, followed by those from West Wales, Hamtun and the Essex weald. They knelt before the King before being assured in turn, of their new Lord's favour.

Alfred and his older companion joined the queue of lesser thegns, duly repeating their vows.

"Who is he?" whispered the King to the elderly Bishop sat beside him on the dais, indicating Alfred. "He wears my brother's colours."

Overhearing the loud whisper, the unfortunate Bishop being somewhat deaf, Alfred was obliged to advise the King of his fore-bears, whilst hastily removing the diadem in question. He gave the King details of the work he had done for his elder brother over the past four years, and that the lands of Uddings and Didlington he now owned in Dorset were confirmed by grants made at Cheddar by King Edwy.

Edgar was thoughtful for a moment. "Uddings you say. How far from the palace is that?" A clerk whispered something in the King's ear.

"No more than four miles my lord; Is there something you would like taken there, or a message?"

"I will see this man tomorrow," announced the King. "In the meantime he will be given my colours to wear. How old is my brother's horse? I must admit a new destrier would please me immensely but that is a matter for later."

An armed guard stepped forward briskly with the coloured headband, presented it to the King and returned to his former position. The King folded the diadem to reveal his own colours of red and gold and placed it in Alfred's outstretched palms.

"My lord Edgar, I thank you." Bowing quickly, he left the King's raised dais conscious of the whispers. He returned hastily to stand beside Brithric whose position as keeper of the forest of Cranburne appeared to be secure.

"What was he asking about? Why have you been summoned to attend the King? You may be asked to provide some service or maybe he wants men for the army," he guessed. "It couldn't be anything more sinister. Come, share my quarters tonight."

"It may be something to do with a new horse but then he changed his mind but tomorrow will come quickly enough!"

When Alfred met the King the following day he was relieved to find other Dorsetshire men had also been ordered to attend the meeting, and nodded briefly to those from East Dorset with whom he was already acquainted. Without turning his back on the King, he raised an eyebrow at one particular friend who responded with the slightest shrug of his shoulders. Realising that he was not the only one who was mystified by the summons he took his place on a stool. He bowed briefly to Hugh, the new shire reeve of Dorset and then to Bishop Wulfric who now looked so frail both in body and spirit. His thin, knobbly fingers gripped the head of his cane so tightly that the knuckles showed strangely white beneath the age mottled skin of his hands. Hunched forwards, neck muscles straining to keep his head erect, the Bishop's bright eyes watched approvingly as the Dorset thegns acknowledged his presence, bowed to the King and quietly found a seat.

When most of the stools were occupied King Edgar raised his hand for silence, looking briefly at each man as if to imprint every individual face in his memory. Some shifted uneasily, uncomfortably beneath this scrutiny while others like Alfred returned the King's stare more directly.

"I want to build a fleet, on the Southern shores, to be kept in readiness at all times." He paused dramatically to add weight to his wishes. "Dorsetshire has many skilled fishermen on its coast and rivers. They must build bigger ships to carry armed men. Do not think that yours is the only county to be so charged. Mercia already has such a fleet to prevent invasion up their rivers. West Wales' estuaries are guarded and the coast there is steep and rocky. Dorset has always been the chosen landing site for these heathen marauders from the North. Set up watchmen to guard the high places with firewood ready to give warning to those inland. It will not be fair for only the coastal people to provide this guard, so I propose to charge each of you to supply men and arms for one month each year from your immediate lands or estates so that the work is shared. No man should suffer great loss to his living."

The thegns mutely nodded their agreement to the King's command. They had been given no advance warning of the reason for their gathering and many were hastily calculating who could be spared to carry out yet another duty particularly if this was in addition to his forty days of duty in the King's army.

Bishop Odo of Sherborne muttered a prayer under his breath. He was much younger than Wulfric but his face had already paled at the thought of raids and invasions. "My Lord, are churchmen to be included in the rota you have suggested.

"No-one is excluded," stressed the king. "After all, the church is often the target of these heathens. Only the sick and lame will not be armed. Hugh, my lord of Dorset, you will take charge of the forces and report to me in confidence. The property of those on guard duty will be tended by those who remain in the villages and hamlets. You will oversee that also. Those who serve in the coastal guard need not serve in the army. Each captain of the guard will hold my seal and pass it to the next group. Their needs will be provided in turn, payment to be made by Lord Hugh who will account to me for all sums expended on my behalf."

The senior thegn of Dorset raised his eyebrows meaningfully, assessing the extra work which had just been imposed on him. Other men glanced at their neighbours at the mention of exemption from fyrd duty. Many grinned briefly or made gestures of approval.

"I will account to you for all monies my lord. Shall I see your treasurer before I leave for Wareham?"

The King nodded briefly, dismissing the Dorsetshire men. They left the King's quarters, barely restraining their urge to discuss the task ahead of them. Quelling the babble of voices, the Sheriff summoned them all to a corner of the hall where a rough plan was outlined and agreed with varying degrees of enthusiasm. Men would return to their estates to assess the surplus corn harvest, others to calculate their own contribution of both men and supplies.

"At least King Edgar is spending tax monies on sensible things not wasting our hard earned silver," muttered one man in a studied monotone voice. Heads nodded in agreement for it had been the rumours of the late King's wastefulness and dissolute behaviour which had made him so unpopular.

Few men could argue that the King's reasoning was sound but providing men for guard duty instead of the normal nomination of two soldiers for the army would still impose a severe burden on those who had a small labour force.

Lord Hugh, erect and youthful in appearance with a clean-shaven face, demanded the numbers each man could raise, making marks on an old skin which had obviously been re-used many times.

"As I have men immediately available, courtesy of the King, they will take the first watch and be relieved in one month. Tents will be erected in small groups as there is a long coastline to protect. I will send messengers to each of you in turn to warn each man of his time of duty. God go with you all." Hugh swept the bits off his parchment before rolling it up. His staff of office was thrust under his arm, his gold collar reflecting the flickering torchlight. He strode off to the treasury, leaving the Dorset landowners free to talk among themselves. There were many relieved faces, Alfred's among them, as he contemplated the work that needed doing at home and the arrangements for his wedding.

At Uddings preparations to receive the lord's bride were already well advanced. Wall hangings had been cleaned before being hung back on the newly whitewashed walls. Most of the remaining windows now had covers. Hal had learned to prepare the lamb cauls when he served at the Kingston farm. It was a delicate task but had been completed without accidents. Already those who ate and slept in the hall had noticed the warmth. The thin membranes had been cleaned to insure that they would no longer be attractive to the hordes of flies which always rose from any animal parts left lying around.

"Perhaps they are not as clear as glass would have been but by all that's Holy, a great deal cheaper," announced Alfred when he had inspected the young man's work. "Have you any more such tricks to teach us?" he joked as they both withdrew from the crowded hall where the women fussed with the stools, the settle and Grandmother Galena's old loom which still stood in the pool of light from one of the windows. It still had warp threads held by its weights, the flints polished by many years of use. Alfred had not asked if Brith would be bringing her own, it being normal for looms to be passed down from one generation to the next.

The bower at one end of the hall had already been furnished with a newly carved bed frame containing a woollen bed mattress stuffed with the smallest feathers and soft, washed, fleece tips. Two ox hides formed a new door curtain reducing the draught and affording privacy. A whole fleece, washed and brushed had been laid on the wooden floor, an unheard of luxury or waste according to ones' point of view.

Owenson's wife ruled the household firmly, determined that Brith would find no fault with her preparations. Even the scrubbed trestles in the hall were sanded so that their surfaces were smooth to the touch. In places the delicate tracery of the wood could be seen.

Pigs for the feast were fattened on the thin by-product of the cheese making. Fowl were selected for slaughter and let loose in the ox byre or the stables during the day to clean up any spilt grain. Fresh rushes and straw were cut to lay on the hall floor despite the fact that they had only been replaced some two months ago, the stems being woven into mats and laid on the crushed bracken. In addition, a rule was re-introduced, that no adult was to foul the floor in future, its transgression to be punished by a beating. Some of the servants grumbled that they would catch their death going out to the midden night or day, but the lack of the familiar ammoniac smell in the corners quickly became noticeable to those who entered the hall so that they soon gave the new rule their grudging approval. Those who remembered Galena knew that she would have approved for she disliked unpleasant smells in her house. They also spared a thought for the honey cakes she used to make, when people used to visit Uddings on any excuse in the hope they might be offered one.

Down by the fast flowing stream the miller worked all day and often into the night to provide fresh flour from the sacks of grain stacked above ground. Using a wooden scoop he removed one portion for Alfred's fee, one portion for the King's reserves, then ground the rest of the corn into fine or medium coarse flour to be returned to the farmer.

Each week Alfred visited the mill to check the stored grain which paid the King for the lands the family now owned. Because he dwelt some distance from the hall at Didlington the miller sometimes was the last to hear the gossip and news. These visits were his opportunity to catch up with the affairs of the estate.

"It's passing strange that you be marrying a maiden from Cranburne and our flour is sent there. My son may recognise your lady for he takes the cart with the King's flour," the miller stated in his heavily accented English. He rarely made conversation preferring to listen to others. "Besides, my wife does enough gabbling for the two of us," he often replied laughing heartily at his own sense of humour. His barrel chest threatened to burst his jerkin at the seams, his huge arms which could hoist two sacks of grain at the same time, appearing to fit skin tight to his tunic.

"A branch of the apple tree must be cut this autumn," Alfred said to the miller one morning while letting the grain run through his fingers.

"It bore so much fruit that it cracked. To ensure that it does not go for firewood, you should send your son to do the sawing. I am told it must be cut for the water wheel while it is fresh. The carpenter will come to work here so that you can supervise and be sure it will fit the wheel."

The miller nodded, appreciating the small compliment that he would be required to oversee the work on the new paddle. He brushed the flour dust from his jerkin, allowing it to fall in misty showers onto his boots.

"You'll be wanting fine flour then my lord, for Christmas time? My wife would like to bake her special pasties for the feast. Not wanting to offend Lady Edith, I thought I would mention it beforehand."

Alfred rested his hand on the miller's powerful shoulder. "There is little fear of offending my mother! She has already banished me from the kitchens and the brew-house for tasting her preserves and barley ale before they were ready! Aethelflaed was slapped for putting too much salt in the brawn. She went off in tears vowing never to set foot in the kitchen again!"

Both men laughed heartily, agreeing that women and their store-rooms were out of bounds to mere men at some times of the year.

Talking of times of the year reminded Alfred of the rota for the south coast guard. It had been agreed in October after King Edgar had issued his decree that those estates nearest the coast would provide the winter guard so that there would be less distance to travel on the muddy roads. Grumbling at this arrangement had been quickly countered by those who had drawn the lighter months pointing out that their absence from the spring planting, breeding and harvesting on their lands were equally onerous.

The new King had made a law banning the keeping of slaves except for convicted felons. It was announced by the new priest at St Mary's, an energetic young man with a fresh face. He amused everyone by enthusiastically waving his arms to illustrate stories from the Bible.

Newly freed bonded persons were to be encouraged to stay with their present lords by being provided with bed and board, clothing and tools of a trade, the priest had announced hoping that the monastery would not be inundated with requests for alms from malcontents and beggars who had left their masters.

Alfred had shrugged when he was told of the law, not having any slaves. This was something else he would have to check when he was sent to other towns and villages to hear minor court cases. Grandfather Udda had never approved of keeping slaves, and had given each man his freedom after one year so that whenever possible the children of that man had been born into freedom.

"He bore the marks of the slave shackles to his dying day," he remarked to no-one in particular. "Freed Owen long before he had to, before my grand-father's sister gave birth, I believe."

There were still a few in the hall who had heard the sad story of Owen's handfast woman and her child. The tracking skill of the old Lymer dog kept the memory alive for it had sired a long line of pups which still worked on both estates. At that very moment, two of the most recent russet-coated litter were fighting over a scrap of meat below the tables.

One of the men bent down to pick up one of the squabbling pups and was rewarded by a nip of the needle sharp teeth. His companions laughed at his discomfort while he swore under his breath. "Let's hope its nose is as sharp as its teeth!" he muttered sourly, rubbing his finger on his leggings.

New Year, still the first day of September in country shires, passed with celebrations for the harvest, and people turned their attention to stores of grain and meat for the winter. Church services emphasised the grateful thanks which should be given to God Almighty for the bounteousness of the fruits of the field, bush and stock. Sheaves of barley, oats and wheat adorned the altar while baskets of fruit, beans, peas and roots were also placed so that they could be admired. The priest took these offerings as an additional tithe, hardly able to contain the anticipation of the meals which his housekeeper could produce from such munificence. The Lammas Day service, which gave thanks specifically for the corn harvest and featured the first loaves made from the new grain had passed the previous month but so many loaves provided by housewives outdoing each other with patterns, shapes and flavours meant that many were not eaten by the priest and were given to beggars.

Gatherings on market days of this month frequently turned into musical entertainment, the young men and women mixing with less stringent control from their parents. Daughters seeking husbands wore their finest gowns trying to look demure and biddable while fathers who looked for healthy, capable maidens for their sons eyed the girls as if they were stock to be assessed for breeding purposes.

"Thank God I have never had to parade myself like this," stated Aethelflaed walking round the market hand in hand with Hal. He grinned broadly before replying. "My boldness got me the pick of the crop. Mind you, my father always said that if you teach a woman to read and write, her head will be overflowing with unseemly ideas. For myself, you are the prettiest girl of them all and I shall always feel that way." His smile, with just the corners of his mouth lifting, evoked strange, exciting emotions within her body. They continued walking slowly passed the stalls oblivious to the shouts, the squeals of piglets and the music makers hoping for small tokens of appreciation.

October was always one of the busiest months for everyone working the land, usually rewarded by the freshest food served in large quantities. Salting of meats for the leaner months and clamping of root vegetables which could not stay in the ground were essential tasks. Nestled in straw, then covered with a woven mat and earth, stored turnips and the like could be added to winter dishes. Every housewife had already prepared pots of ointment based on the grease from the pigs which was used to heal chapped fingers, syrups of betony leaves for coughs and healing balms for wounds.

At Uddings the mares had already been separated from the stallions so that the three year olds could start their training without distractions. Owenson still supervised all the horses, but now several men and boys were free to assist him. They slept in the room adjoining the stables, bedding down in thick straw with woollen blankets. A strict rota ensured that there was always a man on duty at night to guard against thieves. The punishment of an offender was extremely severe, probably because the cost of a horse was still more than most could raise. They were mainly bought by men whose lands were held in return for providing armed men to serve the King. When King Edgar had assured everyone that all appointments granted by his elder brother would be honoured by him Alfred had never doubted for one moment that this also included the breeding of horses suitable for a King to ride.

"They have been given or sold to Kings for more than fifty years now," commented Owenson with pride. "Most of them descend from one old warhorse 'Thor'. See, they all carry their heads high. Many regard our horses as having the best temperament as well as being able to carry a man all day. Of course that is down to the way we handle and pet the foals when they are young."

"Tell us of Thor," begged a young stable boy cheekily, knowing that once the head horsemaster started on the story, the rest of them could be idle for a few minutes.

"Later maybe," replied Owenson never loathe to tell the tale of the King's legendary horse. "First there is harness to polish."

Crestfallen, the youngster returned to his work with a barely concealed sigh, his friends scowling at his failure to obtain respite from their work.

The sheep too had thrived under the care of a devoted sheepward who lived out with them but whose family had a new thatched cottage.

Although Alfred owned most of the flock many of his servants and field hands now possessed a ewe which ran with the main flock and was served by the same ram. Each man marked his animal with a coloured mark so that its fleece could be identified. After shearing, he could decide if the wool was required in his home or if it should be sold with the estate wool, in which case he received a portion of the monies or produce in exchange. For many this was the only money they ever possessed, a matter of great pride, flaunted when they bought a jug of ale after church or a new household item at the Shambles market.

Many of them now lived in small cottages consisting mostly of single rooms which had been built on either side of the main road from Cranburne to Wymburne. Even quite small children worked in the fields or helped in the gardens, learning their skills from their fathers. Several of the minor disputes settled each month were the result of sons wishing to learn another trade or even leave home to work in Wymburne.

"I am not keen to have unwilling labour on my land," Alfred told Owen. "Occasionally it is necessary to agree to a man's request to seek another lord. Like those two brothers who spent all their time fighting. When one asked to move, I know we were not at all loathe to part with him! Just as often another turns up looking to find a place at Uddings. I check at the Moot that he is free to move and if possible why he came to me. At least there is little possibility now of runaway slaves being involved."

"Quite so lord. Most of our workers are content. They have all the Saints' Days free, Sundays and days for special celebrations," he added pointedly referring to Alfred's forthcoming marriage. His face was split by a broad smile knowing that the man he addressed as lord was counting the days, even the hours until he would be with Brith.

It was chilly in the late afternoon, the light almost gone for the day. Both men wore thick felted woollen cloaks to ward off the cold as they walked slowly back to the hall along the ridge between two bare fields empty of crops.

Towards the end of December when hard frost gripped the earth, a messenger arrived from his future father-in-law bringing the news that the wedding party would be setting out in one week. Alfred immediately insisted that his hair was cut in readiness for his wedding, unwilling to appear unkempt on the great day. Edith too was affected by the excitement and frequently took supplies of her preserves and herbs over to the store rooms at Uddings where she was relieved to find all in readiness for the arrival of her son's bride. Even though travel by ox cart was slow the ground had remained hard, each evergreen leaf on the small bushes edged with frost. Wrapped in a woollen blanket and the pots bedded in straw she found the short journey was a welcome break from the steamy heat of her kitchen.

Edith knew that Aethelflaed and Hal held hands at every opportunity; she thought him a handsome young man but without prospects. As yet he had not even had the chance to gain riches in battle and if King Edgar had his way there would be no wars.

"Tis time they too were married," Edith reminded Alfred one evening. "Has anything been negotiated?"

Not having seen Hal's father again since the court case he agreed reluctantly that the matter should be discussed. "I am not entirely happy that she should marry a landless man. There are many young men at the King's court who would make her a good husband. It's my fault for not keeping her with me on my journeys to court or on the King's business.

He is undoubtedly a pleasant young man but he must seek favour with the King to get position and status. The time has come to nudge him in the right direction. Life here is pleasant but it is too easy for a young man who could go far."

Edith immediately regretted her lack of supervision of her daughter these last few months. While she had her own doubts as to how Aethelflaed would cope with married life, being untidy and some might say undomesticated, she had enjoyed watching their love blossom and had heard no complaints of undue forwardness.

Hal was sent for the following morning before starting work. Aethelflaed was curious, but was told sternly that a man's business was of no concern to her. "You still have that hide to finish; you cannot expect the other women to do your work for you."

Aethelflaed pulled a face behind her mother's back. Cleaning the fat and veins from the inside of a sheepskin was one of the most unpleasant tasks. She picked up an old brown tunic and pulled the loose-weave fabric roughly over her head before flouncing out to the pegs which held the offending hide. She did not notice the dappled light falling through leafless trees or hear the small bird scavenging for tasty morsels in the leaf-mould. "I shall have servants to do all this," she muttered taking the guard from the curved knife before making the first sweeping pass with the blade.

Chapter Four
AD960

"Your brother suggests that I should find a new lord. There is little more to learn here. He is right; he keeps me in food and ale, clothes, shoes. None of this gives me a home to offer you."

"Why now? Will you return to your father? How can we see each other or be together if you go away?" retorted Aethelflaed aghast at the suggestion that Hal leave Uddings and Didlington. Tears streaming down her cheeks she ran pell mell for the hall where she accused her brother of condemning her to spinsterhood at worst and being a hand-maiden to his new wife at best.

"He has not offered for you, sister," retaliated Alfred when confronted by his outraged younger sister, her eyes wild with anger, her cheeks flaming in a very unbecoming manner. "Neither has he the means to do so. He is a younger son and must make his way in the world or the church. You are too old now to be frolicking around with young farming men and will come to court with me in the spring. There are young men there who serve the King and travel with the court. You will be well dowered, as much as a man in my position can afford, and are attractive."

"I would like to go to court, but you would not force me to wed a man I did not love would you?" Her eyebrows were raised with concern, lips open ready to object then quickly closed when her brother shook his head.

Somewhat mollified by this opportunity, Aethelflaed's protestation that she only wanted to marry Hal was not said as forcefully as it might have been. Wistfulness showed nakedly on her face, but Alfred hardened his heart and was tempted to mention that marrying a man without prospects was no way to ensure she had the servants she desired to do the many household tasks she disliked.

"There are many young men at court. Some like me have performed a service or fought well for the King and been rewarded. There are others who were born of a great lord. They feel that they are better than men like me, purely because of their birth, but King Edgar treats everyone equally. Thegns and men like me even hunt with him. Sometimes he asks one or two to sit with him. Of course they are likely to be from Mercia or Northumbria where he has been King for four years. Men from the other shires will be given positions when he has fully established his court. There will be opportunities to meet many after the main meal of the day. I would remind you though; scowling, moodiness and temper have no place there. Besides, when you smile your face is almost pretty!"

Aethelflaed aimed a slap at her elder brother which he dodged easily. They parted laughing, she, to ask her mother for a new gown and Alfred to visit the mill.

Hal left early, just after daybreak, for his father's home, dressed in a new, warm, fleece jerkin as his old one was not only in a state of considerable decay but several sizes too small. Greying dawn light was illuminating the furze bushes and prickly leaves of evergreens. He used a stout stick with a ram's horn decorating the end as his only weapon to keep himself safe. Well muscled from all his outdoor work he had refused the offer of companions to walk with him. He promised fervently to make good somehow and return to claim his love. Edith understood her son's anxiety to see Aethelflaed well married, but also sympathised with her daughter at being parted from her young man.

"Alfred is right to introduce you at court. You will have a choice of suitable men who have already established themselves in the King's favour. Maybe Hal will offer to serve in the King's guard. He could do well to rise in the army or join young Lord Hugh's force and travel all over the shire. Many men are rewarded for their services, but it is not in your brother's power to make another's mark for him."

Aethelflaed had to be content with her mother's practical explanation although she brooded, shedding tears in private or when she thought no-one was looking. To counteract her daughter's moodiness Edith ensured that she had little free time, keeping her daughter busy with household tasks from dawn to dusk. After church a very subdued girl followed her mother round the market hardly raising her eyes to greet acquaintances. The joy had gone out of her life and everyone could see it. When anyone spoke to her there was no smile, just quavering sighs as if her heart was breaking.

On a bright winter day, with small clouds scudding across the pale blue sky the wedding party arrived with servants leading baggage ponies and an ox cart loaded with household goods. Edith greeted them, enfolding Brith in a capacious hug. "You are both so welcome! The entire household has been in a state of anxious turmoil all week. I tell you, even the youngest child has made excuses to come and ask questions, everyone looks forward to meeting the master's bride."

Even as she was leading the way into the hall, curious faces peered round the corner of the kitchen. Brith looked around and smiled broadly when children were hastily pulled back out of sight. Picking up the skirts of her new gown she followed her new mother in law and father into the hall wondering why Alfred had not been outside to greet her on this important day.

"Had I been in the yard there would have been no decorum in my greeting! As it is there is an overwhelming desire to pick you up and whisk you off the bridal chamber! Hardly suitable at this time of day, let alone that we are not yet married. My love, you have never looked more beautiful. I do not have the courtly words to tell you how much I love you and want you beside me for all time."

Alfred subsided into embarrassed silence, but continued to look directly at Brith. Her eyes shone, almost glittering in the dappled sunlight inside the hall. Neither of them noticed the servants unloading the cart, spreading the bride goods on the cloth covered trestles. They were holding both hands outstretched, drinking in the sight of each other from head to toe. He with his newly cut hair and King's diadem, his best green tunic and leggings; her with just a narrow scarf securing her long hair in a single plait down her back and a new dark green robe with panels of lighter green to emphasise her slim waist.

Edith broke the spell between them, coughing politely to remind them that they were not alone in the hall. Anything that could be scrubbed or polished had been done countless times. Cobwebs had been removed from the rafters and the stones around the central hearth had been whitewashed like the walls. Around the walls boughs of evergreen and holly had been arranged in preparation for the Yule Day celebrations. Their scent added a spicy perfume to the atmosphere. The huge log which would burn for the twelve days of the holiday season lay beside the hearth.

"I must compliment you on the quality of the bride goods, my dear. Look they are now arranged. Did you do the stitching on the wall coverings yourself?"

Brith pointed to the ones she had done and those which had been made by her late mother. Alfred chatted in hushed whispers to his father in law Brithric, aware that his attention often wandered as his eyes followed Brith as she walked beside his mother.

Aethelflaed fussed round rearranging jewellery, comb and belt buckles so that they were shown to their best advantage.

At the same time a cup of finely brewed ale was passed round by Edith who had already been fondly embraced by Brithric as soon as he had finished supervising the unloading of the last pony.

"They will be wed at noon," she said, "then I return home. I shall be glad to have just the one household to look after!"

"My lady, if I may escort you to Didlington it would be an honour. There is private business I would discuss with you," murmured Brithric. Smiling broadly, he took her arm to lead her away from the laden tables. Dressed in his best tunic and short cloak he was a striking figure with merry eyes set in a tanned face. Although his hair and beard were grizzled with silver they only served to emphasise the authority in his demeanour. Edith felt girlish in his presence, an emotion which she had not experienced for years. Their private conversation was interrupted when Alfred announced that the priest from Wymburne had arrived. This individual had once again brought respect for the church back to the townspeople of Wymburne. His clean dark robes and shining, fresh faced complexion only added to his aura of competence when leading a service. Now he greeted everyone with open arms and a cheerful smile including servants in his salutations. He accepted a glass of ale, immediately complimenting Edith on the valuable drinking vessel with which she had honoured him.

Servants scurried round with the last dishes for the feast while Brith and Aethelflaed withdrew to the room which would become the bridal chamber to prepare for the ceremony. Alfred's young sister could not prevent herself from admiring the girl who was to become her brother's wife. "You are so beautiful; I am not surprised that my brother has been worrying these last few weeks in case anything went wrong with his arrangements. Everytime anyone visited he feared it would be orders which would take him away from home."

Happiness had given Brith's complexion an added lustre. Her eyes shone with joy so that it was infectious. Helping Brith prepare for this important moment in her life made the younger girl forget her hurts. The sulky looks vanished to be replaced by a genuinely welcoming smile, small dimples, inherited from her mother, appearing in the rosy cheeks.

"My mother wore this at her wedding to my father," Brith sighed unfolding a length of linen woven so finely that it had little weight to it. It was edged with gold thread which caught the light, falling just above Brith's eyebrows.

The fine gold circlet was adjusted to hold the veil in place while Aethelflaed watched in wonder as her future sister was transformed from a maiden with uncovered hair to a married woman with a household to run, her hair completely covered by the veil.

"You look lovely sister." Aethelflaed could not disguise the admiration in her voice. "Come, the priest will be ready and I know my brother is impatient!"

The two girls giggled nervously arranging the skirt of Brith's dress quite unnecessarily.

In the hall Alfred was indeed more than ready to proceed with his wedding, almost hopping from one foot to another as the minutes passed. As many servants as could be spared from their duties had filled the hall to witness the marriage of their lord. Someone had flung a handful of scented leaves on the fire so that the hall was filled with a perfumed haze.

It was through this haze that the door curtain was drawn back revealing Brith dressed in a deep blue robe, the underskirt showing light blue as she slowly walked towards the assembled company and her father.

Stopping in front of him, they embraced formally, clearly an emotional moment for them both. Brithric led his daughter to Alfred and placed his daughter's hand on her future husband's outstretched arm with the traditional words "I give her to you willingly."

He returned to Edith's side, discreetly feeling for her hand as the priest stepped forward to bless Alfred and Brith in front of the jostling witnesses. "Do you Alfred take this woman, Brith, daughter of Brithric willingly?"

"I do, most willingly" he responded, his eyes shining with just a hint of a tear so great was the emotion of the moment.

"Do you Brith; take Alfred, son of the late Lord Udric and the lady Edith, willingly?"

"I do indeed!" responded Brith, conscious of the sense of occasion, the hush in the hall, the exhaling of many breaths when she agreed to take Alfred as her husband. Even the dogs who had crept in by the hearth sat with pricked ears as if they too understood the solemnity of the oaths they had witnessed.

The priest's arms were wide apart as he spoke a final prayer in English which everyone present could understand. He called on God to bless the union, the house, and everyone in it; his beautiful, clear voice being heard by even those at the back of the crowd standing on stools to ensure a good view of the proceedings.

When the ceremony was over, Edith took the two iron keys of the Uddings store chests to Brith, signifying the transfer of responsibility for the household. With tears in her eyes, Edith embraced her new daughter affectionately.

"These now belong to you daughter. I give them to you with love and honour."

Taking the huge keys as if they were of gold, Brith undid the loop of her scrip and slipped them into its depth where they would be safe.

The light wind caused the candles to waver, flickering shadows dancing on the newly brightened walls. Cheers erupted from the servants before they scurried to fetch the last few dishes from the kitchen.

The feasting lasted until well into the dusk when servants cleared the hall. The shutters were closed and additional wall lights lit providing both warmth and light. There was dancing and music, loud enough to drown the sound of the coarse jokes at Alfred's expense. Most of the guests left after escorting the bridal pair to the small room, wishing the young couple a long life, happiness and many children, the latter added in suggestive tones, quickly stifled.

Having been prepared for their first truly intimate encounter by willing helpers Alfred and Brith were alone at last in the small private chamber transformed with small flowers from gorse bushes into their nuptial haven. Only two candles lit the cosy interior, a small wrought iron brazier providing a little warmth to take the chill off the December air. Standing close together on the fleece beside the bed, Alfred stroked his new wife's neck and shoulders, nibbling the lobe of one ear and then the other. She arched her neck so that the ties of her new shift could be undone more easily. His kisses had already fired her blood, unfamiliar sensations of warmth and wetness in her innermost secret places flooded her body. In a moment of wantonness she touched his manhood causing them both to gasp.

Their progress to the bed which Alfred had planned to make slow and courtly so as not to frighten his new bride was instead a rush, dignity thrown to the winds as two passionate bodies sought release in each other.

Now that the hall was comparatively empty save for servants, Edith was tired after many days of preparation in both kitchens. Most of the field hands and cottagers had already left for their own hearths because tomorrow would be a busy day. It was nearly dark but she was anxious to return to her own bed rather than sleep in the more cramped guest room at Uddings. True to his promise, Brithric called for his horse and escorted Edith and Aethelflaed from the hall, unaware that those who remained were smiling to themselves at their elder's obvious attraction for each other. The track was well trodden, the edges having been marked by the judicious placing of whitewashed stones. They left to rousing cheers, their parting lit by fleeting glimpses of the new moon.

Gradually Brith took over the management of the household. She had a lovely nature, offending no-one as she introduced small changes to the routine in the kitchens and hall. Her dower goods were added to the well equipped furnishings while the jewellery was locked carefully away in a strong box beside their bed.

Owenson and his wife now had their own cottage close to the hall, each of them having been assured that Alfred's marriage did not affect their standing in the small community at Uddings.

Brith too was glad of their friendship and support, especially when she was left alone while her husband attended the quarter sessions. Stable boys vied for the opportunity to accompany their lord's wife when she rode out to familiarise herself with his land. Her mare, a dainty moorland pony, had quickly become a favourite in the stable, Owenson longing to ask for permission to put her in foal by the remaining stallion.

News from court mentioned the land which had been restored to the church, apparently at the request of Dunstan, the King's advisor. Having been restored to favour, the devout churchman had first been appointed Bishop of Worcester, then of London.

"He is now Archbishop of Canterbury," reported the clerk, a small man with permanently ink-stained fingers. "The previous minister was frozen to death crossing the Alps on the way to Rome! Dunstan plans to depart in mid summer."

The King gave permission for the abbey at Hortune to be built for the Benedictine order. The site had already been chosen but now cartloads of materials trundled up the gravely track spitting stones into the fields alongside. Stone from deep in the earth showing its reddish iron content gradually rose as substantial walls. The heliers from Wymburne awaited their turn to work on the site as carpenters and joiners sweated to fit huge rafters on which the roofing slates would be secured. Alfred watched in dismay as his boundary road, for which Didlington was responsible, gradually wore down. After rain the chalk, without its flint and gravel content, degenerated into clinging, grey mud. Children collected the stones from the fields, extracted those which could be used with the countryman's weapon, the sling, and threw the remainder back onto the road.

As in Wymburne, there was one building for housing nuns and a separate less comfortable one for the monks. The latter worked as manual labourers, pausing in their work to send songs of praise towards heaven. The Wymburne men shrugged their shoulders, looking forward to the end of the working day when most of them would walk home.

Following the agreed rota, Alfred was summoned to supply men for the coastal defence watch for one month. Choosing the men from Didlington who would serve as guardsmen, many admitted that they had never seen the sea. Indeed, some had never been to Dorchester but had kin who came from villages near Bleneford on the far side of the King's palace beyond Wymburne. It would be an adventure, an experience to tell others who had not been asked to go on this first duty.

"We are lucky in a way. The ground is hard and frosty so wear the warmest clothes you have. Ditching will have to wait this year, I'm sure you won't mind! We will join men from Cheneford, Holt and Chalburie to make up the quota required, but at least our time will be up before the spring planting. Weapons must be sharp and rust free don't forget. We leave on Sunday!"

Alfred was thrilled when his mother told him of her intention to marry Brithric the following year.

"I would rather choose a husband than have one forced upon me by the King," she said. "Now that Dunstan is the Archbishop he may not have time to bring my widowhood to my lord King's attention but another advisor will if only to gain notice for his efficiency. Besides, seeing you and Brith so happy has made me feel so lonely again. I miss Udric, although the pain is dulled through time. I never thought to have a second chance of happiness."

"Your contentment is what is important. Actually, your decision to wed again, to a man whom you love is timely. Be assured that you have my blessing. When I return we will all go up to court. The King will be pleased for you, especially as he has recently married himself. Besides I promised to take Aethelflaed."

He did not add that according to the Bishop Brithelm of Sherburne the royal marriage might not be legal. Lord Brithelm had already been demoted once for criticising the King and was not anxious to spread rumour, so had impressed on Alfred the need for keeping these thoughts to himself for the time being.

Reluctantly he left Uddings and his beloved Brith who was now expecting her first child for the shore-line watchtowers of Dorsetshire. Already there was a small swelling of her normally flat abdomen, her breasts rounding in preparation for the new child within. Their last night had been spent wrapped in each other's arms, spent, sweaty and content after slow, sensual mating.

Alfred's newly sharpened seax hung in its broad scabbard over his back. Hanging from the pommel of his saddle was a spiked mace wrapped in hide, a blow from which could fracture a man's skull like eggshell. Most of the men had bows and sheaves of arrows, the weapon with which they were already familiar. The waxed thread for the bow was kept dry in scrips hanging from stout leather belts. Rations for his squad followed slowly in an ox cart, thick blankets and a tent had also been made to give shelter. There had been no information as to what was provided for the guards even though tents and rations had been promised by Lord Hugh.

Alfred was anxious that his field-workers would have at least some of the comforts of home.

The men found the air cold and were quickly bored watching the sea once their astonishment at seeing such a huge expanse of water had waned. As far as the horizon was grey, dull pewter coloured broken only occasionally by white spume or a flash of silver when a creature from the deep leapt above the surface.

Alfred resorted to leading practice sessions with arms and horse races or other games for those not actually on watch to alleviate the men's boredom. Even those who had never ridden before were taught the rudiments, their fellows laughing at the discomfort of those who fell off.

"Surely you do not let your field-hands ride such valuable beasts?" queried William, the leader of the men from Chalburie, a haughty individual who had been antagonistic right from the start of his duty. With dark, brooding eyes and a long thin nose the man had criticised the tents, food and lack of home comforts.

"Of course they do not usually ride horses but I breed them for the King and have workers who do nothing else but look after them. Some however are natural riders and they can ask to learn more. At Uddings each man does what he is best at, I find that the men are content."

"Huh! You are too soft. Treat them like the low born peasants that they are. Mine know who is master!"

Alfred could feel anger swelling up into full blown rage at the overweening pride and boastfulness of the elegantly dressed young man before him. He sucked in an outraged breath determined not to let his rising temper fool him into making stupid responses. He regretted not having worn the King's diadem that day, having replaced it with a more practical plain band of fabric matching his tunic and cloak. Bowing abruptly, granting the minimum respect he could, he turned and left the Chalburie lord standing alone, a puzzled look on his dour face.

"Blast the man!

The fresh fish brought up to them by the coastal fishermen was greatly appreciated as an addition to the food which they had brought with them. Day after day, sometimes in strong eye-watering winds, a watch was kept on the grey-silver expanse of the sea. They saw nothing, not a single suspect vessel was spotted, no striped sails, no sleek, oar-powered ships. Alfred missed Brith as well as the amenities of Uddings so he was not the least surprised when several men had to be punished for leaving the camp to visit girls from the fishing villages. He was later to realise the outcome, when news was brought that several girls had given birth to children, some nine months after his turn on duty.

Handing over the King's seal to the next watch commander, he led his men back to Uddings. There a message ordered him to report to King Edgar who was travelling to Dorset. Having been away from Brith he could see the changes which had already taken place to her once shapely figure. There was a soft glow to her face, the bloom unique to portending motherhood. The other mothers gladly gave their support and encouragement when morning sickness made her weak and exhausted.

"There is more to child-bearing than I ever knew," she complained in the privacy of their room, "when I need to rest he decides to kick in protest! Feel it, there, now."

Alfred gently rested his palm on her swelling belly. Beneath her warm skin he could feel small movements, gentle pushes against the light pressure. His eyes widened in surprise, a huge grin breaking across his face at the wonder of the new life being created.

"My love, it is a marvel. I can feel the kicking…"

His descriptive words were interrupted abruptly when Brith adjusted the pillow to support her shoulders. "Oh this is nothing, wait until we go to bed tonight. I swear it knows when the last candle has been blown out!" They laughed together when he described his month away on coastal watch and she told him of her early attempts at some unusual household chores.

"I started weaving some extra soft cloth for the baby. A Wymburne woman came and helped me to set up the loom. This is one skill my mother never taught me because she died when I was only a small child. I suppose father has bought the clothes or cloth we needed. Anyway, hopefully it will be a useable length of fabric. It was nice to make a friend in the town. I will introduce you on Sunday if you have finished with the King's business by then."

Soldiers at Kingston confirmed that some guests had already arrived. All the mills had already been ordered to provide the necessary flour for the bake houses, the cart from Didlington having delivered Alfred's quota during his absence. Sheep had been driven to the slaughter place in preparation for the arrival of the court.

There had been no orders to take any horses from the Uddings' fields so Alfred confined his initial visit to finding out from the clerks exactly when he would be required to attend the King. He admired a new litter of puppies nestling beside their dam in the stables before returning home in the pink tinted dusk.

The ideal opportunity to present Aethelflaed to the King had now arisen without the need to travel or stay in Winchester. She was now twenty-one summers old and should have been married several years ago. "I have neglected you shamefully," he admitted. "Let me speak to the King about a husband for you. Lord Hugh may be coming to the feast and bring men from his household. Surely there must be a man who can out-shine all the skills and handsomeness you attribute to Hal!"

Excited at the prospect, Aethelflaed washed her hair and brushed it till it shone, determined to enjoy the experience, all the while insisting that she loved Hal. Brith plaited her new sister's shining tresses into three sections before interweaving the three together, sun-lightened strands interspersing with the darker hair.

Wearing a new overdress with her mother's enamelled torque around her neck, Aethelflaed proudly accompanied her brother into the King's hall. "It is just like the hall at Uddings which grand-father built," she remarked immediately. "It is bigger but the windows and doorways here are also whole tree trunks. Have you seen the cooks' quarters? They are so big!"

"Remember, many people will look at you and judge your whole family by your behaviour. No listen, and don't pull that face! Drink very little for the King's ale may be stronger than mother's; talk of general matters to your neighbours who may be the wives of thegns or the King's officials. Do not under any circumstances leave the hall without another woman, it could be misunderstood. Now come and I will find you a place where you can see the high table."

A great feast was held in the evening of the King's arrival at his Wymburne palace. All the Dorset thegns were present together with the Bishops of Winchester, Bath and Sherburne. Alfred was congratulated on his marriage to Brith who was now obviously pregnant. He found a seat for her with another mother-to-be and left her talking of women's matters while he renewed his acquaintance with other Dorset thegns. Welcoming everyone, King Edgar ordered that there be no ceremony, for he had come to hunt, not to conduct state business.

Aethelflaed was introduced to many young men who surrounded her eagerly under Edith's watchful eye. "Keep them all at a distance," she advised, "your behaviour here must be beyond reproach, especially as your brother sometimes represents the King in this county."

"Most of them are also younger sons and landless. No different to Hal's situation really, and there is not one who has his fair hair or bright eyes!" retorted Aethelflaed who had quickly grown tired of making polite conversation to young men who had few topics apart from bettering themselves in the king's service.

Setting her daughter a good example, Edith smiled politely as the dishes were passed along the table, helping herself to a little from each. They could see all the brightly dressed nobles and churchmen seated at the raised table, most of whom outdid the clothes King Edgar had chosen to wear. In the torchlight a number of vulgarly large jewels flashed and the gold threads in their cloaks glowed. Beneath maidenly lowered lashes, Aethelflaed was astonished to notice the large mouthfuls one churchman endeavoured to swallow, wiping dribbles of gravy or grease from his mouth with fat, podgy be-ringed fingers. The man beside him had obviously noticed his neighbour's greed and turned his head away. He caught Aethelflaed's eye and smiled conspiratorially. Aethelflaed blushed not realising that her glances had descended into open staring.

The King's wife was present despite being more heavily pregnant than Brith. The two women talked together, resting comfortably supported by cushions.

The last time Alfred had met most of the other landowners was when the King had ordered warships to be built and a watch set on the coastline. Comparing their experiences carrying out the recent guard duty, one remarked how dull his turn had been. "I could just as well have seen to my own fields," he grumbled.

Alfred also admitted to having been bored but pointed out that Dorset was often thought to be an easy target because of the number of rivers which could be navigated inland. "We have some which come many miles into the land, especially through Twynham. The old watch towers of King Alfred are not sufficient. After all the fishermen of Poole come right up to Wymburne or Hame if the river runs deeply. In the summer they can still get to the ford at Longham."

The others nodded solemnly, their conversation interrupted when a tall stranger approached them.

"My lord wishes to call council tomorrow," he said, "at eight of the clock before the hunt." Bowing slightly, the man turned and left them to speak to another group. His blonde hair was long, held in a knot at the back of his head. On his bare arms were bracelets which only served to emphasise the bulging muscles.

"Who was that? His speech was not like ours."

"I met a northerner who spoke like that," commented Alfred, "but let us join the womenfolk again or I'll be accused of neglect."

Laughing and nodding, the men returned to the main group in the hall where the servants were busy clearing away the trestles.

Having broken their fast with bread, cheese and ale, Brith, Lady Edith and Aethelflaed were ushered into the Queen's quarters, a pleasant room with sun-lit windows and comfortable settles. Other ladies made space for them before returning to their gossip. Aethelflaed's face had once more relaxed into its familiar pout. "There was not a single boy there of any interest at all," she grumbled. On looking round she discovered to her dismay that she was the only woman with unbound hair. "How long do we have to stay here?" she whispered loudly causing one or two women to break off their conversations and stare in her direction.

Brith and Lady Edith exchanged knowing glances, having suspected that the girl would have made her judgement quickly, her heart already content in her choice of Hal as her future mate. The fact that she had received no word of him since he left Didlington had not dimmed her hopes, her love or her determination. She stood up and strode to the open window. Outside horses, huntsmen and dog handlers milled round in disorganised chaos, everyone waiting for the king to close his meeting. More horses were brought from the stables, including the King's horse, Thor. Standing taller than every other mount, Aethelflaed recognised the famous horse from endless descriptions of it by first Owen then Owenson.

At the council the King, a diminutive figure, being smaller than many of those present, called for silence. Even standing on the dais gave him little advantage. "So far all reports from the Dorset coast have been only of innocent traders or fisher-folk but that has not been the case in the North East. Raiders have attempted to disturb the peace of this land, some-times aided and abetted by the people of the Danelands and their allies. For this reason Lord Sigferth, the King of Northumbria travels with my court ensuring the loyalty of those lands." The King waved his arm in the direction of his companion beside him.

Alfred quickly looked around the men gathered in a circle about the King. There was a quick flash of understanding between several of them. The stranger sat on a chair only slightly less ornate than Edgar's, a thin gold circlet about his brow.

Having been introduced, the hostage Prince bowed briefly and left the hall his head high, the cloak over one shoulder swinging in step.

"The man who spoke thickly," muttered the man sat next to him, nudging Alfred quickly.

The King continued, ignoring the whispers. "I have brought peace and the Christian faith to all parts of the Kingdom. My right hand, Bishop Dunstan, is on his way to Rome to receive the Pope's blessing. My Lord Bishop Aelfwold has returned to his former see in Bath and Sherburne as he had not the stomach for the work. According to our wishes, many monasteries have been set up with strict rules so that men may learn the love of God and honour him."

Some were used to these homilies of the King. Others were astonished at the strength of their ruler's feelings expressed so openly.

The King continued in his praise of Dunstan's work, both as chancellor and as leader of the reformation which had been brought to the religious houses of the land.

"I will have every child christened in the faith. The clergy will not marry, but devote themselves entirely to service, healing and divine meditation."

It seemed as though King Edgar would continue to lecture the Dorset men on their Christian duty for some time. Many grew restless, but none dared interrupt. They could hear the horses being readied for the hunt, harness jingling and hooves stamping on the packed earth. Still the King went on with his monologue, ignoring the tempting sounds around him.

Even while he spoke a young servant entered the hall, paused nervously and then approached the King, clearly terrified of a stern rebuke. Almost crouching as he made his way forward, his close cropped head ducked as if to avoid a blow, the young man only straightened himself with difficulty.

"My lord, my lord," began the man clasping his hands together in his agitation. "T'is Lord Sigferth; he is dead!"

Edgar rose up suddenly, his face reddened with anger. The servant stepped back several paces and collided with those men who had been closest to the King.

"Dead?" queried the King, "by whose hand?"

A number of the men rose to their feet and rushed to the far corner of the hall where a guard stood over their weapons. Swords were snatched up, some even raising blades in readiness.

In an instant the King had forgotten his peace-loving, god fearing attitude, calling for his own sword. Without waiting for guards he led the men out of the hall shouting for the assassin to be caught and brought before him.

"The man was under my protection," he lamented to anyone who cared to listen. "Where is lord Sigferth's body?" The hall was in pandemonium, men struggled to fasten belts, cloaks dropping to the floor to ease the task. Dogs rushed around barking excitedly, infected by the sudden increase in activity and tension.

Led by soldiers to the guest quarters, the body of Sigferth lay face down across his bed, his blood slowly congealing around it.

A priest pushed his way in to the room and gently turned the body over. A dagger protruded from Sigferth's chest and had clearly done its work well.

"Who ever did this shall die," declared the King vehemently.

"But my lord," pointed out Alfred boldly interrupting his liege lord, "T'is his own dagger. He used it at the feast last night. I swear it is his own knife." Men pushed forward to see the bloody scene more clearly.

The priest drew back from the body as if it had suddenly become an evil thing, exclaiming that it was a sin against God to kill oneself. Everyone crossed themselves hastily, mumbling prayers in hushed voices.

"He killed himself!" pronounced the priest again, obviously on the point of expanding on such a sin.

"My guest will be given an honourable burial. Dress him decently, priest. Have this removed and order restored," he said pointing at the bloodstained bedding and rushes on the floor. "Clean the knife; put it back in his belt. He was my guest; under my protection and I have failed him."

Needless to say the hunt was cancelled as a mark of respect leaving everyone wandering around aimlessly, talking in shocked whispers of the death.

The King spent hours on his knees in the little church accompanied by a succession of Dorset dignitaries while messages were sent for a grave to be prepared in the great church at Wymburne. The old Bishop of Sherburne was ordered to attend the King as a matter of urgency.

"Thank God the women are safe with the Queen. Just because a man has a knife in his chest does not mean he did it himself. He could have known the killer and greeted him in the guest room." Alfred confided to a friend.

Despite the protests of the priests that a man who had obviously killed himself should not be given Christian burial, the body was taken by ox cart to the church the following day and laid to rest inside the church. All men bowed their heads, many crossing themselves fervently. Candles had been lit on all the sconces so that the atmosphere was filled with the smoke so particular to wax. A small boy waved an elaborate incense burner, wafting clouds of perfumed smoke around the congregation. By the time the mass ended many men had become cold in the unheated atmosphere. King Edgar, a small figure in robes which seemed several sizes to large for him, led the congregation out into squally gusts of wind laden with freezing rain. Men raised their hoods, pulled on gauntlets then paused as the King remained bareheaded among them.

A sullen crowd of townsfolk had gathered outside the church fearful of the large number of guards who waited with the horses, stamping their feet and blowing on their hands in an effort to keep warm. They had not been allowed inside St Mary's but rumours abounded concerning the burial of a possible suicide in their church. Only recently they had accompanied a man and his children to the place where two roads crossed to place the body of his woman in a shallow grave beside the track. Her mind had been disturbed after losing a much longed for son. She had bled to death from deep cuts leaving two girls and their father to grieve, their sorrow increased because she had died unshriven and her resting place was unhallowed. They muttered among themselves but fell silent when the King had glared at them before mounting the huge horse, using a servant's back as an aid.

The women folk in the Queen's private room had taken no part in the funeral. They emerged for the evening meal which was subdued, the shadow of the suicide hanging over the whole court. There should have been hare and deer on the menu but the cook had been forced to prepare mutton, yet again. The King declared that he was fasting as a penance for not protecting Lord Sigferth while in his custody.

Alfred was approached discreetly by several would-be suitors for permission to court his sister, but she had already made it clear that she had not been attracted to one more than another.

"My sister is honoured by your interest. She is with the Queen's ladies, but this is no longer the time to be thinking of courtship."

He knew that only the most persistent would make another attempt to ask his leave.

Conversation lapsed into more mundane matters as the evening progressed. Brith and the King's wife, accompanied by many of the ladies and unwed maidens retired early while the men gathered into groups to talk amongst themselves. Some talked in hushed voices about the apparent suicide of the northern King while others contented themselves with talk of crops or livestock. Many wished themselves back at their farms instead of attending the King's court which had proved to be so lacking in advantage or preferment. The King had given no gifts to his loyal thegns or landowners, indeed apart from brief praise for their share in guarding the coastline, there had been little gain for any of them.

Alfred managed to speak to the King privately as he crossed the courtyard the following day. At a quick glance lord Edgar was unchanged but as he came closer, it was obvious that his face was pinched and drawn; the eyes which normally noticed everything were now hooded and dull.

"My lord, forgive me for approaching you in your grief but I need your advice." Alfred had learned the best way of getting the King's attention by watching the senior members of the court at Winchester.

"My sister is unwed and has formed an attachment for the younger son of Vann of Woodcutts at Sexpenna Hanlega. He is skilled with sheep having learned much here with your own sheepward. His father let him spend some time at Uddings as his father's land grows barley. Hal put sheep on my meadows for some weeks before we sowed the corn and the crop was the best raised."

"He worked here you say?" replied Edgar thoughtfully.

"Yes lord. Your steward gave good reports of him. He is well formed, presentable, and respectful to his elders, but as yet without land or position. His elder brother intends to marry shortly and will have the farm when his father dies. There is no room for both of them. Hal must make his own way. He is fond of Aethelflaed and she returns his affection." He added with an attempt to lighten the tone of their conversation.

The King nodded, taking a moment to wrest his mind from the more serious matters that needed his attention. "Walk with me then Alfred." Guards hovered discreetly behind the two men, the King waving his hand dismissively in their direction.

Linking his arm through that of his companion, the King talked generally of the situation in the Kingdom, and of his constant fear that the current peaceful situation would be broken by rebellion or worse, an invasion.

Alfred commented quietly from time to time but without interrupting the King's concentration. The fleet was being built as ordered; the courts supervised the laws of the land and with some exceptions, the church kept its own house in order. "It is an envious state of affairs according to the occasional news from France and the Saxon states across the water."

Nodding his agreement, Alfred wished the King would turn his attention to his own problem. "He must come to court," said the King suddenly. Presuming that the King was now referring to Hal, son of Vann of Woodcutts Farm, he replied that he was grateful for the suggestion. "If the Sheriff of Dorset has arrived, send him to me."

Taking that as his dismissal Alfred bowed gracefully and left his lord to his meditation, hoping the King would indeed summon Hal to court. The guards nodded to him as he went back to the hall in search of Lord Hugh.

The postponed hunt took place the following day to replenish the stocks of deer meat, a welcome change to salted pork or mutton with the usual barley pottage. All were welcome to attend the meal so that every villein who could leave his land had trekked to Kingston for the feast.

William of Chalberie was among those who arrived with his uniformed guards. He nodded condescendingly to those he considered worthy of notice and was observed to push his horse towards those of the visiting earls and greet them with all the appearance of close friendship.

"It's a good thing he was not here earlier," commented Alfred in a brief moment alone with his mother. "I had the opportunity to ask Lord Edgar if he would give Hal a chance to make a name for himself. The King linked arms with me; his guards nearly had multiple apoplexies! What would my haughty neighbour from Chalberie have made of that I wonder?"

Edith, had hoped that Lord Brithric might have attended the King's court in Wymburne, smiled weakly. "How soon can I go home? There seems little point in hanging around. Aethelflaed is being her usual miserable, moody self. I feel like knocking some sense into her head but I can hardly do that here." Her normally rosy face looked strained with disappointment. The crisp white wimple now drooped, mirroring her own feelings. She had got used to having some small measure of privacy at Didlington and found sleeping cheek by jowl with many others in the King's hall was not conducive to a good night's rest.

"It was only because of the death that the hunt and feast were delayed. Tomorrow hopefully we can all leave. I too look forward to going home. Brith finds it tiring, even though the King's lady is kindness itself. Now it is time for me to ride out. Having asked the King for a favour he would be irritated if my absence was brought to his attention. It would not be beyond William's prideful nature to do just that. We'll be back soon enough, hopefully with fresh meat." He gave his mother a quick hug before fastening his cloak and striding towards the stables.

Once again the courtyard was crowded with horses, hunt servants and lymer dogs straining at their leashes encouraging men to mount and move out. The women watched, recognising their spouses or sons following the King out of the high gates. Spare mounts and baskets of refreshments followed at a slower pace, the solemn face of the head stableman dictating the dignified exit under his charge.

No sooner had the courtyard been cleared of men and beasts than the steward appeared to order the mess to be cleared. Sounds of the butcher sharpening his knives penetrated the sudden lull, broken by the rhythmic sweeping of the courtyard under the eagle eyes of the scowling steward.

Servants put up the trestles with hardly enough room between them for a man to walk. Visiting servants gladly helped while women sipped small beer and chatted to their friends around the hearth. Many were in awe of the size of the building, lifting their eyes frequently to the massive oak beams and the smoke hole, or curiously fingering the woven hangings on the wall. Outside the sky was veiled with thin cloud and there was no heat in the sunshine but the day still felt festive and the prospect of a portion of forbidden deer meat was a magnet for those who could leave their labours. The smell of stale food and body odour was quickly dispelled when the dried leaves of herbs were scattered on the green rush mats and crushed underfoot.

Despite the recent suicide of the northern hostage, visiting minstrels played quietly while storytellers told many sagas of the glories of the King's ancestors, of battles fought and deeds of valour. Fires were discreetly fed with logs brought in huge baskets by strong servants. Maidservants and pages replenished ale mugs and dishes of sweetmeats. King Edgar refused the latter, murmuring that he could not treat himself while Sigferth's body was hardly cold in its grave.

Lord Hugh, Sheriff of Dorset sat beside Godwin, Earl of Wessex apparently deeply involved in conversation. The former's dark eyes revealed little of his thoughts but missed little of the activities at the trestles set below the high table. The Earl of Wessex in contrast, was a large, florid faced man in bright robes. He flaunted his wealth ostentatiously, a large garnet brooch on one shoulder and elaborately worked gold chains around his thick neck. More gem stones were set in rings half buried in the pudgy flesh of his fingers. Each expansive movement of his arms seemed designed to show off the ornaments.

"Hasn't anyone told him of Sigferth's death?" commented one of Alfred's neighbours who like most of the other diners still wore the green or drab clothes in which they had hunted.

"He obviously eats too well. I suppose he can afford to with all the lands he owns. Mind you, no-one can accuse the King of over-eating. Who is on coast watch at the moment?" The quick change of subject may have been due to those on the high table rising to their feet, sweeping glances over everyone. Heads turned, hands paused as silence fell, allowing men to hastily swallow.

The King announced his departure for Shaftesbury to pay his respects at the nunnery before going to London for the remainder of the month. "I would prefer to have spent more time here among my friends." He paused to beam expansively at his Dorset subjects. "Yes, I would far rather spend longer hunting but my council constantly remind me that there are matters of importance which require my attention."

This time it was the turn of those counsellors who had joined him to quickly look regretful and apologetic. Earl Godwin belched loudly and shrugged nonchalantly when giggles could be heard in the hall. The musicians broke into another melody as men and women prepared to leave. Exhausted servants were chivvied into one last effort, clearing the tables, finding lost items of clothing and helping others to pack saddlebags.

"I believe the King intends to call Hal to attend him," Alfred confided to his mother as the horses were prepared. "In the meantime several young men have asked if they may court Aethelflaed." He was stroking the huge horse's head, pulling its ears gently. Thor's gentle brown eyes surrounded by long eyelashes half closed in ecstasy, his warm breath on Alfred's shoulder.

He helped his wife to mount while the steward held the bridle. He admitted that the extra length of time everyone had stayed had stretched the servants to the limit. "Mind you, now the larder is full again everyone is leaving, even the King. We shall eat well here! Not that you are a stranger to venison!" he added quietly, "The fencing has been repaired yet again and I intend to set a watch."

Alfred nodded to acknowledge the steward's warning and waved a cheerful farewell, shepherding his womenfolk before him.

Brith was anxious to return home as she now tired easily. There were signs of strain and dark shadows beneath her eyes. She too had not found it easy to rest comfortably at night. Used to the sounds of woods and heaths after the sun had gone down, the guards metalled boots striking paved or cobbled paths during the hours of darkness seemed loud and intrusive. Servants started work early, the clatter of cooking pots breaking into the pre-dawn stillness before birdsong announced the start of a new day.

They rode companionably side by side, Alfred's stallion matching its stride to that of her pretty mare.

"The King is very pious," commented Brith who had not seen the King close to before. Her father and brother had both spent time at court, and told her the exciting stories on their return, but apart from attending the communal meals in the late afternoon, she had found the experience of attending court rather boring. "The lady Aethelflaed is quiet, modest and god-fearing but idle. I have much to do at home."

Alfred laughed, remarking that they would be home soon, "no doubt to find a whole week's worth of problems to be dealt with. The steward mentioned that dratted fencing again. No-one at Uddings has owned up and only the occasional deer strays and is quickly chased off."

Edith and her daughter followed slowly walking with others from Wymburne who had been to join in the feast. Now that she was on her way home Edith was brighter, animatedly describing a brief conversation with the King's seneschal, a man of many skills and an infinite knowledge of status.

"He has to seat everyone in the right order or someone feels slighted. If a man has an exaggerated sense of his own importance it is his task to correct this but without hurting feelings if he can. How the kitchens managed to feed so many people is quite beyond me. No wonder the cooks start baking while the stars are still shining and the rest of us still abed."

"I for one will not be sorry to return to my small household," responded one Wymburne lady. "We were mystified though, how a man of importance can be buried in church when everyone knew he had taken his own life. It is the gossip of the town." Puffed up with righteous indignation, Edith and Aethelflaed could offer no explanation beyond that it had been the King's wish.

Sorry now that they had agreed to walk part of the way with the townswomen, Edith politely made her farewells but was ridiculously pleased to draw her daughter away towards the ford. Lifting up their skirts the two kept their feet dry by jumping from stone to stone, glad that the winter rains had not yet flooded the crossing.

Chapter Five
AD 963 - 973

Yuletide passed with feasting, singing and music. Everyone who could join in the celebrations at Uddings made their way down the track along which poles had been placed. It had snowed heavily so that no work could be done outdoors, men spending time carving wooden spoons, dishes and children's toys. Although no wolves had been seen for many months the domestic animals were sheltered close to the houses. There was still no news of Aethelflaed's young man but she was adamant that none of the young men she had met at the King's palace were to her liking. "Milk sops, all of them! Hal is more handsome and brighter. He talks of ideas, of improvements he would like to make. All the court men could manage was their family and how much their land was worth." She wrinkled her freckled nose in disgust, and then flashed a smile to include everyone.

At the church service they heard the news of the burning of London when the great church of St Paul's had been raised to the ground. Apparently Archbishop Dunstan, now safely returned from Rome, and filled with renewed religious fervour, had put its rebuilding in hand the day after the fire.

"As long as he does not want extra tithes from everybody," laughed Alfred having admired the priest's new painting of the Miracle at Canaan on the wall of the nave. He had been greeted like a special friend with knowing winks and slight digs after he had apologised for Brith's absence due to her imminent lying-in.

Brith's father had also heard about Dunstan's construction dreams. He came in the spring to be present at his grandchild's birth and to marry Edith. His whole demeanour softened at the sight of Lady Edith, dressed once again in matching robe and cloak, the inside of which showed contrasting hues of deep red.

The ceremony took place in Wymburne, Alfred, wearing his royal diadem and Aethelflaed, for once beaming delightedly, being among the witnesses at the church door. Brith was forced to stay at Uddings as her time was so near but greeted the newlyweds with a welcome cup on their return.

"I would take Edith back home with me," Brithric stated after the wedding feast. His broad hands gripped the delicate glass drinking vessel which he had already admired. "My wife, my dear wife, will find my house has lacked a woman's touch these last few months, but no doubt it will be restored in her capable hands." His eyes twinkled with merriment as the two men enjoyed a last jar of ale before joining their wives in the sleeping quarters. In view of their age and status, there had been no bedding ceremony, but his eagerness to join Edith was not lost on Alfred, even though he could no longer share a bed with his own wife.

They still cuddled close to each other, Alfred collapsing in giggles when a well-aimed kick from the unborn child almost un-manned him. He rubbed her shoulders with perfumed balm and helped her dress as she could no longer see her feet. Brushing her long hair with the new brush he had managed to purchase at the market was another way of cementing their loving relationship now the ultimate closeness was denied all but the most ignorant of men.

News of the birth of a Prince eventually reached all parts of the land. Bells were rung and services of thanksgiving held by even the smallest chapel. Amid the celebrations in Dorsetshire the incredible story swept through the townspeople that on his journey from Wymburne King Edgar had called on the nunnery at Wilton, and had ravaged a young nun there!

"But he was so pious," exclaimed Brith relaxing on a well stuffed mattress in the hall. Covered with rugs and wrapped in soft fabrics she watched a new litter of puppies playing in the crushed bracken on the floor. It was impossible to use her spindle or to stand and weave even a few rows of fabric. The slightest effort resulted in swollen ankles, breathlessness and acute nausea. Rather than be shut away in her private quarters she preferred to be in the hall propped up on well stuffed cushions where she could chat to anyone who entered.

During the summer and autumn months the story was told and retold, many of the details becoming wildly distorted and exaggerated. It was disbelieved by many as being so contrary to the reports of the King's piousness. That the King had promised to undergo public penance was also thought improbable.

"I did not see the flogging myself but spoke to one man who did," confirmed Hal on his longed for return to Uddings having served in the King's guard. "I believe it is to be carried out each Sunday at several churches in turn. I certainly saw the blood on his tunic for he allows no salves or ointments to be administered to him."

Now a captain of the Dorset forces, proudly wearing a diadem of the royal colours, he led his men wherever the King needed an armed garrison. His face had long since lost its boyishness and been replaced by leaner, slimmer looks. With the dignity of battle-earned rank, he requested permission to court Aethelflaed, offering as bride price the harness from the plundered stables of a rebel in East Anglia.

"The King took the beasts themselves of course, but I have harness for more than a dozen; saddles, bridles, scabbards and weapons. These were my part of the forfeited goods. Most is of superb quality," he boasted eagerly. "There are brass buckles and gem encrusted browbands. I can think of much better places for jewels than on the bridle of a horse. Garnets make a pretty bauble for a wife!"

If he had gained in dignity the same could not be said for Aethelflaed. Since her mother's marriage she had been left in charge of the manor house at Didlington. Alfred asked Owenson to send his fastest rider to fetch her. When she saw Hal, admittedly the love of her life, she burst into noisy tears and flung herself into his arms. He covered her wet face with kisses holding her far closer than was correct for an unmarried couple. Even when they momentarily drew apart it would have been a cruel man who could have interrupted the flashing darts of love which sped between them. "I have dreamed of this for so long my sweet. Now, with your brother's permission we can be together. All the nights on the hard ground did not stop me thinking of you. I can hardly breathe my heart is thumping so much."

Neither of them noticed that the hall had emptied. "Mind you Owenson, the sooner they are married the better!" The Uddings' steward grinned, showing gaps in his teeth. "Ah, to be young again! My son tells me that I am too old to train horses now and that his son will start work in the summer. What cheek! That will be alright with you won't it? I bet the young rascal has not asked you. No respect sometimes these children as you are about to learn!"

Owenson smoothed his grizzled beard thoughtfully. Like his father, he still had a full head of short hair but all trace of blackness had long been replaced by silver-white.

After the blessing, when Aethelflaed's expression of joy was contagious so that everyone watching was quickly smiling, the young couple went to live at the now vacant Didlington house. Hal would be in charge of all the sheep on the two estates as well as soldiering when the King required him. The sheepward who might have been jealous quickly appreciated the young man's knowledge and sang Hal's praises when others asked if he minded his apparent demotion.

Some week's later travellers mentioned the name of the lady involved with the king. Lady Wulfhere, formerly a professed nun was now reported to be living in comfort in one of the King's own houses.

"She might be high-born, but if she had taken her vows, well, surely that is a sin!" condemned the travelling merchant.

"And the King's lady-wife?" enquired Brith who still nursed her son born soon after Prince Edward, the king's heir. "What news of her?" She kissed the top of her baby's head, breathing in the scent of his scanty hair.

"Ah, she was a lady of true goodness," responded the man wiping the ale froth from his lips. "She never raised her voice to a soul. Mind you she died soon after the aetheling was weaned; some do say that Lord King Edgar had put a divorce in motion and that she died of a broken heart.

The King has a new wife now, the daughter of ealdorman Ordgar of Devon. Elfrida is her name, a real dark haired beauty she is." The man's eyes gleamed appreciatively. "Mind you, she was married to Ethelbald, ealdorman of East Anglia. He died fighting against our King," he stated reflectively.

Brith crossed herself rapidly on hearing of the death of the former queen. They had talked intimately of their pregnant condition at Kingston and become friends. She herself had little trouble giving birth to baby Udric, named for his grandfather, who smiled toothlessly as she hugged him firmly to her bodice.

So many children died in infancy, and mothers too, but she had liked the quiet manner of the King's wife, mourning her passing.

The messenger from the King's chancery, prominently carrying his baton of office, escorted by the Bishop's men was given refreshments after the monies from court fines were accounted for. It was not a task Alfred enjoyed, preferring to find a solution which did not involve taking money from hard-working farmers and labourers. Before leaving with his armed escort he mentioned that the King's second wife had now given birth to a son, immediately proclaimed to be the heir. Even the most simple minded calculated in seconds that insufficient time had passed for the couple to have waited for a legal marriage before consummating their union. Grateful that he did not have to provide another horse for the pompous clerk, Alfred waited silently until the party had left his boundary.

"How can a second son be the heir?" Brith asked, puzzled by the news. "Surely the King's elder son has the right." She had hardly waited for the collector of the taxes to leave Uddings before raising her question. They were seated on a settle beside the fire, a screen sheltering them from any draught which might penetrate the heavy leather door curtains.

The female dog left her well grown puppies and leant against Brith's legs. She stroked it absent-mindedly waiting for the answer to her question.

Not really knowing the answer Alfred shrugged his shoulders and took Udric onto his knee. The child pulled his father's beard gleefully; his tiny moist hands gripping surprisingly fiercely until tired with the game he settled down to stare at the firelight before falling into a contented sleep. His parents continued to sit quietly beside the big stone fireplace, previously the cooking fire, which now kept the family quarters warm. Only in the hardest winter had an extra brazier been lit.

For many seasons the country remained at peace, so that yeomen and thegns alike prospered while their weapons gathered dust. The earth at Didlington was now so fertile that harvests improved each year. Only once did the stream fall so low that the mill wheel would not turn. In that year, nine hundred and sixty eight after the birth of our Lord, the sun burned day after day without relief. Hay dried quickly and was safely stored before summer storms broke without warning. Tracks which had been made on raised ground became muddy, water-logged and virtually impassable. The ford in Wymburne disappeared beneath a raging torrent of foaming water which had already spread over the low lying fields. Carcases of sheep and goats which had not fled to higher ground fast enough tumbled and rolled as the river sped towards the sea. Some houses were flooded and when the water receded, the filth of many years was swept out with the wet rushes.

The steward of the King's Tun was kept busy allocating funds from the hardship and welfare monies he had collected on the royal estate since it was ordered by previous Kings. The storm had been of such savagery that people knew it must be heaven-sent in response to sins committed. Once again the burial of the foreign lord in their church was debated, and the taking of a nun from a sacred house was high on the possible causes of such retribution.

"To say nothing of the rumour that the King's wife used to be married to the East Anglian ealdorman and that she conspired with the King for her husband to be foully slain."

The gossip could not have been more pleased with the reception of this salacious morsel. There was a shocked silence then subdued whispers, men and women checking who was within hearing before discussing the accusation. The Steward had heard the woman but chose to leave the gloomy interior for fresher, undefiled air. He too had heard such tales and chastised the tellers of such stories, threatening them with a whipping if the subject was mentioned again. He was appalled that an ordinary woman, probably the wife of a trader, had been bold enough to talk of such treasonous matters.

"God forgive me, but please let her stay away from Dorsetshire." His fervent prayer must have been heard by the Almighty for there was no message waiting on his return to his tiny office alerting him to the King's imminent arrival. His attempt to find the culprit who was trespassing in the hunting forest had so far been unsuccessful and he was frustrated by the failure. A well worn track was evidence that it was habitually used and he determined to bring the subject up at the forthcoming moot.

The King's lady, Elfrida, had another son and called him Aethelred, a sturdy baby which endeared himself to everyone. With deep blue, slightly protuberant eyes, his tiny head was covered with downy red hair above rose-bud lips.

Prince Edmund, her first born son meanwhile caused concern, being pale and undersized. Prince Edward, although apparently no longer destined to be his father's heir, having been born, some said, out of wedlock, was still treated royally. He had his own servants and often travelled with his father around the Kingdom.

When the shocking news of the death of Prince Edmund reached Dorsetshire, Brith hugged her own son tightly to her despite his boyish struggles. She had lost one baby and knew the grief this caused while acknowledging that it was not seemly to show one's sorrow in public. "Even if a child is born weak a mother's love is never less than that given to a more robust baby. So now her second son becomes heir," she stated frowning slightly.

Relaxing together in the evenings, they talked quietly as the child slept nearby. "Is it true that Lord King Edgar murdered Ethelbald, the queen's former husband? Some say that she helped the King to do the deed, and why does the King call her Elfrida now?" asked Brith while she stitched a cloth by the light of a torch on the wall behind her. The servants had long departed for their own hearths, the shutters were closed and the fire burnt down to little more than a red glow. Occasionally a log settled sending out a flicker of flame before subsiding once more to smouldering crimson.

Neither of them believed such a tale but the story persisted and had been talked of in hushed whispers after church only the previous week.

"We may never know the truth of the matter, but if she did agree to the killing of her husband, did she also have a hand in the death of the aetheling Edmund seeing as he was sickly? We do not know how she persuaded King Edgar to make her own son the heir." Alfred frowned as he voiced his doubts, looking round as if he feared being overheard.

"Sometimes I am glad that my only involvement with the court is accounting for the fines and my portion of them. I need no other reward for doing the King's work. I certainly don't wish to be involved in rumour-mongering or petty squabbles."

Brith retorted that murder was hardly a squabble, before changing the subject to talk proudly of their son who was now learning to ride under the stern eye of the horsemaster.

Returning some time later from a visit to Lord Hugh at Wareham, also the official town of the ealdorman of the county, Alfred was in a state of great excitement. He could hardly wait to dismount from his horse, throwing the reins to a young lad with barely a pat for the beast. His face was flushed above the ties of the thick cloak which he impatiently cast aside on the settle. With shining eyes and a radiant smile he announced the news which had induced such excitement.

"The King is to be crowned at Bath, on Whit Sunday. We are all to attend. It will be a great ceremony and a huge feast is to be given afterwards." All thoughts of the Queen's possible crimes were apparently forgotten. Since the hunt several years ago, Alfred had not had direct contact with King Edgar. Now he and his wife had been invited, together with the highest in the land, to attend the long postponed crowning of his King.

Brith shared her husband's joy and immediately arranged an excursion to Wymburne. The strong box set in the floor beside their bed was pulled from its niche and opened carefully. Money from the annual sale of fleeces and his percentage of fines was kept in small leather bags securely gathered and tied with plaited flax fibres. Alfred gave his wife a handful of silver pennies. When her face fell at the small amount she held he added several more. "We farmers tend to be careful of our coin love! Go and buy yourself some cloth. Why not get blue to match your eyes. It would not do to be seen in the same gowns you wore before!"

"Flatterer! But it will be lovely to have a new cloak. Where is Bath? Is it likely to be cold?"

"To tell you the truth all I know is that it is west of here but North of Somersetshire. With luck we can find someone else going from perhaps Cheneford and join their party. Now go and spend my money before I change my mind!" He aimed a playful smack at her bottom and they both ended up in a fit of giggles, Udric pressing against them both trying to be included in the embrace, his sun tanned, chubby arms clutching his mother's legs.

The lower half of many of the properties abutting the High street was a shop, wares being displayed on counters inside the window opening.

Stout shutters were fastened back against the wall during the day providing space for items which could be hung from pegs. With the coins secure in a small cloth bag inside her scrip, Brith purchased coloured woollen cloth for new cloaks and over skirts after having fingered the texture of several bolts in shades of blue from gentian to the mauve of the heathland heathers. The shoemaker was instructed to make slippers for herself in a matching shade and sturdy shoes in tanned leather for Alfred and Udric. New breeches and leggings completed their outfits for the occasion which was rumoured to be the first time a separate ceremony had taken place whereby the crown would be put on the King's head during a formal church service. In this year of our Lord Nine Hundred and Seventy Three, Lord King Edgar would be thirty years of age, and on the whole, had proved himself worthy of a formal coronation.

"Maybe he feels that he is now mature enough to accept a proper crown. But it could have been pushed to the back of everyone's mind with so much else to do. At least the country is at peace again. Hopefully his penance for past sins is complete; mind you I cannot think what came over him taking a woman from Wilton like that! Not that she minded for she has lived in far more comfort since. It is a good thing Archbishop Odo is no longer alive – he would be turning in his grave!"

Enjoying spring sunshine outside the hall Alfred and Brith sipped from the valuable glass beakers, enjoying the smooth lustrous surface. He often pointed out that they had been a gift to their child's namesake. Udric was out with the other children having been sent to gather the winter bracken before the green shoots of new growth made it too difficult. The main harvest had been brought in shortly after the sap died back but there was always more to be found and carefully stored for the stables.

New fresh green leaves were unfurled but not yet full size, the sunlight showing the veins and lobes, forming patterns on the leaf mould. A puppy scampered after one of the fowl and was quickly cuffed by a woman from the kitchen. It ran off howling, looking for comfort from its bored mother while the fowl strutted off with the self righteous walk so characteristic of someone who knows they were in the right.

The monthly moot was held but if anyone had harboured petty grudges or had complaints about another man they had all been forgotten. It was only the steward who called attention to the laws of his master's forest glaring at Alfred as he did so. No-one liked to be the object of complaint especially when he had made every effort to discover the cause on his own side of the boundary. Returning the steward's accusatory stare in full measure Alfred determined to set his own watch.

The King's reeve, elected by the estate tenants, made no secret of his invitation to attend the ceremony. "It is recognition for all the work that is done. The King could visit his royal estate at any time. As far as I know each man who works for the crown or provides a service has been instructed to be present." He glanced round at the Steward and received a nod in acknowledgement.

"Hardly an invitation then," joked one man from the town.

"Well I wish I was going. The King rarely comes to Wymburne even though Prince Edward has come here a few times. He bought a belt from me the last time he came." The leather worker was fingering his own belt as he spoke, the intricately worked strands formed like metal links, many stained with grease from his fingers.

Few thegns would not be attending the celebrations, the man whose turn it was to guard the coast grumbling that he would not see the greatest event of his lifetime. "I have to join with the men from the outer villages. Perhaps we could have venison, Master Reeve?"

The reeve grinned ruefully in response to this normally outrageous request. "Actually, you could be in luck! An injured animal was seen only earlier this week. I will send the boys out with the dogs and see if they find it. T'would be a shame to waste the carcass wouldn't it!"

Everyone was apparently joining in the anticipation of the happy event. There were lots of enquiries after wives, new babies and proposed matches of teenage boys and girls. The wheelwright was grinning broadly at the blacksmith, normally bitter enemies because sometimes the latter poached business, repairing the outer ring of metal at his hearth.

Not knowing what accommodation would be available, Alfred took the precaution of arranging to share a tent. They would travel west with those from Cheneford, Wymburne, Twynham and many other small estates, protected by soldiers from Kingston who had drawn lots to form part of the King's guard.

News of the event spread throughout the whole country. A state of excitement and anticipation prevailed, for even those who would not actually attend the coronation feast would doubtless be treated to roasted meats and other delicacies on the day. Guards on the coasts and forts bribed others to take their places in order to join in the merrymaking.

"Why has it taken so long for the King to be crowned?" Brith asked her spouse as they travelled westwards along the Ridgeway. Her mare picked its way carefully along the stony track, harness tinkling at each nod of its head.

"He is old now and has been King for many years."

"Nearly as old as I am dear wife," replied Alfred laughing. "It could be that at thirty years old a priest can be ordained. I hear that the penance he undertook was to last for seven years; the end of that time may well have come."

Brith nodded and fell silent. Other travellers could be seen making their way towards the city of Bath. At night, camped roughly beside the track-way, people told stories of the cures that could be obtained by drinking the water which flowed from underground springs. They heard how some still called the city Ake Man's Ceastre, the place for invalids and the sick to visit. Not being in need of the curative waters themselves, these stories were of no particular interest, but tales of the Romans who had lived there, the wonderful old buildings and the heating system fascinated Udric who was wide eyed with excitement.

Not yet old enough to ride alone he clung to his father's back, gripping handfuls of felted wool and sitting astride on the cloak. From time to time his small head slumped forward, the gentle rhythm of hoof beats and the warm spring air producing a soporific effect on the small boy.

Surrounded by soldiers from the King's palace at Wymburne, the long cavalcade which wended its way towards Bath had no trouble from the bands of brigands and thieves reputed to prey on lone travellers.

"How many old soldiers and outlaws are still free to roam is hard to know. No-one asks too many questions if a worker offers his labour. One of our cottagers may have been a soldier. Owen pointed him out and he would know an old soldier having served twice in my father's place."

"You must tell me his story one day. All I know is that he was Owenson's father and served your grandfather many years ago."

"Mmm, right now I am more concerned with the present. The town looks full to bursting."

Finding space to erect the tents in the city itself was difficult. It seemed as though the entire population of the land had thronged to Bath for the crowning of their King. Branches of colourful leaves had been used to decorate archways, pillars and porches of the many churches within the city boundary. Shields displaying the King's colours were much in evidence, while every noble was flying his own pennant above a veritable tented city. In a gentle breeze every colour of the rainbow was represented in flags showing lines, crosses and circles in many different combinations. One or two horses were unhappy with the constant flapping and cracking of the fabrics, jinking and side-stepping nervously.

The tent was full to capacity but as the crush was only for the one night no-one complained too vociferously. "I'm surprised Lord William from

Chalberie is not around. Mind you, he's one man we would not want to be sharing with." Alfred and Brith were whispering quietly, Udric already asleep between them, both for warmth and for his protection as their neighbours were both large. They had eaten a rather basic meal, some of which had suffered from being squashed in the saddle bag. Tomorrow the ceremony would take place, Brith's new gown hanging from a makeshift peg above them.

Chapter Six

Leaving a servant to guard the baggage horse, Alfred obtained places beside a pillar from where they could see the proceedings in relative safety. Inside the grey stone building every candle had been lit, the pure globes of light pointing heavenwards. Clutching the youngster firmly, they watched in silence as the King, his head bowed, walked slowly down the aisle toward the altar. Silver and gold chalices reflected the light of the pure beeswax candles. Coloured robes and tunics filled the nave of the church, everyone craning to watch the solemn proceedings. Singing boys sang a melody, their treble voices filling the entire building with pure notes.

The ceremony, beneath the arched wooden roof, involved a mass led by Archbishop Dunstan wearing some of the most beautiful gold embroidered robes Brith had ever seen. She marvelled at the colours and the intricacy of the stitching, contrasting so greatly with the simple robe the King had chosen to wear.

There was complete silence as the Archbishop paused dramatically, holding the crown above the King's head. As it was placed on his head a huge cheer broke out acknowledging Edgar, their King.

"I actually wondered if the Archbishop was waiting for the Good Lord to strike the King dead if he was not worthy of the crown. He waited so long, holding the crown at arms length. I am sure it weighs a good bit so Dunstan is not the weakling he appears to be, only eating bread and water!"

"Mm, many held their breath at that moment," whispered Alfred as he escorted Brith towards the King's hall after the ceremony. Their son had been left in the care of a matron from Bleneford who had volunteered to mind the children of several thegns for a small sum. There were many treats in their saddlebags to ensure young Udric behaved himself while out of their sight.

"At least he will be able to tell his children that he had seen a King crowned. No-one complained of his presence. I did not feel him wriggle once. But did you see his eyes? They were so wide with the wonder of it all."

The streets of Bath had been cleaned so that the usual piles of ordure, butchers offal and rotting carcases did not produce the smell that most big cities suffered from. Cobbles of a type had been used to pave the main road which led to the biggest hall in the city.

"I wish now that I was not wearing these fancy slippers!" commented Brith as she leant heavily of Alfred's arm for support.

"It's so crowded that one could be carried along without taking a step and still not fall over."

At the feast that night the young Prince Edward sat beside his father, clearly the heir apparent despite the fact that he may have been born before his parents were married. He was wearing a gold circlet with a brilliant gem set in a roundel on the front. Hugh sat at the high table with the Sheriffs and ealdormen from all the other shires including Ordgar from Devon who towered over them all. While each wore a diadem decorated with the King's colours, their tunics were of a dazzling variety of hues; every colour but purple, a colour everyone knew to be reserved for those of the royal house.

The other Dorset men were grouped together on a lower table. Brith saw her father and waved to him happily. She mouthed silently that they would see him later for the noise of hundreds of guests would have made it quite impossible to hold an intimate conversation. Alfred proudly introduced Brith to those she did not already know, - thegns like himself from each part of the county, and the churchmen from Sherburne, Dorchester, Wareham and Wymburne, the King's own church. Each of them had responsibility for keeping the peace or seeing to the souls of the King's people. She joined their ladies, confident that Udric was happy among the children his own age in the matron's nursery.

"So where is the King's lady?" queried a lady from Shapwick having already admired Brith's new gown and cloak. "She might not be too happy for Prince Edward to be sitting alongside his father."

"Hush, but I agree, the Prince looks every inch his father's heir. It is difficult to understand why the first born son is not next in line. He looks noble and smiles easily enough."

At the mens' table news was exchanged, bargains made and the coastal rota revised. Some grumbled at the continued need for such service but were quickly silenced by the majority who pointed out that such a guard had obviously prevented invasion on the Dorset coast, whereas the shores of West Wales, where the watch had been discontinued, had not been so fortunate. Many men had lost their lives or been maimed in battles to repel invading forces.

Horse races were held the following day, when many Uddings bred stallions or their progeny were winners. Sweating mounts and their riders paraded before the crowds who had gathered to watch. Gusts of hot breath punctuated the chilly morning air, snorts and shouts interrupted all other conversation. Delighted at their success Alfred was thrilled when King Edgar personally ordered a new stallion together with a suitable mount for the aetheling. "I need a horse of stature but biddable. My legs are so short that if the horse is nervous and jerks I am likely to take a tumble!"

"Gladly, my lord King," responded Alfred, hastily bowing in an effort not to laugh. Visions of Edgar being catapulted over the head of a big destrier should have been amusing but to the man who was in charge of the breeding at Uddings, such a picture spelt disaster. "We have horses bred from 'Thor', your father's old horse. There is one which is light grey in colour, but the most like Thor is coloured like the most precious wood brought from overseas. You could send a message with your man to tell me which you prefer.... Perhaps the aetheling wishes to choose his mount himself?"

After Prince Edward's visit was arranged, he hurried through the crowd to tell Brith, who had already left the arena with the other ladies and their children. His eyes glittered with excitement and hope of further advancement, if not for himself, then for Udric. He was not boastful by nature but could hardly suppress the bubbling rise of triumph which seemed to invade his entire body. If he had not been among so many decorously behaved Dorset people he would have swung Brith round in a wild, whirling embrace. Nothing however, could prevent the wide smile with which he greeted her.

"We are indeed honoured. How soon can we leave without causing offence? There is much to do if Uddings is to be ready to welcome the aetheling. We should say our farewells to our parents before we leave. They are in the hall with the King's clerk."

News was quickly exchanged with Edith's father and Alfred's mother who were on the point of leaving the hall. He noticed that his mother's hair framing her face despite the discreet wimple of finest linen was now silvery-grey. This sign of ageing however, was belied by her obvious new-found happiness which had put a girlish spring in her step, revitalised the dimples in her cheeks and produced a sparkle in her eyes. Promising to visit soon, Brith and Alfred returned to collect Udric who had played himself to a standstill with all the other children.

The journey homeward beneath a veiled sun across acres of common land grazed by small, hardy sheep and goats, involved a series of farewells as people left the slow procession for their own homes. With promises to meet again soon and talk of greater protection for each man's estate in case invaders came inland, the men from Shapwick, Cheneford, Holt and Wymburne separated on the road below Badberie to use the old Roman roads to their homes.

The coronation was the talk of the entire nation for several weeks after the event. Those who had actually attended told others all about the ceremony, the food, the clothing, the colours and the gossip. Details were elaborated, exaggerated and embroidered as the tales were retold again and again. The King's steward, who had probably had a better view of the crowning than many other Dorset thegns, was able to add the small details which coloured the imagination of those who were still curious. At the palace he found himself being waylaid. An hour of questions and answers changed the routine for both him and the workers who took the opportunity to lean on their tools until chivvied back to humdrum tasks.

Udric waited impatiently for the day of the Prince's visit, his waking day filled with tasks so that the time passed quickly. He helped groom the horses, took his turn as guard in the fields and learned the basics of how to choose animals for breeding stock.

At night he returned exhausted to the hall, ate supper and fell into a deep sleep. Brith too, anxious that she should not disappoint the hopes for their son's advancement, kept the household in a constant state of readiness.

"What happened to my father can happen to any boy who takes the aetheling's fancy," stated Alfred. "My father had lessons with princes, was taught to ride, hunt, hawk and fight. Until his death he was their friend. I was told he saved the life of King Aethelstan. He was close to death after being knifed when protecting the King. I saw the scar on his chest, a knotted, white patch surrounded by shiny pink skin. Actually, come to think of it, that was the first time he saved a King's life. The second time was when he put his arm up to save the king from a weapon thrown at him. He died of his injuries. The man, sent by the King, who brought mother's share of treasure, had seen him fall and the burial of the arm with his body thank goodness.

I can read, but only because my father taught me. It is time Udric learnt. We must think of setting time aside for lessons."

"I too can read a little," responded Edith. "If we got a retired priest or an educated younger son of one of your friends to teach Udric, maybe my own learning could be bettered."

Without warning the King's ordered that all old coinage was to be surrendered. Having now been crowned, a new silver penny bearing his image was to be minted by the licensed moneyers. Alfred sighed with frustration. He had hoped to be at Uddings when the prince came to try the horses. "I have to collect all old coins, noting the amounts, so that they can be exchanged. I need all the treasure chests we can find.

The Bishop is sending two guards but I'll take my own man as well. Hal might lend me that huge man who came last year. He has a cottage on the northern boundary."

The fact that he would be carrying out the collection was advertised after Mass on Sunday. It was the only way important news could be circulated reliably. Alfred could feel his shoulders sag, his watchful eyes becoming more suspicious. "Talk about letting every criminal in the area know that big sums of money are about to be transported from Wymburne to the King's treasury! It is an open invitation for vagabonds and thieves."

As he visited each household in turn, starting with his own tenants, he found many were reluctant to part with their carefully hoarded wealth.

"But it is all I have lord. Until the sale of this year's fleeces there is nothing else. My wife needs needles and salt."

"My Lord Hugh gives his word that fair exchange will be made. He is the King's officer for the whole of Dorsetshire. I will bring your new coins as soon as they are ready, but the old money is needed to make the new," explained Alfred carefully keeping the tone of his voice moderate. He was quite sure that some villeins had not surrendered all their coinage but could do little to force them obey the King's orders. Marking the sums on tally sticks which were then split so the cottager had a matching half took time. Alfred scratched the figures on the re-used parchment together with his version of the man's name. Ink splattered from the badly cut quill but the record was readable and would have to suffice for the clerks.

Putting the coins in leather saddle bags, the laden horses travelled under armed guard to the treasury at Winchester. Alfred admitted to being mightily relieved when it had been safely delivered and tallied with his own figures. The black robed clerks of the treasury department scowled and tutted, dramatic sighs emphasising their responsibilities and onerous work as they placed piles of the silver pennies on the tables. A fee to cover his time and effort was arranged, to be collected at the next quarter day. He noticed that their fingers too, were stained with ink, shavings from scraped parchment littered the front their robes like heavy falls of dandruff.

He had only just returned to Uddings hoping to make some enquiries to find a tutor when he was ordered to accompany the Bishop of Sherburne on his tour of the chapels and churches in the area. Meeting the genial cleric at the priest's poor lodging in Wymburne, he knelt to kiss the huge red stoned ring on the churchman's finger. "But my lord Bishop, I know little of churches and nothing at all of church law."

"Leave the law to me," replied the Bishop firmly. "You have got yourself a reputation for good sense and fairness. It is for that reason I have asked for you."

Memories of several of his judgements flitted quickly through his mind. Many were not profitable for him or the crown and could have led to criticism by men of a greedier nature.

The Bishop explained that they were authorised to settle disputes over the boundaries of church land where it joined common or another's land. Those charters which were unclear were to be sent to the chancellor for clarification with their findings so that friction among neighbours was kept to a minimum. Sealed writs copied out by the King's writers would be returned in due course to be treasured by the owner as evidence of his ownership of land and property.

The Bishop's tunic and robes of rich quality contrasted dramatically with the clothes of villeins who owned a few acres. Many wore stout boots without leggings below a tunic of coarse fustian. A sheepskin jerkin tied with a leather thong completed a man's protection from the cold. If he was lucky a woollen hat which also wrapped round the neck completed a working man's clothing. The Bishop's sensitive nose could not fail to notice a smell of sweat and dirt which arose from the men who bowed over his Episcopal ring.

Life was hard when one could only work a few days on ones' own land. The other labour days were on the land of a lord, especially in harvest time. Some grumbled that by the time the tithe produce had been set aside and the lord's portion in another sack, there was barely enough for the householder to keep his own family. Few could store more grain beyond what was required for next year's seed. When times were hard, or the harvest failed, the amount available to keep body and soul together was very little.

One point which was mentioned frequently had nothing to do with legal boundaries.

"Lord, deer from the Cranburne Chase cause damage to our croplands. Many of us have strips which border the King's preserve yet it had been made law that it is an offence to harm them. I lost peas and beans this spring when the shoots were only a hand's span above the earth. How shall I feed my family, let alone keep stock through the winter without decent haulms for their forage?"

Alfred suggested palings and hurdles should be used to protect a man's fields. The Bishop agreed that such a remedy would be acceptable, in return for which each hamlet would receive a full grown deer once a year, complete with its hide, for a feast or for division amongst the people as they decided. "Make a note of this judgement clerk," he ordered, praying fervently that he had not overstepped his authority. "The king will have my hide, let alone that of the deer, if he does not like it. The keeper of the forest should also repair the palings that are in his charge."

Taking the Bishop's comment referring to King Edgar's uncertain temper on occasions, Alfred hastily busied himself with his own affairs but wondered who would be sent to remind Brithric to have the gaps in the fencing repaired. After the last case he excused himself politely from the bishop's invitation to admire alterations to church buildings, pleading pressing business at home.

"The aetheling is here," shrieked Udric at the top of his voice. He had taken to climbing the tallest trees to keep watch for the first signs of travellers on the southbound road. Scrambling down from the oak the boy's clothes were soiled, green smears streaking the newly brushed tunic. Brith's annoyance had to be hastily hidden by a welcoming smile. The King's own guards reined in their horses around that of the young prince. Harness rattled as the beasts were taken to the stables by lads whose faces and more than likely, their necks, had been washed for the occasion. Round eyed, they watched their lord as he went forward to greet and bow to Prince Edward.

Although the King had sent his son with provisions and a colourful tent in which to sleep, Alfred and Brith moved out of their private room off the hall and gave their bed to the Prince. Udric followed the young, fair haired man wherever he went, showing him the litter of puppies and the new born colts playing around their mothers in the field nearest the hall.

At the feast Udric proudly carried the basin of water and a fine napkin for the Prince to wash his hands, a task which would normally have been allotted to a far more experienced boy. Prince Edward had brought his own servants with him but had dismissed his page while in a towering rage over some minor incident. The royal temper was well known. Many senior members of King Edgar's court had reported his rudeness and spitefulness to their lord. Much of it had been brushed aside as youthful spirits but if he had been punished then the young prince often held a grudge against those who had complained.

The smaller horses were selected for the Prince to ride the following morning. While the soldiers relaxed in the lee of the stable, Edward mounted one horse after another, cantering round the field accompanied by Uddings' horsemaster. Sitting on the fence post,

Udric admired the Prince's undoubted riding skills, holding his breath when a sudden gust of wind blew a ball of dry grass across the paddock in front of the Prince's horse which sidestepped suddenly. He was seen to apply his spurs quite viciously to the flanks of the frightened pony.

"Gently my lord Edward," called Alfred from the fence. "He is but a youngster and has much to learn." Indeed the horse had never been spurred before and returned to the stable with its eyes rolling and flecks of blood on its sides where the spurs had grazed the shining coat.

Owenson was clearly in a towering rage. Whiteness showed above his lips which were compressed into a hard line. That one of his charges had been ill-treated for no other reason than vanity brought bile stinging to this throat.

In the hall Alfred quickly called for small beer to be brought. He pushed the incident to the back of his mind as the horses were discussed. The Prince eventually chose a dark bay pony stallion and ordered that his own harness be fitted to it immediately. Young Udric applauded the Prince's choice and was rewarded by Edward suggesting that he accompany him for a walk.

Raising his hand to prevent the soldiers joining them, the two left the courtyard. "It is good to get away from the guards and the churchmen who surround my father," he sighed, then took a deep breath of clean air. The biggest dog followed closely at Udric's heels, reassuring Alfred that it would warn of any strangers approaching or threatening the Prince's safety while at Uddings.

Udric showed the Prince his favourite place in the stream while the red coated oxen stared at them solemnly.

"My oxen are white," commented the Prince as Udric led the way to the sty where he knew a litter of piglets were housed. They giggled together at the antics of the young pigs, each trying to suckle from the fat sow. Udric told the story of how his forefather Udda had trapped a forest boar and crossed it with a local pink pig to produce the hairy two coloured pig which was now bred widely in the county.

They returned to the hall still deep in conversation, two heads side by side, momentarily equal beneath the blue sky, to find a messenger from the court waiting impatiently to recall the Prince to Winchester with all haste. "My lord Dunstan commands my return," sneered the Prince, "but I would like to visit again soon," he added, smiling at Udric. "I like your dog too! At court they are either hunting hounds or lap dogs. That's a man's dog, a companion. I don't suppose father will be keen, even less my step-mother, but a dog like that is a guard and friend all in one."

He bade farewell to his hosts, thanking them for the hospitality of Uddings. He rode his new pony, now decked out with his own colours, while a servant led the King's new horse, a grandson of 'Thor'. They moved off at a smart trot sending fowls scurrying for safety. The foot soldiers formed a column and marched briskly away, the Prince's banner flying proudly at the front. Staring at the departing Prince's back, Alfred was pleased to see the young man turn in the saddle to raise his hand in salute as he trotted towards the Cranburne road.

"Thank the Lord that he does not appear to have noticed the blunting of his spurs."

The young ironsmith glanced at Alfred, their exchange of glances were of relief and at the same time conspiratorial. Owenson joined them, hands on hips. "Little turd! You should see the welts on the black pony's sides. I for one am glad that his spurs have no points now. Princes perhaps are never whipped so he does not know the pain caused by them."

His son nodded his head in agreement. He was proud of the training and gentling the horses in his charge received with hardly a slap or raised voice being used. He felt the same scalding contempt as his father for a rider who needed to use pain and fear to get the best out of a beast.

With the visitors gone, Uddings seemed quiet. Brith was anxious to replenish the larders which were almost depleted.

"How the court is provided for day after day I do not know," she complained. "It is no wonder the King has to move round the country for we have almost no stores left." She rubbed the back of her arm where a recent bite still itched.

Exaggerating a little, for her housewifely skills had been learned well, she bustled off to oversee the kitchen servants. For a short time they had basked in the admiration of their men-folk having prepared a meal for the prince.

The massive figure of Ordgar, earl of Devon called at Uddings on a courtesy visit, striding past awestruck field workers. He was an enormous man, fat as a hogshead with great jowls. His face was red with weathering, his dark eyebrows rising outwardly towards his temples. Dressed in an elegant but not ostentatious tunic which barely contained his vast stomach, he had a surprisingly melodious speaking voice.

Together with his giant of a son they were on their way to visit the newly completed Abbey at Hortune.

"We come from Tavistock, where our lands are quite similar to here," he explained waving his arms expansively. "There is a fast flowing, clean river which tumbles down from the high tors where the old Britons used to farm."

Brith found it disconcerting to look up so high into the face of his son, Edulph. He had refused the offer of a stool saying that he would break it. "And lady, my knees would be so high in the air that I might fall backwards! I did ask if the church door could be made high enough for me to walk through without crouching but the masons laughed and said it was not possible."

Udric could do little more than stare at the huge visitors, his eyes wide in wonder. "Can he ride a horse?" he whispered to his father who had honoured his visitors with the two glass beakers of ale.

"No lad, I do not ride a horse, some say the horse could ride me for I am the bigger!" Edulph laughed at his own joke, the giggles echoing to the rafters. Udric looked down at the giant's feet seeing massive toes peeping from strong leather sandals. For all his size he was a gentle man and had stooped to caress the head of the bitch that had been curious to inspect the huge intruder.

"The church will be consecrated shortly then the nuns will arrive. It is good to know you have a mill here for I feel sure they will need flour for their bread. The King's reeve told me you had a good man here, a part-Dane I believe, Hal. He recommended that I sought him out; or rather the lay servants who will work the land at Hortune may need his advice if you would allow it. The fields are poor but I suppose I was lucky to get a plot so close to the King's hunting parks."

Having explained that Hal was at Didlington and would undoubtedly be pleased to help, Alfred and Brith watched their visitors striding off towards the Cranburne road, Udric having to run to keep up with their strides.

"Well husband, thank the Lord we are of normal stature and that we do not have to feed the pair of them for the larders could hardly keep up with their appetites!"

When Udric returned some moments later he found his parents embracing, exchanging loving kisses and endearments. Raising his eyes in amused mockery, he left quietly to tell the other children of the gigantic visitors.

Some days later Alfred went to collect the new coinage together with his own payments from the King. Brith and Udric, the latter pouting with disappointment at being refused leave to see his princely friend again, accompanied him as far as the mill where the miller was inspecting the wheel which turned the grinding stones. Above, two layers of clouds, one grey and one white blew at different speeds across the blue sky. The artificial mill leet burbled quietly on its way to re-join the river Wym. The water wheel remained stationary, small growths of weed hanging from a couple of the paddles.

With winter approaching it was important to mill the corn before the air became too damp. There was also the autumn slaughter of surplus sheep to attend to immediately after the New Year celebrations which would be more difficult than usual as Hal would be taking his turn on the coastal defence rota.

"The sheepward and I could mark those animals we think should be kept for breeding in the spring. In view of the new people at Hortune it is planned to keep a few more than usual and sell a couple of beasts to them," Hal stated confidently having previously discussed his determination to produce a profit from his new homestead.

"Whatever you think best. Have you been contacted then? The Earl, Ordgar, got his information about you from the Wymburne steward so you must have impressed him! He did say that the land is poor but did not know what used to graze there. I know you think the dung should be from another beast but it's up to you how much help you give them."

Acknowledging the young man's expertise, he watched the Wymburne miller as he prepared to re-surface the huge stone. They discussed other matters of a more general nature before Alfred remounted his horse. Brith and Aethelflaed stepped back to avoid being shouldered by the horses.

"Actually, Udric, I suppose there is no reason why you should not accompany me to court. You will have to ride hard my son for I wish to be there tomorrow night. Do you think you can keep up or will you ride with Owenson's man?"

Udric indignantly refused the offer of a pillion ride, his gap-toothed smile hiding his determination. "My pony is fast. He will keep up with you because I am smaller and carry no baggage."

The man who had been chosen to act as armed guard and servant for the journey grinned, showing several rotted, black teeth. Despite the foulness of his breath he had been reluctant to allow anyone to draw his painful teeth and alleviate the pain.

Brith smiled at her son's faith in his mount. "While you are gone I will stay to help Aethelflaed to press the cheeses, dry vegetables, hang the wildfowl and all the other things we women have to do! Besides Aethelflaed, we can have a good gossip behind their backs. Mind you I cannot imagine how so many cheeses have been eaten since we did the last lot! There must be more mouths to feed than expected." The two women smiled secretively, happy in each other's company. Both were wearing practical gowns with large white linen aprons, Aethelflaed's riding high over her swelling belly. Hal warned them teasingly that he would be expecting a veritable feast that night, pointing out that he had been working since just after dawn and would not finishing until the sun was low in the sky.

Between the two estates, varied provisions for the cold season could be prepared and shared between them. Brith bade her husband and son farewell, reminding Udric to keep warm, mind his manners and obey his father. The young lad twisted round in his saddle to wave, too excited to have listened to his mother's instructions. His dog whined, swishing its tail slowly before slinking back to wait for his young master's return. It gave a long suffering sigh, curled up in a small pool of weak sunshine and went to sleep.

Fats which had been saved during the year were now boiled up to make salves for chapped hands and chilblains, the unpleasant sores of the wet, cold months. Tallow together with any beeswax was melted to make stout candles for the hall in the winter evenings. The children released from everyday work, were sent out to pick nuts and berries as the season turned golden and then brown. Despite the chill in the air, few bothered to wear warm clothes, certain they would have full bellies by the end of the day and be warm enough from their games. Slowly the larder filled up. The lowest part, often cut several feet below ground and stone lined would be kept for those items which needed the chill to help with preservation. On occasions, if the mill wheel was not turning, a block of ice might form in the leet and be brought quickly to the manor larder. Any rats which had the temerity to enter the kitchens were quickly despatched by the dogs, both women known to screech loudly at the sight of any vermin.

Udric, having returned flushed with pride from his visit to court, became the natural leader of the youngsters who now lived on the estate. He often had to be punished for getting himself and others into possible danger.

"The tree is not safe to climb my son," chided Alfed one day when Udric had come back with a rip in his jerkin. Brith smacked her son soundly for his carelessness although she was secretly pleased with the amount of fruit he had gathered. Even now the damson juice was being strained off to use as dye for the newly spun wool while the fruit would be mixed with honey until it formed a sticky sweet. Blackberries and elderberries were also used, though some juice was boiled and reduced to a jelly so that the winter diet could be varied. There was a great deal of work to be done at this time of year if they were not to exist on pottage by the end of the frosts. In the coolest part of the kitchen she took stock of the food stores hanging from hooks on the beams.

"We have enough to feed an army, well a small one," she observed to a servant girl who was busy salting beans in a new barrel. "Where the meat will be hung in November is still to be decided. That's a good weight in there now. Well done."

All surplus eels and wildfowl were either dried or preserved with jelly from the pig trotters, advice she had been given by the King's lady when they had met at Kingston.

"Not that she actually did it herself of course but I was still grateful for the idea." The kitchen maid looked up from her work but finding that a reply was not expected shrugged her shoulders and returned to layering the beans and salt in the barrel.

Brith sighed as she also remembered the tragic death of the Northern King, Sigferth. She had never trodden on the stone covering his tomb in the church, although others appeared to have forgotten the gentle man who could not live with the shame of captivity. It cast her mind back to the stories of Alfred's fore-bear whose mind had been badly affected by bitterness and banishment. 'It obviously affects people different ways,' she pondered as the eels were finally hung from the last hook. Her thoughts were interrupted by the arrival of a travelling smith from Ringwood who regularly sharpened the knives and sold shears, axes, cooking pots and hinges of all sizes. Drinking cups with flat bottoms instead of horns could now be placed with ease on the trestle tables at mealtimes. Some were really beautifully worked, with handles joined invisibly to the body of the vessel. French traders too, had bought glass beakers and jugs to the King's court which had been copied by the less skilled glass workers in Mercia.

"Of course they will not last as long as the pottery jugs we have," admitted Brith, "but I can see the light through this one." She held up a beautiful flask, squinting at the winter sun through the smooth sides.

In the winter of nine hundred and seventy four years after the birth of our lord Jesus, Hal's father had died suddenly at Woodcutts. Although he had only just returned from his turn on coastal guard and was just in time to celebrate the birth of Gail, their first child, Hal had to leave his wife who was still in no condition to travel, to attend the funeral. His elder brother, Vannson and his new wife would now work the farm and hopefully have a long and happy life together. Alfred sent his sympathies but did not attend.

"It is more than likely that my judgement a few years ago is still remembered. Hal needs to feel relaxed at this sad time. Mind you, I never thought of Vann as old!"

As the frost hardened its grip on the earth it seemed as though neither homestead was to be spared bad news that year. A messenger arrived with the news that Brith's father was mortally ill. This time Udric did not accompany his parents as the fastest horses were saddled in the hopes that she would reach Cranburne before he died.

"He's never had a day's illness," lamented Brith through gritted teeth.

Even wrapped in furs, the journey was unpleasantly windy and wet with a bone chilling cold that seeped through every layer of clothing. The tracks were deep in partly frozen mud so that the horses tired quickly.

"Ride up here on the edge of the field," suggested Alfred as he forced his horse up the bank onto the narrow strip of rough ground. Several times earth and stones gave way beneath the hooves of their mounts, spilling down onto the already treacherous roads.

By the time they arrived at Brithric's house their horses were covered from the flanks downwards and the riders were spattered from head to foot with the stinking mud. A chilling sleety drizzle blew in eddies, creeping into any gap in their outer clothing.

Without even casting off her travel stained cloak, Brith hurried into the hall and was immediately directed by an old family servant to her father's bedside.

"He is still alive, but only just," Edith admitted as the bone-weary beasts were led away gently by the stable men. "He keeps calling for his son who has been here since last evening. I wish we could have been reunited under happier circumstances."

As the sleet fell silently from the darkening skies she led her son into the hall where ale had been set out for them. They sat down close to the fire.

He admired the coloured walls hung with brightly coloured rugs. Some of the windows were shuttered while others had skin covers keeping out the worst of the weather. They sipped the mulled ale quietly, giving Brith time and privacy at her father's bedside. Brith's brother studied his boots, picked at his nails and turned the cross at his neck over and over. His face showed no emotion at all until he rose suddenly and returned to the sick room. Edith started to say something about the young man when the peace was shattered by Brith's scream. Alfred almost drew his knife as they both stood up abruptly, the stools falling noisily. Edith led the way quickly drawing back the heavy leather curtain. On a raised bed, Alfred saw the body of Brithric sprawled untidily across the mattress, furs spilling onto the floor. Brith's dress was bloodstained.

"He choked on his own blood, it came gushing out, he...."

Brith gazed at her father with horror, almost frozen with shock. Edith gently closed her husband's eyes before leading the girl from the room. Alfred nodded to Brithricson who seemed stunned by the sudden death he had just witnessed. His eyes were wide and black in his pale face, his mouth shaping an appalled 'O' before relaxing.

"Come lad; let us arrange your father's limbs in a more seemly manner before my lady mother returns."

Pulling legs and arms between them, they managed to straighten the body before it stiffened. Nothing they could do removed the look of agonised astonishment on the older man's face, but at least the eyes remained closed. By the time Edith returned, they had covered the body decently, wiping away the dribble of blood from Brithric's mouth, and gathered up the worst of the blood soaked rushes which were burnt hastily on the brazier in the hall.

"May Jesus Christ receive your spirit, Amen," muttered Alfred as he crossed himself. He opened the shuttered window briefly to let the man's spirit leave the house.

Leaving Edith and Brithricson, still white faced, at the bedside he left the room. Brith was seated by the fire hugging a mug of spiced ale, shivering with shock, the servants sitting respectfully some distance away. One left the hall, returning a few minutes later with the saddle pack of spare clothes. Meekly Brith allowed her husband to replace her soiled over-dress.

"Burn this," he instructed the servant, bundling the stained mantle tightly. "No not here man, find the smith's or an outside hearth." The servant left obediently, holding the offensive bundle at arms length.

"You will keep watch tonight dear?" He asked tenderly. "Would you like company?"

Brith nodded, choked with tears and gulping spasmodically but staring fixedly into the fire. Even this hall brought back memories of her father's powerful presence. She had sat beside him so frequently and listened to his wise counsel.

"Why was there no priest?" she mumbled between sobs. "Will he lie in church land if he was not shriven?"

"Perhaps the priest has already been. We will ask Mother, but not just now."

"I did not even know he was ill." Brith rubbed her hands together in the welcome warmth of the fire. She felt cold, chilled to the bone despite Alfred's arms around her.

Food was brought quietly into the hall for those who wished to eat. Many of the servants were obviously upset with reddened eyes and running noses wiped hastily on sleeves.

Alfred felt guilty as he cut meat and bread for himself, but the journey had been difficult and he was extremely hungry.

They took turns to watch over the dead man's body, a single candle lighting the bedroom. At dawn, when the bell started to toll, everyone rose stiffly to their feet. Brithricson covered the face of his dead father gently, crossed himself and held the curtain back as Edith lead them back into the hall.

After the funeral at the tiny abbey church, attended by all who could be spared from their work, Alfred was anxious to return home. Two deaths in the immediate family in such a short space of time were unnerving. Neither Vann nor Brithric had been very old and the manner of his father-in-law's death had shaken him considerably.

"Will you stay here in your husband's house?" Alfred enquired gently as his mother turned a spindle aimlessly. "It is as you prefer of course, but there is always your old home or Uddings."

After a moment, not getting a reply he coughed quietly to gain his mother's attention.

"Has Brithricson spoken of his wishes? Will you stay here to keep order in the house for him?"

Edith started suddenly, her daydreaming interrupted by the question. "He has already asked me to stay. When he has returned from court I will give the matter thought again. Until then I will keep his house."

Alfred knew that Brithricson would have to inform the King of his father's death so that the land ownership could be recorded properly. "He will swear his fealty to the King, take over his father's position and in turn receive homage from the villeins and cottagers who worked on the land belonging to the hall. Until he takes a wife your position is probably comfortable. Promise you will send a message if you need me."

Privately he wondered what price the King would demand for his continued favour; an increase in rent payment or an extra man's service in the royal army could easily be the cost of a son's inheritance.

"Tomorrow we will return to Uddings," Alfred stated flatly. "There is unrest in the area and I have few full-grown men to defend the estates." Exhaustion was etched into the dark smudges beneath his eyes. Obviously while watching over the corpse his thoughts had been occupied with other matters instead of praying for the dead man's soul.

Edith agreed to let her son know of her decision in due course, but now, once again wearing a white mourning head-dress, she stood alone, with sad dignity, as she bade her visitors farewell.

A particularly vicious frost had hardened the mud sufficiently to allow a slightly faster return journey but even so it was tiring and cold. The sleet had not turned to snow for which they were grateful but the wind blew the old leaves in gusts until they had left the trees behind. They met few travellers, exchanging greetings as they passed, each acknowledging the mind numbing chill.

His return home was marred by reports of further thefts of precious stores from the Didlington hall. Yet more cheese and some newly baked wafers had disappeared from a board on which they had been set to cool. Hal expressed his puzzlement and also reported that a tenant had seen a stranger running towards the woods alongside the road. "If it is an excuse to cover the theft of food I'll have his hide but somehow the man persuaded me that it was the truth. Should we report it?"

"I will see the Steward. If the stranger is on the King's land and causing damage then it is his concern not mine. Perhaps Aethelflaed should tie one of her dogs close by next time she leaves her baking outside. You saw nothing yourself?"

Hal's normally broad forehead was creased with concern. No-one liked the idea of a stranger entering the yard in front of their house without permission. "I've seen no-one actually close to the hall. Several months ago someone mentioned an ill-kempt man near the road but I never gave any thought to it. Perhaps it should have been reported. There's always stories of outlaws or homeless soldiers."

Alfred took a rested bay horse back to the King's palace a couple of days later and found the steward poring over his accounts. "Welhail Master Steward! The sumpter horse is back in your stable ready to work again according to the staller. While I'm here," he paused dramatically, "there has been a series of thefts from the stores at Didlington and sighting of a stranger on two occasions, the man running off towards Wymburneholt forest. Have the keepers mentioned anything?"

Irritated by the interuption the Steward looked up a taunting half smile on his face. "What! Another excuse to blame someone else when you can't control your own tenants. No, I've had no reports and I have no time to listen to such cock and bull stories either. There is no-one living in the forest apart from the woodsmen and those legally entitled to be there. Go home and start pressing for answers. Now leave me in peace. The King's auditors are coming."

With an air of long suffering the Steward rudely turned back to his well thumbed sheets of parchment. Alfred left his hut astonished by the man's abrupt manner and lack of concern. He rode home indignant at the way he had been treated, determined to discuss the matter more fully with

Hal. Suffering mixed emotions of hurt and anger his face was flushed, his breathing short and hard. It was not until he had ridden beside the stream which formed the western boundary of Uddings that his temper subsided. A duck flew up noisily and something further up slid into the stream forming ripples in the widened part where washing was normally done. The horse stopped of its own volition getting little guidance from the rider. Alfred let it drink while he looked round. Everywhere he looked the fields were tidy, the raised pathways pruned of excess grass which had been cut for animal feed.

"Blast the man! Why does he always make others feel inferior? I'd like to prove the man wrong." He left the horse to graze in the paddock putting the Steward's attitude to the back of his mind.

Chapter Seven
AD972

A messenger from Hugh, Sheriff of Dorsetshire, arrived as spring moved into summer, carrying a sealed document. While Brith fetched refreshments Alfred moved to the best light spilling in through a window. Apparently the King had demoted many of his officials in the Wessex, Essex and south West peninsula on the grounds that they were becoming over powerful. Lord Hugh was anxious to refute this charge and had sent messengers to all the minor officials in each Hundred requesting their support.

"He wants me to make representation to the King!" exclaimed Alfred, astonished by the contents of the letter. He could quite understand why the messenger had not been entrusted with a verbal message on this occasion. Brith listened quietly as he explained the news.

"Who will replace him?" she queried, "that is, if the King will not re-instate him? I wonder if Ordgar has suffered the same fate?"

For a moment Alfred frowned until he remembered the pair from Devon, the father too gross to ride and the son so gigantic that there was not a big enough beast in all the land that could carry him.

He thought of all the other Dorset landowners that he was acquainted with but could not imagine any of them taking Hugh's place. "Most of them are busy enough dealing with their own problems, besides, many have young families or could not be spared from their own lands beyond the month already given to guarding the coast. Who wants to move to Wareham even if a castle is provided?" He smiled lovingly at Brith, thinking that she was becoming more beautiful in maturity than when they were newlywed. The idea of moving one's family to the confines of a castle by the sea had no attraction at all.

"I will send my court reports to the ealdorman as usual, and let the King know I have done so. This seems to be the least offensive way of letting King Edgar know of my support for Dorsetshire's leading thegn. I do not know of any wrong-doing. Perhaps the King wants the shire thegns to take a smaller proportion of the monies. If someone wants to keep their position at all costs..."

At the next quarter sessions he therefore reported the yield from the mill, and the King's portion, together with all decisions and judgements he had handed down in the courts to Hugh as usual, requesting that they be forwarded to the King in due course.

"I have received no orders to give my report to anyone else. We should go on as we always have done surely," added Alfred supportively.

In early summer Alfred attended the quarter-day witan or council meeting on St Johns Eve. Any matters not settled by the lower courts could be raised on these occasions which were also an opportunity for the King to reward his loyal thegns. Deliberately keeping apart from Hugh, he joined other men of his own standing to observe the proceedings. Dunstan, now an elderly man, sat to the right of the King, below the dais. He was seen to nod occasionally as if he were dozing, the wispy beard fluttering with each breath. Apart from the wooden cross hanging on its golden chain, there seemed to Alfred to be little difference in the magnificence of the King's robes and those of his chief minister.

Edgar had just returned from Chester where he had apparently received homage from no fewer than eight minor Kings, most of them from Wales. He was looking round the room, catching the eye of some and ignoring others. Guards with spears stood either side of the main door, shields resting on the floor.

"In recognition of their submission," he said, grinning broadly at the memory, "I obliged them to row me down the river Dee. In return we have promised to protect their lands from invading armies. My lord Dunstan here left saintly priests to bring them all to Christendom. Mercian lords will oversee justice to all. Those who were pardoned their crimes must deliver wolves heads as the land is over run with them, ravaging their flocks, killing their children and attacking travellers."

Most of the assembled company nodded in agreement with the King's wisdom while others who had perhaps recently paid a heavy monetary fine for some minor misdemeanour glowered at the King's leniency.

"It is a poor country," continued the King after a brief pause. "Tribute will only be in wolves' heads, three hundred a year, until the people are safe again."

There were more murmurings, but this time even fewer were happy with the arrangements that had been made.

"My lord," queried one thegn, "will their men fight with us in battles if need be? We provide men and arms, or food and shelter. Some must provide both, according to the terms of their land leases."

Many nodded in agreement with the speaker, but any discussion was quickly silenced when the King explained that the Welsh soldiers were fearless in battle and would be called to aid any English forces which were threatened.

The coastal defence watch was discussed in detail. Many of the southern landowners were clearly bored with the routine, arguing that they had not seen a single enemy ship in all the weeks they had led their villeins along the coastal stretches.

"Exactly my friends," rejoiced the King bluffly, rising from this throne in his enthusiasm. "We have let it be known widely that our coasts are defended night and day by alert, well trained soldiers who only wait for the day when they can kill an invader. Word of our forces has spread, even to the Northern men so that not even the most battle hardened Dane is keen to attack this land. Do not let your watchfulness slacken; it is just what the northern warriors hope will happen if they wait patiently."

Reluctantly the discontented thegns acknowledged the wisdom of continuing the watch rota though many continued to mutter quietly.

The King confidently reminded all present that he gave land and could also remove a man from favour. All appearance of bluff cheerfulness had suddenly faded as the king stared hard at particular individuals his narrowed eyes hunting among the crowd like a wild cat for her prey. Ignoring nervous glances among the men standing or seated below him, he swept his cloak back over his shoulders, pacing back and forth along the raised platform. Dunstan struggled to his feet and attempted to climb down the edge of the dais.

"But my lord," he expostulated, "none should be seated if you stand."

On being told to resume his seat, the Archbishop sank back gratefully into the chair, even that small effort causing his heart to thump uncomfortably.

"Some of you," continued the King, "have forgotten that I was chosen King by the Council, some twelve summers ago, and received your homage. You in turn lead men who live and work on your lands which you hold from me, as one of you has already pointed out. While I live, there will be no other leader in my Kingdom. With God's grace I have many years left so that my sons may be mature before they are asked to take on the task ahead. We have had peace in my time so that your womenfolk have been safe, your stock has prospered and the crops have been safely harvested. Any man, and that includes outlaws and lordless thieves, who threatens that peace will feel my wrath and be cast out from the church so that his very soul will be in jeopardy."

With this awful threat the King resumed his own seat. There was total silence in the hall. The King arranged his robes to his satisfaction, apparently untroubled by the fearful atmosphere which had developed. Alfred glanced quickly at Hugh of Dorset. He was looking straight ahead, expressionless, lips tightly pursed as if he was preventing himself from an outburst. The reference to outlaws recalled the scornful words of the steward of Kingston. His stomach curdled sending hot gall up to the back of his throat, the rigid muscles of his abdomen threatening to tear from each other. 'Yes', he thought, 'an outlaw is the most likely disturber of the peace of Uddings and must be dealt with even if it is with less severity than the King threatens.'

A cough broke the silence. One of the King's closest advisors reminded him of other business which needed to be discussed during the course of the day. Edgar nodded, cleared his throat again and turned to his audience.

"It has come to my attention that the meetings in the burghs and vills are not being held regularly as custom decrees. In future these will be held every four weeks so that justice is not delayed and sinners can repent sooner. The ealdorman is to be informed of cases which cannot be judged by local leaders. He will then either say whether the matter can be dealt with by my Justiciars or if it should wait for the half-yearly courts when I and my council will hear petitions or deal with serious crimes. Ealdormen and deputies will continue to attend to local affairs on my behalf, reporting regularly to me. Now I would leave you for a moment." The King rose and left the hall, followed by his council and the Archbishop leaning heavily on his body servant's arm.

Discussions immediately broke out unrestrained by the King's presence, some even managing an attempt at laughter to lighten the atmosphere. Some needed fresh air to cool overheated blood before anger ripped through all common sense and dignity. Refreshments were brought into the hall and men excused themselves briefly during the break in the proceedings.

Alfred had already noticed that Sheriff Hugh of Wareham looked more relaxed. He spent a few moments with Brithricson who had been standing on the far side of the hall. He looked older, thinner, so that his cheek bones seem suddenly to stand out. Enquiring about Edith, he was assured of his mother's continued good health. Their conversation was curtailed with promises to meet again soon when another man claimed his attention.

When the King emerged from his private room, the court was again called to order. Alfred managed to move his stool so that he could lean against a pillar, and settled down to hear reports from all the areas of the southern part of the Kingdom. Those who had done well, bringing revenue or increased produce to the court were praised while those who brought less than expected were encouraged to do better in the future.

There were no further references to the King's doubts as to the loyalty of the thegns of Wessex, or to the honesty of the sheriffs but during the evening meal some made their excuses to leave court.

Alfred sat on the lower benches with men from Wymburne and Cranburne. Many discussed farming matters while others turned their thoughts to women and the food upon the table.

While outside the hall breathing the cool night air to clear his head before settling down to sleep, Alfred saw Prince Edward crossing the courtyard. On impulse he hailed him, asking after the young man's horse.

They talked for several minutes of the skills the horse already possessed and of the new tricks the Prince was teaching him. His voice was animated and enthusiastic, describing how he could hang down from the saddle and pick up a rag bundle from the earth. "It can be used to reclaim a dropped weapon or to fool an enemy," he said proudly. Come and share a jug of ale. Do you need your cloak? It's chillier than expected."

They were standing in the lee of the hall so that the torch in its iron holder was behind them. Above stars shone brightly in the darkness; a young moon, almost on its back, was rising in the sky. They both looked up into the firmaments, Alfred pointing to a line of three stars which shone the brightest at that moment.

Fetching his cloak from the floor space he had reserved, he quickly joined the Prince in his small room. Spare tunics and cloaks hung on pegs in the wall above armour and the Prince's sword in a decorated scabbard. A small brazier had been lit to provide warmth as the youth lolled on his bed while Alfred used an upholstered stool and leant on a coffer with strong iron bands and locks.

They talked until the early hours mainly about horses until Prince Edward fell asleep. Alfred gently covered the boy with a fur rug and left the room quietly, reluctant to call a bodyservant from his rest. Finding a sheltered corner just outside the young boy's screen, he pulled some rushes up to form a pillow and lay down covering himself with his thick cloak.

The following day being Sunday, many thegns attended the church service for the Feast of St John with the King before leaving for their homes. Prince Edward stood proudly beside the King during the mass. On seeing Alfred he waved with innocent abandon before following his father back to the royal quarters, the ladies clutching their woollen cloaks tightly, struggling to keep up with their brisk pace, but equally keen to break the night's fast.

Chapter Eight
AD 975

Aethelflaed's second child still flourished so that the hall at Didlington seemed full of nursemaids. The boy child was to be named Udda in honour of his great grandfather. "We are far from Wymburne, well a good walk anyway," Alfred commented to Brith one night. "Perhaps we need to build our own church. T'is some distance to go for all these christenings! Some of my friends have their own chapels."

He had returned to Uddings in time to help with the shearing of the sheep. The shearers had come from Wymburne and sat in a circle sharpening the blades on whetstones lubricated with accurately aimed spit. When the bleating beasts were corralled and led into the compound without their lambs the noise increased forcing everyone to use sign language. Pulling off the tags of dirty wool was women's work, a back breaking task before the foreman would accept a fleece for rolling and tying.

Talking in a dialect which was strange to the farm workers, the men worked fast, packing the fleece into small bales. Udric worked with all the other farm hands sorting the smelly bundles into portions. Most would go to the wool seller, while Brith needed some for spinning into thread for new clothes for the Uddings' household. Aethelflaed would need soft wool for her two children, while in the cottages many women spun or wove all day to satisfy the need for cloth on the estate.

The wool had to be washed, an unpleasant task usually done during the warm weather by all the young girls treading the fleeces down on a stony part of the stream. There was a great deal of laughing and splashing during the work which took several days.

This year the fleeces were long. They would sell for good prices in the market. Alfred, Hal and Udric accompanied the laden cart to Wymburne promising to buy salt, fresh fish and other necessities before returning.

A young sheep shearer had cut Udric and Alfred's long hair while those less brave watched as their locks fell to the ground in ragged curls. Hal kept his hair long, saying it was warmer in the winter, but on seeing Udric smartly dressed with a colourful headband around his brow, he wished he too had been brave enough to submit to a barbering. Alfred offered to do it for him on their return. "If my hand is steady enough," he joked holding out shaking hands as if he suffered from palsy.

The market in Wymburne was in full swing. Leaving the wool and the cart with a servant, Alfred went to the wool buyer. Making a good bargain, the cart was unloaded and he counted the silver pennies into his purse before knotting it securely to his belt and forcing it between his stomach and trews. Every step he was conscious of the weight of the leather bag as it bumped against his groin. Thieves were rare, punishment being so severe, but it was better not to put temptation in the way of discontents, thought Alfred as he attempted to stroll casually, looking for his son and brother-in-law. Hal and Udric were purchasing foodstuffs which were needed.

Having bought a great deal of salt, fresh fish, iron tools and soft cheeses they were anxious to pack the purchases in the leather bags. Everyone would be free for an hour or two now the chores were completed. Hal also wanted to arrange for his son to be christened.

"Owenson, come with us while the rest of you guard the cart and horses in turns," commanded Alfred. 'The men must lead the ox back so I hope they are sober enough at the end of the day! Now let's enjoy ourselves too."

Standing in small groups, musicians piped reed instruments or plucked strings to accompany singers hoping to earn a living from those who thronged the market where the ale seller did a brisk trade. To add to the noise, stall holders tried to out do their rivals, shouting their wares then cursing the children who dodged in and out between them.

The air became hot and sultry causing tempers to fray as the afternoon wore on. Udric and Hal mounted, leading Alfred's stallion securely between them. It rolled its eyes as thunder could be heard in the distance plunging heavily between the two geldings which were also becoming infected by the excitement of the market. Final bargains were purchased by those who left things to the last minute before running to join the ox cart which was already piled high with baskets, rope, food and children.

The cavalcade finally moved off behind other parties also making their way north, the tracks being mainly dry apart from the area either side of the ford which had already become a quagmire. Some children jumped off to push the cart, shrieking in delight as they splashed in the muddy water.

Their eventual arrival back at Didlington was greeted with enthusiasm. Those who had not been to the market unloaded the cart while Hal and Alfred went into the former's private quarters to settle up the monies from the wool sale. Dropping the bag of coin on the board, Alfred carefully counted out his coins. "I sold all the fleeces in one transaction. Here is your portion Hal , one third of the proceeds, and this portion is due to the cottagers. I'll leave you to see that it is divided fairly. Each man usually receives his pennies and signs a tally with his mark." The horn was blown to summon men from their work. As the vast majority had already heard that the wool had been sold they were poised to run and collect their share.

For many, this was the only coin they would receive until the beasts themselves were sold. While some were slaughtered to provide food for the meals served in the hall, the sheepward received one penny from each man whose animals he tended, while the ploughmen received one good beast each year in return for ploughing the land. As at Kingston, these provisions became set in the unwritten manor laws.

Those who cut wood for others received their share, as did the miller and the smith who had no time to look after their own land or animals. It was late before the last man had finally received his share of the sale money which would be carefully hoarded away.

They left for Uddings, the cart carrying the goods Brith had ordered. The storm had come to nothing but the evening air was still very warm. Rising up the small hill they saw a glow in the sky and were instantly alarmed. The shorn sheep scurried out of their way as they spurred their horses to a gallop.

Fire, the enemy and friend of man, had taken hold of the stables by the time they reached Uddings. The men had already formed a line and were throwing buckets of water at the blazing roof.

Speaking rapidly to Owenson's son who was now the overseer, Alfred quickly assured himself that all the horses had been taken to safety.

"God's Bones! How did it start?" he exclaimed angrily. "I leave for one day and come back to disaster." Brith and the kitchen servants continued to fetch water from the old clay pit which had long ago become a dew pond. On seeing her already dirty and dishevelled, he felt ashamed of his outburst. Letting a villein lead the stallion and Udric's horse away, he threw off his jerkin and helped fight the fire, the leather buckets passing hand to hand to where he stood, legs braced, as close as he dared. Fortunately the stable had been built across the courtyard but he directed that the roofs of the adjacent buildings be dampened down to prevent sparks setting them alight.

It was fully dark before a rumble of thunder could be heard in the distance followed shortly afterwards by a sudden downpour.

"A Godsend my lord," shouted one exhausted man who was quite unrecognisable. When the fire was out the men shambled away to their own cottages, too exhausted to talk. Alfred strode round examining the damage while Udric went with the horse-keeper and his boys to examine the horses in the nearby fields. Although still restive, most of them appeared to be unharmed and were grazing in small groups.

After arranging for a watch to be set for the rest of the night, Udric returned to the hall where Brith had hastily provided meat and ale. A man lay against the wall faintly moaning, his wife beside him wringing her hands as she crouched over him. Sometimes his fevered brain caused him to mutter out loud but his words were garbled until they faded away.

"Is anyone else badly hurt?" she enquired when Alfred strode in. "I have salves and ointments for burns and bruises, but perhaps we should send to Wymburne for a monk to attend."

"I will leave at dawn," promised Alfred almost asleep on his feet. He went to his bed hastily eating a piece of cheese washed down with a honeyed drink. He was so tired that he did not even bother to loosen his belt or remove the knife from its scabbard. He awoke the following morning feeling battered and bruised. His clothes smelt strongly of smoke and sweat. He pulled a face, disgusted that he had slept on their marriage bed in such a state.

Riding to Wymburne to collect an infirmarian from the monastery he was aware of the nagging ache over one hip where he had lain all night on his weapon. Rubbing the spot rhythmically he thought of the meeting he would call during the mid-day break so that he could enquire into the catastrophe. Most of the harness had been burnt along with some foodstuffs which were in the stables. Fortunately the better harness which Hal had taken as his spoils of war was in the guest room. It was far too good to be used during training and would be sold with a horse if a wealthy man ordered one of the stallions.

In Wymburne Alfred had to knock many times on the stout, iron studded oak door. A shutter was pulled back from a small hatch to reveal a newly tonsured monk. Throughout their short conversation the man's lips twitched with a tic at one corner. This distorted the poor man's speech so that it was almost unintelligible.

After some attempts at requesting the Infirmarian be called the young man backed away, his sandals slapping on stone floors.

"Ye Gods no wonder he became a monk," he thought in a dour unchristian moment. "He could do little else, but why on earth is he answering the door?"

A few paces away he could see a similar door through which no man would enter. Smiling wryly he remembered the Abbess' possessiveness of her precious bible when Lord Hugh had held an inquest in the church.

A man tapped him on the shoulder. Alfred whirled round already drawing his dagger. With relief flooding through his body he realised that a monk clutching a large bag was trying to attract his attention. A sorry looking donkey with only a thick blanket to serve as a saddle waited patiently. Together they returned to Uddings, the monk to minister to those who had suffered burns and the little donkey to a good meal.

Sitting at the high table Alfred listened to the overseer explain how a small brazier had been knocked over by an excited mare when she was being led past the stallion's stall. Young boys who helped with the horses after their work on the fields was done nodded vigorously, some still smeared with sooty water.

Required for heating glue or the honey and water for the orphan colt, a small brazier was kept burning throughout the year outside the stable. Fortunately all the horses inside had been freed before the fire took hold. They had been led to safety and only one had suffered a minor scorch, but the man who had gone into the burning building had not been so lucky.

The infirmarian had set to work to plaster the man's extensive burns. What Alfred had taken to be soot on the man's face were actually deeply seared burns from falling thatch. He screamed as the monk's gentle hands covered his face with a healing salve before wrapping a fine woollen bandage over the damaged skin.

"It seems it was an accident and no one is to blame," judged Alfred when the man had finally fainted from the pain. "The man who saved the horses will not work for many months. His work will be done by others until he is well again; his woman and children will feed in the hall and be given bread, cheese and ale for their own use from the kitchens so that they do not suffer for their man's bravery. Have you noted that Udric?"

At Uddings, Udric acted as his father's writer at the regular courts when any man could voice a grievance or query his days of service which were imposed on the cottagers in return for their piece of land on his father's estate. Lower servants did not necessarily have any land but worked all day directly for him in return for their food, clothing and a place to sleep. By working hard and well they could raise themselves, acquiring the right to build a cottage with a small area of land to grow crops or raise fowl for themselves.

Udric had quickly learned reading and writing from a younger son of a landowner at Shapwick. Eventually the tutor hoped to enter the church but in the meantime he would earn a little teaching basic education to those who wanted to learn. Brith's presence ensured that her son would not be lazy or use an excuse to miss a lesson.

The injured man moaned as he was laid on a makeshift bed which had been hurriedly constructed in a corner of the hall. Clearly fevered, his woman was instructed to nurse him while others fetched cool ale and water.

"I asked the monk if he had seeds of poppy but they are not common and he had none. On Sunday I could ask my friend, the weaver who taught me, if she knows anyone who has some. I hate to see anyone or even an animal in pain. It makes me feel so helpless." Brith's face clearly showed her distress. She laid a hand on the woman's shoulder and was rewarded with a quick glance of gratitude even though her husband alternated between thrashing in a fever and unconsciousness.

Outside, work started immediately to clear the debris. Any wood which was salvageable was cleaned and stacked carefully for re-use while the ashes were scooped up and taken to the midden. The slightest breeze blew these back onto the workers coating skin, hair and clothes with grey. Eyes and teeth shone cleanly causing many to laugh at others and then themselves.

"I think we should rebuild further from the house," Alfred declared when he had studied the cleared site.

"Why not use the high land beyond the furlong field? It would drain off naturally in the winter months yet still be near enough to guard," suggested Udric.

Instructing the head horse-keeper to accompany them, they walked rapidly to Udric's suggested position. The dog ran round them in circles scenting a hare which must have run across the paddock during the night. It suddenly stopped, cocking its head to one side before dashing past the men barking wildly, the hair on its back bristling.

Calling the dog to him Udric stared in the direction the dog was pointing. Despite the recent storm a horseman was galloping towards them, raising clods and dust on the track. As one, all three men placed hands on their knives until a horn could be heard and they relaxed.

The rider slowed so that his royal messenger's headband and staff of office could now be recognised. Alfred hailed the man as he pulled the blowing horse to a halt. He tumbled down from the saddle clearly worn out, staggering with fatigue.

"My lord Alfred of Uddings?" gasped the rider as he fumbled for the writ he had brought. Taking the message Alfred untied the cord. Without a word he rolled it up again, turning to the horse-keeper. "This man is to be given a fresh horse and food for his journey to Hamtun. His own is exhausted but will be recovered by the time he returns. Get my own horse ready and one for Udric but get the King's man on the road again first. We ride for Winchester."

Glancing curiously at his father, Udric took the bridle of the messenger's horse to remove the royal insignia from the brow band. In order that the man could claim meat, drink and a mount it was essential that he carried the King's colours. All three walked briskly to the field where the horses had been turned out. Most of them were already clustered round the fencing, eager to meet the new arrival whose tiredness had been momentarily forgotten.

Selecting a similar sized gelding, the horse-keeper led the animal out, bridled it and transferred the saddle. As soon as the colours had been attached to its browband the messenger remounted, collected the bag of food from a young lad, and set off quickly southwards waving his thanks.

"Come Udric we have no time to waste. The horses will be ready in a few minutes and we have much to do." So saying he strode off to the hall shouting commands as he went. There were many curious glances until the steward recalled men to work.

Food was wrapped quickly and ale drawn off into leather flasks while Brith followed Alfred quickly into their private room where he selected his finest tunic and jerkin. Drawing the curtain quickly to ensure privacy he drew her to him, an urgent embrace bearing in mind the haste that was necessary.

"King Edgar has died. Young Edward is supported by many of the ealdormen and the Bishops, but Aethelred is already using the royal title, encouraged by his mother, lady Elfrida. There is to be an emergency Council. Archbishop Dunstan commands Dorsetshire thegns to attend for the Council and crowning of the next King."

"Who will it be then?" she queried, slowly removing her apron, puzzled frown lines creasing her forehead.

"I do remember when Aethelred was born that the King's lady insisted that she was his real wife and that her son was therefore the King's heir. Since then I don't suppose the subject has arisen. After all, my lord King Edgar appeared to be in good health and only recently was saying that there would be many years before either of his sons would replace him."

Struggling to lace the jerkin up while talking to Brith, Alfred's fingers were awkward so that the leather thong became knotted. Brith laughed as she offered to finish the lacing for him.

Udric too was hastily dressing while his dog sat nearby watching, its head on huge paws. Everything had happened so fast no one had made time to reward the dog for his timely warning. Large liquid brown eyes studied Udric as he pulled the green tunic over his head.

The two men eventually left Uddings having had to tie the dog to a stout stake to prevent him following them. Alfred felt that as the court would be filled to capacity and accommodation might be at a premium, the large dog would be in the way and might get lost. One of the other young boys promised faithfully to care for the hound in their absence.

Their arrival at Winchester proved how right he had been. Even to get through the gate was an effort. Buildings had been put up replacing the old high fenced compound that had held prisoners, but even so, every corner which could be pressed into service as a temporary shelter was already occupied.

Giving their names to the guards they were directed towards the church where they left the horses in the care of a young boy. Udric would act as his page during the visit. Alfred would be obliged to attend the formal meeting tomorrow, when the council would vote on the King's successor. Until then, Udric could meet his friends and renew acquaintances.

"Do you think Edward, I mean Lord Edward, will remember me?" queried Udric as his father turned to leave him. "I mean, he was only the aetheling when he chose his horse. I remember how cross he was when Dunstan ordered his return to court. He said something about the man acting as if he was …."

"Hush, not a word more on that subject. Yes, Lord Edward will remember you if your paths cross but since it's not likely I should just enjoy yourself. Go and see his horse for yourself if you are curious. Tell the staller who you are and don't be cheeky. He has boys working for him who have felt the back of his hand no doubt!"

Wearing a headband showing the colours of the late King, Alfred had no difficulty in passing the guards posted outside the King's hall. He was hailed by several Dorset landowners grouped around the ealdorman. Like him, they had removed colourful tunics, replacing them with those of a more sober colour fastened by a jewelled pin.

"Welhail Alfred, have you found room?" called one using the old Saxon form of greeting. Others grinned a welcome and clapped him on the back. Even William from Chalberie was smiling although he could not prevent it being tinged with his haughty demeanour. Ever since his father had been granted the title of thegn he had been led to believe that he was superior to many others. There were few occasions when he had not left someone feeling belittled or ridiculed. For this reason he had few genuine friends and was kept to the fringes of any gathering. Even now, as the Earl of Dorset strode towards the Dorset men, William was trying hard to be noticed.

"My lord, friends - greetings to you all." Alfred bowed, exaggerating the sweep of his arm, certain that he was among friends and loyal comrades.

Sheriff Hugh, now more confident of his own position, suggested that they move closer to discuss the reason for the council having called the meeting.

"We'll get into this corner. Pull up that bench!" Tempering his voice so that only those around him would hear he continued, his tone lowered to reflect the confidential news he was imparting. "As some of you know, King Edgar was buried at Glastonbury as he had always intended, among the saints. Both sons attended as is proper, but in the procession which returned to court, Queen Elfrida rode at the head of the soldiers with Prince Ethelred beside her. She raised his arm as they re-entered the city and acknowledged the cheers, forbidding Edward to accompany them into the King's private quarters. Mercia and the Welsh Princes support Ethelred, while I believe the new Devon and Cornwall ealdorman is undecided.   Suffolk is for Edward, Essex is for Edward, Oslac of Northumbria would have been for Prince Edward had he not been banished, and I support him too," he added with a rush.

"Some say that Edward is not the heir because his mother was not truly married to the King, but my lord Dunstan feels sure that Edgar would not have confessed his sin with the nun, if he had not been married to the lady Aethelflaed or at least held her in very high regard."

"Edward is the oldest son and has already taken men to Wales to arrange the tribute, whereas Ethelred only goes with his mother. Besides he is only a baby."

Alfred did not like to point out that Ethelred had recently passed the age of twelve summers old and could therefore be counted a man.

"The aetheling Edward came to Uddings to buy horses. He has a quick temper I admit, but was courteous to my household and princely in bearing," said Alfred steadily. "I have had no real dealings with the aetheling Ethelred. From his appearance he is not a baby but one hears that the King's lady has much influence with him."

Others related their contacts with both the Princes and it became clear that the majority of the Dorset men favoured the elder son.

"You have helped me with your advice," acknowledged the ealdorman, pushing his thumbs into his belt. "I will speak for Edward tomorrow. Now let us find a place in the hall to eat."

Alfred beckoned Udric who had been standing apart from the thegns. "We go to eat son. Stay close until we see if there are places for all. Remember you act as my body-servant. No doubt my lord Hugh has his own man, but he may need attending at the table. Leave me my best knife if you are called on."

Seated with the other Dorset thegns Alfred was relaxed in the company of friends and acquaintances. Young Udric was relegated to the narrow trestles closest to the door and therefore probably in the draught. Guards stood beside the doors, spears inverted to signify the death of the King. Their faces were masks of concentration, eyes flicking rapidly over the assembled diners in case of trouble.

During the meal heated debate could be heard as to the rights of the succession. Ethelred and his mother, both wearing gold circlets and dressed in bright, embroidered robes, left the hall immediately after eating their fill while Edward made no appearance at all, apparently being closeted with Archbishop Dunstan in the private quarters.

As soon as the aetheling and his mother left, fighting flared up between the rival factions causing the womenfolk to shriek in fright. As all weapons were outside the hall missiles were confined to mugs or even pieces of manchet bread, but as knives were drawn, people began to leave hurriedly calling for the Captain of the guards.

"Come Udric, we will away to bed," decided Alfred when two men close to them started shouting at each other, their table knives held threateningly. Although not lethally sharp, neither wanted to be involved in a fight. He had always preferred to consider both sides of an argument, taking time to make decisions after due thought. Some may have thought him slow to anger, having enormous self control but in reality Alfred's anger could rise and erupt without warning if he was genuinely riled or provoked.

Their temporary accommodation lacked comfort, privacy and cleanliness. In the morning both men were scratching from the numerous flea bites they had suffered during the night. They dressed hastily, shaking the outer tunics and cloaks thoroughly to avoid carrying the vermin with them.

"God's blood father, I'm eaten alive," exclaimed Udric vehemently, rubbing his wrist savagely. "T'is not fit for a beast let alone men! I am glad I did not bring the dog with us." His hair was tousled with bits of straw. He ran his fingers through it leaving deep groves in its thickness.

"Better than sleeping outside, but come now, we have to go but try not to scratch or others will not want to stand next to you."

They made their way back towards the hall in plenty of time for the Witan meeting. There was no sign of the previous night's violence. Benches had already been set up for the council, the trestle table covered with a richly covered tapestry. Udric would have to leave the hall before the meeting began but in the meantime he kept his father company as men from all parts of the Kingdom came into the hall, some in groups, others singly.

"I will leave you now, the hall is getting crowded. I will wait where the horses are stalled, unless you send for me."

Bowing briefly to his father, Udric left the hall inconspicuously, making way for men entering.

The councillors filed in, their cloaks billowing out as they turned to face the assembled representatives of the Kingdom. Archbishop Dunstan, wrinkled and gaunt, and the Bishops took places in either side of the council, their grim faces set in a determined expression.

The two Princes entered, Ethelred preceding his elder brother, causing many eyebrows to lift in astonishment. The lady Elfrida, styling herself Queen, would have followed her son into the hall but was restrained by the guards. She could be heard shouting angrily as the bodyguards and soldiers prevented her from even watching the proceedings of the meeting. The doors closed firmly as the bar was lowered into its position. The royal bodyguards stood solidly, legs apart, guarding all entrances, weapons head down into the rushes.

Some men smiled, feeling that Ethelred's cause was harmed by his mother's behaviour. Others who backed the younger Prince, scowled at the delay in starting the formalities.

"Silence," called the leading councillor rising to his feet. "The Archbishop will pray that our deliberations are guided by the Almighty."

Archbishop Dunstan duly rose slowly, recited the familiar prayer invoking God to look kindly upon the men present and to guide their thoughts towards Christian unity and justice, keeping them from all harm, especially from invading heathen-folk.

Nominations for each of the Princes were quickly noted by the writers scratching noisily on new parchment before the arguments for each of them were presented. The ealdormen had obviously rehearsed their arguments well.

Dunstan reminded them of King Edgar's will, hoping to influence those who were as yet undecided. Those who had been insulted or annoyed by Edward made much of their affront, while his supporters ridiculed Ethelred's obvious continued dependence of his mother.

The hours passed, men discreetly shifted their weight, coughed and scratched. The councillors and Bishops had access to ale which they sipped throughout the morning.

Alfred, who had forgotten to break his fast heard his guts rumble noisily in the comparative silence of a momentary pause in the debate. His neighbours glanced hastily in his direction before hiding their amusement behind a hand. Neither faction had made any impression on the supporters of the other when a second vote was taken.

Archbishop Dunstan stood up while another man was speaking. The speaker paused, put off by the interruption. Taking advantage of the man's discomfort the Archbishop announced that he would hear no further arguments.

Taking Edward's arm, he hobbled quickly out of the hall followed immediately by some of the Bishops who had greedily finished their ale, and many of the leading ealdormen.

Thinking that there was to be a break in the proceedings Alfred gratefully made for the cookhouse to snatch a quick bite of food and a mug of ale. Many of those leaving the hall followed him until the cooks, besieged by hungry men-folk, were obliged to supply bread, cheese and ale on a makeshift table. Everyone noticed how quickly servants slacked when their master was absent. The courtyard was once again liberally spattered with stable muck, mud and vegetable waste which should have been taken to the pigs. Shoes attracted the worst of the dirt, further spreading the aroma of the stables and decay.

Alfred made his way towards the new Minster to stretch his cramped legs, munching the bread as he went. He wiped the welts of his shoes on tussocks of grass, swearing softly when the stinking mess stuck to the leather.

Hearing voices inside the new cathedral he peered curiously into the dim interior only to gasp with amazement.

Archbishop Dunstan appeared to be in the act of crowning Edward. Adjusting his sight to the gloomy interior Alfred walked quietly into the nave of the church momentarily astonished by the sight of the elderly prelate holding the wide gold circlet above the Prince's head, muttering Latin prayers to the Almighty.

The ealdorman of Dorset inclined his head towards Alfred, briefly acknowledging his presence but the Kentish and Northumbria men ignored his intrusion. Making his way quietly behind Hugh, he was surprised to feel Udric grip his arm beside him. Without turning he pressed his son's hand to his body.

"By the grace of God," pronounced Dunstan, "I anoint you and crown you King of all the territories of England and Wales, of the waters in and around the land."

The crown was finally placed on the young King's head, pressing down his fair hair. Raised to his feet, Edward looked slightly bemused but smiled graciously at those who had attended his crowning.

Dunstan was the first to offer homage, followed by the Bishops. The ealdormen too pressed forward, putting their hands between those of the King while repeating the familiar words.

Alfred and Udric hesitated, unsure whether they too should kneel before the new King now or wait until the more usual occasion when the oath was taken by all the lower ranks simultaneously.

"Do you hesitate my lord Alfred, and you too Udric?" asked Edward when the last senior thegn had sworn.

"No my lord King," responded Alfred hastily, embarrassed at being singled out. "We would indeed offer our homage to you. Our hesitation is only due to the fact that we are here by chance. I mean my lord, that we would not presume to take your time or draw attention to ourselves. Besides my son is not quite of age."

The King laughed, held out both hands and bade father and son kneel before him. Before the ealdormen and senior Bishops of the land, Alfred and Udric made their vows together. Later they would describe the event with wonder. Udric was quite sure he was so close he could have touched the crown itself!

"Now my Lord, elders, Bishops and ah, thegns," added Dunstan, "we must return to the hall." Although Archbishop Dunstan's eyes were cloudy white, an enigmatic smile spread across his ascetic face, a hint of the satisfaction he gained from this unusual course of action.

With one phrase the Archbishop had re-introduced solemnity to the atmosphere. The sun shone briefly through the large window directly on the men below who were straightening tunics, cloaks and headbands. To Udric it seemed like a good omen. "He did remember us! Do we follow them back to the hall?" he whispered to his father.

"Aye, but let us stay well behind and slip to one side as we enter the hall. There are those who would envy our attendance at the ceremony. Most of those present were ealdormen of the shires, not thegns of my class. Were the horses rested?"

Udric nodded as they followed the dignitaries out of the church, the procession appearing to grow in regality as they entered the door of the hall. The soldiers stood to one side gaping at the young Prince wearing the crown of his late father. They hastily swung their spears upright, banging the wooden poles onto the floor.

"My Lords, and all of this land, I present your King." Dunstan spoke clearly, emphasising his words.

Alfred pushed past the outer ring of soldiers and gained the back row of those entitled to attend the Council. His entry was only noticed by those he brushed against, everyone's attention being taken by the announcement that the Archbishop had just made.

At first there shocked silence only broken when Ethelred blustered and attempted to leave the hall until restrained by his own supporters. Commotion followed as realisation dawned on men at differing speeds of understanding.

"By God brother, you will regret this day," vowed Ethelred savagely. His face was blotched with angry red patches, his slightly protuberant eyes narrowed to angry slits.

Men either congratulated each other on their chosen heir being made King or blustered outrage at the Archbishop's boldness in taking matters into his own hands.

With Edward now seated on his father's ornate chair and the Archbishop standing formally behind, together with the supporting ealdormen, the councillors called the meeting to order again. It took several attempts for calm to be restored so that an announcement could be made. "The King will now accept the oath of homage from all present."

One by one, some more willingly than others, the dissenting ealdormen spoke their vows and took the King's hand in open and witnessed acknowledgment. Prince Ethelred too knelt before his older brother who embraced him warmly so that they appeared to be reconciled before the full council. The doors of the hall were flung open admitting those who had waited patiently outside.

Alfred and Udric lined up with all the minor thegns and land owners surrounded by the guards who were attempting to establish some sort of order to the proceedings. Feeling that it might be unwise to advertise the fact that they had already given their allegiance to the King within the Minster the two of them approached their lord again as their turn came.

"Again Alfred, and you too Udric my young friend, son of Alfred? Are you doubly loyal then?" The newly crowned King's head was tilted slightly to one side, his eyebrows raised questioningly.

Assuring the young man of their good intent they took their oath again in the crowded hall and were rewarded with a warm handfast grip from the new King, grateful for their genuine support and friendship.

No-one pointed out that Udric was not yet a man so he stayed beside his father trying to look as tall as he could, adjusting his browband to raise his hair beneath it. It was dusk before the ceremony was finally over. King Edward left the hall surrounded by advisors, bidding all welcome to his table that night. The guards fell in to form a troop behind their new King, their captain barking out orders quite unnecessarily.

As soon as the royal party with the bodyguards were out of ear-shot, noisy discussions broke out again. Servants trying to put up the tables for the coronation feast had to push their way through the quarrelling crowd of men.

"Let us take a short walk my son," suggested Alfred. "We have witnessed amazing events today." Placing one hand on his son's shoulder they made their way out of the hall into the last of the sunlight. Slanting shadows reached across the courtyard which had been hurriedly cleaned.

The horses still seemed content on the horse-lines, but they agreed to make an early start the following morning. "That is of course if no further dramatic events change our plans! Now for some food, my belly complains again."

Feasting lasted for many hours without any apparent rancour from those who had supported the younger Prince. The lady Elfrida made a brief appearance, bowing her head and offering her good wishes to her stepson so that a cheerful atmosphere prevailed all evening. Archbishop Dunstan proposed a toast to the young King during the meal which outwardly was drunk by everyone present.

It was clear that the Archbishop had appointed himself chief advisor to the young King, but this was not an unexpected development bearing in mind the sudden death of King Edgar, and Edward's little experience of rulership. He had fought in minor skirmishes, presided over shire courts but never been responsible for the laws, finance and general well-being of the population. The restraining hand of the prelate would temper the impetuousness and naivety of the new King. Many were pleased that the old man had apparently elected himself guardian. They hoped however, that less land would be given to the monasteries and churches. Many now had church-lands adjoining their own which led to disputes over the upkeep of the nearby roads, the church deeming itself to be above such mundane tasks.

Alfred and Udric rode off early the following morning leaving many with thick heads, some still oblivious of the dawn. In contrast the journey home was unexciting, although both were glad to leave the crowded city with its noise and smells. Alfred could not believe that the apparent signs of friendship displayed at the feast were more than a temporary truce between the rival factions.

"I thought they would come to blows," he said as they stabled the horses in the temporary stalls behind the hall. "My Lord of Mercia was almost beside himself with anger. I thought he would choke on his own bile when he swore his oath. If looks could kill, our young King would have been felled on the spot!"

They spent the rest of the evening talking over the events of the past two days. Udric related how he had been waiting for his father outside the hall, following him when he had come out for a quick walk during an interval in the proceedings.

"I recognised Lord Dunstan but did not realise what he was going to do. Then a servant produced the crown and we were there, watching a King being crowned!"

Brith listened to her son, excited by the visit to court and the ceremony he had witnessed. Her own report on Uddings was unimportant compared to the momentous events which her husband and son now reported.

"We were asked to take our oath of fealty there and then, in front of the ealdormen and Archbishop Dunstan. I took the King's hand and knelt before him in front of Hugh and three, no four Bishops," he corrected himself.

"You will tell these things to your own children one day," said Brith when Udric paused for breath. "Now I must tell you of the stables and horses".

Both men gave her their attention although Udric's eyes still shone with excitement. She told them that the main timbers had now been prepared by the woodcutters. They only awaited Alfred's final instructions on the site to begin work on the construction. As to the horses, only the grey with the scorched flank was giving cause for concern.

Despite several applications of salve, the animal was still distressed. Owenson's son, the head horse-keeper, was with the horse night and day, hand feeding her with choicest grain, but there did not appear to be an improvement.

"First thing tomorrow I will see the horse myself. If it is in great pain then it must be killed. I cannot stomach an animal gravely hurt."

He called for a servant to sharpen his knife, before retiring thoughtfully for the night, laying aside his best doublet and tunic before embracing Brith and falling asleep, his arm around her.

It was late the following morning when Udric enquired after the mare's health.

"She is indeed gravely sick. She is so hot but still seems reasonably strong. We will inspect her again tomorrow."

Udric went to look at the mare. She was indeed fevered but greeted him with a whinny. "Why don't we take her down to the stream? The water could be cooling if she would let us pour some over her sides," he suggested.

At the meal that evening he mentioned that the mare had seemed a little better after her bath. They discussed the merits of such treatment, Owenson recalling that his father, Owen, used to take horses suffering from hot feet down to stream below the place where the water was taken for drinking. "They were apparently tied up in the cold water for most of the day, only being released to feed at night. The swelling used to go down so that the animal could walk more easily," he recalled. "Not the same ailment I know but cold water will reduce the heat of the burn. She can be hand fed though, there is no need to keep her on short rations."

Alfred agreed that the cold water treatment could be continued, as long as a horse-boy was with her at all times. Other matters were raised as they sat round the fire relaxing after the meal. Hal announced that he had selected strong rams from his brother's small flock to ensure new blood this year. "The lambs are not all white but the wool is longer. It can be dyed darker colours," he added. "My brother assures me that the meat is good so the women will be happy!"

The wool buyer had already visited the fields and made a bargain with Hal to take the fleeces directly from the barn when they were ready. He had agreed the deal in principle with Alfred the previous summer when many flocks had died, forcing fleece prices higher than usual.

"I hope that will not mean that there will be no day out for the womenfolk after the clipping. You know how everyone enjoys the wool market at the end of the year."

Alfred hastily agreed that just because his own wool would not need to be carried to the market, the outing would be allowed as usual. "After all the owners of the sheep will actually benefit as the money will be paid to me before they go to the fair instead of waiting for it until I return. Mind you, King Edward will make his own coins in due course."

He stood up and stretched, remembering the carpenter who waited to start the stables. Owenson's son walked out with him, his face a picture of concentration. The ground in front of the house had been swept clean. There was only the faintest smell of horses. Fowl pecked in the earth, scattering as the two strode across to the waiting men. Last winter's drainage channels had almost disappeared but would be dug out again to prevent mud being taken into the hall.

"Until the stables and feed rooms are finished we will have to pile the hay in a big stack. Cut bracken and lay it thickly, about so deep, on waste clods of clay if you can," Alfred demonstrated the desired depth along one arm before continuing, "it keeps the rats out, and another mat will make a thatch for the top to keep the stack dry." Owenson nodded that he had understood and watched carefully as the site of the new stables was scratched out on the earth.

"The men have just finished work at the church in Wymburne. For months, no it feels like years, we have trodden in mud and mess to get through the door. Now they say the tower and new side aisle are completed, with glass in two of the windows! We shall see the side of the church without all the scaffolding poles and piles of material that has been around for so long."

"I would like it even better if pigs were not allowed to forage on the old burial ground!" retorted Alfred who was watching the carpenters carrying planks onto the ground marked out for the new stables. One was holding an angled piece of wood and scoring the ground more heavily to make sure that the corners of the building would be square.

During the next two months everyone worked steadily towards the climax of the year. The sun shone brightly on the corn ears turning them golden, while children gathered dandelions and elderflowers for winter drinks. Both the oxen gave birth to bull calves while the mare with the scorched flank made a full recovery, new hair soon covering the raw patch.

During the following year travellers brought tales of friction between towns and villages in Hampshire, Wiltshire, Somerset and West Dorset, where many people were still in favour of the aetheling Ethelred being King. His mother, Elfrida, continued to incite unrest and dissatisfaction wherever she could, even daring to ridicule the royal counsellors.

Although Archbishop Dunstan had not persuaded the young King to give any more to the church, some counties were realising that vast areas were now under the control of Bishops, monasteries or churches in another county.

"Gods Blood Owenson, haven't people got more important things to do than worry about who is King. Personally I like Lord King Edward;

he has a sense of humour. Did I tell you that we gave him our oath twice?"

Owenson politely nodded because he had heard the story several times. His own memory recalled the adolescent prince's treatment of a young horse. "Does he treat his horse with more kindness now?" he asked hoping to change the subject. "He liked Udric's dog and was kind to it."

"Mmm, he seems to have grown up since then, but of course he is very much under the influence of his father's Archbishop, Lord Dunstan."

There had already been fights between small groups of men supporting opposing points of view and general unrest at the disproportionate amount of land under the control of absentee landlords, who apparently paid little tax while those whose lands lay alongside found themselves having to repair roads and pay tax.

The lady Elfrida still encouraged her son to demand his royal status, punishing those who offered the slightest sign of hesitation. She had moved many of the best hangings to their own quarters and kept royal state even though Edward was entitled to those quarters by right of succession.

Alfred attended the local moot meetings where the rivalry was discussed, more as a matter for debate than because anyone local was involved. The ealdormen had made his loyalty to Edward plain. "Since the King owns much of Eastern Dorset, providing a living for many local families, it is not in the interest of the inhabitants of Wymburne to voice a contrary allegiance. However, further north where the land is less populated their absentee landlord does not inspire such loyalty," stated the King's steward.

Alfred had recently attended the Hundred court of Canendone, in the very east of the county. "The mood in the north and east of the area is indeed less supportive of Archbishop Dunstan's young protégé. They say that it is not actually the King who is disliked, but the influence of the prelate who has virtually taken control of the realm."

The Wymburne men nodded but had already listened to the steward's advice. St Mary's now boasted a tower and other improvements, all done at the expense of the church. Some of them had supplied fittings or carried out work for which they had already been paid. "We have no argument with the church here. Many of us supply food or services for the nunnery and they cause no trouble." There were some sniggers of amusement since it was well known that the Abbess forbade any contact with her charges.

"I make ink in many different colours and even the Bishop says it is of excellent quality," boasted one man whose fingers and tunic could have advertised to anyone which trade he followed. There was always a variety of stains on the fabric giving his clothing a parti-colour appearance.

Others agreed that they too had no quarrel with the church. In Wymburne it owned two or three small properties and a couple of meadows which it leased to townsfolk.

The meeting broke up when there was no further matters to discuss, men leaving in groups to return to their own homes before dusk fell.

Alfred had made no mention of precise names of the malcontents when making his report to the Ealdorman. He had taken Udric as his page in the hopes that he might one day be appointed to take over his tasks. Wareham had stone walls rising to more than thrice the height of a man which had been built in the time of the great King Alfred. The shire-reeve lived in the castle, a gloomy, cold building with arrow-slits instead of windows. One large room was set aside for business purposes, Lord Hugh sitting in a large carved chair to receive visitors and people like Alfred, bringing reports from other areas of the county. Using his baton of office, they had spent two days travelling to Wareham accepting hospitality for both themselves and their horses from thegns who had the misfortune to live immediately adjacent to the main road to the coast.

The lighter evenings meant that everyone retired to bed late and rose early. If Udric missed being with people his own age he never mentioned it. "Will you ever be given a post like Lord Hugh's?" he asked when they had returned to Uddings and were once again enjoying Brith's food and ale.

"It is most unlikely because King's choose wealthy thegns or those of noble birth. If a man has his own income he is less likely to accept bribes. We make a little money from the sale of our fleeces and from the horses when the King gives permission for one to be sold but it is not enough to live on without doing some of the work myself. From time to time the King notices us. After all he came here to buy a new horse and we both gave our oaths twice over if you remember but I am not an advisor or in his close circle of friends. Here at Uddings I try to make the land work for us so that we do not have to buy corn or forage for the beasts. Luckily we have woodland to provide hurdles, acorns, beach-mast, the occasional mushroom and timber but many do not and they have to spend their money for those things. This means that we save a little each year. After all, one day you will need arms and armour which cost a great deal. Actually, you should be practicing archery far more than you do."

Udric pulled a face at the thought, remembering how even the short sessions at the butts above Wymburne made his shoulders ache. Even with a leather guard on his forearm he had bruised the tender skin many times. He would far rather practice with a sword or spear even though the former was the weapon used only by thegns and nobles.

There was no longer any need for hides to be taken to Hamtun for tanning as there was now a tanner in Wymburne with a shoe and harness maker at Didlington. The fact that this man had been an outcast from Wiltshire at first made Alfred reluctant to admit him to his lands, but his skill with leather had been useful. The original boy with the club foot had succumbed to a winter fever and his skill was missed. The new man now trained a crippled boy in harness making so that he too was now a useful member of the community.

Having mentioned that he employed an outcast and cripple during a conversation within the hearing of William of Chalberie, Alfred had made no secret of his disgust when William had suggested that all cripples should be strangled at birth. Once again he had attempted to make himself out to be superior. On this occasion Alfred had been riled, retorting that he hoped William's wife never gave birth to a less than perfect child. Pointedly stroking the King's baton and mentioning that he was employed by the county officers to hear small disputes at Moot courts, he made it quite plain that he would take great pleasure in arresting William should any of his children die shortly after birth.

"Oh I would not do anything like that. At the moment my father has not found a suitable wife for me but when he does we will have children of course."

They parted, Alfred regretting that he had risen to William's provocation and William leaving with a glimmer of new respect for the thegn of Uddings.

During his travels with his father Udric had taken time to look round similar sized estates. He had been appalled at the treatment of malformed children or adults who had lost a limb. On some farms they were condemned to turn the spit by the kitchen fire all day or mix food for the swine, one of the least attractive tasks in any household. Idiots too were frequently used for sport or entertainment after the evening meal.

Alfred felt uncomfortable during such visits but was not in a position to criticise what other lords did to their own villeins or servants. He could only set an example among his own people, keeping his word, even on the smallest thing.

Once again the shearers came and went, leaving piles of fleeces stacked up for which Alfred paid them in coins. When they left with promises to return the following year, they too mentioned the unrest they had experienced in their travels from the Essex hills.

The honey collector, dressed from head to foot in thin suede, took combs of honey from the bees' nests in the wood every year. The children enjoyed the sticky sweetness left in the bucket after Brith had stored as much as the pots could hold. Dabbing the man's stings with soured milk, he too mentioned the wavering of loyalty he had sensed during his usual round of the heathland settlements.

"I hear that Archbishop Dunstan has ordered an increase in coastal watches," he said as he flinched when Brith removed a sting from his neck.

Certain that her husband had not received such orders she asked the man where he had heard such news, and how many more men were to be provided for the task.

Shrugging his shoulders he gave no further information but thanked Brith for her ministrations. Accepting her offer of a night's accommodation she hoped Alfred would return shortly so that he could question the man more closely. Repeating the rumours to him when he returned, the honey collector grumbled that like many others, he would find more fyrd duty or time away from his work difficult to deal with. "They still want honey each autumn, all cleaned and carted to court in covered jars. Every year they demand more honey, more wax, and now Lord Dunstan wants the best wax given to the monks. The trouble is they do not pay any more for getting the best."

Sensing the man's dissatisfaction with the new ruler and his advisors, Alfred and Brith glanced quickly at each other. They sympathised with him over the demands which were being issued, sometimes in the King's own name but others were only in the name of Dunstan and the council. It was difficult to know whether these were orders from the King or not.

Putting his own point of view quietly, Alfred pointed out that the King was untried, inexperienced and above all, young. "It is hardly surprising that he needs advisors, as indeed Prince Ethelred would, had he been crowned. Sometimes I think it is the young prince's mother who seeks to make things difficult. King Edward seems to have the patience of a saint whereas we lesser mortals would have lost the argument long ago! Perhaps the late King's wife will leave court; she might even re-marry!"

On a light note, everyone having dissolved into giggles at the mere thought that any man would want to take on such a harridan, Brith and Alfred retired to bed, a place of harmony, a private space for intimacy and loving happiness which he missed so much when he was away from Uddings.

Chapter Nine
AD 975 - 978

Needing to visit the midden before going to bed, Brith was horrified to see a bright light travelling rapidly across the sky. Forgetting her dignity, wearing a cloak over her shift, she called out to Alfred who came running out, his knife already drawn. Pointing at the bright light she clutched her husband's arm in alarm. Her stomach had instantly cramped and twisted; her eyes, in which the light of the celestial object was mirrored, were wide, dark pools, enormous in her white face.

"What is it? What does it mean?" she queried gripping his wrist fiercely, so great was her fear. "Dear God in heaven defend us!"

Others spilled out from the hall and nearby cottages in various states of dress and wakefulness. Men and women wrung their hands in terror while the dogs barked, causing further commotion. Children cried out as mother's snatched them from their cradles.

One old servant cried out that his father had told him of such evil signs. "We will all be killed," he shrieked. "It is the devil leading our souls to his dwelling place. Even the King will die! No one will be saved."

The old man fell to his knees praying aloud, convincing others to beseech God to pardon their sins, but as the light faded, the normal night sounds resumed, the dogs settled and people drifted back inside to discuss the strange event.

"What in heaven's name was that?" queried the bee keeper who had intended checking his hives on Holt heath the following day. "Like the old man said, it has happened before and the world did not end. Perhaps it is just a strange phenomenon in the heavens."

"Well I will have a last look round just to make sure that everyone has settled down and that the beasts are content. It is strange, the dogs did not bark until my lady started shrieking! No more visiting the midden late at night for her." He was grinning, more with relief than at any attempt at humour.

It was late before the hall was quiet, the doors once more secure. Alfred had quickly toured the kitchens, horse paddocks and store rooms to reassure the fearful servants before joining Brith in bed where they talked quietly among the fur rugs, all thoughts of romance dispelled.

Throughout the following day there was an atmosphere of fear. Many were convinced that the light moving across the heavens was a sign that great evil was to follow. Others believed that the light was similar to the star which showed the three wise Kings the way to Christ's birthplace in the stable and that a second coming was imminent.

The bee keeper had left early to check his skeps on Holt Heath, but promised to be back in time for the harvest feast that night. During the winter he wove new nests for the bees from long stalks of barley fastened with thin alder strips. The conical structures offered protection from the worst of the winter weather but collecting the honeycomb often meant that many bees died. For this reason he tried to be first to collect a swarm and re-home them in his artificial nests. His son would be checking other hives on the chalky lands beyond Shapwick and also stealing the honey from the nests of wild bees just as he had done the previous day.

Everywhere small groups of people discussed the event of the previous night. In the kitchens at Uddings the preparations for the harvest feast were in full swing under the direction of the overweight cook, a widow who had been delighted to take on the task. There were far too many people milling around for any stranger or outlaw to risk trying to steal food. For once everyone gladly took a turn with the cooking of the whole pig roasting on the spit. New bread and ale had already been made for the occasion and summer fruits jellied or stewed sweetly with honey. Soft cheeses which did not keep well, boiled mutton, wild fowl and rich gravies were all put ready to serve when the last labourer had arrived and found a place in the hall. Children sat on their mother's knee so that more space was available for the adults to sit closely one against the other.

For a few moments, the comet was forgotten as the meal was eaten. Alfred rose to his feet when he judged the time was right to ask for their loyalty for another year.

With a shout the men in the hall rose to their feet. Some were less agile than others, sending trestles and drinking cups flying in their haste to be at the front to repeat their vows of allegiance to Alfred and his sons after him. Glowing with pride in the spontaneous cheers which filled the hall, he toasted Brith and bade everyone enjoy themselves.

As the men returned to their places he quietly gathered a large plate of the tastiest morsels and left the hall for the pastures where he knew the youngest son of Owenson was guarding the horses. Carrying a torch above his head, a dog at his heels, he called to the boy to eat his share of the feast. Wrapped in several layers of wool and sheepskin, the dark haired boy, the image of his father, leapt to his feet when he heard Alfred call out to him.

Despite his fear that another light might appear in the night sky, the boy ate his food eagerly, asking questions between mouthfuls.

"When will the horses be kept in the stables again?" he mumbled as he pushed even more meat into his mouth.

"Only when the building is finished; it would not be safe before the field and the stalls are secure. There will be room above them for you and the other horse-keepers to sleep, a store for the feed to be kept safe from rats, and a dry place for hay to be stacked for the winter months. The woodman is making new racks for the harness so that mice cannot nibble the leather, and there will be shelves for salves and ointments for all the animals."

The boy appeared to be satisfied with Alfred's reply and nodded, dreamily wide eyed with the prospect of sleeping above the horses.

Leaving him to his lonely vigil after assuring himself of the lad's comfort, Alfred returned to the feast, leaving the dog to keep the boy company and no doubt, to finish off the huge plate of food he had carried out.

No part of the winter cull of sheep was wasted as the bones were carved into handles, fasteners, spindles, combs or ornaments during the winter months. Children played games with the bones of the back, catching one in the air while snatching another off the floor. The hides were strung up tautly between trees or frames for the womenfolk to cure as they had done for hundreds of years.

There was time too for Brith to sew clothes in good daylight beside the women endlessly spinning yarn for the weavers. They chatted comfortably while their men-folk worked, calling out to each other cheerfully.

"I swear my son is a weed," Brith grumbled to the woman sat beside her. Taking a knotted cord from her pocket she placed it carefully on the sheepskin stretched on a work-worn trestle. "Look, this fleece is not big enough for the back of the jerkin. He out grows his clothes before they are worn out. Is there another fleece ready for sewing or shall I ask Aethelflaed if she has a larger skin already cured?"

Hal and Aethelflaed had held their own harvest feast exchanging many foods with Uddings. Her children were still quite young, Udda, named for his great grandfather, being a frequent visitor to Uddings because he loved the horses. The mill still served both estates and the cottagers who had their small holdings alongside the main road to Cranburne. It was now in the charge of the miller's son, a huge, red faced lad of enormous strength whose jollity guaranteed any feast would be a happy event.

He had been among the volunteers putting up scaffolding for the new tower at the church holding a tree trunk upright while small boys shinned up and tied cross poles in position. His booming voice would have made him eligible for town crier, the man who spread news, the King's decrees and for a fee, advertised a trader's wares at the market. Fortunately, he was quite content to work at the Didlington mill, built as a condition of the charter long ago.

Alfred watched the new colts start their first lessons between hours spent teaching Udric how to use his sword, the bent blade of a seax enabling powerful sweeping strokes and stabbing to be very effective. There was still an atmosphere of suspicion and discontent in the land so he was relieved to know that there was now another armed man on the estate when he was away on the King's business.

"Personally I think that many more people should learn to use a sword, not just those born to the nobility or like me, granted the position for a service rendered to the King. No, you have left your chest unguarded. Let me show you."

Men at the moot court complained of demands for taxes and service in the fyrd which were un-reasonable. Some who had previously allowed monks on their territory had now expelled them, causing enmity between the powerful Abbots and their neighbours.

"It is not right," they complained. "Writs were issued by the King in my father's time and his father before him. Who does Lord Dunstan think he is ordering us about without leave? He has no authority to demand anything. There are many of us who cannot respect the king's officers as we used to."

"I thought that those who had served in the coastal watch were exempt from the forty day service. The King's steward should get this matter brought to the Lord King's attention," suggested Alfred who had listened to a great deal of grumbling.

"We are told that the King relies heavily on the lord archbishop Dunstan but he is an elderly man. It is possible that the King has given him permission to issue orders, but does he know that there is unrest throughout the land. He is a God fearing young man but many feel that the church is favoured above those who serve in the fyrd, guard the coasts, mend the roads and bridges, or grow the food for the King's tables. I will ask Lord Hugh to put our case to the King." The steward packed up his clay tile, closing the cover carefully and fastening the pretty cord in a bow. He rarely had to contact the Earl on behalf of Wymburne townspeople and the local farming community. He did not look forward to dictating a letter to the clerk outlining the dissatisfaction with the current state of affairs in his small area. So far he had dissuaded the more vociferous tradesmen from their threat to withhold taxes from the royal collectors but having a large nunnery which paid no tax and a community of monks who never volunteered to help with road mending or garrison duty was pushing the traders to the limits of their tolerance.

So many complaints were reaching the King's court that at last a formal Council was summoned to Wiltshire. For once the order from Dunstan was not criticised by the King's subjects.

"Will you tell the high and mighty lords and bishops that we can pay no more taxes? My children go hungry to pay for their greed," stated the cooper, a new-comer to Wymburne. "I paid in Hamtun before my family came here with me. Now there are new demands. Rent for my workshop and tax for the King. It leaves a man with little reason to get out of bed in the morning, let alone set the fire beneath the cauldron. One man on his own can only make three barrels a day and that is if the wood is already shaped."

"That's right," interrupted the smith who was profiting from the new arrival. "I make the iron bands to hold the staves. Now the tax men say that he must pay a fee for each one because they hold liquor or some such excuse."

Alfred had walked to Wymburne with Brith and Udric to hear mass at St Mary's. Throughout the service there had been an undercurrent of discontent despite many being fascinated by their arm-waving priest who brought bible stories alive.

Outside he had quietly informed one or two traders that he would shortly be attending the King's Council meeting at the palace in Calne, near Devizes. "I expect Lord Hugh has been summoned and he will put our case to the Council. It is not my place to speak at these meetings although all thegns have a vote. Rest assured, the Earl will be reminded of Wymburne's unhappiness. And it's not just the taxes, we have outlaws in the forests north of the town. They need to be dealt with and it's the sheriff's responsibility."

Brith dressed with care before going to Mass. Now she waited with other women while their husbands talked of taxes, and trade. The young men had already left for the butts, followed by the less closely chaperoned girls. Other maidens waited patiently for their parents to leave for home, chatting quietly beneath a grey sky. Some had been promised in marriage and were nervously excited at all that it entailed while others were either too young or had not yet been spoken for. Wymburne was a small town and though almost self-sufficient, had suffered with epidemics of the sweating sickness or water borne infections. Several had seen Thegn Alfred's son striding off to the butts, a bow and quiver of arrows over his shoulders but so far no-one had been able to hold his attention for long. There were collective sighs for he was good looking, an only son and therefore likely to inherit his father's farm in due time.

The Council meeting was to be held in the upper chamber of the great hall of the King's palace. Set on a small rise in the Wiltshire countryside, the high wooden walls provided security and a far reaching view should any threat arise.

The majority of the nobility and land owners had answered the call to attend the extraordinary session, crowding the roads and tracks until the dust rose high, coating everyone, whether they were mounted or on foot.

Having found a wall against which a shelter could be erected, Alfred and Udric staked their claim for the night. It was not comfortable but Alfred was quickly ready to take his place, diadem neatly positioned across his brow, among the lower ranks of men at the far end of the upstairs room. He could see Lord Hugh amongst the crowd, William of Chalberie apparently having his complete attention for the moment. He swore under his breath knowing that William itched to be included among those who worked for the Earl.

Forced to bang his staff on the table to obtain silence before his words could be heard, the Scottish Bishop made a long and impassioned plea for unity. "I am aware, that there have been arguments between the supporters of my lord Archbishop Dunstan and those who are against him and the council having such powers over the King. I pray you hear him."

There was a momentary silence when he sat down until Archbishop Dunstan rose unsteadily to his feet.

"More priests," said someone loudly, mocking the old man as he struggled for breath. "Where is the King?"

"My Lords," started Dunstan quietly, "I have taught your King the Lord's Will. Now my time of labour is past. I desire to retire to Glastonbury to live out the remainder of my life in peace, seeking comfort from the King of Heaven. I trust that the power of that heavenly being will be sent against men who have shown enmity towards those who chose a Christian way of life."

As Dunstan raised his arms high, closing his eyes in prayer, a man could be heard decrying the Archbishop's apparent saintliness.

Suddenly the whole building shook, the timber cracked and a hole appeared on the far side of the chamber. Many men fell through to the hard floor below screaming in terror, beams and timbers continuing to rain down on them. Alfred flung himself to the wall behind him as men scrambled away from the gaping hole.

When the noise of falling timber had ceased, those who were mocking and critical of the prelate, had all gone. Only shortly before, they had been standing immediately opposite the Archbishop's chair. Dunstan had not moved, continuing to pray while the monks' eyes were wide with shock. Servants and guards could be heard below, moving beams and floor timbers off the bodies of the dead and dying men. Grunts of effort mingled with moans. Instructions were called out brusquely, a contrast to the quiet tones of a priest offering the last rites to the dead and dying.

The wall lights, having wavered when heavenly retribution had suddenly fallen on the un-godly, once more threw steady flames which lit the ghastly scene from above. Dust coated everything. Men sneezed time and time again. Brushing it off a cloak or tunic, the pale cloud settled, until another swept it off his clothes.

Alfred crossed himself hastily, praying silently that the rest of the floor would remain strong. Making their way slowly round the edge of the hole everyone got out of the upper room safely. Lord Hugh and thegn William also appeared to be unharmed although both were unhealthily pale and shaky. The Archbishop, leaning heavily on his stick walked slowly away with his supporter, leaving the monks and infirmarians to tend to the dying.

Staggering down the stairs, with shaking legs, some men were barely able to hold the weight of their body above. Some covered their ears to muffle the awful screaming of the fallen thegns.

Alfred stared, horrified at the chaotic scene which met his eyes. Mangled bodies, pierced by wooden splinters or broken by the weight of the falling beams, were piled one atop the other. Guards toiled silently to release the living from their hellish torture. Screams and moans from the injured were now the only sounds apart from the whispered last rites being given to the leader of the faction which had only moments earlier been taunting the Archbishop.

When the double doors were unbarred and opened, the dust cloud billowed out as if there had been a fire. Every man who came out was choking and coughing. Eyes streamed with tears fending off the irritating particles of old wood and painted plaster.

Safely outside Alfred joined many of the thegns who had been close to him at the back of the room. He brushed the dust from his tunic again, still dazed with shock.

"It was the Mercian men who fell then?" queried one man.

"Aye, against Edward from the start, and worse since Dunstan took control of the taxes and fyrd orders. It's always been the King who directed where the army should go and how many men from each shire were required. Now we get demands from someone with not a mention of the King's name."

This latter point seemed to sum up the whole matter which had given rise to the discontent around the country.

"He says he is going back to Glastonbury now," commented Alfred.

"The King is a man now. He will give orders and rule the land so that no man need fear the wrath of the church if he needs the King's justice."

The crowd of curious townspeople, attracted by the sudden activity and screaming, parted to let the nobility and thegns through, many being anxious to put distance between themselves and the dreadful scene of carnage at the hall, while others felt the urgent need to return to loved ones.

"Pack up boy, we'll eat as we travel or stop at a guest house. There will be no further business here today." White faced, his eyes already reddened from the irritating dust, Alfred swallowed several gulps of ale from a leather bottle before hawking a great gobbet of mucus onto the ground. "Lord save us Udric. Fasten my sword belt. My hands are all of a dither; anyone would think I had the ague."

It did not take long for the pack horse to be loaded and the riding horses to be fully saddled and bridled for their journey. Udric wisely remained silent although he was curious as to the cause of his father's grave face. As they rode out they met up with many of the Dorsetshire thegns.

Lord Hugh, still obviously suffering from shock, stammered that the King had arrived at the hall with several young companions. "He says that messages will be sent to each ealdorman in the near future. I will send copies to each of you but for now, all I want to do is to get back to my own hearth. There could be changes if the archbishop retires. The King is old enough to rule in his own right. We were not the only shire to complain of the high taxes. Lord King Edward may take notice of the sheer number of pleas he has received and ask the exchequer department to look into the matter, and the collectors," he added so that only a few heard the last cryptic comment.

The King had quickly taken charge, arranging for the dead to be returned to their kin with all honours, while carpenters had been summoned to rebuild the upper floor as a matter of urgency. Of the Aetheling Ethelred and the Lady Elfrida there had been no sign.

"Did Dunstan come back?" asked someone behind Alfred and Udric. No-one had seen the elderly prelate since he had been assisted down the stairs after the accident.

"A sign from God," "the wrath of God," and similar comments were murmured as they made their way along the river bank while it drizzled steadily until cloaks were sodden, and spirits dampened. Men and horses were tired, muddy and hungry. Few talked as they huddled into wet cloaks, legs becoming chapped against the sodden leather of their saddles.

"Had the lady Elfrida been nearby she would have been blamed. It is a good thing that women are not allowed to attend such a meeting. She would have been right in front of Dunstan; after all he took matters into his own hands and crowned Edward while most stood in the hall squabbling," stated Alfred boldly now he had recovered from the shock. "They said that when he was young he fell from a great height when he was in a fever and was unharmed. Did he think that those who spoke against King Edward and himself would also be unhurt? Can it have been a trick? Lord knows but I tell you Udric that grown men in that room cried with relief that they were unharmed."

Although relatively close to home, those from Wymburne, Twynham, and Bleneford decided to seek a bed for the night at the nearby hostelry at Cranburne. There was slightly greater comfort in the guest rooms than in former times. The straw paillasses smelt fairly fresh and the floor covering of neatly plaited rushes had been renewed recently. "I could sleep now if I wasn't so hungry. I see every scrap that your mother put in the saddle bags has already gone and she always packs enough for an army!"

Udric managed to look completely innocent of any implied suggestion that he had finished off the food while he was waiting for the meeting to finish.

"The horses have been stabled so at least they are out of the weather. The hay is not as good as ours but it smells alright." Knowing his father's concerns for the beasts, Udric adeptly changed the subject and suggested they went to the dining hall. Although only pottage, there were identifiable pieces of meat among the barley grains and it was served hot with herb bread. The appetising aroma brought the other travellers hurrying into the hall. Alfred nodded to his former companions, most of who had managed to brush the worst of the dust from their cloaks. Their news was eagerly sought by the residents who listened in silence after the guests had eaten.

Udric too heard the full story for the first time. As the tale was told by the Bishop, he emphasised that those present had had a miraculous escape and should give thanks to God.

"How many died?" asked Udric quietly when the Bishop's exhortation had finally ended.

"At least ten, and they were all men who had supported Prince Ethelred, and recently had criticised Edward's dependence on Dunstan. They had gathered together in front of the chancellor's chair and were shouting abuse at the old man. The screaming, it was terrible, gut wrenching, but I'll not tell your mother the details. Now eat your food. Have mine too - I have no appetite."

Local affairs were discussed briefly after the meal but they were of little interest when compared with the results of the Divine intervention that had apparently just been witnessed by the travellers.

As they lay down for the night in the driest bedding from their packs, Alfred suggested to Udric that they might call on Hal's brother at Woodcutts Farm before riding south in the morning.

"It is very close by, and we can give him news of Hal, Aethelflaed and the children." Murmuring his agreement, Udric slept soundly beside his father amid the men of Dorset.

Striking eastward in the early morning mist, they quickly reached the road marking the edge of Woodcutts Farm. Remembering the stories of long ago, Alfred reached for his horn to warn the householder of his arrival. The young man who appeared from the barn was an older version of Hal, fair haired, strongly built, and ruddy faced, all characteristic of his Danish forebears.

"Hail young man, we are kin of Aethelflaed, your brother's wife; we bring news of Hal."

The young man's face split into a wide grin at the mention of his younger brother. Inviting them to dismount, Vannson made them welcome in the small thatched house.

"Did you get your well water cleaned?" asked Alfred after he had given the young man all the news of his brother's family.

"Oh yes. My neighbour did everything you said. The funny thing was that others came to help and we made a sort of game over it. He now prepares hides on the far side and has proved to be good at it."

They discussed the outcome of the judgement over a mug of ale, chatting easily. Vannson told them that his wife had died giving birth, leaving him to manage the farm on his own with casual labour from Sexpenna when he could get it.

"I am due to take my turn on fyrd duty over the Christmas period. That is what really worries me," he confided. "If someone takes my place I am honour bound to do his work as well as my own and there is more than enough to do here." His broad brow was creased with frown lines; he sighed, his shoulders drooping.

Agreeing stoically between them that life could sometimes be unfair, Vannson walked his guests back to their horses.

Arriving at Didlington, Udric rushed to find his aunt and tell her the exciting events which had occurred at court.

In the hall, sat beside the hearth, Alfred explained to Hal the difficulties his brother was in, running Woodcutts Farm single handed. "You could take some time over the Christmas period to help him, with perhaps one or two of the younger men. The miller runs the mill well without supervision, but you must leave a trusted and skilled man with the sheep here. Since the sickness in some flocks, I would not want ours to stray beyond the heath onto the road where others pass."

Staying with his sister long enough to be polite and admiring the children over a mug of ale, Alfred had difficulty in disguising his eagerness to return to Uddings to reassure Brith of his safety.

"Bad news somehow travels faster than good news. Somebody making an earlier start home from Winchester could have spread word of the accident, causing unnecessary alarm. I've no doubt that you have already heard all the gory details from Udric so I will be on my way. Let me know what you decide to do with regard to your brother won't you Hal."

Having greeted her husband affectionately, Brith listened in silence as he recounted details of his latest visit to the King's court. They were sitting side by side on the settle, the last rays of the sun lighting up the swirling dust motes.

"You say Dunstan asked for divine intervention against his enemies, and then they fell through the floor?"

"Aye, some prayer like that! There was a crack, and the centre of the floor broke away. I was at the back, near the far wall. Lord Dunstan, with the rest of the council was on the other side of the room. It was the Mercians in the middle, calling abuse, who mostly fell to their death."

"Thank the Lord!" muttered Brith with heartfelt sincerity. "Presumably Udric was safe enough outside?"

"Yes, he and the other pages and servants sat with the horses. Mind you, they probably took some calming. Even when we Dorset men got out the dust was still rolling out in clouds."

It took several days for the news of Alfred's miraculous escape to reach all parts of both the farms. Prayers at church were more genuine than usual during the coming weeks, Udric frequently being the centre of attention when the young boys met afterwards to practice with their weapons.

It was several weeks before the subject was dropped, and more immediate needs of everyday life and events in Wymburne assumed their usual importance. Reports that a woodsman in the forest of Wymburnholt had been beaten senseless brought the matter of outlaws back to the forefront of men's minds. Some criticised that no-one had taken the opportunity to demand that Sheriff Hugh send a posse to catch the criminal. Others had also reported glimpses of an unkempt man and food had been stolen from storehouses and even from the kitchen of the King's palace. The steward had apologised in vague terms for accusing Alfred of being responsible for breaking the fencing down. "What was I supposed to think? The breaks were always on your side, your boundary and no-one had seen anyone, least of all an outlaw who could be blamed. When the sheriff comes he will want every available man. I presume you will be available?"

For a brief moment Alfred could feel his anger rising. That his word had not been trusted and that his many reports of stolen cheeses and bread had not been thought evidence enough riled him. When he replied he could feel that his voice was brittle and taut as if the muscles were reluctant to allow words to pass.

"Yes I will join the sheriff's posse. Now that one of your own men has been attacked you have the proof. This accusation has hung over me for months and I'll be glad enough to have the matter finished."

The steward had the grace to look ashamed, his eye lids lowered as he muttered under his breath. By the time he looked up Alfred had walked away trying to disguise the disgust he felt.

A man had suddenly been possessed by devils. In the middle of a service he had started shouting that there was no God; that he had sold his soul to the devil and there was nothing any priest could do about it.

The church elders and the priest were completely at a loss. The man's wife was distraught.

"He does not mean it. He cannot mean it! What can I do, he will not eat or drink." She was tearing at her wimple in her distress, the grey hair beneath tangled and dirty. Other women crowded round her offering comfort. Men approached her husband who mouthed obscenities and blasphemed alternately, a length of spittle flying from his mouth. The miller, whose strength was legendary tried to wrap the man in his arms to pull him away from the stone wall. The man's head was already bloody from beating his forehead. With no more than a shrug, the miller was flung off, his round face expressing his total surprise.

"He must be tied up for his own safety," suggested the priest when the possessed victim once more attempted self harm.

"And how do you suggest we do that? If miller here cannot hold him then there's no chance of any of us getting a grip on him." The smith was himself a strong man. One had to be tough to bang a hammer on an anvil all day. "Why don't several of us rush him? Who has a decent rope?"

Men scattered to hunt for lengths of rope. Alfred hesitated to interfere, not being from the town. Brith had already helped the woman to sit down further away. Although she was still in earshot of the demented man, the fact that fellow townsmen were now dealing with her husband had reduced her distress.

"Is there some prayer to rid a body of the influence of the devil?" Someone asked the priest while other men argued whether to try and pinion the man's arms or to trip him up with the rope.

"Never been done before! A bishop might have done but I've never heard of it. No, it is not something I could do." The priest waved his arms about but in a crisis had been revealed as utterly spineless.

Alfred sighed with frustration. Four men were creeping up on their victim whose face had now disappeared beneath a bloody mask. His lips were torn, revealing blackened teeth; strips of skin hung down from wattled jaw bones.

Children were now gazing in awe at the scene. Some found it frightening while others encouraged the four would-be captors with yells and screams.

"If you cannot get rid of his evil spirit then what will you do with him? He is obviously sick in his mind. Last week he was weaving material, this week he is crazy."

The priest continued to shake his head. He had no suggestions to make, was not strong enough to subdue the blasphemer and kept inching back towards the safety and familiarity of the church.

"Say a prayer, priest," shouted one woman whose stance showed everybody that she meant business. Arms akimbo, feet apart, she had a voice which could be heard over the hubbub of the crowd.

Dressed in faded blue, a stout belt around her middle, her coarse features were reddened in anger when the priest again refused to offer spiritual comfort to the man who now lay tossing on the ground. He had been virtually wrapped in the ropes but still managed to scream.

"If you are not capable of praying for this man or of ridding him of his demons, then perhaps the Lady Abbess will." Alfred and many others were in awe of the lady. He spat out the last few words in an effort to shame the priest. The latter waved his arms about, raised his eyes towards heaven and slunk back into the church.

Once more, refusing to dwell on the spineless character of the priest, Alfred found himself knocking on the stout oak door. The window opened so quickly that he knew that someone must have been observing the events by the church.

"The Lady Abbess is needed at St Mary's. A weaver is demented, saying all sorts of ungodly things. Would she…, well …. Will she come and do what she can for him?"

Not normally lost for words, he now felt awkward, unsure if even an Abbess could cure or heal a sick man's soul. It was not an emotion which he often felt and it humbled him and made him feel inadequate.

The Lady Abbess, tall, dignified and impressive in her noble demeanour, glided through the open door which was immediately shut behind her with a resounding bang. Despite the dirt and rubbish left strewn around the street, she proceeded towards the patient. Now frothing at the mouth, so demented that many thought he would die of an apoplexy before anything could be done for him, the man struggled against his bonds.

"Clear a space," she demanded glaring at the crowd who had gathered closely round. Children, who only a moment before had been taunting the man by poking him with sticks, fled from her presence.

Drawing herself up, the Abbess raised one arm above the helpless man. "Begone foul spirit; leave this soul and depart to the depth of hell where you belong."

The crowd was completely silent, stunned with a mixture of awe and admiration for this apparition of cleanliness who had appeared in their midst.

"Oh Lord in Thy mercy; renew the faith of this man. Take from him all wickedness and grant him peace in Thy Love for the sake of Jesus Christ, the son of God."

Most of the crowd was by now on their knees, hands clasped together in an attitude of prayer. Alfred too, bowed his head and had surreptitiously crossed himself half a dozen times.

All eyes were on the man on the ground. He was no longer struggling, no longer frothing at the mouth. Through bloodied lips he asked for a drink in a perfectly rational, though hoarse voice.

"Fetch him a drink for God's sake someone," Alfred ordered when he had got over his astonishment. The man was attempting to sit up despite his bonds. It was impossible to see the expression on his face for the blood which now attracted flies.

The man was eventually un-bound and assisted to his feet. Unable to stand unsupported, men rushed to help him and half dragged him to the Infirmarian of the monastery.

"Thanks be to God," said the Abbess in such work-a-day tones that Alfred could not help a smile forming on his face.

Turning about, the Abbess returned to her sanctum, a small smile raising the corners of her mouth. The door opened and closed behind her silently.

"What a woman!" Alfred had already put his arm around Brith's shoulders and hugged her to him. "Poor man, but even the Devil is frightened of the Abbess!

People say court is exciting but Wymburne has its fair share. Not that I want to witness another scene like that. Where has Udric got to? He'll be mad that he missed all that."

Their return to Uddings should have been quiet, a time when people rested, pursued hobbies, saw to their own gardens or sat about chatting with neighbours and friends. Instead they found the shepherd from Didlington exclaiming loudly that Lord Hal's girl child was missing.

On seeing Alfred he loped across the paddock and vaulted the fence stumbling as he landed.

"Master Alfred, the lass has gone, taken by a man. He was stealing and Gail set up such a wailing that he took her so that we would not attack him. I loosed a dog but it too has gone. Master Hal is all for following but the man went into the forest, the King's forest and we dursen't go there!"

The man's distress was so obvious. For all his tanned, lined skin, the softness below his eyes was wet with tears.

"She's only little for God's sake. How could he ...."

Alfred was already running to collect a saddle and bridle. His voice, shouting instructions and orders faded as he neared the hall leaving Brith to comfort the shepherd and send him to the gathering of men already armed and waiting for Alfred to lead them. Snippets of their indignation and intentions towards such a man drifted towards Brith.

"What must her mother be feeling?" she mumbled as she re-fastened her boot. "He should swing! I hope they take a rope with them."

Leading the horse the men strode off towards Didlington followed by the grizzled hunting dog, its feathered tail waving slowly. Brith watched them go and stood with the other wives, many in the stance which is recognised all over the world as beligerent, arms akimbo and feet apart. Chins poked forward as the men reached the northern boundary of Uddings and disappeared from view.

No-one mentioned eating and few spun their spindles as the women, mostly mothers, imagined the distress that Aethelflaed must be going through.

"We don't even know if the child had wandered away from the hall. If he was seen stealing then he must have been close, or even in the store-room," the ploughman's wife added. She had wide-set, honest eyes and regarded her companions calmly. It was past noon, a misty sun high in the sky but little shadow was cast. The birds sang and the insects buzzed, all such normal things for the time of year but the abduction of a child from her home had thrown normality to the winds.

As children returned from their games they were hugged and kissed more lovingly than usual. Udric too received his share of affection although Brith knew that he had now reached an age when hugs and kisses embarassed him.

"Your father has gone to Didlington. They think that the outlaw who has been stealing has taken her. Well actually," she corrected herself, "to be truthful, they know that a man abducted her to prevent the shepherd attacking him. He raised the alarm and then ran over here to gather our tenants. You are of an age now that does not need to be shielded from unpleasant things."

She watched him wriggle with eagerness to be off. To gallop along the track and follow his father would be uppermost in his mind. "I know you are itching to ride off, but the most valuable thing you could do now is to ride to Kingston. Alert the steward; call out the garrison. If they enter the forest from the western end and your father has gone in from our end, and I've no doubt he has, King's hunting forest or no, then between the two posses they will catch him. Actually it could be them! Either way, hurry now. Go across the old tracks it will be quicker than using the river-side road."

Udric needed no further encouragement. His face showed his determination, his eyes alight with excitement. He grabbed a bridle from a peg on the side of the hall, twisted round and sped across the deserted courtyard to his pony. It too was affected by the unusual events, the shouting, the hurried passage of armed men, and then Udric's hasty arrival. It tossed its head, sidling excitedly as he vaulted across its back and took off at a clattering canter down the slope towards the stream.

Brith closed the gate thoughtfully hoping that she had done the right thing involving the Kingston steward and the garrison. For months Alfred had been bleakly miserable that he had been unable to counter the steward's suspicion. She had seen him pacing, his distress over his inability to find real evidence that someone other than a tenant was causing the damage leaving him tired and irritable.

'Surely if a child is involved any man would want to help!' she thought as she walked slowly back to the hall. 'T'is done now. If he's annoyed so be it. The main thing is to find Gail, a terrified little girl who might be in the hands of ....' Her thoughts tailed off, not willing to let her mind conjure up the worst scenario.

The wails of a child led the men into deep, tangled undergrowth. The dog pushed through the knotted briars and set up a deep baying. If any game had been within earshot it had long since left for quieter copses.

"Over here, over here!" came the triumphant shout. The miller, whose deep and loud voice was legendary called the Didlington men to his side. From the southern side the Uddings men also heard the call and crashed through the close-set trees to join their friends. Hal called to his daughter, his voice almost breaking with over-stretched nerves.

"Call the dog, shout at the dog; he'll bark again. She's close but this damned undergrowth is so thick we can't see a thing."

Advice from all and sundry came to an abrupt stop when Hal shouted his daughter's name. A reedy response was heard by everyone, paused as they were in the gloom below the tree canopy.

"Ah lovely! Gail my lovely!" Scratched but beaming with triumph Hal emerged backwards from the bramble den. Runners clung to his legs, his hair and shoulders as he sheltered his daughter's face from the vicious spines. Willing hands pulled the tendrils from his clothes as men almost cried with relief. The child's head was tucked into her father's shoulder but finally a tear-stained face emerged. She was scratched, bruised and frightened but basically unharmed and men grinned stupidly, slapping each other on the back.

They were still in this state of euphoria when the steward of Kingston found them.

"This the child?" he demanded rudely as the garrison soldiers gathered round.

"This boy demanded we come and that's what we've done," he stated rather obviously. "Not seen sight nor sound of an outlaw though." He would have continued in this vein had not the Didlington shepherd interrupted.

"Well I saw him, I saw him take the child and carry her in front of him when I approached him. Always carry a staff I do and know how to use it! Oh aye, there's an outlaw and probably more than one seeing the amount he's been stealing. We can't guard the storeroom all the time, got work to do. I saw him; a dirty beast an' all." The normally taciturn shepherd had got himself all worked up, his face was red as he faced up to the steward. The other Didlington men had arranged themselves behind him, a phalynx of stalwart support with Hal still holding Gail beside him.

The soldiers seemed quite happy to observe the interaction between peasant farmers and the steward of Kingston. Udric now crossed the space between the two parties and joined his father.

"Did I do right? Mother said that between you at this end and the soldiers the outlaw would be trapped. Is Gail alright?"

"Yes lad, she's fine now. We'll take her home and leave the soldiers to look for the man. We've got what we came for. Good day to you steward."

The Didlington and Uddings tenants crowded round Hal with his precious burden and retreated from the hostile atmosphere. Once in sight of the fields beyond the deep ditch Alfred sent Udric running to tell Aethelflaed that Gail had been found. "She'll be in such a state so the sooner she knows the child is safe the better," he explained to the silent men. The steward's attitude had damped their joy. The shepherd fulminated into his beard, snippets of curses on unbelievers and suchlike followed him all the way home. They dropped into the ditch and clawed their way up the far side, willing hands pushing and pulling Hal who could not put the child down. She screamed and shivered with fright on the only attempt he had made. Neither would she be passed to Alfred when he offered so Hal accepted the rough and ready handling in order to get out of the King's hunting ground.

The welcome home was tearful, the tenants tactfully returning to their homes leaving the parents to lavish affection on their child in the privacy of the hall.

Alfred and Udric walked back across the heathland as the sun began to set. The horse snatched at the new growth of heather, jerking back suddenly when an adder reared up.

"That's all we need, bloody snakes!" swore Alfred still irritated by the Kingston steward's sarcastic words. "We'll get your horse tomorrow. God keep you all and thank you for your efforts. One day that outlaw will hang and I will be there to see it!"

Chapter Ten
AD978

Stories of the King's hunting expeditions and riding exploits spread across the Kingdom, from town to town, through the villages to the smallest hamlets. His half brother, the Aetheling Ethelred, accompanied him on many of these exploits, all enmity between them apparently forgotten. It was only in the presence of the Lady Elfrida, mother of Ethelred, that an atmosphere of malice and jealousy was evident. She still made every effort to influence the King in her own son's favour, demanding land and treasure at every possible opportunity.

With his chosen companions, it was apparently the King's practice to ride off into the countryside visiting outlying villages and farms in disguise. He was then overjoyed when his identity was discovered by his hosts. Sometimes he allowed a close friend to ride his own magnificent horse, watching as people addressed its rider as King.

Alfred smiled when he heard tale of such adventures. He knew the King's horse well, having sold it to his father, King Edgar, shortly before his sudden death. It would now be in its prime, capable of siring a line of quality offspring if Lord Edward would send the horse back to him. "Mind you he is not likely to. It's well known that the King insists that the greatest care and best food are given to his precious stallion. It would not take long to serve a few mares if they were around the horse at the right time! Everyone would ride their mares to court if they could get a foal of that quality."

Working on either manor where he was needed Udric had taken the sacks of milled flour to the hunting lodge hoping that he would make the delivery in advance of the royal visit to the forests of Cranburne. Unfortunately the King had already arrived with a huge retinue. Most had been forced to erect tents on the level ground beside the hunting lodge. He drove the ox cart carefully then led it as close to the building as he could. Hastily he swung the sacks into the kitchen where they would be kept dry and out of the reach of vermin.

Preparing to take up the reins for the return journey, King Edward strode past the hunting lodge, a short cloak swinging from his shoulders. On seeing the cart and Udric about to manoeuvre the ox to start his homeward journey, he paused beaming widely.

"Ah, doubly loyal er.. Udric isn't it? You ride but you have probably never hunted. Come and join the hunting party."

"Lord, I would be honoured to join you, but my father would be cross if the cart was delayed on its return. We are somewhat short-handed because Hal is at his brother's farm while he is on fyrd duty. Besides I am not dressed to ride with you," he added nervously by way of further explanation, glancing down at his drab tunic, suddenly conscious that he was prattling to his King.

"Well said Udric. I would not have your father's wrath upon my head, but return tomorrow, early if you can."

Udric bowed; partly out of respect for his King and partly to cover his astonished expression.

Leaving the King laughing at his own joke, Udric was frustrated by the slow pace of the ox cart as the animal plodded slowly along the road pulling the empty cart. He shouted at it to the effect that he could run faster than it was walking. With the tally for the sacks of flour delivered to the royal household carefully fastened in his jerkin, he was excited by the prospect of an interruption to the normal pattern of life at Uddings where providing food and training horses took priority over everything else. Even Sunday arms practice had lost its attraction since they were rarely allowed to fight each other with real weapons. Admitting to himself that he was bored, he shouted at the ox, urging it to hurry.

From his earliest childhood he had heard stories of how his great grandfather had met Galena and brought her back to Uddings long ago; of how Udda had fought to clear his family's name after his father had been mistakenly banished for murder. Some of his Wymburne friends were already married but not all were happy like his parents so Udric was content to wait. 'Mother is always saying that I will know when I meet the right girl. Sounds a bit fanciful to wait for a bolt of lightning or some such exotic thing but I'm in no hurry.

It's strange that grandfather's birth place is the farm where Hal has gone. Such a different landscape to the woods of Uddings,' thought Udric whose imagination was flitting from one subject to another.

He had not realised that he had been talking out loud, deep in thought so that sheepwards who waved as he crossed the heath received little response from him. The ox flapped his ears to move the irritation of the flies never breaking stride as it plodded steadily home.

Seeing his father breaking-in the colts he hurried across the yard towards him. Alfred was gentling a young black colt wearing soft leather harness. Knowing better than to call out suddenly, Udric was forced to contain himself in patience until the training session was over. As a young boy returned the beast to its companions, Udric was at last able to blurt out his news, his eyes shining with youthful excitement.

"The King has asked me to hunt with him at Cranburne, father! He wants me to return without delay."

Being at the stage when the male voice see-saws between childish treble and adult baritone, Udric's exciting news ended with an embarrassing squeak. He giggled, regarding his father with beseeching eyes. Already with his imagination running riot, he was galloping after a buck, shooting it cleanly with one arrow while other hunters applauded.

"Well you had best do his bidding then and be quick about it. Have you told your mother?" Alfred smiled to see his son so excited at the prospect of hunting with the young King. Whether it was the thrill of the chase and the speed involved or the thought of being in the presence of his King, he was not sure. Either way, the boy's eyes almost sparked with eagerness. Friendships with ordinary people had made the King popular and Udric had probably been one of his first, when at Uddings the two boys dashing from the piglets to the foals all those years ago, the dog their only guard.

Shamefaced, Udric admitted that he had not stopped to speak to her but had come straight to him.

"Your mother will be proud of you too. She will no doubt tell you to take care. The King is not much older than you but is unpredictable sometimes. Serve him well, with honour. Go with God son."

Udric acknowledged his father's blessing, which gave him permission to go, but could hardly contain his enthusiasm to join the King. Word spread rapidly of Udric's invitation. His horse was quickly groomed until its coat shone and the harness burnished. As he dressed, he briefly described the meeting with the King while waiting for the royal panterer to check the flour delivery.

"He called me his 'twice loyal servant', father. He remembers me, us both, I mean."

The sun shone as he left Uddings, having been told as expected, to take good care of himself. Despite the cold wind he had dressed in his best jerkin which was better fitting but less weatherproof than his working clothes. He had also changed into another tunic, fastened a wide leather belt around his slim waist and put his knife in the scabbard which hung on one hip. Unsure if the King hunted with bows or just a spear Udric quickly strung his with a cord so that it would fit across his shoulders with his quiver and put spare strings in his scrip.

A cloak was rolled up tightly and secured behind his saddle having refused to wear it as it would cover up the intricate patterns Brith had embroidered on the front of his jerkin.

Cantering steadily across the heath Udric took time to greet the shepherd and his boys, calling out cheerfully. Lambs ran fearfully to their mothers even though he was riding around the flock not through it as he had seen many who gave no thought to their well-being. He sang a bawdy verse he had learnt from one of the stable lads at Calne in Wiltshire while he waited for his father at that ill-fated meeting.

The road was hard from the overnight frost but he could still clearly see the marks of the oxcart. Either side of the track the gorse bloomed, its musky perfume blowing in the lightest of breezes. Small blue butterflies flitted from one flower to another while above a small hawk hovered, its head unmoving as it waited for the incautious appearance of a vole.

Slowing down on the outskirts of the King's land, Udric pulled the jerkin down so that it fitted snugly over his chest and sat up straighter.

Introduced to the other young men surrounding the King, Udric soon became friendly with them, enjoying the quick repartee, the good humour, and the slight air of competition. Some of them, like him, were sons of men who owned land but were not churchmen or noble. It had always been his father who had been commanded to attend the King; now he himself had been summoned. It gave rise to a strange emotion, a mixture of pride and fear that he might disgrace himself in some way. He was almost too excited to sleep, especially after he had drunk more ale than usual and his stomach felt queasy. He had rolled his thick cloak around him on the cleanest rushes he could find. The practice of relieving oneself in the corners of the hall filled the darkness with its unique unpleasant smell. 'No wonder mother has banned the practice at home,' thought Udric as he settled down with the other young men.

Riding in the thickly forested slopes hunting deer in the King's company, Udric felt exhilarated. His horse was fearless beneath him so that fallen trees presented an opportunity to jump them, not an obstacle. Alfred had taught him do so many manoeuvres without any bit in the horse's mouth that he only needed the lightest of touch upon the reins to guide the beast. He was undoubtedly a better rider than Edward but quickly realised that it was politic to let the King overtake him when they galloped after a beast. A pack of hunting hounds had accompanied the royal party from Winchester under the care of the hunt master, a man of great experience. Like his dogs he had grizzled hair, dewlaps hanging from his jaws above a stringy neck. He held two dogs on each leach with strength of sinew rather than bulging muscle.

Only one stag was taken after being held at bay by the hound dogs. Of course, the beast's fate was sealed by a poorly thrown spear. It was then humanely dispatched while the hunting party celebrated the kill, drinking from wine skins hastily provided by the servants.

When Edward's quick temper led him to shout at the man, Udric felt sorry for him and made a point of visiting the stables when everyone returned to the hunting lodge. The dogs were in their stables alongside, tails waving slowly as if uncertain.

"It's always the same young man, 'tis always my fault or the dogs, never the fault of the horse or rider. When a dog gets killed, it's called a mistake, never anyone's fault. However I will rest the dogs now and feed them, ready for tomorrow."

Wishing the man a good night's rest, Udric spent time with his own horse rather than rely on the casual labour which was hired in during the King's visits. He did not rejoin the others until he was quite happy that his own horse and the King's stallion had been fed and watered properly and that neither was showing signs of strain or other injury.

Another huge meal ended the day. Vast supplies of meat, pastries and suet dishes followed one another and were consumed with great appetite, after which messengers from the court brought dispatches for the King to approve. These he read through briefly before making his mark on the page. Some more confidential than others needed to be sealed up before they were given to the council's messenger.

"Is there wax here?" he demanded petulantly, holding out his hand expecting to be given the glossy red candle stub.

The servants looked at each other in dismay. Every bit of sealing wax had already been used on his previous signing session and no-one had thought to renew the supply. Fearing the King's wrath no-one wanted to be the one to admit that there was no sealing wax available.

Udric excused himself from the King's table, disliking being a witness to the discomfort of the servants. Racking his brains to work out an alternative, all he could think of was fat and flour which was used in compresses to heal bruises.

"The mixture sets reasonably hard after a time. If it has to be red then there must be plenty of blood in the kitchens. Of course it may not take an imprint of your ring but might be sufficient to seal less important documents. A supply of real sealing wax could be brought with the next batch of documents which come from your councillors."

Edward laughed heartily. "We have a statesman in the making! Send to the cook for Udric's concoction, it might work well enough. I do not know why the exchequer cannot wait a few days for their writs and writings." The King had not yet learned that a ruler's face should remain inscrutable. Edward's reflected every emotion for all to see. Now, having laughed only seconds before, he was frowning, annoyed that matters of state followed him no matter where he was. "I thought here, in the depth of Dorsetshire that I could relax and hunt and be with friends for a few days. But no, all the trimmings of state have to come with me." He was stroking the chased gold surface of a goblet set with semi precious stones. None of them flashed in the flickering torchlight but even in the poorly illuminated hall, no one could mistake the quality of workmanship involved in its making.

Having calmed the King's temper, Udric quickly became a favourite of the servants. Extra bedding appeared for his comfort at night, his horse was cosseted and harness stripped down, cleaned so that it felt like soft lambskin.

Edward spent the last day sporting in the forest wildly galloping from one glade to another as if he was desperate to snatch the few hours away from responsibility. Enough venison had been killed to fill the lodge store rooms as well as to give the local villagers their annual beast as a reward for repairing the palings which surrounded the hunting forest.

As the baggage train was prepared to carry all the bedding and plate which accompanied the King on his travels, some of his friends prepared to accompany him back to Winchester.

"Will you come with us Udric? I would value your company. You have an honest way with you, no flattery or requests for rewards. Here, I give you this ring as a token of our friendship and esteem." Edward struggled to remove a large gold ring from a finger. It came off with a jerk making them both laugh. Udric took the ring and fitted it on to his own finger.

"My lord, if I can be of service to you at any time, I trust that you will ask me. I will gladly come with you, though I have nothing but my horse and a bedroll!"

Dappled sunlight and the first of the autumn leaves fell on the courtyard where servants bustled round laden with food for the journey. The hound keeper grinned at Udric, his dogs relaxed after several days of hunting. He would walk all the way in his simple green tunic, everything else being on a cart.

They left with the armed soldiers forming a guard around the King, the baggage train behind them. The naked spear blades flashed even though the day soon became grey and overcast. Even as rain threatened, the ox carts were still raising dust on the road coating everything behind in fine, chalky grit.

Brithricson glowered at the departing procession. There had hardly been a word of praise for the condition of the Chase. He yearned for the crowded capital and the busy exchequer conveniently forgetting his dislike of pressing people to pay their taxes. He had watched all the activity but remained a bystander, not part of the King's hunting expeditions, not seated on the King's table with the laughing boys and young men. He turned on his heel his grim expression advertising his unhappiness, his eyes merely slits of resentful rage.

At Winchester, entering the city through the high wooden gates, the procession was greeted with enthusiasm by the citizens who bowed or cheered as the King passed by. A trumpet sounded, its strident note tailing off into breathy, discordant tones before the musician tried again to sound a welcome salute.

Riding just behind Edward among the other companions, Udric had time to look around as they approached the royal palace. The guards saluted smartly as the horse keepers rushed out to relieve the riders of their mounts. Hoping that his own mount would be tended carefully, Udric cast a glance at its departing haunches, conscious that the other young men seemed careless of anything besides their own comfort and entertainment. His concern for others caused him to be the butt of jokes that evening but he bore them well, discreetly stroking the ring which the King had given to him beneath the table. Sat below the raised dais, Udric studied his companions. One or two had noble faces with high cheek bones and long straight noses while others like him had rounder, more open characteristics. Edward had made little distinction between them, riding first beside one and then next to another as if sharing his favours and company equally.

Prince Ethelred joined them at supper, sitting next to the King. His hair had darkened slightly to a more manly shade, but his pink lips often pouted if he was not the centre of attention. Every finger sported a ring; his gold circlet gleamed in the torchlight. The Lady Elfrida, wearing a broad gold circlet to secure her veil, smiled at her son as she picked daintily at the food. No-one present could have found cause for criticism in her dress, manners or speech but her presence was undoubtedly the cause of a slight atmosphere. The two days hunting had been relaxed, full of boyish humour and pranks. Now, returned to the formality of court, that gaiety had been replaced by caution and wariness. Udric occasionally felt her eyes upon him and blushed to the roots of his hair. She had the type of glance which tried to penetrate a man's mind. There was no hint of sexuality, purely a weighing up of one's worth or value to her. His discomfort was relieved by the entry of a dwarf, who after bowing to the King, acknowledged the Lady Elfrida as Queen. Edward appeared to ignore the use of the title, preferring to watch the antics of the clown as he tumbled skillfully round the hall between the trestles, occasionally stealing a bite from a plate of food.

"Enough Wulfstan," commanded the King holding his sides with laughter. "You have earned your supper tonight."

Elfrida dismissed her diminutive servant, leaving the hall shortly afterwards with her ladies. Ethelred studiously avoided catching his mother's eye in case she demanded he retire too, but she swept past with the barest of nods in the King's direction.

Immediately she had left there was an almost tangible lightening of the atmosphere. Dogs crept from hiding places to clean up spilt food, and even the guards were less expressionless, allowing a smile when they overheard a ribald joke. The young men soon had the high table to themselves. Talk turned to boasting of their conquests with womenfolk to which Udric listened avidly. Having had little opportunity to try out his sexual prowess he found himself fascinated by the stories of willing daughters, reluctant servants and blushing dairy girls.

"We will find a maiden for you Udric," they suggested as the boasting became wilder with the drink. "It's time he was bedded, is it not my Lord?"

Edward merely smiled, suggesting that they all retire before heads became too thick. Putting his arm round Ethelred's shoulder, the two half brothers left the hall laughing together. Udric was pulled to his feet by the others.

"To bed, shared with us tonight, but tomorrow could be a different matter!"

For the next few days Udric was on tenterhooks in case he was suddenly presented with a companion for the night. He wondered if he would suddenly be lanced by cupid's arrow of fairy tales or be embarrassed by his amateur fumblings. There had been no summons from the King to assist with anything; no task was set for him to carry out. In fact, considered Udric, he was not sure why the King had asked him to return to the capital with him.

He found he was unashamedly interested in the workings of the court. Since he had nothing to do of any importance he spent time finding his way round the gloomy, cold corridors of the royal palace.

In the writing room Udric watched as clerks made neat copies of the judgements handed down by the King or his shire deputies, writs granting lands or benefits to a person or church. Most of the writers were monastery trained, still wearing simple robes and tonsured hair. In the dim light he watched the careful strokes of the nib, the control necessary to form the figures upon the tautly stretched parchment. There was no comfort at all for those who worked here. Udric was quickly aware of becoming chilled but the clerks were either inured to the conditions or cared little for their own comfort.

While Alfred had had the advantage of being taught to write by the same tutor who had taught the King's father, Udric was less practiced in the art although he could read well.

In the counting house, formerly under the control of Archbishop Dunstan in his capacity as Chancellor of the King's exchequer, he admired the quick reckoning of tallies. A collector would bring in the records from the shire, all marked to identify the source. The sticks marked with strokes recorded receipts of silver pennies or goods to the equivalent value, while those marked with burned scorch marks represented goods taken in exchange, or silver paid out. The senior clerk placed counters on black or white squares to represent the marks on the sticks; eventually calculating the amount received or paid out by the king's treasure chest. At times the table was covered with coins before they were carefully placed in leather bags and put into the chest guarded by the biggest men Udric had ever seen. Unblinking, the soldiers wore full armour and carried spears with newly sharpened edges. Udric nodded briefly to the clerks as he backed out of the chamber. No one had questioned his presence as he stood watching the intricate calculations, until his cold feet forced him to return to the fireside of the hall.

In his absence, the King had asked for him. Hastily brushing his tunic with the flat of his hand, Udric walked quickly to Edward's private quarters. The guard admitted him without hesitation.

"My lord, my apologies for not coming sooner. I have been watching the workings of your court. The writing room was freezing!" so saying, Udric took the liberty of warming his hands by the glowing brazier. "You have clever men in the chancery too. They were reckoning the monies from Wiltshire." Udric hesitated before asking what the King had wanted of him. Edward was pleased that he could now talk to someone his own age about the economies which his councillors were insisting he make. "The fact that you have just been to the chancery is sheer good fortune. You will probably understand better than me. They tell me I must spend less on hawks and hounds, dress more sensibly. They do not even like the import of wines from abroad. They are even advising that taxes be increased," he explained. "They make much of young lord Alfhere of Mercia who has turned all the monks off his land, replacing them with his own people but refuses to pay money or service for those lands. He is a powerful man with many armed servants. He had a fright when he was injured at the court in Calne, but seems to be unrepentant. He guards his own borders with the Welsh and Northern people but contributes nothing to the weal of the realm."

The King sighed, depressed by the weight of the responsibility which fell on his shoulders. "I hardly dare send my shire reeve to his lands. Each month the revenue is less than it should be. Messengers are mistreated or ridiculed so that even my toughest captains are unwilling to act as escort. The army cannot be used against my own people. I could not ask them, yet there is no money to hire mercenaries." Edward appeared defeated; he slouched over the cup of wine staring moodily into its deep ruby depth. Occasionally he ran his hand distractedly through his hair which showed signs of needing a cut and above all, a wash.

Udric sympathised with the King's dilemma but having no experience in these matters, felt unable to give Edward any constructive advice. Sitting astride the bench, Udric watched the King as he sorted documents into some order.

"Pardon me for the suggestion my Lord, but do you personally visit his territory as you visit Dorsetshire, Wiltshire, Somerset or the Essex and Weald shires? As I understand it, some men in Wymburne who own their land do not pay money to the exchequer but provide services or food for a given number of days in the year. So the courts you hold around England are supplied with stores due to you from the surrounding townsmen, farms and mills. The gamekeepers and woodsmen too, have to bring their share. My father tells me that all the supplies needed to provide you and your councillors, soldiers and servants with the things you need are demanded by the ealdormen at the hundred courts. So for instance, we were told last month that a quantity of flour was needed at Cranburne for your visit. We told the miller, who keeps the portion of milled flour due to you. Within a day the sacks were delivered to your controller of stores. It is part of the service we pay to you in return for the land my father holds."

"What you are saying Udric, is that we take the whole court to Alfhere's land so that the expense falls on him. What a marvellous idea! My councillors have been racking their brains to think of a way to bring Mercia back into the fold. Even Dunstan said that if the ealdorman had not realised the error of his ways when he recovered from his injuries, then there was little that could be done unless I wanted civil strife to break out again." By this time the King was grinning broadly, his eyes glinting wickedly at the thought of causing the errant earl such expense.

"I have to visit Dorset again very shortly, but in the summer the court will descend on Alfhere! What a wonderful plan; perhaps we should hold a Council meeting there too so that there are even more visitors for him to accommodate."

The King chuckled gleefully with the thought of the whole court, of councillors, soldiers, servants and visitors all being fed at the expense of the reluctant ealdorman.

Continuing more seriously he told Udric about the planned visit to the coast of Dorset. "Corfe is a vital defence position but a bit isolated. My advisors think that my presence is needed, bearing in mind that the Lady Elfrida has taken up residence in my late father's hall there. Poor Ethelred lives a dog's life you know, most of the time she does not let him out of her sight. I like to take him about with me a bit. He is my heir after all."

Both men crossed themselves hastily. It was almost tempting fate to mention one's successor. One could be in good health one day and die of the sweating disease the next.

Whenever Udric and Edward met during the ensuing few days they exchanged conspiratorial glances. Messages had already been sent out to Alfhere's halls that the King would grace them with his presence for an extended summer visit. Meanwhile preparations for the more immediate visit to Corfe were well in hand.

A late snowfall delayed the departure for a few days which gave Udric the opportunity to send a message to his parents with the guards who were being sent down to relieve the soldiers at the King's Wymburne palace. He took great pains with his writing having begged a small piece of parchment from the Chancery clerks. Sitting at an empty desk, he dipped the quill into the ink bottle and wiped the surplus off the nib before carefully writing his greetings and telling them that he was still with the King. He dusted the wet ink with sand, tipped the grains back into a barrel and rolled the thin parchment up before tying it with a cord. Entrusting it to a captain he asked him to get a message back to him by one of the returning men as to his parent's health and wellbeing.

The pack train was being loaded in the courtyard which was a scene of organised chaos. Udric watched with fascination as bedding, furs, clothes, tableware and jewels were all packed with care under the guidance of the supervisor of the King's wardrobe. The clerks prepared their own panniers as did the Chancellor's department.

"Have you remembered the sealing wax?" joked Udric, remembering the difficulty in sending the messages and writs back to Winchester from the hunting lodge at Cranburne.

Initially scowling with annoyance, the chief clerk looked up but smiled when he recognised Udric for whom he had developed a liking. "Oh yes, that will not happen again." He held up two large sealed pots before dropping them into the pannier on the sturdy garron pony. "Your paste seals served their purpose. After all, when the document is opened, the seal is broken anyway. The bits fall off, usually into the rushes or straw, so no-one in the future will know that the King pressed his ring into unbaked bread will they?"

Servants bustled round preparing the final chests to be loaded. Udric watched from the doorway with some of the King's friends, commenting when they saw their own bedrolls being fastened onto a horse which already seemed to be well loaded.

"At least bedding does not weigh much!" commented one young man whose highly polished shoes showed that he had not ventured onto the courtyard which was quickly becoming muddy. Dogs roamed loose, darting under carts and barking at the activity.

"There is good hunting quite close to the main hall I am told. I hear there are white deer to be found. Edward's father once let one go near Sherburne, and then a thegn killed it against his orders. He fined the archer a hundred shillings. An expensive hart!"

Dressed warmly for the ride, the friends watched as the last baggage ponies were led off to start the slow journey to the south coast. The courtyard was cleaned of droppings by an army of labourers wielding brushes and shovels before the King's horse was led in prancing and sidestepping so that its harness jingled. The saddle blanket of felted material was edged with sparkling gems, the cantle covered in the same fabric so that the horse looked as though he was carrying a throne. Udric's horse, standing quietly, looked drab compared to the magnificence of the King's stallion.

Twice the King was called back to attend to last minute business, causing one friend to voice his impatience.

"It seems our Lord would rather not go to Corfe after all."

Although he joked, Edward scowled, irritably bidding him be silent. He mounted lightly, still a small figure on the huge horse.

"Thank God we do not have to move from our homes so often. No sooner has Lord Edward settled into a routine here than his counsellors insist that he visit here there and everywhere. The servants as well as the King must be sick and tired of packing up, loading carts, riding in all weathers. We would not be doing it now unless he had asked us to go with him. Have none of you ladies you will miss?"

There were a few shamefaced glances as they mounted their own horses. Officials and councillors stood by the hall watching as the King finally mounted and left his capital.

"I shall call on Ethelred while we are down there, but first a few days hunting. We shall have good sport and fill the stores at the same time. What could be better! I see the writers put many pots of sealing wax in their chests Udric. Was that your idea?"

Laughing, the riders trotted southwards, guards keeping a distance from the royal party while no strangers were in sight. Due to the delay in leaving Winchester the party stopped at Shaston for the first night as guests of the Abbess. With her nunnery's royal connections there was little sign of austerity or poverty in the guest house where the meal was wholesome if less varied than one served from a royal kitchen. In deference to their surroundings they attended a short service in the chapel before retiring but were not disturbed by the bell which summoned the nuns to services in the early hours of the morning.

As soon as the King's treasure had been safely stowed, and the bedding replaced on baggage ponies, the party headed southwards. The March winds blew in gusts making many of the horses restless, shying when someone's cloak billowed about them. Scudding clouds were evidence of forthcoming rain so they hurried to Sherburne to take shelter, soldiers galloping ahead of the King to give warning of his impending arrival. When the royal party made its entry up the hill into the town the people stared from the safety of their doorways. There was no welcome for the King, the streets were un-cleaned and the elders still at work, ignorant of his coming.

"Whatever is going on? The King has never had such a poor reception. The people look, well, frightened. And by all accounts, my nose tells me that the middens need cleaning!" commented the man with the shiny shoes. He was studying the road, the filth and mud which had accumulated over many weeks. Unless he was carried to the hall, there was no way to avoid coming into contact with the loathsome mess. An open drain flowed sluggishly down Cheap Street which was still covered with the detritus of the market. Pigs rooted in the filth adding to the overall unhealthy smell.

The elderly Bishop had been extremely disappointed when King Edgar had removed him from the office of Archbishop of Canterbury in order to replace him with Dunstan. Not however a man to harbour a grudge against Edgar's son, Bishop Aelfwold hastily welcomed Edward, bowing low to hide his nervousness.

"My Lord welcome to my humble hall. You do me much honour."

Edward entered the Bishop's hall and immediately admired the unusual wall sconces, putting the old man at ease. Udric gripped the wrists of his father's elderly friend in greeting before kissing the huge amethyst ring on the churchman's bony thumb.

"We may have time to speak privately," murmured Udric discreetly as he moved to let another address the Bishop. He was sure his father would wish to be remembered to the elderly cleric. His attributes may not have been in statesmanship which was probably the reason he no longer held high office, but the man was undoubtedly godly. The hall was comfortable but had few luxuries. There were no tapestries or fine carpets adorning the plain whitewashed walls. Candles smoked indicating that they were not of the finest wax which was used in the King's courts.

Servants hurriedly built up the fire, sparks rising as they tried to create more flames. A welcome cup was brought and passed round among the visitors, as bedding rolls were brought in and stacked in the corner.

"Lord preserve us," swore one young man, his nose wrinkling at the poor quality of the ale. He passed it quickly to the man standing at his side and dramatically wiped his mouth with the back of his hand. The King scowled darkly, both at his companion's comment and his uncouth manners.

"We have given my lord Bishop no warning of our coming. There are many of us to squeeze into his hall but at least we are not being drenched by the rain."

For several minutes there had been a drumming noise on the roof. Now drips fell from gaps in the tiles into the rushes below, the odd spot landing on the fire which sizzled in protest. Servants closed the wooden shutters casting the hall into deep gloom until more sconces were lit.

At the hastily prepared feast, conversation was somewhat stilted initially as the Bishop was known to favour a more moderate approach to the religious institutions than Dunstan had demanded. Edward reassured him that while no further strictures were to be placed upon those who chose monastic life, neither had he any intention of increasing their lands or privileges.

"There have been many disputes over these matters my lord Bishop. My father was overly influenced by the great Dunstan. The chancery is now in the hands of men who are not connected to the church. Some have trained solely in accounting. I have no great understanding as you know, but my counsellors tell me to make savings."

The Bishop nodded, pushing a bowl of tart apples towards his royal visitor. Any embarrassment on either side was quickly dispelled with light hearted, non controversial chatter so that the remainder of the evening passed quickly, a musician playing softly amid the buzz of conversation. A servant brought in some of the King's own wine, a big improvement on that which was served at the table.

"I would value your opinion my lord. It is from Gascony and has travelled well but some find it too sweet. Perhaps I can leave it with you."

For such a young man with so many other cares to deal with, the Bishop appreciated the King's tactful gift.

Leaving the town early the next morning after the Bishop had blessed the royal party's endeavours; the riders reached the hunting lodge by late afternoon to find that preparations were well in hand for a feast. With whetted appetites they need no urging to change into fresh tunics before finding their way to the hall. Servants bustled about directing the visitors. As the trestles were being erected Prince Ethelred arrived, embracing his half brother with real affection. He was smiling broadly, but obviously not dressed for any formal occasion.

"My lady mother is indisposed so I slipped away with a couple of guards," he whispered conspiratorially to his half brother. "Can I come tomorrow?"

"I know that the Lady Elfrida would forbid you to accompany me and my 'wild companions'. Why don't you meet up with the hunting party? You had better say that you wish to ride, rather than admit that you will be joining me and my friends. Not exactly a lie, you understand, just not the whole truth."

Watchful that Ethelred did not drink too much before returning to the palace with his understanding guards, the feast was a great success. For a few hours there was little formality, Edward changing seats several times during the course of the meal so that the local thegns were impressed by his geniality and hospitality.

Some spoke hesitantly of beatings, maimings and other punishments meted out by the Lady Elfrida for what she deemed to be the slightest infringement of duty or respect to her.

"When my daughter married, she insisted that my finest ox should be delivered to her," recalled one weathered headman. "I only have two, for pulling the plough you know, so I protested and offered her more labour days for a year in its place. Shortly afterwards my ox was ham-strung, dying in agony from its wounds. Of course I can't prove it was the Lady's doing, but who else would harm a man's ox?" The man's face was weather beaten but was without a trace of guile. No one answered his question, knowing that there was no suitable response.

Edward sympathised with his dilemma but having given the rents of the land to the Lady Elfrida, she could treat her cottagers and servants as she chose. "Udric here is my trusted friend. Go with him to the clerk of the treasury. He will give you silver so that you may buy a new ox for the plough. Udric will vouch for my command and be witness."

The villein gabbled his thanks emotionally before following Udric to the room where the clerk guarded a small treasure chest under his trestle table.

Somewhat annoyed at being required to dispense silver late at night, 'as if he were a common clerk' the clerk's good humour and his sense of dignity were only restored when the King's gift was received with grateful thanks.

"Let it be known that the ox is from the King," suggested Udric as they returned to the hall. "That way no-one will dare harm the beast, meanwhile keep your silver safe."

Agreeing that Udric's suggestion was wise, they slipped back into the hall quietly where most of the men had bedded down for the night. Those who were still awake talked quietly beside the fire.

"She says honeyed words to my face, but has the heart of a she-devil. It is said that she charmed my good father with magic," mumbled the King as he relieved himself in a corner. "Poor Ethelred dare not cross her any more than the servants. Most of them believe the rumour that she had a hand in the death of her former husband."

Not having a suitable reply to this confidence, Udric changed the subject, enquiring about the hunt the following day. The other friends joined in the conversation vying with each other to relate the most fantastic story about their hunting exploits.

Next morning, despite some thick heads, everyone was up early, anticipating a good days hunting in the surrounding woods. The kitchens provided ale and manchets of bread for those who could face food, while meats and cheese were packed into panniers to accompany the hunt.

The trumpet sounded, alerting the entire household to the King's departure. All the horses were excited so that the leash-men were nervous for the safety of their hounds. Two large lymers on leather leashes were almost pulling the handler along in their eagerness to track their quarry. The mood was infectious, causing even the youngest servant to turn away from his work to stare at the magnificent procession now setting out from the hunting lodge.

The chase was long and hard, sometimes across open ground and occasionally through thickets of trees. Despite alternating dappled light and deep shade, many of the riders cursed trees on which they had either banged their heads on overhanging branches or the horse had gone through a gap which accommodated his own width but not that of the rider's knees. Two big stags with fine antlers were shot, the King's arrows being returned to him when the huntsman had cut the animal's throat.

It was only when the party paused for refreshment, that it was realised that there had been no sign of Ethelred.

"He was obviously not allowed to ride out today though we made enough noise for him to find us. Poor boy, he gets no fun at all. Always under the eye of his mother or her close cronies. Carry on the hunt; I want to see another couple by tonight! If he cannot get out, then I must seek him. Leastways, I suppose I should pay my respects to my late father's wife." He made an expression of distaste then shrugged his shoulders.

Refusing the company of the guards, and of his friends, Edward rode off towards the lady Elfrida's palace. Udric inspected his mount's leg which had become inflamed. A guard offered to walk it for him so that he could ride a spare horse but Udric refused saying that he would start walking back with the servants who had already trussed a deer to the carrying poles.

By the time he approached the hunting lodge there was no doubt in his mind that his horse was lame. Each step the horse dropped its head; Udric muttered comforting words and patted its arched neck.

It took a little time to prepare a poultice for the affected limb and by the time he returned to the hall the afternoon was well advanced but no-one had returned. He borrowed a spare horse, retracing his steps towards the hunting party. The woods may have contained plenty of game but all the small creatures and the birds stayed silent, hiding from the hunters.

"Did you leave the King at the lodge?" they asked seeing him coming from that direction.

"I have not seen the King since he left to visit Ethelred and the King's late wife. We should go after him and escort him back before the light goes."

"He should have more sense than to go into the Queen's lair on his own," growled one companion. "I would not go without guards behind my back."

"Nor me," replied another whose face was red from exertion. "She has the sort of stare which either turns my legs to jelly or sees into my very soul. Let's go and get our King back!"

They cantered towards the palace, joking and teasing each other about the day's sport. When one man's horse stopped abruptly so that he was catapulted over its head, they initially laughed at his discomfort.

Furious with his mount and red-faced with embarrassment, the young man attempted to remount but found great difficulty as the horse was extremely distressed. Dismounting Udric threw the reins of his borrowed mount over a branch and checked his friend's horse for injury.

"There is nothing obvious," he said. "I will walk him a moment if you will take my horse." As he passed a thick clump of holly the horse again shied and stood still, its eyes rolling in terror.

A low moan broke the eerie silence. Udric called the others to him, suggesting that there was perhaps a wounded deer in the thicket. Parting the prickly branches the men gasped in horror. "My God, the King's horse!"

Everyone ran to the stricken beast. "T'is true, I'd know that horse anywhere," said Udric dropping on his knees beside the fatally wounded beast. "Someone has tried to cut his throat!" Regardless of the blood soaked earth, Udric cradled the beast's head on his lap.

"I'm going to put him out of his misery. There is nothing we can do for him."

Drawing out his knife, Udric quickly pulled the stallion's neck taut and drew his blade quickly across his throat. Its eyes fastened on Udric, perhaps in gratitude for his merciful act, before it gave up its feeble hold on life and died with a final sigh.

Having known the horse since its birth some seven summers before, Udric was visibly upset, wiping his sleeve across his eyes before standing up to face the others. He wiped the blade on some leaves before replacing it in the leather scabbard, taking a few moments to get over the shock. One of the men vomited in the winter leaf mould, not because he was not used to the death of an animal but because fear was now gripping him, knotting his innards in a vice like grip. "We should never have let him go alone," he moaned.

"The King, where is the King?"

The friends frantically searched the surrounding wood, half expecting to find the mortally wounded King. They called his name, sometimes just one voice, sometimes in unison.

"We must call the guard," suggested the man whose horse had stopped abruptly. "I'm going back to the lodge to call them out."

He left on a horse which was keen to get away from the smell of death, leaving the others mounting up to follow the trail of blood which the King's stallion had left on the forest floor.

Not far from the palace the ground was disturbed. Signs that the horse had dragged a rider were evident for the King's gauntlet was beside the bent grasses. One of the men dismounted, picking it up gingerly. "The stallion must have been frightened. It has never bolted before."

He led the way on foot following the drag marks. Occasionally there was blood, particularly as they neared the stony outcrop. The palace was in sight but not one of them elected to proceed further without armed guards. Of the King's body there was no sign and the light was fading fast, a blood red sunset falling below the western horizon.

A chill settled over them all as they waited for the soldiers. Harness occasionally jingled as a horse stamped its feet, but there was little talk between them, each being wrapped in his own private thoughts.

The sight of torches approaching at speed was gladdening to the young men whose pleasure in the day had ceased so abruptly. At the head of the column was their friend who had called the soldiers from their guardhouse.

Explaining the situation to the captain, the gauntlet was examined closely.

"Go back to the lodge. We will ride to the palace and find out the truth of the matter," instructed the senior officer.

"You can do no good here in the dark. We will bring the King back if he be not mortally injured," he added dourly, drawing his sword slowly from its leather sheath.

Dismissed by the authority in his voice, Udric turned his horse gently, guiding it back the way the soldiers had come. It led them unerringly back to its stable, glad to be back in the shelter with food, water and hay.

In the hall the companions picked at the food the kitchen staff had provided. There was an atmosphere of suspicion, even among themselves. They kept glancing at the big carved chair, willing its occupant to return safely. Every time a dog barked the men looked up hopefully. Some ventured outside hoping to see torches lighting up the blackness. There was no moon, just one torch lit to guide the missing men back to the lodge, its flames casting leaping shadows in the nearby woods.

"We should have insisted on going with him," said one man, voicing the blame they all felt. In the ensuing silence each man searched his conscience. They recalled with some relief, how the King had expressly forbidden anyone from accompanying him on his visit to Ethelred. Waiting for the returning guards, they only spoke in nervous tones, aware of the slightest sound.

The captain of the guard marched in without ceremony bringing them all to their feet. White faced, he stood blinking in the brightness.

"Where is the King?" "Is he injured?"

"My lords," began the captain trying desperately to maintain his dignity. "The King apparently called at the palace. On finding the Aetheling away from home, he rode off. No one knows where."

"A horse does not cut its own throat," growled Udric. "Some one must know who tried to kill the King's stallion. My father bred that horse, he was brave but steady. He would never have sold him to the King unless he was a safe ride. Someone botched the task then left the beast to suffer."

"No-one mentioned the stallion." The guard commented. "As soon as dawn breaks I intend to take a search party out to look for the King. Will you help? I would be obliged if you would all assist my men. In the meantime I have sent a rider to Wareham to fetch the ealdorman. The horse-keeper is the fastest rider so he has volunteered for the task. Even so, he cannot expect to be back with lord Hugh before tomorrow night."

Long before dawn the friends were ready and eager to ride out. They had not slept well, tossing restlessly on straw pallets during the darkness. Udric again had to rely on a borrowed horse, his own being stiff from the previous day's injury. The marks of the stallion were examined again and followed back to the palace gates. They looked everywhere, calling at the small cottages, demanding to know if the King was within, or had been seen by the occupants.

Passing one field, Udric recognized the man to whom the King had given the price of an ox. Explaining his presence and briefly what they had found so far, the man immediately dropped the plough handle to join in the search. "My lady can do what she likes; my King has my love and my loyalty." He was almost weeping with emotion as he dusted the earth off his huge hands.

Udric rode on to the next cottage, his heart heavier by the minute. They had searched for hours but no-one had seen the King. Cottagers expressed their concern but few dared leave their work for fear of earning the wrath of the Lady Elfrida whose reeve had eagle eyes.

Determined to go over the stallions tracks yet again, Udric rode back through the forest to the place where the King's horse had been discovered. The noble beast still lay in the thicket, stiff in death, flies crawling round the wide nostrils. His borrowed mount snorted, diverting Udric's attention for a moment. He had a momentary glimpse of a short man grinning at him before a crashing blow felled him to the ground in tumbling blackness.

When he returned to consciousness, dazed and confused, his horse was nuzzling him gently. Moving cautiously he pulled himself up using the reins which still hung down. Muttering his apologies for using the animal's soft mouth so outrageously, Udric finally stood up. His head hurt abominably, faintness threatening to overtake his senses once more. Torn between clutching his head or his stomach, nature resolved the matter for him. He was violently sick, shaking as if he suffered from an ague. The horse nuzzled him sympathetically. Udric was grateful for its warmth for he was chilled to the bone.

The King's stallion had gone. Even the bloody leaf mould had been swept away. Udric blinked and looked again. The dead horse was definitely not there. No harness, no gilt bridle, just woodland debris.

'Perhaps this is not the right place,' thought Udric looking around. It appeared to be the same thicket, so he checked the spot again. Something sparkled among the leaves. Looking round carefully before bending down, he retrieved a small gold tassel from the stallion's bridle. He put it into the bottom of his scabbard with his knife for safe keeping and remounted thoughtfully. The effort made his head swim. Making his way back towards the hunting lodge, swaying unsteadily in the saddle, he let the horse find the best path. He met two of his friends with soldiers searching the undergrowth. One of the Lymer dogs had been unleashed in case its sensitive nose could find the king.

"Whatever happened to you?" called out the man who saw him first. "Did you fall off?"

Feeling extremely dizzy Udric found it difficult to speak clearly. Once again the blackness descended as he fell slowly from the saddle.

The next time he recovered his senses he was being tended by a young woman wiping his brow with a damp cloth. The captain of the guard sat on a stool nearby.

"Where is my belt?"

Presuming that he was still delirious, the girl pressed him back on the straw paillasse.

"Someone has taken the King's stallion. Gone, completely gone," he repeated. "You must believe me. I was staring at the poor beast when a man hit me. Where is my belt, my scabbard?"

Passing the sheath and belt to Udric, he drew out the knife and tipped the guard up. The small gold tassel fell out onto his palm. Showing the captain, Udric explained that he had found the ornament on the ground, from where even the bloodstains had been removed.

"They must have missed this. It is off the browband. I know I was looking in the right place."

For the rest of the week the countryside was scoured. It was rapidly becoming clear that an accident had befallen the King.

No-one voiced their true suspicions. Now recovered, Udric told the Ealdorman about the attack, taking him to the place where they had found the mortally injured stallion.

"I had intended to follow the hoof prints back towards the palace to see if I could find the place where the King might have fallen off."

Before mounting up, the Ealdorman spoke to the grim faced men gathered around him. Calling them closer, he looked round carefully before speaking quietly.

"We need a trusted man to take the hunting dogs. Too many round here are in the pay of the late King's lady. Apart from the guards, who can work the dogs?"

"There is the man from one of the cottages. He is a loyal King's man. He has no love of Elfrida I swear," prompted Serian, the oldest of the guards. "I will send a man to fetch him, and leave a guard in his place so that his absence will not be noticed. He used to work in the King's kennels."

Glad to be of real service to the King, the cottager expressed his eagerness to work the dogs in an attempt to find the King. Requesting an item of Edward's intimate clothing, he wrapped it briefly round the dogs' noses.

"They know what they are looking for now," he said confidently, pushing the garment into his jerkin.

From the place where the stallion had fallen the search party back-tracked. Some signs of the stallion's headlong gallop still remained but heavy dew had washed away most of the blood stains.

The dogs confidently led their handler away from the main tracks towards the outlying buildings of the palace. Some distance beyond the outbuildings which appeared to be deserted, they came on a clearing. The dogs still pointed, pulling eagerly so that the pace quickened, the cottager running behind them. The ealdorman, having initially doubted the dogs' instincts, now pushed his mount to a trot to keep up.

"Used to be the best well for many a league," commented a local guard riding alongside the nobleman. "Dried up or cracked in my father's time."

Sure enough, the old well wall still stood in parts. Obviously some of the stones had been looted for other purposes, but the dogs circled the well head, pausing to scent the air and the mossy masonry. One sat down, looked enquiringly at the cottager and uttered a loud wail. The other lay down, head on paws, its task obviously completed.

Initially inclined to scoff at the dogs abilities Lord Hugh was on the point of waving everyone on, to continue the search.

Dismounting, the soldiers approached the well cautiously. The dog handler pulled the hounds away to make room for the guard who peered into the hole.

"There is nothing to see my Lord," he started. "No, wait, a piece of wood perhaps or ....My God t'is may be...."

Others crowded round anxious to confirm or deny the guard's suspicions. The hole was dark and smelt slightly dank. Ferns grew abundantly out of the disused stonework obscuring the view.

"We will need a rope. Someone will have to go down there. It may be nothing but that dog seems to know something is down there." Leaving two soldiers to guard the well the search party returned to the hunting lodge. The cottager was sent back to work, richer by two silver pennies, but warned to say nothing of the day's work.

The ealdorman ordered the guard to fetch ropes. While waiting for someone to find a strong rope the kitchens provided food although few felt like eating much.

Udric, as the lightest man, was unanimously elected to search the well although the prospect of being lowered into the darkness filled him with foreboding. Since a small child he had not liked small enclosed spaces. When playing hide and seek with other children he had never chosen the darkest corners beneath mangers in the stables or the cubby-hole at the mill. He had always preferred to find a hiding place above ground level, hence the numerous tears to his tunics or jerkins for which he had been punished.

"God preserve my soul," muttered Udric as the guard fastened a knotted loop around his waist. He crossed himself rapidly before sitting astride the broken stones.

Now he was lowered jerkily into his worst nightmare. The darkness increased, a cloying dampness invaded his clothes even before he reached the bottom.

The water was cold, covered with green weed and scum. Gingerly he stretched out his arm to grasp the protruding object. A hand rose out of the slimy water. On it was the King's ring, identical to the one he had been given so recently.

Calling back up to the guard, Udric grimly reported his gruesome find.

"Here is a second rope," called down the soldier lowering a thick hempen rope down to Udric who had managed to wedge the toes of his shoes into a crack in the stonework. "Tie it round the body. Under the arms if you can."

Udric reluctantly felt round the clothing of the corpse until he had the rope securely round Edward's chest. Tying a fast knot without one hand to steady himself caused him great pain as the rope around his own chest tightened. As soon as the body was tied, he ordered the guard to haul it up.

Slowly, dripping water and weed, the body of the King was pulled up the well sides and over the top. Udric waited to be brought up, the pressure of the loop around his own chest becoming increasingly uncomfortable.

Above he could hear shouting and the clash of arms. Attempting to pull himself up the rope he was horrified when it slackened.

Fear, bordering on panic gripped him. "Pull me up," he demanded. Scrabbling with his toes to get a grip on the stone work, he fell back into the water, swallowing and choking on the rubbish that had been stirred up.

Udric was now extremely frightened, inwardly screaming hysterically. Most of the rope fell down on top of him further hampering his efforts to get a grip on the side. A head peered over the top moments before the body of a guard was hurled down on top of him, followed in quick succession by three more until the water was full of unresisting limbs and torsos. Udric extracted himself from their unfeeling grip; the corpses' eyes wide open in silent accusation.

A head appeared over the top again, lips curled back in a wide grimacing leer. "Rest with the king's bastard, whelp!"

Udric recognised the piping voice of the dwarf who belonged to the Lady Elfrida. With a flash, he realised that it was the same person who had struck him down when he had found the stallion, the small man who had dealt the savage blow to the side of his head. He could only reach that high, thought Udric bitterly. He could not even make a proper end to a dumb animal.

Taking stock of his own situation as the light above began to fade, Udric began to realise the seriousness of his position.

There had been no answer to his shouts and the chill of the cold water was becoming penetrating so that his teeth chattered. Anger gripped him as he fumbled in the foulness for the soldier's dagger. It would be quicker to end his life with a blade, than wait for the cold water to close over his head. Locating first one knife and then a second he stuffed them inside his sodden jerkin, bitterly regretting that he had stripped off most of his clothes before being lowered into the well.

Time passed in the blackness. Using a knife in each hand he managed to wedge himself against the stonework by pushing the blades into the old mortar. His head nodded and jerked back into wakefulness as his face touched the cold water.

The first light of the false dawn appeared above him as he dozed. During a brief spell of wakefulness he heard rustlings above. Fearing that the dwarf might have returned, he initially feigned unconsciousness. "By Christ," a voice swore. From the corner of his eye Udric saw the cottager's head appear over the rim of the well.

"Udric, Udric! It's Wain, the ox driver! God's blood, what evil happened here?" Clearly not expecting an answer, the man's head jerked with shock when Udric opened his eyes and groaned loudly. His teeth were locked solid with cold, speech impossible.

The knotted end of the rope had snagged some distance down the well, beyond the man's grasp. The head drew back, but reappeared with a branch a few moments later.

Lowering the forked end down the opposite side of the well, the cottager gently hooked the knot in the twigged shoots. With a quick twist, he turned the branch so that the rope was looped twice around the makeshift pole, and pulled it back over the side of the hole.

"Is it still tied to you?" he whispered. Udric grunted what he hoped was an encouraging reply. Gingerly his rescuer pulled on the rope, gently at first. Udric pulled one knife out of the wall and hastily pushed it into his doublet. The other he had to leave as he was pulled slowly out of the cold water. The dawn air was even colder than his waterlogged skin. He shivered involuntarily, unable to help himself as he was hauled, dripping foul water, up the steep wall of mossy stone.

The cottager was grunting with effort, his breath wheezing noisily as he pulled Udric's dead weight up from the grizzly depth of the watery grave.

With a final heave Udric found himself at the rim in the comparatively bright light of the dawn. Urgently Wain pulled him away from the dangerous edge before collapsing on the ground overcome with weakness. Both of them lay gasping for breath. The rope had tightened around Udric's chest to a dangerous extent, threatening to cut off the air supply even though he was on God's good earth again. Fighting to extract the knife from the doublet, he cut feverishly at the fibres which gripped his chest in a vice-like grip. He glimpsed red flashes interspersed with wavering blackness as he sawed through the strands. When at last the rope was cut, the air surged into his body renewing his energy.

"Thank you my friend. My life, I owe you."

The cottager too had now recovered and was rubbing his calloused hands which had rubbed raw and bleeding on the coarse rope.

"Let's be gone from this evil place. But leave no trace or my life will not be worth a candle." Staggering to their feet, both men straightened the grass around the well to hide the traces of drag marks. Wain pushed the mossy stones into the well because the greenness had been torn by the rope, hurling the rope down after them to look as though Udric too had drowned after all.

"Come, lean on me, but we must get away before that hell-sprite comes back to gloat over his evil deeds."

By the time they reached the cottage Udric had regained fairly efficient use of his bloody, scraped legs. Ducking below the door frame they entered the smoky warmth of Wain's dwelling. His wife was crouched over the small fire but looked up quickly when her husband entered.

Her first words of surprise were silenced when Udric sat down on the dirt floor utterly exhausted.

"Hot gruel woman, this man is hurt," commanded Wain gruffly. "I must go out with the oxen or my absence will be noted. Keep him here with you until I return tonight. Let no-one see him, and speak of him to no-one. T'is the Lord's work wife, and as I love you, keep you both safe this day."

Wain left, pulling the leather door curtain down behind him.

Udric greedily drank the weak soup, feeling its warmth restore his own body heat from within. He could not keep his eyes open. A drugged sleepiness overcame him as he sat beside the fire. The leather of his boots had been leached of all colouring. Even the fingers on which the King's ring still fitted were white, his nails soft. Fearing that he would fall into the flames, Wain's wife hauled him to his feet and roughly marched him to the only bed where he fell soundly asleep. She pulled off his boots then covered him with the only blankets that she possessed.

Waking only to relieve himself into a pot which she held for him, Udric slept throughout the day. He was too exhausted to be embarrassed by the intimacy which had been involved. He was not even aware that she had stripped him of his sodden tunic.

Wain's loud greeting to his wife from beyond the walls of the cottage brought him back to full consciousness. With a start he sat up, finding himself firmly wrapped in a white wool blanket. Reacting with horror, he pulled the shroud off, then realised that he was naked beneath it. Udric blushed, suddenly feeling awkward, grabbing the thin fabric as it fell to the floor.

Wain entered to find Udric clutching the shroud to his manhood while his wife attempted to look unconcerned as she boiled a thick pottage in her stew-pot. Her lank hair was partially covered with a small scarf, thin wrists protruding from a shabby gown.

"His clothes were too wet to sleep in husband. Yours do not fit, so I used what God provided to cover him."

Seeing the funny side of his circumstances, now he had got over the shock of being dressed prematurely in a shroud, Udric laughed. He wrapped the material round his body securely and greeted Wain more formally.

"We owe you an explanation," stated Wain as he eagerly sat down to eat. Between mouthfuls, Udric and his host related the events of the previous night to Wain's wife whose eyes became wider with astonishment.

"I swear my arms are longer by a hand-span," joked Wain holding out his battered palms. "He may only look like a stripling but his weight pulls like a wayward ox."

"I owe Wain my life," confirmed Udric, having related the details of being lowered into the well to retrieve the body of King Edward.

"Your husband's life and mine are in danger. We may be the only two alive who know the truth about the corpse. It should be wearing this fine shroud, not me. It is fit for a King."

"If I leave, then Elfrida's men will know that I have learned their secret. You must go, but in darkness. You need a horse. Are you, er... were you a friend of the King?"

Udric nodded mutely suddenly unable to speak. His throat was sore and his breathing hurt with emotion.

Recalling his own mount stabled at the hunting lodge, Udric decided to go secretly to reclaim it.

"Any horse would do, but I trust my own horse. God willing he only suffered a sprain and is healed now. He would find his own way home if need be."

They discussed the plan well into the night. Udric's clothes had dried stiffly but he forced them on, tying a cord round his waist with a makeshift scabbard for the dead soldier's knife.

Despite the risk, Wain wanted to accompany him to the lodge, saying that he must know if Udric got away safely. Thanks were said inside the cottage as they both knew that there would be no opportunity for talking once they were within earshot of the guardhouse.

"No doubt it will be presumed that I and the guards have all met our deaths. For certain, the Lady Elfrida has already taken the treasury on behalf of her son."

The ealdorman and the late King's surviving friends would all be gone by now, leaving soldiers loyal to Prince Ethelred in control, thought Udric bitterly. He had no warm clothing, no cloak, only seething anger and bitterness at the treachery which had undoubtedly taken place.

"With luck my horse will have been turned out to graze. As long as a bridle can be fashioned, we will get away somehow." The unspoken words 'or die in the attempt' hung heavily for a moment or two.

They left Wain's wife in the darkness beside her loom and walked quickly to the edge of the woods. From there they made their way to the lodge, silent in the windless night. Faint stars were outshone by the moon which shed enough light for them to approach the stables noiselessly. A dog stirred but was instantly hushed by Wain who was known to them.

Alongside the kennels were the store rooms from where the sound of a woman weeping could be heard.

"T'is my daughter, I know her voice," whispered Wain. "She married a guard. Oh my God, her husband could have been murdered too!" The sudden realisation hit him as if he had been thumped.

"I will look for my horse, you see to your daughter. God go with you."

There were no guards on duty and no horse-keepers sleeping with the stabled beasts. Udric's horse whinnied softly on his approach but the others were unconcerned. Even the harness and saddle were still on the rack. His eyes were completely accustomed to the darkness of the night, putting the harness on his horse by touch and familiarity. As he led the horse out of the stable he expected at any moment to be challenged. Knife at the ready, he put one foot in a stirrup and mounted quickly. Wain slipped out of the shadows whispering that his daughter had been locked in the store. Her man had indeed been killed. "The Queen told them there had been a hunting accident and that all were lost over a cliff edge. My daughter has been told she has to marry again - one of the Queen's palace guards: she says she would rather die."

Clearly distraught, Wain was wringing his hands, oblivious to the pain of the huge festering blisters.

Reluctantly, Udric felt that he had to leave; his presence could be discovered at any moment, his life forfeit.

"Go to your priest, Wain. Surely he would not see your daughter forced unwillingly into a second marriage, at least not until a decent period of mourning has passed. We need time. If you need me, send a message to the Bishop of Sherburne, refer to me as 'Udda' for God's sake, I am supposed to be dead. God be with you and your family Wain."

It was with some reluctance that Udric pressed his mount quietly towards the East, out of the jurisdiction of the Lady Elfrida, a bitter smile on his lips. If Ethelred succeeded to his murdered half-brother's throne, then nowhere would be beyond the reach of the woman. She would be the most powerful mother in the land.

Hiding in woods near Dorchester during the day, he mounted up again at dusk. Apart from a few desiccated nuts he had not eaten since leaving Wain's house. Water was no problem and the horse was happy to graze, but Udric's stomach grumbled at its unaccustomed emptiness.

Skirting the city by the fields beyond the gates he was on the rising ground as day broke. The skyline was empty of woods, forcing both man and horse to continue wearily towards Wymburne across common land and then on the public road. Everywhere was grey, the sky, the clouds and the mud. The drizzle was being blown in eddies by occasional gusts of wind, the dampness quickly removing the slight stiffening of his clothes.

A forest in the distance promised shelter and a hiding place. An ox cart plodded along the road, the driver unconcerned but making him nervous however innocent he looked.

Without being rude, Udric bade the man a good day, turning his head slightly away and effecting a crouched position to disguise his appearance. The man drove on without stopping the cart. Udric breathed a huge sigh of relief when there was no challenge.

During the following night he reached Uddings. Leaving the unsaddled horse in his usual stable with a hastily pulled bundle of hay, Udric crept along the familiar walls until he found his father's room. For some reason, at least until he had discussed matters with his father, he felt he should get into the house without the servants being aware of his presence. Knowing the routine of the night watchman, Udric ducked out of sight when he approached. The dogs yipped but were stilled quickly. Udric tapped urgently on the board of his father's window. "Father, let me in, quickly. Tell no-one," whispered Udric hoarsely when his father demanded to know who was disturbing the peace of the night.

Somewhat astonished at his son's request, Alfred nevertheless unbarred the door and let Udric into the hall. Brith appeared with a warm cloak around her shoulders. She started to chide Udric for his unkempt, wild appearance, but he silenced her with a gesture.

"Later mother, I need food. Can we talk privately in your room?"

Neither of them remonstrated with him for his abrupt manner. Now he was home safely he felt his fear melt away. His stomach grumbled loudly and he belched rudely. Reddening, he realised that the aroma he could smell was his own dirty body. His skin had dried after being in foul water but he could smell the filth in his nostrils and shuddered in disgust.

Brith felt tension in the atmosphere and went out to the kitchens taking a small flambeau from the wall to light the way.

Following his father, Udric first apologized for waking his parents in the middle of the night. "I need help. My life is in danger," he started, breaking off suddenly when his mother returned with a basket of food. Suddenly ravenous, Udric snatched meat and bread, cramming them into his mouth.

Normally a fastidious eater, his parents were astonished by the greed with which he ate and drank. "I have not eaten for two days," he muttered between mouthfuls, "my apologies!" Udric finally told his parents what had occurred since he had sent them word that he was going to Corfe with King Edward, swearing them to secrecy.

"So you see, there's only Wain and me who know exactly what happened. The King had been stabbed several times in the back and thrown into the well. The body must have been snatched back and then all the witnesses killed, except me," he added. "If I speak of this matter, I am as good as dead." He told them of Wain's bravery, and then of his daughter who was to remarry on the Lady Elfrida's orders.

"I have told Wain to send a message to the Bishop of Sherburne in grandfather's name. If anyone saw him rescue me, or even realises that he did so, then he too will be killed. The Bishop remembers you kindly father, I forgot that he sent messages of good wishes in my, er…, predicament."

Brith and Alfred had both sat down with the shock of their son's news. His mother had partially covered herself with rugs from the bed but both Udric and Alfred saw her shiver.

"They will have to call the Council, a Witan. He cannot just become King because he is the King's, I mean late King's, half brother," said Alfred correcting himself. He got up and stirred life into the small brazier. The reddish glow was somehow deeply comforting.

"Where is the King's body now? Ethelred could not have been involved personally. He is too young and not yet full grown, but the Lady, she had always hated Edward for becoming King. It is rumoured that she killed her own husband to marry Edgar."

"God knows! I saw his body hauled up from the well then all hell let loose. Dead men were thrown down on top of me but they were the King's guards. Where his body is now I really do not know," he shrugged. "They killed his horse too, or tried to. I had no choice but to dispatch him properly." Udric sniffed, trying to prevent the tears leaking from his eyes which pricked and stung.

Crossing themselves rapidly at the mention of the late King's father, they talked for the rest of the night without coming to any real decision. The only matter they did settle was to let it be known among the servants at Uddings that Udric was ill and would be staying inside for a day or two. There was no way they could disguise his homecoming so a few days illness would cause no comment among the servants or the cottagers.

"We could tell them the whole matter but sometime it would slip out. For now, the least they know of the danger you are in the better, though there's not one who would fight to protect you," added Brith proudly.

Days later when Udric had recovered Alfred told him of the sheriff's arrival in Wymburne with his own guards and most of the garrison from the King's palace. "He was recruiting men to join the posse. It seems that the steward had received reports of food going missing from other people. A man was seen at the rear of the smith's forge and another, or perhaps the same outlaw was almost caught when he stole food from a mercer's cottage. They scoured the hunting forest and eventually caught three outlaws. Two of the men, including the one who was seen abducting Gail according to the shepherd, came from, you'll never guess where!"

Udric dutifully looked puzzled.

"That ersling William of Chalburie's manor! He was the man who suggested that all deformed babies should be strangled at birth. The third was a soldier who had never returned to his lord somewhere west of here. Anyway, they were apparently dragged by the feet to the Hangings and swung without any trial or excuses. I was not summoned but I hope their souls go to hell. Any man who takes an innocent child and then abandons her in the middle of briars deserves no less." Having delivered his own verdict on the fate of the outlaws Alfred nodded confidently, his only regret that he had not been there to see justice, however summarily handed out, done to any outlaws who had been terrorising the neighbourhood for years.

"Let's hope they found all of them. There was talk of a large band of outlaws at Cranburne chase not so long ago. We never saw a glimpse of them with the hunt but Mother's brother, Brithricson, mentioned them and tried to get Lord Edward to do something about them. Of course he was too busy hunting but I believe a clerk made a note of his request."

Udric crossed himself, an enigmatic smile crossed his face as he remembered the wild galloping along the grassy avenues which had been cut between the tall trees of the forest. How he had jumped the fallen logs, the streams and up banks. It already seemed a lifetime ago.

In a few short weeks he had become a man, a man who probably had a price on his head. He sighed and returned to whittling the bone whistle fingering the smooth polished surface thoughtfully.

It was the end of the month after the Lenten fast that a Witan was called. Instructions arrived from the council for all thegns and owners of one hide or more of land to attend. Alfred reluctantly made preparations to attend.

"Knowing what I do, about the death of King Edward, I mean, it will be difficult to swear fealty to a boy who might have been involved in murder."

"Dearest heart, you must go. If there is the least suspicion that our son is still alive, then he will be killed for that knowledge. If you stay away, even the Bishop will be curious. Absence without good reason will cast doubt on your loyalty perhaps. I do understand, really I do, but you must attend. If you have to swear then God will understand that you do it to protect your son. Besides, I thought Ethelred was still a child. Udric thought he was only ten summers old when he last saw him. Who will be on the council? Surely they will not allow his mother to have too much authority!" Having set out her reasons as to why her husband should go to the Witan, Brith set to brushing the heavy cloak he would need both for the journey and to use as a blanket at night.

In Wymburne everyone grumbled about the poor diet they were forced to endure during Lent. The price of fish always rose and the whole town seemed to smell of the salted fish which was sold at the market. They were puzzled about the rumours that their late King had suffered an accident while out hunting. Alfred and Brith attended Mass but were unusually un-talkative at the usual gathering outside the church. They excused Udric's absence on the basis that he was seriously ill and must hurry back to him.

The priest had lost much of his popularity over the incident with the sick man, the congregation continuing to chat among themselves while he intoned the prayers. There were no small gifts left for him on the steps of his modest dwelling and no smiles or invitations to share a householder's meal.

Udric stayed at Uddings during his father's absence. Seeming outwardly physically unaffected by his ordeal, he found himself starting nervously at strange sounds. He stayed close to other people, taking dogs with him if he walked alone in the fields.

"I feel wretched letting father go off into that viper's nest. Just because they did not see the King stabbed to death, everyone will know that she had a hand in it. Why he insisted on going alone is still what mystifies me. We should have followed but at a distance. That dwarf she keeps to amuse her killed the horse, or made an attempt to do it, and it was he who threw the rope back into the well. The lady must have soldiers who are loyal, either from fear or because they have been promised rewards.

Oh, and there is Wain's daughter. Her soldier husband was killed by Lady Elfrida's men. When I crept from the stable near the hunting lodge, her men had locked the girl in a store-room. I had to leave Wain, the man who rescued me from the well, to deal with it on his own."

"Your father knows the risks all too well. He talked of finding an excuse but his absence would be questioned. The last thing we need at the moment is to draw attention to this family. If the Lady is as vindictive as you think, then she will use any excuse to have the land taken away from us at best, and have you killed at worst. Your father has gone to protect his family." Brith burst into tears, her face quickly becoming wet. She wiped her eyes with the sleeve of the over-kirtle she wore during the day.

"Any oath that he has to take is not one from the heart. It is almost under duress. He is protecting us, and God will protect him," she finished stoutly, drawing Udric into a hug so that the two of them felt comforted.

At the court, the Lady Elfrida proudly presented Ethelred already dressed in royal robes. She told the council that Edward and his companions had died in a hunting accident and the bodies had been buried at Wareham. She gave them few details and there was little sign of regret in the tone of her voice. Men looked around at faces they were familiar with. Now there was doubt and suspicion in the very air of the hall.

Without giving anyone time to raise questions she left, sweeping dramatically out through the double doors which had been opened to admit her son. An escort of her own guard formed around her.

The ealdorman of Mercia was visibly shocked. He sat down on the nearby bench as if all air had been punched from his chest. "What about the lying in state or royal funeral rites? Why was he buried so quickly? Was nothing decent allowed for our late King? My head is whirling. Was the body so mutilated that even the church did not insist on a decent interval?"

From a man who only months ago was defying the King the sudden concern for proper formalities sounded strange. One look at the ealdorman however, would have proved that his anxiety was genuine. He was pale, obviously shaken to the core.

No-one answered the questions which were on everybody's lips but which few would have had the courage to ask. Previous Kings in living memory had lived short and violent lives. Some shrugged as if they were disinterested while others studied their feet or cleaned fingernails with the point of the short knives which each man had for use at table.

Reminded by the men of the Council that the business of the day was to elect a new King, Alfhere, ealdorman of Mercia, sat down reluctantly. Ethelred still stood in the centre of the hall looking rather bemused. To many he looked like a little boy dressed in a grown-up's clothes. Because the late King had died without children, being only sixteen years old, the council had no other nominations so the vote was unanimous. It must have been noticed that the traditional "Aye" lacked enthusiasm and volume. Men whose minds are otherwise engaged automatically make the correct response but in a voice lacking feeling. So it was when the small boy found himself being hailed as the King of England.

Chapter Eleven
978AD – 980AD

A coronation date was arranged, to be held at Kingston, near the source of the great river Thames. The 14th of April in the year of our Lord nine hundred and seventy eight was chosen to give time for everyone to make arrangements to travel. Obviously the court needed to move so that the Winchester palace could be cleaned and prepared with new provisions. The Council therefore chose another palace with the facilities to accommodate the mass of thegns, townsmen and even princes who would be invited. All subjects who could attend must do so, the Councilmen stressed and this was the order cried in the market place at Wymburne some weeks later.

The oath of loyalty was taken collectively, for which everyone was grateful, raising the right hand to swear allegiance. It was thought that taking each man's individual statement would be too tiring for the young boy. Ethelred still seemed unaware of the drama taking place around him. He fingered the royal robes as if they were strange to him, stroking the fur as if it belonged to a favoured puppy, looking round with his slightly protuberant eyes as if he were seeking someone familiar.

Alfred left court as soon as he felt it was possible, anxious not to call attention to himself or Uddings. He rode in company and if any noticed he was quieter than usual they said nothing about it. No-one asked questions, perhaps because they thought Udric had been killed in the hunting accident. Many of the late King's companions that day in the woods around Corfe, who had enjoyed an innocent hunting party, were no longer mentioned. Their fathers were silent, grieving for lost heirs, lost opportunities.

Several weeks passed before a writ arrived at Uddings directing Alfred to attend the shire court to deputise for the sheriff on the new King's behalf.

"I must go for not to obey such a command could lead to trouble. Our lands are held of the King and we must be grateful that the late Lord Edward's former officers are still needed. No doubt several towns have been asked to send the man used by the sheriff in the past." Strain was showing on his face; his eyes had become wary, smudged with dark tones.

Brith held him tightly, concerned that almost overnight he had aged.

She kissed him full on the lips, assuring him of her love and loyalty. They stayed wrapped in an intimate embrace while Udric crept out to ready his father's horse.

At Dorchester there was more concern about building up the ravaged sheep flocks than over the recent election of a new King. A message asking Alfred to call on Bishop Aelfwold as soon as possible alleviated the boredom of the minor cases they had to hear. He hurried to the Bishop's quarters before the daylight began to fade. A servant took him to the private solar where he found the cleric wrapped up warmly in bed.

"Alfred," croaked the old man, "I am sick unto death but must pass on a message. It is a message for 'Udda.'"

Alfred looked up in surprise, then behind him to see if others were present. He had not been addressed by the old form of his name for many years.

"Come closer for my voice is weak." The Bishop's hands were frail and age-mottled, the eyes sunken and watery. Kneeling down, Alfred took the old man's hand.

"Wain the ploughman is dead. His daughter Emma begs that 'Udda' take her, as a servant if need be. I have no idea what it is all about, although the priest who told me this seemed ill at ease. The girl is widowed recently. You would have to buy her if her father was a bondsman. Will this man 'Udda' do that?"

Alfred struggled to remember what Udric had said, how he had used a long dead ancestor's name to protect himself. Obviously the Bishop thought he was party to a romance, not in a conspiracy. He may even have remembered that his grandfather was named Udda, for most introductions involved stating one's family line.

"My Lord I cannot deceive you. You sponsored me when I was but a boy, my own father killed in battle at the King's side. May I confess to you now?" With difficulty the Bishop raised himself on the fur covered bed, and held out the ring for Alfred to kiss.

Telling the Bishop of Udric's narrow escape from death and of the assassination of King Edward, Alfred felt the lifting of a great burden from his shoulders.

"So you see my lord, if my son openly buys the woman from Lady Elfrida, questions would be asked. How did her father die?"

"Ah yes! The ploughman's hands became infected and he died of a great fever, so the messenger informed me," replied the Bishop suddenly remembering the details.

"The rope burns!" Alfred recalled Udric mentioning how bad Wain's hands had been after pulling him out of the well. He was not aware he had spoken aloud until the Bishop spoke again.

"If she remarries or becomes a servant, her mother must be part of the bargain for the cottage will have been given to the new plough hand."

"Could you ask her wait in a nunnery? Women do visit for comfort don't they? It would delay an unwelcome marriage that has been suggested for no priest would marry a girl who has arranged a visit to a house of God. In that way my son Udric would not be involved directly with the King's mother or her clerks. The girl and her mother will both be welcome at Uddings. Their man saved my son's life and they have lost him. Would you arrange this for me?" Alfred looked up into the Bishop's pale eyes. He had not realised that the man who saved his only son had lost his life doing so and felt strongly that he owed the family all the help he could give them.

Obviously impressed by Alfred's impassioned plea the Bishop agreed to put the suggestion into effect. Asking him to call his private clerk, the Bishop dismissed him with a blessing, saying that he would pray for Lord Edward's soul.

For the rest of the week Alfred continued to hear cases with the men from other towns acting as deputy sheriffs, but had great difficulty keeping his attention on the matter in hand. Fortunately no-one seemed to notice his pre-occupation, presuming that he was deep in thought over the matters before him. The jurymen stood patiently waiting for his summing up, a few moving closer to the brazier when the chill of the day began to penetrate even the thickest cloak.

It was shortly after his return to Uddings, while struggling to write his reports accounting for the small fines, that a messenger bearing the Abbey colours arrived with news of the death of Bishop Aelfwold, and the appointment of another in his place.

"My Lord Aelfwold bade me tell you that 'all was done as you asked'. He lies in the Abbey, God rest his soul."

Not realising the impact of what he had just told Alfred, he was surprised when he was asked to repeat the Bishop's message, but presuming the recipient was becoming hard of hearing he repeated his former lord's message more loudly.

Alfred did not have the opportunity to give the news to Udric until after the meal when they were able to discuss the plight of the women. Udric shared their small private room on the grounds of safety. Each night he dragged his paillasse across the doorway, deliberately turning his face away from his parents to give them privacy.

"I owe it to Wain to take in his womenfolk. I realise that to go to the nunnery and demand they come back with me would look more than passing strange. But then, it is not really for me to say that they can come here father. I beg your pardon for presuming..."

"It never crossed my mind to refuse aid to the man's family Udric," interrupted Alfred placing a hand on his son's broad shoulder. "As you say, to get them out without calling attention to you or Uddings for that matter, is going to be difficult. Let's hope the women will be patient."

It was not until the harvest was over and the autumn chores well under way that the sheriff called Alfred to Shaftesbury to join him at a difficult court hearing. Needing a guard for the journey, Udric was able to accompany his father without calling attention to himself. He took the precaution of wearing clothes with muted colours. Indeed even his father commented that he looked like a servant, even though he was wearing a sword which would normally denote a higher status than he possessed.

"But that is exactly what I hope to look like. What if the Lady still has spies? Even though her beloved son is now king, which has been her lifelong ambition, she may know that I escaped from the well if the bodies were removed. Her dwarf will know that my corpse is not among the dead."

Two men from the garrison had been hired to act as guards, the steward having allowed them time away from their duties at the King's palace. His curiosity had been aroused but apparently satisfied when Alfred explained that he was acting as a magistrate and that might make him unpopular. Guards would increase the solemnity of the occasion and be returned as soon as possible.

Leaving the temporary court room after the last session, Alfred and Udric casually made their way to the Abbess's lodgings beside the nunnery. Sited on the top of a bluff above the town, the view across the valley was magnificent. An elderly ostler took the horses, grumbling at the number of beasts before directing them to a neat, two storey house built of the same grey stone as the perimeter walls.

Seated on a high backed chair, beneath an elaborately carved crucifix, the Abbess imperiously dismissed the novice to the far corner of her chamber with a flick of her wrist. Bowing low, Udric and Alfred introduced themselves.

"My lady, I believe the late Bishop of Sherburne sent a young girl and her widowed mother to you for shelter. We are here to conduct them to Wymburne if they are willing to accompany us. Their man was a distant relative of mine." Alfred crossed his fingers behind his back and hoped that God, in the circumstances, would forgive the lie. He tried to keep his face neutral, almost bored as if having to take a kin's womenfolk into his own household was an imposition which he would doing out of Christian charity.

Having taken the two women into the nunnery on the Bishop's command, and having received no funds or treasure on their behalf, the Abbess gladly sent for Wain's widow and her daughter.

"I cannot force them to leave with you, but two extra mouths to feed is a burden. There was no explanation for their arrival here and I have asked for none but..."

The Abbess was interrupted by the arrival of her unwanted guests saving Alfred further justification for their need of shelter. Alfred embraced the older woman, expressing his heartfelt sorrow over her husband's death. He held her for moment longer than was proper reminding her in a whisper of his identify. She brought her daughter forward, still wearing a coarsely woven scarf.

"Emma my dear, this is your father's friend. He wishes to take us to Wymburne with him. Are you willing to go with him?"

Udric had not said a word since the girl had entered the room. Although her head was modestly lowered, he could see her clearly defined eyebrows, dark hair and shapely hands clutching the shawl. Under the dirty tear marks her face was delicate, with high cheek bones. She nodded her agreement, biting her lip with nervousness.

Aware that the Abbess was watching them closely, Alfred hastily decided to take charge of the situation by emphasising that they would be leaving shortly while daylight lasted.

"May we collect our possessions, Lady Mother?" They both bobbed a curtsy to the mother Superior before Emma and her mother left the room.

"I believe they are good weavers," commented Alfred to fill the silence. He hoped to give the impression that the women would be servants.

The Abbess nodded, clearly anxious to bring this meeting to a close. She had not even offered them refreshment. Calling a servant to let his party out she smiled grimly as he put some silver into the offertory box by the door and took his leave. Taking Emma's arm, Udric ushered her to the spare horses which were already harnessed for the return journey. Seeing their consternation Alfred realised that neither of them had ridden a horse before, a complication which he had not foreseen. They were eventually placed on the cruppers of the two reliable geldings, seated behind the guards. The party set off at a walk, Udric constantly glancing behind at Emma. Turning South on the Cranburne road, Udric and his father cantered on to Uddings, leaving the soldiers to ride more slowly with the women.

Horns announced their arrival beneath a grey sky, the sun obscured by billowing mist. All day the clouds had built up and now threatened a storm. Udric hoped fervently that the women would arrive before the rain.

They joined Brith in the privacy of the sleeping quarters. "Emma and her mother are riding pillion behind the Steward's men," said Udric in a matter of fact tone. "They have not spoken much. I do not know how much she knows of what her father did for me but I feel badly that his hands were so badly hurt that they festered."

"They will be here any moment. Do I welcome them as guests or new servants?" enquired Brith practically.

Discussing this point, Alfred repeated that he had purposely given the Abbess the impression that they were to be servants so that little importance would be given to their leaving.

"I suggest that for now they occupy the room next to the store room. It is comfortable and dry. I will have mattresses made now. We can find out what they can do shortly. Emma and her mother are still in mourning. The girl's husband was one of the soldiers who were killed at the well. I doubt if Wain told her that her husband's body was thrown in. She may believe that he died in the hunting accident, the same story told by Lady Elfrida."

Udric left to help prepare for the arrival of Emma and her mother. The moment he saw her he had felt himself short of breath. She was no lowly or cowed servant girl in his mind. Despite bowing her head in the presence of the Abbess, when she turned to leave the room he noticed that her head was erect. She almost seemed to glide when she had followed her mother. He reddened, remembering his nakedness when the white shroud had slipped in Wain's small cottage. Thank God it was not before the girl, he thought as he energetically stuffed fresh straw into the mattresses.

As soon as he had gone, Alfred turned to Brith, the corners of his mouth rising in an enigmatic smile. "The girl is comely. Udric was quite tongue tied. She really is a beauty. Of course she is still wearing her shawl, but in a few months she will relax. It's not right to put a widow out when her husband dies. The Lady Elfrida wasted no time in enforcing her rights. A new plough hand moved in almost before Wain was cold in the ground. Our message through the Bishop must have been a godsend." His voice had developed an edge of anger when he spoke of the late King's step-mother. Brith put her hand on his arm, showing her support but simultaneously urging him to be calm. With a sigh as the tension left his shoulders, they embraced, tenderly renewing that loving bond which they both valued so much.

Rumbles of thunder sounded in the distance as the two guards and their passengers made their way steadily down the track to the house. As soon as they had dismounted the two men saluted Alfred and cantered off hoping to out-run the storm and get back to the palace before nightfall.

Udric arranged that he was first to greet Emma when she arrived.

"I hope the ride was not too uncomfortable? Come inside out of the weather. You have got here just before the rain."

Emma smiled at him, thanked him for his concern before asking if she and her mother should see the master or the man in charge straight away.

After the initial introductions and greetings in the hall, Alfred lowered his voice so that only the four of them could hear. "My wife is a lady of great compassion but also very practical. She will help you all she can, as will Udric and I, but hear what Lady Brith has to say." He glanced reassuringly and lovingly at his wife who's ready, dimpled smile acknowledged his praise.

"We think it best if we say that you have come to Uddings to make hangings for the hall. You both know the importance of saying nothing about the recent events at Corfe. The Lady Elfrida is now the most important Lady in the land and she is known to be spiteful. Forgive us for directing that you spend time in a nunnery. At the time it seemed the safest place." Brith smiled at the two women, both of whom wore homespun kirtles and shawls.

"With the King's coronation at Easter, the mystery over the death of Edward will fade from memory and we will all feel a great deal safer," said Alfred. "You will take your meals in the hall with the others who have no hearth of their own. Tomorrow we will make a start on the looms you need. God willing, you will be safe here and can grieve in your own time. Your man saved my son and for that you have my greatest thanks."

The two women acknowledged both the thanks and the wise advice of their hosts. Initially the widow's speech was accented and difficult to understand but as she relaxed she spoke more slowly, emphasising words with her hands, coarse from hard manual work.

"Come, I will show you a private chamber. It was a store room so it is secure, dry and close to the hall. Until a cottage can be built we hope you will be comfortable here."

Udric led Emma and her mother to their room. Warm covers had been laid over the soft mattresses. The small window had stout shutters but two cresset oil lamps lit the snug quarters which would now be theirs.

There were no other comforts in the tiny space which even after all this time still had that smell of new wood. Pegs were already fastened to all the walls which had previously been used for suspending baskets of food high above the reach of any vermin. The floor of packed earth would be cold underfoot but similar to the family accommodation which they had been forced to vacate.

The short winter days passed with cold winds, snow, rain and fog. Emma and her mother were indeed skilled weavers, producing fine lengths of woven cloth from the summer fleeces. Much of the yarn had been dyed in soft greens, browns and deep red. They worked so fast that more women were asked to spin at home. Using lengths of wood wrapped round with the warp threads instead of just hanging stones, the length of the pieces had been extended. The wooden weight was turned to release more thread as the fabric was woven. Instead of standing all the time the two women had high stools, objects of curiosity as far as other weavers were concerned.

Udric continued to admire Emma from a distance. She still wore her mourning shawl and it would have been improper for him to make overt advances towards her until she chose to put it aside. For months neither she nor her mother had encouraged friendships, keeping very much to themselves and talking in low voices as they threw shuttles from one side of the weft to the other.

A little concerned that Udric was possibly attracted to the girl out of regard for her father who had saved his life, Alfred spoke to his son on the subject of a wife.

"You should look around you at court as soon as it is safe to return; many young women accompany Lady Elfrida or the Ealdormen's wives. You might meet a girl at the coronation. After all, the nobles and large landowners are expected to attend. Many bring wives and daughters to the celebration."

"Mm…, that is on the fourteenth day of April isn't it? Do you think it will be safe for me to attend? Poor boy, Ethelred is not much more than ten years old, still a child; I would not be in his shoes and especially not with a mother like his!"

Udric said he would bear his father's advice in mind, determined to be more discreet when he cast wistful, longing glances in Emma's direction. His dreams at night were mixed, sometimes waking sweating in fear or finding himself with a burning hunger, clutching his cloak in his longing for a bed companion.

The journey eastwards to Kingston in April would take upwards of three days. With newly brushed clothes, freshly trimmed hair and gaily ornamented harness for the horses, the party from Uddings left in good time with a suitable retinue of servants, guards and a baggage pony.

Before leaving, Alfred moved his treasure chest to Hal's house. He and Aethelflaed now had three growing children, the hall echoing to excited shouts or laughter. Gail seemed to be fully recovered from her ordeal at the hands of the outlaws growing up with flaxen hair like her father but with her mother's brown eyes and slender features.

"It will be up to you, Hal to protect the family lands and deal with day to day problems during my absence. It is a responsibility you have never shirked, and of course the stewards are there to help. I now have to concentrate on Udric's safety attending court for the first time since the death of King Edward. You know we have two widows working for us. Take extra care to see that they are safe. Owenson's boys have been given the same instructions."

With the youngest child in his arms plucking at the fur trim on his cloak, Alfred had difficulty sounding composed and suitably like a conventional father in law. He blew teasingly on the child's face before putting the little boy on the floor where he promptly popped a thumb in his mouth.

"While you are away there will be no reason for me to leave the land. I gave you my oath and I fully intend to keep it. Your stock, treasure and people will be safe. Not that people should have been last on the list! No, really, go with assurance that all will be here when you return."

Hal and Aethelflaed watched the group of riders make their way to the road. She, hoping that Udric would be safe and he, vastly pleased that he had been trusted with the entire estate.

The nights that April were extremely chilly but dry; wrapped in thickly napped woollen cloaks the travellers slept fitfully beside a fire. There were so many travellers that erecting a tent beside the road was hardly practical. Most were muffled to the nose with their warmest garments, in an effort to keep warm.

During daylight they made steady progress towards the head of the river Thames where Kingston, another of the royal palaces had already developed into a city of colourful tents.

On their arrival Alfred was forced to pitch his own some considerable distance from the centre. Soon there were more camps beyond his, each with its own cooking fire. Brith had come well prepared, her food carefully packed into lidded bowls sealed with wax to guard against spillage.

Udric stared about him at the tents in all shapes and sizes, some decorated with coloured pennants, separated only by the temporary horse lines. Already the air was redolent with the smell of leather, horses, sweat and that universal odour produced by ill-drained middens.

So far he had only nodded a greeting to others of his age. None had been among the companions of the late King. Guards stood round chatting with each other while grooms brushed their charges more ostentatiously than usual, each anxious to emphasise their own lord's wealth.

That night many people renewed friendships and acquaintances or passed on new gossip. There was still some speculation as to King Edward's end, few believing that it was an innocent hunting accident. The majority however, seemed content to accept Ethelred, the second son of Edgar, as their rightful King despite the fact that he was so young.

"Not just in years you understand, but in experience. He has never led an army, never held a trial or made a judgement," said one man conversationally. "He'll learn soon enough," he added as he turned to inspect a friend's horse.

There were to be races and competitions after the coronation. Udric was disappointed not to be riding, but dare not be noticed. He was also aware that he was missing the odd glimpse of Emma.

"It is too dangerous. You will call attention to yourself," whispered Brith. "Be content to watch this time. Your father needs the favour of the King to continue as a shire thegn with duties on the sheriff's circuit. Do not take unnecessary risks at this time. Has anyone commented that there are few of the old King's friends around? I saw a guard staring at you, a fairly old man with a gap between his front teeth. Is that anyone you know?"

"Oh Lord, that sounds like Serian, the leader of the King's guard, or used to be. No doubt he has been pensioned off by now. I did not know what happened to him but like me, he will not be drawing attention to himself. The lord Hugh and he must have got back to the hunting lodge safely and not realised that the King's body was found, and then lost," he added miserably as if the loss was his fault. "No, Serian will not be pushing himself forward if he wants to keep his head on his shoulders." Udric felt thoroughly depressed, his shoulders sagged dejectedly. He kicked a clod of earth viciously showering those sat by the fire with grains of earth. They complained loudly but accepted his apology graciously.

Udric walked off his irritation, glancing critically at many of the horse lines as he did so. The animals were mostly stocky brown or grey garrons, shorter than the Norman horses bred at Uddings. Still slightly wary of the royal guards wandering round the busy encampment he returned thoughtfully to his parent's tent.

'If the new King's mother could plan the assassination of her stepson, a king, then the murder of a thegn's son who happened to know the truth of her wickedness, would pose no problem.' To most people she appeared charming, few realising the intensity of the dislike she had harboured for Edward who had taken precedence over her own precious son. Udric had seen her eyes blazing with hatred for the older prince. Edward had ignored many of the slights and taunts in favour of keeping the peace and a harmonious atmosphere at court. 'Perhaps he felt sorry for the boy, always at his mother's beck and call. Maybe that is why he put up with her behaviour. To most people doing that would qualify them for sainthood.'

The coronation took place on Sunday. Stewards endeavoured to direct people to places according to their rank. There was some muttering when rivals for the best view or a grander position occurred. Colours which nature never intended to be seen side by side clashed violently as men and women were crushed together in the vaulted building. Cloaks lined with fur, embroidered jerkins and flowing robes of finest wool were pressed up against each other as people craned to watch. The church was decorated with a multitude of candles. A young boy walked up and down the centre of the nave waving a silver incense burner. The spicy smell hid the odour of so many bodies crowded together.

Crammed together beside a pillar, Udric pointed out that Dunstan was obviously going to officiate at the service. "I thought he'd retired. He must have been forced to act at the ceremony despite his age. Poor old man, he looks so frail. Ah! He's going to do it now." They craned over or between those in front of them as silence fell.

As the late Archbishop of Canterbury placed the golden circlet on the young boy's head he was heard to mutter, "Even as, by the death of thy brother thou didst aspire to the Kingdom, hear the decree of heaven. The sin of thy wicked mother and of her accomplices shall rest upon thy head, and such evils shall fall upon the English as they have never yet suffered, from the days when they first came into the Isle of Britain, even until the present time."

Apparently the young King had blanched, almost fainted, but his mother stepped forward hastily to explain his weakness saying that it was excitement. Not being well placed at the actual ceremony Alfred had to rely on hearsay, but realised that the elderly Archbishop knew the truth of the murder. Indeed it was now common knowledge that the

Ealdorman of Mercia had already left for Wareham. He made no secret that he intended to find the body of the late King and give it the honour that was due, followed by a Christian burial.

"I'm glad of that. A man, King or peasant, deserves a decent burial. What did the lady fear? That he would marry and have heirs of his own I suppose. In the future probably but the man I knew had no thoughts in that direction. He was happiest hunting with a few friends, but women were never mentioned. I hope his body is found and given proper, respectful burial."

On hearing that others knew of the assassination of the late King, Udric was glad he had been persuaded to remain inconspicuous at the celebrations. Men and women spilled out from the church, the latter trying to avoid the mud and dirt which had been stirred up by so many people.

The Queen's guards abruptly mounted and rode out of the palace scattering the throng making their way to the race course. There was a mood of muted expectation among them as they hoped for enjoyment of the festivities which had been planned. Men grumbled when they were roughly pushed aside and sworn at by uncouth soldiers.

"She wants to stop the Ealdorman," muttered many people in the crowd. There was a general feeling of horror and shock now that the assassination of the former King was widely known. The young Ethelred was deemed too young to have been physically involved in the killing himself. The people laid the blame entirely on the shoulders of the self-styled Queen. No-one was brave enough to accuse her openly of the crime, after all, who had proof? The celebrations were muted, overshadowed by the rumour. The curse muttered by the old archbishop were repeated, exaggerated and embroidered at each telling.

Alfred and Brith watched the horse-racing but took little pleasure in the triumphs even though some of the competitors may have been riding stallions which had been bred from Thor, the exceptional horse ridden by King Edgar. The Lady Elgiva cheered her own men, persuading the new King to give prizes. There was little of the enthusiasm that normally accompanied such events although it was colourful as usual. The grinning dwarf hitched himself onto the very rail of the course, falling off frequently to the applause of many who watched his antics.

"Curses on his head," muttered Udric from his inconspicuous position far from the course. "Widow-maker and worse, but God knows the truth." Realising that people were close by and had recognised that he was muttering, he closed his mouth so tightly that a white line showed below his small moustache. His thoughts continued in the same vein but now he was guarded, his eyes flicking from one face to another, praying that they would all be strangers.

During the spring there were blood red rays of light during the night, foretelling doom and death for the inhabitants of the land. The strange curse which the Archbishop had uttered at the coronation was often repeated so that people became nervous, distrustful of strangers and discontent.

New coins were issued by Ethelred in the first year of his reign, although many of Edward's silver pennies were never exchanged. Many kept them as good luck charms or just as mementos of the young King.

Ethelred was quickly made aware of the people's distrust and dislike of his overpowering mother. In Wymburne where there was nobody with a good word to say for the King's mother, the dislike simmered into open hatred. Even the new Steward of the King's palace was distrusted on the basis that he had been appointed by the new King. When he appeared at Mass or in the market place, the conversation either died away completely to be replaced by ill concealed hostile stares or the subject of discussion was changed.

"No doubt he's got spies out. Well someone's ears are going to be burning. If my beast was so bad tempered and spiteful it would be beaten soundly. Someone needs to tell her to let the council do its job. She should get on with her sewing." The man stared morosely into his beaker of ale, the tips of his ears burning red where they peeped through his lank hair. Men nodded at his sentiments but looked round warily. "The trouble is we don't know the man, or his cronies. Are there other people up there who she has appointed?" The 'She' was emphasised; everyone knew who 'She' was.

The young King was persuaded to send the Lady Elfrida to a nunnery where she would live comfortably, but less in the public eye. His councillors nodded approvingly, certain now that the inexperienced king would be more malleable in future without her influence. The lady had left her son's court with dignity but tales of her tantrums and curses circulated quickly leaving fearful clerks and tearful ladies behind until they were sure she would not return.

Gossip travels fast, hurried on its way by pedlars, guards and travellers. Within days of their return to Uddings Alfred and Brith were in Wymburne for the market. With great relish the salt seller, a dour man who had little imagination, relayed the news that Ealdorman Aelfhere, a Mercian lord and former supporter of the Lady Elfrida, had eventually found King Edward's body in Wareham. He had left the coronation ceremony as soon as he had heard the curse laid upon the boy-king Ethelred by Dunstan. His conscience had apparently smitten him like a blinding light forcing him to endeavour to put matters right.

Apparently a soldier who had helped bury the corpse was encouraged to confess to his part in the crime and led the search party to the spot where the corpse had been hidden. The same man also admitted to having taken part in the assassination on the orders of Ethelred's mother. He described how King Edward had arrived at the palace calling for his half brother. The dwarf Wulfstan had capered about, attracting the King's attention, and the Lady Elfrida herself had offered him a welcome cup which the King had accepted. No sooner had he put the drink to his lips than soldiers had plunged their daggers into the King's back.

The guilty soldier had protested that he had not made the fatal blow. He struck the horse with his knife. The stallion bolted with the King slumped in the saddle bleeding from many wounds. Some time later the King must have fallen from the saddle trapping his foot in the stirrup. The horse was frightened and galloped away dragging the body roughly across the stony ground. When it finally stopped the Lady Elgiva's guards pulled the body away and threw it down a disused well behind the outhouses. Wulfstan had been ordered to dispatch the stallion in case it returned to the hunting lodge; all blood stained, and gave the alarm.

Apparently Lord Aelfhere had been sickened but wanted no more killing. He told the guard to get out of his sight.

"The lady is in a nunnery. Let her repent of her sins. The ealdorman had the late king's body carried in state to the nunnery at Shaftesbury. But this is the strange thing! Apparently it was not rotted, the knife wounds being still clearly visible. After washing and wrapping in the finest wool shroud a service was held. The burial finally took place in a fine tomb, paid for by the thegn. There were few mourners at the service, the fear of displeasing the new King keeping all but the bravest beside their hearths." The salt seller's voice was thick with emotion when he had relayed all the news to a gathering audience. Women hushed their children realising that there was a ring of truth to the story. Men crossed themselves with sincere feelings. Alfred nodded thoughtfully. He was deeply moved by what he had just heard. So much of it duplicated what Udric thought might have happened to the King, so much of it told of the horror of assassination, the evil deeds of men in the employ of the new King's mother.

"God forbid lord Ethelred turns out like his mother," he confided to Brith as they walked slowly home hand in hand. The ford was still passable with care, the two of them convulsed with giggles when Alfred had made a great play of attempting to lift Brith in his arms to carry her across the river. "The sooner Udric is aware how much is known and that Elgiva is safely tucked up in a nunnery the happier he will be. Come to think of it," he added, the thought just having occurred to him, "so will our two weaving ladies."

At Uddings the news that the late King Edward had finally had a fitting funeral and that the details of his death were now widely known were a matter for great relief and discreet celebration.

"He deserved a decent burial," stated Udric as he walked home after arms practice.

"He deserved a decent death," countered his mother sharply. "No one deserves such traitorous treatment. I pray for his soul, although I am sure it has gone to heaven." Her normally full, pink lips were pursed with disapproval. She rolled her eyes towards the grey skies emphasising her hopes for the late King's soul.

The gory details became widely known throughout the following year although Udric still felt it wiser not to admit that he had survived the attack. Pilgrims and loyal subjects flocked to pay their respects, reporting miraculous cures of their ailments and other wonders.

A couple of times he had caught the garrison commander's eyes during his brief stay at Kingston on the banks of the great river. Neither acknowledged the other and Udric realised that Serian's wise silence must be adopted by himself for ever, however unjust and disquieting for his conscience.

The council called a meeting to be attended by all in authority. Messengers galloped throughout the shires relying on their staff of office to afford them changes of horses and accommodation. The new King had demanded that his emblem of the gold martlets in each quarter of a gold cross on a blue field be painted on saddlecloths, pennants and flags. It represented the arms of Wessex but never had it been so blatantly paraded round the country.

Dyers of threads and embroiderers throughout the Kingdom took advantage of the decree, charging huge sums to supply surcoats, pennants and smaller worked panels for those who wished to request a favour or grant from the King. The guards at Wymburne were supplied with their tabards but the Steward was expected to buy his own, a matter of great injustice he felt.

Once more Alfred prepared to attend a meeting called by the king's councillors. Despite aching limbs and a hacking cough which often beset the elderly, Brith had tried every cure she possessed in vain. His hair was now grey-white and thinning rapidly. Normally of tanned complexion, Brith had noticed that his face was now very pale with patches of red above his cheek bones. After a coughing fit his eyes remained bloodshot causing her great concern. Many of her prayers were directed to the Virgin Mary in the hopes that she would intercede and restore her husband's health.

"Perhaps you should call at the tomb of Edward on your return," suggested Udric thoughtfully. "It is said that many are cured of their ills. May I come? I would pay my respects to my friend."

In the King's hall the council had to call for silence repeatedly. As usual guards stood at each door, now wearing the newly made sur-coats which introduced splashes of colour among the more sober coloured robes and cloaks of the thegns.

They made great efforts to quell the muttering of nobles and thegns, banging knife handles on the cloth covered trestle. Many stood below, on the floor of the hall were still resentful of the manner in which the young Ethelred had inherited the throne of his half-brother. Whether the young man who sat before them had been involved in his half brother's murder was the question which still dominated conversation in manors and cottages alike. The young King himself sat impassively on the great chair, his bulging eyes and slack jaw not endearing him to his delegates. The crown did not sit evenly upon his head, nor was he looking at his liegemen with interest. Eventually he spoke, nervously at first, prompted by a Bishop, not to convince them of his innocence, but to announce that he was henceforth demanding service of fully armed soldiers from each noble, thegn and landowner.

"For each five hides of land or portion thereof, you will provide a trained soldier, with horse, fully harnessed, a sword, a spear or lance, a helmet and byrnie, a knee-length coat of mail. I must have a fully trained army ready at all times, not a half trained rabble of farm labourers who would far rather be harvesting or ploughing the land.

When a man dies his armour will be given back to his lord so that it can be fitted to another. All this you will put in hand immediately at your own expense. Those with less than five hides will provide a soldier for part of the year according to his lands while cottagers, bondsmen, vassals and hired men will provide a portion of their produce to feed my army. Further, any man who fails to provide the due number of soldiers or tithe will forfeit his lands."

There were gasps of shock and anger, causing the King to pause in his speech. He continued when the council had once again restored order, gradually gaining confidence.

"In return, these nobles, vassals and loyal subjects who provide me with mounted soldiers and who lead their men in defence of my realm shall be given honours. Indeed these men will be the Cnihts of the shires, answerable only to me. They will sit with me at the high table in the hall, carry my standard before them and be respected by all the people of the land. How say you men of England?"

There was an instant cheer from almost all those present. For the past few years there had been few rewards for service given to the King, no finely wrought swords, cups, jewels or most prized, rings worn by the sovereign himself. The fact that the King's voice had not yet broken to adopt the lower tones of a man had initially lessened the impact of his decrees. The thought of gaining rewards in recognition of services however, swayed the most disapproving thegn in favour of the demands.

Alfred thought of Udric's ring, his most prized possession given to him by the late King Edward. As far as he knew it had been hidden on the shelf inside the old oak tree behind the stables along with his own father's treasured items. He knew that there was no way that his son could possibly wear it openly where it would undoubtedly lead to questions. To many, the hope of royal reward was an enticing prospect. The expense of providing a fully equipped soldier and horse would be onerous, affecting large land owners most.

Mentally he calculated what he would be obliged to provide. One hide at Uddings, five hides at Didlington. That would mean one soldier for a year, a helmet, spear, sword, byrnies, and two stout horses with saddles, packs, bridles and colours. In addition, rations for the King's army.

"Cost more than forty shillings a man," calculated his neighbour obviously doing his own sums.

"How are people to afford horses? Even the meanest garron is more than five shillings. I have a couple of cross-bred Norman horses just about ready but usually the King gives permission for these to be sold or given to a favourite. Mind you, Lord King Ethelred has not bothered to send any instructions. He probably already has a horse but the Earl of the shire could find out if I am allowed to sell them. There is enough business in our Hundred to keep the Wymburne smiths in business for a long time." Alfred pondered on this matter ignoring the discussion and chatter around him. A chain link coat would be a laborious undertaking especially if the local smiths were not familiar with the process. There was a skilled metal worker at the King's palace but whether he was still there he did not know.

After further debate the King's orders were accepted, albeit reluctantly by some. The Bishop of York bowed slowly and painfully in the direction of the small figure occupying the man-sized throne before facing the crowd.

"Raids by the Norsemen have been occurring in the north east of the land, mostly by Danes wishing to join their compatriots already living in the area. We have heard rumours of the war-like character of the Danish royal family. These tales strike fear into the hearts of many coastal dwellers where the rota of guard duty has fallen into disarray. When it is not strictly supervised people have become lulled into a false sense of security. The new decree means that the King's army will be ready at all times for the call to arms. They will train together under a leader, preparing for a disciplined defence of the King's land rather than just their own immediate locality," explained the Bishop who sensed that there were many who were not wholeheartedly in favour of the King's proclamation.

After a blessing, the meeting broke up thoughtfully. Each man collected the King's colours for the number of soldiers he was obliged to provide. At the same time those who owned five hides or more were to have a more ornate headband. It was to be worn on formal occasions as a sign of his status as knight of Ethelred's Kingdom.

Some immediately tied the band ostentatiously in place, frequently touching it to draw attention to their position of authority. Others examined it closely as if the woven strip might have some deeper meaning. There was an underlying feeling of anger developing as men streamed out of the hall and gathered in the courtyard.

"Tax, tithes, loans and now a bloody army!" exploded one man who had a large land holding at Hame, the other side of the river Stour. "God's blood, I shall be leeched dry before I go to meet my maker. There are four holdings between mine and the coast. Between us we will be supplying a god-damned garrison!" The man's face was suffused with angry red blotches. Fearing that he was losing control of his temper, several Dorset men endeavoured to calm him but were shaken off irritably.

Alfred waited until he had rejoined Udric before placing the ornamental diadem round his own forehead. There was still sufficient daylight to start their journey, neither of the two layers of rolling grey and white clouds looking particularly threatening.

Explaining the King's orders to his son as they rode towards Shaftesbury, Alfred recounted the effect of the orders on the larger landowners.

"I thought Aelfhere was going to have a fit," he recalled cheerfully. "He has so much land, some taken from the monks; he has to provide more than forty soldiers for his greed."

"Do you think there will be a volunteer for this service?" asked Udric when his father's breathing had returned to normal. "I mean at Uddings or from Hal's tenants? Both of them made suggestions as to which of the cottagers or servants might want to become a member of the elite armed force. For the rest of their journey, His father's coughing increased to frightening intensity in the cold air. Even with his woollen hat pulled well down over his ears and the tail well wrapped around his neck, every draw of breath was painful.

Outside the stone church the crowds were thick. Cripples limped or were being carried towards the door. Some were queuing to enter the sanctuary, others milling around advertising the cure which had occurred or the miracle they had witnessed. Peddlers sold relics or sweetmeats while stall holders noisily shouted their wares at the nearby market. The ground was already churned up by many feet, but even so sick people lay on the ground waiting for their turn to thrust a limb into the vault of the martyred King. Unusually the perfume of incense hung over the muddy forecourt. A man was being punished in the stocks, the word 'thief' scrawled on a wooden board around his neck. No-one threw rubbish at him. People concentrated on getting forgiveness for sins, hoping for a cure from some loathsome disease or ailment. There was no wish to add to the distress of another. Many averted their eyes preferring not to notice his discomfort even if it was self-inflicted. Even the children were quiet and well behaved, aware that the whole place was sacred, special, and not an extension to their playground. It could hardly be otherwise in the presence of nuns.

On becoming aware of the royal colours Alfred was wearing, the crowds parted respectfully allowing him to enter the church without delay. The soaring roof over the nave must have been designed to reach out to God. Candles lit every pillar, beneath which grateful sinners had left offerings. Pennies and half-pennies littered the floor, retrieved by a nun with gentle smiles for those who prayed silently. Someone had arranged a newly slaughtered hen in a basket with green leaves. Beside it lay a beautifully worked scabbard for an eating knife. A monk gently drew up those who had difficulty getting to their feet, sending them on their way with a blessing.

Beside the tomb Alfred knelt down and prayed. Udric watched from a distance, pleased that Edward's body now had a fit resting place. While waiting for his father his attention wandered, his personal problems being as yet unresolved. His admiration of Wain's daughter had made no progress. How slim her neck was rising from softly sloping shoulders; her erect head carriage spoke of pride, not in the sinful sense but as a valued member of a community. Grey eyes pierced his heart with each tiny glance, perpetuating the strange stirrings of longing which had sprung up on first sight of her.

Emma still ignored his advances although she was quite content to be pleasantly friendly. Both women admitted that their sleeping accommodation and the food they ate were better than at Corfe, but far more valuable than bodily comforts was the friendly atmosphere which they had not experienced on the Queen's estate. His musings were interrupted when his father returned to his side.

"Do you feel any better?" Udric enquired.

'I admit that I have not coughed since leaving the Church. Let's mount now. I had intended to call at Woodcutts farm as a courtesy to Hal. His brother should have his farm properly under control now. He shouldn't have to serve in the fyrd again for quite some time."

Stopping briefly beside the ale sellers stall, Udric quickly purchased several flasks of the best liquor the man could provide. He tied them securely to his own saddle horn before joining his father and the servants who had ridden a little way ahead. Dusk was now falling, the grey sky turning blue-green for just a few moments. Gorse flowers almost glowed in the last of the light but the air was too chill to allow their musky perfume to be appreciated by the riders.

They stayed much longer at the farm than intended, discussing the implication of the King's new decree. "Not owning my own land does not mean that a vassal farmer will necessarily be exempt then? I have no silver to buy food from others. My flock was almost wiped out by murrain two summers ago. I reared two orphan lambs that Hal provided and had to give the best ram in rent. Perhaps I would be better giving this place up to serve in the King's army." Vannson sighed, his shoulders sunk in depression. Since they had last seen him, the young man had aged considerably, lines on his face betraying the worry and stress affecting him night and day. Even his hair and beard were unkempt, the fine blond hair greasy and lack-lustre.

Deciding to spend the night with Hal's brother, the servants quickly fetched food from the panniers. Brith often entrusted one of the servants with pennies in addition to the small purse which Alfred always carried to pay for accommodation or meals if they were needed. The servant had taken the opportunity to visit the market at Shaftesbury, purchasing fresh cheeses, sour dough bread, mutton rissoles and saffron cakes. He would normally have taken these novel items back to Uddings where Brith would have added them to her own supplies, delighting in learning new recipes. Now these purchases were used to feed the hungry travellers and their host, with the addition of the ale.

"Well done!" praised Alfred biting into a cake but looking at the servant whose foresight had provided a veritable feast. The man reddened at being singled out but admitted that he had thought the party's return to Uddings might be delayed. He basked in his lord's praise for a few moments before accepting food for himself.

Despite the fact that the servants were present in the crowded farm cottage, the discussions about the King's new tax continued unabated well into the night. On a full stomach the problems facing Vannson did not seem so overwhelming. Alfred promising to talk to his brother Hal as soon as possible.

Arriving back at Uddings, he was in a thoughtful mood and sent a message to Hal that he should also come as soon as possible. Although he had not coughed, his breathing was still painful. Brith brought a small mug of medicinal syrup in the hopes that it would reduce his discomfort.

Explaining to the steward that the King required the estate to provide a fully armed soldier for a year from now on, they discussed which of the bondsmen would be most suitable or want to represent the estate in the new permanent army.

"Have the smith start making chain mail, each roundel linked to the one below. We can use woollen cloth stitched to fit, with thick leather pads for the shoulders, and elbows. It will be a communal effort to prepare equipment before harvest time but with your help it can be done."

Leaving the overseer feeling pleased that his skills were vital to the well being of the estate, Alfred waited for Hal to arrive, rubbing his throat gently.

Udric pushed aside the curtain looking pleased with himself. "I have selected a number of horses which could carry a fully armed soldier. There would be one for our own man and we could sell the others to men who cannot spare a beast. Did you ask the Earl to find out if that is what the King wants us to do?"

He picked up a biscuit and chewed it thoughtfully, recalling the slaughter of the late King's stallion. It had been exceptional, but disappointingly many of its line were already gelded.

His rather morbid thoughts were interrupted by Hal's arrival with Aethelflaed and the children. After greeting his sister and swinging the youngest child high in the air until he was begged to stop they went through to the kitchen with Brith. The cook quickly supplied them with honey cakes and other sweet meats while their father was discussing business with his brother in law and Udric.

"Any man could be ordered to go into the King's army on my order. It is my right as landowner to give such a command, but from experience I know a volunteer would go more willingly. I think it would be best to call a meeting of all the bondsmen, cottagers and servants on the two estates," he suggested.

After some time the three of them still had no suggestion as to who might be spared from their duties, let alone those who might actually be keen to join the king's permanent army. "I would not force a man to go for surely an unwilling man would not fight well. We just do not have very many single, well grown men. As soon as a man comes here he finds a wife! There must be something in the water!" Alfred laughed but it quickly turned to a choking noise. He eased the fastening around his throat again, aware that the ties constantly felt tight, constricting his breathing.

Sitting next to Hal at the meal Alfred modestly informed his brother by marriage of his new status as a 'cniht' of the King's realm. Cutting short the hearty congratulations, he reminded him of his brother's problem which had come to light during the recent visit to Woodcutts Farm.

"Vannson will have difficulty in providing his portion of produce according to the land he rents. You know the farm well. What can you do to help him? There are only some poor sheep on the land now, not like the quality beasts we bought some years ago."

Hal considered for a moment, scratching his chin. "I have already mentioned to my brother that the land is sheep-sick. It needs to be turned over with pigs or the plough, then possibly left fallow for a year or more to regain its heart naturally. I will go and see him and explain my ideas yet again.

In the meantime wool must be brought down from the fleece store for the spinners and weavers. The steward told me that chain mail has to be made. We need strong cloth for the body armour, much thicker than wool for tunics. I can explain it better to the women who actually do the work than tell you about warps and wefts!" He laughed at Alfred's puzzled expression. "I will go and see the women, and leave you to consider the problem of providing a fully armed soldier for the new army!"

Sunday afternoon was the time when most people relaxed after working hard all week. Young men and girls courted, made up riddles or made wooden toys for the children. Some even took the opportunity to wash if the weather was clement. Attendance at church was more or less obligatory, as was arms practice for the men. This week the talk among the Wymburne men was all about the new army King Ethelred wanted to raise.

"Well we do not have to supply a man but according to the King's reeve, a bossy fellow, we traders have to supply money for hay and oats, food and arms. As yet no-one knows what that will amount to individually but I tell you Alfred, some of us are only just scraping a living. It is all very well being self sufficient. We have butchers, dyers, smiths, fishermen, weavers and many other trades so that the nunnery can been supplied with what they need but there are few further orders for our goods. We need to sell our produce further a-field, say Bleneford!"

Other traders agreed that they too needed more custom pointing out that when their sons wanted to trade on their own account, competition would become intense. The debate continued, even after Alfred had left for home with the other people walking to Uddings or Holt.

The meeting in Alfred's hall was a noisy, good natured affair with food and ale for everyone, unlike most landowner's courts which were called regularly, purely to hand out punishments to those who had not worked hard enough or had fallen behind with rents.

Calling for silence, Alfred told his vassals of the new tax which had been imposed on the estate. Many people, he explained, would share the work involved to provide the equipment needed. What he now required was a willing man to join the armed force proposed by Lord King Ethelred.

The initial response was total silence. Each man turned to his neighbour enquiringly, some frowning at the mere possibility of being chosen while others were obviously weighing up the prospects involved.

To everyone's surprise, Udric stood up noisily and volunteered to join the King's army, to be the soldier his father had to provide. Held in affection by his father's bondsmen and freemen alike, there were cheers of approval when he sat down. Brith tried hard to hide her concern, adjusting her veil to cover her emotions. She left her place, excusing herself by mentioning that she had vital tasks to see to in the kitchen. Alfred had harboured a suspicion with regard to Udric's intentions but when the offer actually came had been momentarily shocked. There had been no discussion, no debate, no warning that his only son would want to fight in the King's army. He experienced a premature sense of loss, as if part of his own soul was splitting away; trying to smile when inside he was hurting, his eyes pricking with unshed tears.

Other matters concerning the well being of the estate were discussed light heartedly before the meeting closed. There was little enough time for people to enjoy themselves.

Udric took the opportunity to walk with Emma. During his absence her shawl had been removed to display long, burnished brown hair kept off her brow with a strip of intricately woven fabric of many colours. She now seemed to find his advances more acceptable since his announcement that he would be going to war. Knowing that his mother would prefer him to be married and his wife already breeding before he left to serve in the army, he asked Emma to marry him. She accepted him gratefully, a small smile playing round her full lips. "Although lord, I am only a humble ploughman's daughter." Holding her close, Udric assured her that he had loved her from the moment he had seen her.

"Had you been a Princess I could not love you more. Shall we tell your mother the good news?" Laughing, hand in hand, they went to tell their parents and received their wholehearted congratulations. Brith immediately wrapped the girl in a motherly embrace beaming broadly, the dimples appearing in her downy cheeks.

"A daughter in the house again! T'is always mens' talk, of crops, yields and such like. Come into the kitchen, we must start planning the feast for all our cottagers expect to celebrate with us. Do you have relatives to join us?"

The wedding took place almost immediately, there being no reason to delay the ceremony. Wearing a kirtle of autumn brown with a new leather belt and a veil of finest linen, Emma glowed with happiness which was infectious. Udric's heart thumped as if it would burst his rib cage, his joy obvious to all. A curious crowd gathered in the graveyard of St Mary's in Wymburne as Udric and Emma were made man and wife in the porch. With much cheering and some teasing after the Mass had finished, the young couple returned to Uddings to further celebrations.

As wife to the heir of the estate, she would not be expected to work at weaving all day but rather learn from Brith how to run the domestic side of the estate. Her shy manners endeared her to all but the most cynical. Asking questions of the women who cooked and others who spun the wool her mother wove, Emma endeavoured to learn from their answers but frequently asked Udric to explain things to her when the two of them were alone.

Taking her place beside him at meals, she copied his manners and watched Brith take small bites of food cut from her portion. Emma now had a fine table knife, her wedding gift from Udric, and used it skillfully after some practice. The sad circumstances in which she and her mother had come to Uddings faded gradually. She blossomed in Udric's love, her heart swelling with gratitude and pride; even though she knew that soon he would put on the newly made armour and go off to face the hazards and perils of battle.

A child was indeed already on the way before Udric obeyed the summons to arms. Proudly showing the royal colours on his headband and wearing the home-made byrnie, he mounted his horse for the journey to the shire meeting place. Each iron ring linked to the one adjacent so that the whole garment flexed with each movement. It had taken the smith in Wymburne many hours of back-breaking work accompanied by swear words his wife was sure she had never heard him utter before.

Hanging from his leather belt was his grandfather's sword, honed to razor sharpness. Across his back was his own bow beside a sheaf of arrows specially made from the straightest alder twigs that could be found. Each had an iron tip bound to the shaft. Spare bow strings of gut were coiled in his scrip to keep them dry. In the scabbard that normally would have housed a traditional eating knife was a long bladed dagger, its handle ornamented and covered with hide which had been scored to form a diamond pattern. Even when wet his grip would stay firm.

As he mounted he experienced a dizzying mix of emotions; excitement at the unknown, regret at leaving his new wife so soon and fear that he might not return.

Emma joined her parents in law in waving an emotional farewell, the wind blowing her veil so that he could not see her tears.

"God keep you safe husband. Foolish, foolish man, there were others who would have offered to go if you had not stood up. What if our child grows up without a father? Oh, go with God Udric but come back to me."

Those who had stood and watched turned away and went back into the warmth of the hall. Emma sobbed quietly until Brith suddenly remembered a chore that needed to be done.

"Come, keep busy. It makes the time go faster. Udric will fight well. On Sunday we can say a prayer to Our Lady for his safety." With a motherly clucking noise she led the way to the kitchen to put dough in the oven to bake. Udric had taken a good slab of bread with meats and a leather flask of ale in case rations at the meeting place were inadequate.

Soon after his departure, news of Danish invasions at Hamtun reached the household at Uddings. According to fleeing peasants flocking into Wymburne in search of shelter and medical help, they reported that nearly all the people had been killed or captured. Many of them bore horrific axe wounds, broken limbs and blood soaked clothing. Apparently the army had arrived too late to prevent the slaughter there, but had driven the Danes off, preventing the raiders from coming further inland. The Northlanders' boats had been seen heading out to sea, laden with slaves, silver and stock. With admirable calm, the townsfolk had directed the refugees to the monastery where they would be cared for.

"So the Archbishop's curse is already starting to come true," stated Alfred running his hands through his thinning hair. "For years this area has been safe; men could travel to the ports to buy goods and return home without fear. Now, according to the in-comers, the heathens came screaming and yelling, trapping people in their homes and murdering whole families. If Udric was part of the army he would feel so frustrated to see the ships leave with plunder and hardly a blow struck in defence."

"Where will these people go? Their homes are gone; many women have lost their children and husbands. Will the King give them land somewhere or do they just go back and live in the wreckage?" Always compassionate, Brith was concerned for the women who had fled the carnage. She was frowning as she considered the problem which although not hers, still troubled her thoughts.

Emma was weaving an intricate length of cloth, no more than two fingers in width, for a new belt. Her tongue was gently nipped between her teeth in total concentration. "My mother and I would have become refugees as you called them. The new ploughman came to our cottage with the Lady's steward, ordered us to leave and gave us no alternative to sleeping on the floor of the barn. It was a Godsend that the message from the Bishop arrived, in the person of one of his own guards I might add, and he escorted us to the nunnery. There was no provision for food or comfort for my mother. Absolutely nothing; as far as the Lady was concerned we were of no use to her after my father's death and she wanted us off her land." Emma's colour had risen as her anger and sensation of injustice had increased. "Forgive me mother, but God rot the woman and her offspring."

She raised her eyes to see Brith watching her, dark eyes full of understanding. Neither of them could tolerate injustice nor oppression.

"We only had time to grab our few utensils, lengths of cloth, the loom weights and the tiny hoard of silver pennies under the bed. These people didn't even have time to do that. They have lost everything. The King's steward should take those who are not in the infirmary up to the palace until it is safe for them to return to Hamtun."

Alfred had left the hall to go and watch the horses. He clicked his finger to the dog which padded out after him, nosing his hand for a caress.

The crops were ripening, turning from a dull green to the light golden brown of readiness. Insects stirred in their thousands chased by small black birds wheeling and diving high above the ground. Everyone who grew grain would be trying to recruit extra labour for harvesting but between Uddens and the Didlington manor there were enough men to wield the scythes and plenty of women and children to form the stooks and collect spilled grains. He smiled when a robin darted down and grabbed a tiny worm in its beak. The tiny, beady eyes checked that he was no threat before flying off to feed on a twig.

Now that Lent was over the market was once again full of odours other than fish. Brightly coloured lengths of cloth hung from the frames of the stalls like huge butterflies above the drab greyness of earth and faded wood. Children released from the strictures of diet and behaviour of the last month ran between adults and market traders playing the age old game of trying to touch each other. A few strangers, remnants of the Hamtun population who had sought sanctuary wandered round still slightly dazed by their change of circumstances. Some had found work but under conditions of virtual slavery getting no more than a place to lay their head and food in return for dawn to dusk labour. They had no money to buy the goods on offer and could only watch enviously as Wymburne matrons fingered bunches of herbs, leather purses and belts, knives and a hundred and one other items on sale. The market steward, accompanied by a strong guard, collected his dues officiously, determined to make his investment profit. Peddlers brought novelty items to tempt those with a jaded palate, shouting their wares in strange accents. A few spices enriched the air with a tang which overlaid the familiar smells of blood from slaughtered beasts and fowls in wicker cages flung carelessly beneath the stalls.

The new stones of the church tower were mellowing but still showed the rusty redness of the iron content. Children kicked a stuffed pig's stomach among the graves, shrieking with delight when dogs joined in the fun.

The harvest would soon be gathered, larders and store rooms filled for the cold, dark, winter months. There would be no idle hands in Wymburne for anyone could find work for a few weeks and share in the feasting when the work was finished. Meanwhile faces turned to the sun for warmth, houses could be aired and clothes dried after their annual wash. It was a time of gladness for the earth's bounty, the fruitfulness of the apple trees, the brambles, elderberries and later, the fruits of the forest.

Some weeks later a wounded soldier returned to Hame. Before his death from a wound induced fever he had told of the horrors of battles in the northern shires. Great warriors with axes and iron helmets had attacked a defenceless population, sacking churches and stealing all manner of riches from abbeys. Among those killed in the horrors of hand to hand fighting was Ealdorman Aelfhere, the man who had reburied the murdered King Edward. His son, an unpopular youth according to his father's soldiers, would succeed as leader of Mercia. The population of Cheshire had fled from fierce northern fighters leaving their cattle and goods to be taken by the invaders.

Yet more disasters and horrors afflicting the lands under the rulership of King Ethelred were spoken of in whispers among the town's men and women.

Archbishop Dunstan, ruler in all but name until recently, died still bitter over the Church's loss of influence in the country. Few mourned his passing but monks wrote poems reminding people of the miracles he had wrought, referring to him as a saint.

"Apparently he cursed the King at his coronation," commented one traveller. "I heard that Dunstan was so annoyed with the Lady Elfrida that he had to be forced at sword point to take part in the service at all."

"He must have worked for hours on the words in that curse or been inspired by God. Whatever, he knew the truth about our late lord Edward of blessed memory. People flock to his grave you know. I've heard of cures and not just through paying with silver. They just pray at the tomb and they see again."

So the stories of wondrous miracles continued and spread so that the people now referred to him as Edward, the Martyr.

"It must be quite galling for lord Ethelred to hear how his half brother's praises are sung. Mind, he's not half the man. He does not even lead the army himself," summed up one traveller putting his ale tankard down quietly on the scrubbed table.

"I heard that the King's mother is now repentant. She intends to found a new nunnery where she will live. God rot her! We had peace and made a decent living under Lord King Edward." The man crossed himself, wiped a moustache of froth from his upper lip and continued, "now we have fear, killing and everyone looking over their shoulder. I did a turn on the coastal watch but you don't hear much of it now. Does the King think that the army will protect the coast of our shire as well as fight the northerners? Deserters are living rough in the forests and attacking unwary travellers. Such thievery was hardly heard of in good Lord Edward's time."

Men nodded, agreeing that the country was less prepared than in the previous King's time.

"Unless we get a huge amount of rain after the harvest the raiders will not be able to get boats up to here from the coast which is a mercy, but half the time they just descend on a village or town and put the whole place to the torch. How would we stand here in Wymburne, if raiders came? Apart from a bow and one narrow bladed knife I don't have a weapon in the house! Tell me, how would we defend ourselves?"

Occasionally new decrees were sent out by King Ethelred, but he never commanded the respect which had been given to his father or late half-brother. People grumbled that he did not travel round the country to hold court at his various palaces. He preferred to keep his treasury guarded at Winchester, to where everyone had to go if they had business with the him or his counsellors. Wagons now traversed the county to collect food rents, a retinue of armed guards accompanying the loads of produce returning to the capital.

Cranburne now had its own priory, a natural development of the manor's own farm and guest house which for years had accommodated travellers from the south on their way to Winchester. The King may not have given much to the church, but those wishing to safeguard their souls continued to provide money or land and many small religious establishments were founded in a short space of time.

"It always was a miserable place," commented Alfred wheezing as he sat by the fire. Plain food is alright but the guest house was flea-ridden. Maybe it will improve if the Christchurch priory has taken charge there. Didn't Udda go there on his way here with Prince.....? er I forget. The one who kidnapped a nun from our nunnery in Wymburne," he finished quietly having no audience for his reminiscences. The dog at his feet twitched an ear then settled, leaning against his bare legs.

Once again the mill at Didlington swung into action after the summer overhaul. Carts of grain arrived for milling or to be stored in the barn which had been built on a raised platform to deter rats. Fowls and pigs would be allowed to scavenge on the fields until autumn. The harvest festival had been celebrated in churches decorated with greenery and sheaves, the Bishop holding a special service at St Mary's. Wearing a scarlet robe trimmed with an embroidered band the churchman seemed almost dwarfed by his clothes. Above a scrawny neck the Bishop's face looked gaunt, not because of age for he was a relatively young man but through his ascetic life-style. Formerly an admirer of Lord Dunstan this churchman did not appear to be living a life of luxury. His speaking voice was so at odds with his physical appearance that the congregation took notice of what he said. The final blessing seemed to be totally heartfelt and ended with a beaming smile encompassing even the meanest servant loitering at the back of the church with the beggars and old, sick people.

Even as he rode away on a be-feathered pony surrounded by his personal guards the townspeople felt that their lives had been enriched by his visit. He had assured them that living a righteous life would protect them from heathen invaders. The last of those who had fled Hamtun had already left to seek work in their own shire or they might have disagreed with his sentiments. Wymburne settled back into its busy, self contained pattern of life. Only the odd miscreant deserved time in the pillory or stocks. The church court held inside the new side aisle punished those who's wilful disobedience or contempt of the marriage laws deserved public exposure, a cause of gossip for a few weeks.

Chapter Twelve
981AD - 997

Woodcutts Farm became empty when Vannson finally joined the army. Hal and Aethelflaed prepared to move to his family home, leaving Didlington free for Udric, Emma and the boy child they had called Aelfric.

Aethelflaed was not wholly in favour of the move seeing it as a downwards step to a two roomed cottage. In private she had raged against the perceived injustice. There would be no servants to cook, sweep and spin. Had she not still been so totally in love with her blond haired husband there might have been more fuss. Even the children, taking their cue from her, pouted and threw tantrums when told that they were going away.

Brith tried to comfort her sister by marriage saying that the farm was not far way. She would be taking a riding mare with her so could visit when time permitted. "But my dear, Udric and Emma need their own place now. I have taught her all the household skills she will need. Hopefully you will all come back for big festivals. The children are nearly grown now and need to think of their own futures. If Hal does not take his father's farm then it will be given to another and lost to him."

They hugged affectionately although Brith was not totally convinced that her opinion had been valued. Aethelflaed left tearfully, convinced she would never see her brother again. His shortness of breath had frightened her. Back at Didlington she packed up the woollen carpets which had taken her hours to make and which would bring a semblance of luxury to her new home.

Taking a plough with oxen and seed, Hal hoped to restore Woodcutts to its former productiveness. "May be you will sell me sheep in a few years time, but for now the fields need ploughing deeply before I can even plant seed. The fowl will be penned for the time being so we will have eggs and if they breed so much the better."

Reminded that they should send messages frequently, Hal, still fair haired, led his small party northwards with a pack pony laden with preserved foods to see them through the first months. Aethelflaed was conscious of mixed feelings as she waved to her family, tendrils of brown hair escaping from her head-shawl and blowing in the light wind. The lumbering ox pulled the cart laden with the plough, hurdles, household goods, new mattresses and two wicker cages of protesting fowls. The sun was already warm, burning off the mist, a silvery haze into which the party disappeared before they had even left the boundaries of Didlington.

Alfred mused thoughtfully on the strange turn of events. "Udda, the founder of the estate, was born at Woodcutts. Now his great, great grand-children will inherit the birthplace which he was forced to leave so long ago."

"It will seem strange without the children," complained Brith. "I hope the oxen calves soon so they will have milk. I sent a large cheese, flour and smoked pork," she listed, counting the items off on her fingers.

"You sent them off with enough for an army," laughed Alfred squeezing her ample waist affectionately. "There will soon be a toddler under your feet again. Young Aelfric grows each day. His father will not know the child unless he comes home soon."

Breaking off with a fit of coughing, he wiped the bloody phlegm onto a cloth which he hid in his capacious scrip in which the small phial of holy water which had been purchased at the market was carefully wrapped. No matter what linctus or balm Brith tried, the lung hacking cough disturbed his sleep. He now spent most of the day propped up on a cot near the fire in the hall. A pot of boiling water containing pine needles seemed to be as efficacious as anything else, the steam wafting towards him in vaporous curls.

A strident horn blast had everyone on their feet, tasks momentarily abandoned. Udric was coming home, riding easily on the track between the empty fields and the paddocks where the mares grazed. Field hands dropped spades or hoes, the weaving women rushed to the door of their cottage, broad smiles on sunburnt faces.

Stable men rushed to see to the horse leaving Udric to embrace Emma and be introduced to his son, a small dark haired boy with eyes like deep pools, overshadowed by a fan of dark lashes. The welcome drink was ignored as the two parents gazed longingly into each other's eyes; a look which was private and which promised much for when darkness fell.

Greeted as a hero on his return, Brith hastily organised a feast for everyone. As it was early winter the main dish would be potage as in every other household. The stores were raided for the tastiest meats to add to the barley and vegetables. Eels, a fowl and a large side of mutton quickly filled her iron cooking pots to the brim. Honey cakes, buns filled with soft fruit preserved in mead, and fritters tossed upon a griddle were stacked on glazed plates fetched from the sideboard for the occasion. Men, women and children came from all the cottages, often bearing small gifts. Carved wooden or bone toys for the young toddler had been laboriously fashioned by candlelight when most working people had already retired to bed.

Emma graciously thanked the tenants for their kindness. "Come in and welcome. My lord husband is returned. He has news for us all. Fortunately Aelfric is already tucked in his bed or we would not hear a word. Thank you all."

Brith smiled to herself. Less than two summers before this young girl would not have said boo to a goose. Here she was, confidently welcoming guests on the return of her soldier husband.

The benches were filled to capacity, some even raising a laugh by falling off because of the press of bodies.

Udric, his young face marked by weathered lines, related tales of the fighting forces in the King's army. "I saw such bravery and courage. One man fell and as the Dane stepped over him he still had the strength to use his dagger. That Norseman will never have children I assure you."

There were good natured sniggers from the men. Udric waited for the laughter to die down before continuing. "We fought until the ground was slippery with blood. Men's brains were spilled, limbs smashed. We need shields with sharp bosses. So many injuries were inflicted by not much more than a push with that point. It penetrated a man's chest; the man fell, and died in his own blood. If I describe the horrors of battle and it sounds full of bravado, let me tell you that my first sight had me puking up my breakfast like a milksop!"

There was another titter of nervous laughter from some of the men, probably because their own courage was not sufficient to have prompted them to volunteer to go to war. Women's eyes were wide with horror as Udric's descriptions of injuries became more graphic. He was standing like a story-teller, using his arms and facial expressions to illustrate his tale. Weird dancing shadows were cast on the walls adding to the drama. Candles flickered and smoked, the upward trail curling on itself before reaching the rafters. The fire settled as someone discreetly added wood to the glowing embers, unwilling to interrupt the enthrallment of the listeners.

Udric took a long draught of his mother's light ale before launching into further description of his time away.

"The Danes had invaded in several places at once taking women, animals, stored crops and valuables. They rampage through the countryside killing haphazardly, looting churches, property and terrorising the inhabitants for miles around. What we need is advance information so that we know where they are going to land. That's where the coastal guard was useful. A man could not set his sail anywhere without it being spotted by the guard."

"Is no one on coastal duty now then?" asked Alfred. "I know we have not sent men for some months now, but I thought it was not yet our turn. No doubt the King will order a new rota. A man in Wymburne mentioned that he had not served for over a year. Mm, perhaps it will be brought back. When Lord Hugh was Earl of this shire he organised it well but the new man hardly gets out of Wareham as far as we know."

As darkness fell, the tenants wandered back to their cottages. Many of them were too thoughtful to chatter. Without exception they had cheered Udric when his tale was told. It was the women who had offered to pray for his safety when he returned to duty.

During one leave Udric went to Uddings and told his parents of the unrest in Mercia which was keeping King Ethelred occupied. The young earl who had inherited the title from his late father was proving to be a thoroughly unpleasant youth with a supercilious air and haughty demeanour.

"Actually father, I need to buy a new horse. My own needs a long rest for he has carried me faithfully. Every day we covered miles of hard ground. Several men have ruined their mounts. They have little feeling for the beast then wonder why it baulks at ridges of rock or swimming a river for them. I would not have mine treated in such a manner so he has never been lent to another man. He was stolen from the horse-lines on one occasion but found the following day and the man punished so this time it should be a gelding and not a pretty one. There is too much envy of a good horse. If a soldier falls during battle the victor takes a man's arms and his animal even though it might be tethered well behind with the baggage carts. We fight face to face and hand to hand: it is kill or be killed with the Viking warriors. There is no honour, no rule or mercy. We pray for a quick death as the heathens do. They have to die with a sword in their hand to enter heaven."

"You are talking as if that is going to happen to you," interrupted Brith grimly. "God willing you are still whole and will stay that way."

Emma was learning to ride so that when he was away she could get round the Didlington lands without having to resort to an ox cart. A pony had been found which would carry her and young Aelfric in safety.

Despite their fairly humble upbringing, she and her mother had both adapted to their raised positions. Emma was now the wife of the heir to the estate, and her mother in charge of the training of weavers. The estate fleeces would mostly be sold as ready-made cloth in the future. Some was dyed using the resources of the land, the word being passed round that the men's urine should be collected for this purpose. The juice from whynberries produced a sought after deep red. As these only grew on heathy land the Uddings cloth of this colour was popular in the Wymburne market although there had been considerable opposition from the weavers who lived and worked in the town.

The matter had been raised by the oldest weaver at the Hundred Moot court where every freeholder of property attended. Sometimes there were less than the required number and sometimes more according to the number of deaths from fevers or injuries sustained in battle. The King's steward at his palace led the meeting because most of the land was owned by his master. The Wymburne weaver complained that he was working all hours for little reward and then women at Uddings, who had little else to do, were hiring a stall at the market and selling their products cheaper than his. His tone of voice was little short of scornful.

"How say you Alfred of Uddings? Is this right? How do the buyers know that the cloth will hold its colour? I do not deny that the colours are attractive but they are not serviceable. The women of Wymburne wear more natural colours, of leaves, grain and well, nature." Frowning, the weaver chewed his bottom lip. Normally a man of few words, the loss of sales had unleashed a bitter hatred towards his rivals. It had simmered for days and now had an outlet. His voice became more and more strident as he condemned the injustice of the state of affairs which he was not going to endure. "I will go to the sheriff if necessary. It is grossly unfair that a man who has learned from his father and his father before him should be pushed from his trade by women." The last word was stressed with hatred and bile.

Beside him other men were starting to feel uncomfortable. Their efforts to calm the weaver only antagonised him. Suddenly he leapt up and flung himself at Alfred who was in the act of recovering from a fit of coughing and had a bloody cloth in his hand. The older man was pushed over landing heavily on his hip, all breath driven from his body.

"Hey, you can't go round attacking people Master Weaver. Control yourself and apologise. The steward helped Alfred to his feet and took up a position between the two men. The weaver was glaring at everyone, his eyes full of hatred. Then he blistered the air with oaths that soldiers might use, not an upstanding man of the community and certainly not a Master Weaver. Everyone was astonished, open mouths and raised eyebrows were mirrored and repeated on each shocked face.

Alfred brushed grass and mud from his cloak. His hip hurt abominably; he wanted to be sick. What had started out as a mild complaint about a trader losing a sale to the rich, deep coloured fabric which had been produced at Uddings was turning into a personal battle between himself and a man beside himself with fury.

The steward was inadvertently continuing to stoke the fire of the weaver's fury with ill considered words. Others stared at the scene unfolding before them, unsure what to do for the best. Usually traders competed on an equal basis and this was no different except that everyone knew that the weavers involved were women.

"There is no law against weaving one's own cloth and selling the surplus. You mentioned complaints but no one has come to me with any dissatisfaction over the Uddings cloth. Go home, Master Weaver and calm that temper of yours or it will lead you into trouble. I feel sure Alfred here will forgive your violence this once but if it occurs again there will be serious consequences. Who is here from his tithing? Well you are responsible for his behaviour." The two men who had reluctantly admitted being members of the same frankpledge, the dozen men who took turns serving in the army, turned away behind the weaver. Now that there was a permanent army the fyrd would become less important from that point of view but as guarantors of good behaviour the King's steward had brought it to the fore.

Money was becoming more important in trading rather than the old barter system. Udric had to carry coin with him during his months in the army in case his equipment needed to be replaced. Some of this was provided by the coin paid for the horses which, as he had predicted, had sold well. He also received pay from the King's exchequer, each man lining up in order of rank to receive coin from the Quartermaster. Most made their mark in the column. At first Udric made the mistake of signing his name but had been teased mercilessly for this skill. He resorted to signing his initials instead which was a half measure, satisfying his fellow soldiers but keeping a little bit of pride.

At Uddings, Alfred usually kept his treasure chest at the foot of their bed but with the increased fear of invasion by the Danish raiders he decided to build an underground store. Finding the best location for the hiding place was difficult, the ground being clay under the top layer of earth. He put the problem to Udric during his next leave from army service.

"Why not try the old oak tree behind the ox shelter? It has stood there for a very long time. There is a hollow inside, above the height of a man. After all, it is said that Udda took shelter there. It's ages since I went inside," suggested Udric helpfully, aware that his father now limped painfully.

During a break in the weather, Alfred and Udric went to look at the aged tree. Lop sided from having lost several of its massive branches over the centuries, the ivy grew thickly up the trunk almost hiding the opening. Pulling the stems carefully aside, Udric put his arm up inside the trunk, he felt round with his fingers for a ledge. Something fell down heavily but he could not retrieve it from the accumulated leaf mould at the base of the tree. Heavy drops of moisture fell from the glossy ivy onto his tunic. He shook them off irritably trying to peer into the darkness of the hollow centre. It smelt of leaf mould, earth and the white deposits of roosting birds.

"There is a small ledge which I can reach. It would hold a bag of coin safely. Something fell down, probably a bird's nest or perhaps a clod of earth. I will have a proper look when it is drier. Do you want to put your silver in there tonight?"

They were walking back to the hall when a servant called to them that a messenger was waiting for master Udric.

"I am not due to report yet," commented Udric as he held the curtain back for his father to enter the building.

The King's messenger bowed low to both men as they entered. "My Lords, the King sends greetings to you and bids you both attend him. Thegn Alfred is requested to join the sheriff and attend the Council at the end of the month, while Udric will join the garrison of the palace guard as soon as possible." He handed writs to both men as proof of the King's demands.

Refusing to rest properly, only accepting a mug of ale and some biscuits, the messenger left to deliver more orders on his pre-arranged route, leaving Alfred and Udric calling for servants to prepare for the journey, all thoughts of hiding the treasure in the old oak tree forgotten.

Brith grumbled fondly that Alfred was far too old to be gallivanting all over the shire. She kissed Udric quickly before he left to return to Emma at Didlington and from there to the King's court. "Go with God, son. Tell Emma to send a message or to bring the boy with her if she is lonely."

Obedient to the King's orders, Udric left hurriedly the following morning, determined to find warm, dry accommodation for his father's visit. He had spent all night comforting Emma who had taken the shortening of his month's leave very much to heart. In the privacy of their new bed he had stroked her cares away, loving her gently until she fell asleep.

Having received such an order for himself he was beginning to feel more confident that his being a witness to the fate of King Edward had never been common knowledge. The dwarf employed to amuse the Lady Elfrida was not at court. A weight was lifted from his shoulders; he no longer needed to fear every shadow or someone recognising his face. He waved cheerfully to the workers in the fields, his greetings being acknowledged with shouts of recognition. The silvery dawn had long since lightened to the greyness of a winter day. The trees looked black against the cloudy sky, only a few stubborn leaves still spiralling down in the light wind. Above a buzzard circled lazily hunting for prey rising in the draughts on the windward side of the small hills. In the distance rose the faint outline of the grey stone walls of the capital, mellowed with lichen and many winters of rain.

Alfred rode more slowly, his cough irritated by damp air or by jogging when the horse trotted. Even though he was wrapped in the thickest cloak, lined with fine napped woollen fabric, the chill air seeped into every bone. His hip ached, his chest hurt and the wind made his eyes water. On the way he was joined by others who had been summoned and passed the journey discussing possible reasons for the meeting but even their best guesses were nowhere near the truth.

A horn blew loudly summoning everyone to the King's hall. There was an undercurrent of curiousity as men filed in to fill every available bit of floor space. Some were no more than the length of a man from the dais on which the King and his councillors would sit. After a formal greeting, the King called for his guard. Now that his voice had dropped, its lower tones sounded more manly even though his physique still lacked the muscle and stature of a full grown man. Every head turned as the curtain was drawn back.

Four fully armed guards marched in surrounding a prisoner, his hands manacled. Compared to the tall stature of the soldiers who performed this duty, the man in their charge was relatively short. The young Earl of Mercia, his face showing every sign of outrage, shrugged off their restraining hands angrily as he faced his King.

A council elder rose to his feet waving a parchment roll. "I have here a charge of conspiracy against King Ethelred."

The audience gasped in collective astonishment. Scowling at the interruption the counsellor continued, holding the parchment with both hands so that he could read the words.

"Ealdorman Aelfric, son of Aelfhere, you have encouraged the Scottish and border peoples to rise in rebellion, pillaging and burning northern properties disguised as the King's soldiers. The frightened inhabitants therefore unjustly blamed your King, Lord Ethelred, for the damage to their homes." Ignoring the muttering which had now started at the furthest end of the hall, the official continued, his voice grave with accusation.

"Further information has come to us. It reveals that you have been rebellious for some time, encouraging quarrels, suing neighbours over small boundary disputes, accusing servants of poaching, stealing or cheating."

Heads turned among the crowd of men as they digested the string of accusations against the young man. Alfred of Uddings proudly noticed his son standing impassively beside the accused, sword gleaming; hair neatly bound in the royal head band. For a moment his attention was diverted from the business in hand. A neighbour prodded him gently so that he concentrated on the serious business before the court, for that was what this meeting was all about, to deliver judgement on a man accused of treason.

The vote was taken on the options to punish the ealdorman. Some voted for death, some for a huge fine, but most, that he be removed from the realm.

After a short discussion in low undertones with his council the King stood up, all sign of youthful softness gone. He grew up in that instant, became a King in mind and body. The transformation was there for everyone to see and to heed in the future.

"You have broken your vow of loyalty to your Lord." Ethelred thundered. "I decree that you be banished from this land, your lands and property forfeit. Death was the alternative punishment; take this nithing away before I change my mind."

The soldiers roughly turned their prisoner round between them before marching him unresisting out of the hall. The king sank down on his great chair, his shoulders sagging; eyes vacant as if the short burst of decisiveness had exhausted him.

Some men unwisely took the opportunity to ask the King how he intended to prevent future Viking raids. Ethelred blustered about his army being able to fight them but was hesitant about putting into effect firmer controls of the coastline and restoring the coastal guard rotas.

"With the greatest respect Lord King, the army has not prevented the raids by the Viking heathens, only seen them off after great harm and damage to property and your subjects. Surely we should bring back the coast guarding rotas. Now men do not serve forty days in the army most would be prepared to give time to guard the coast." The ealdorman who had spoken up waited for the King's reply. So did the rest of the nobles and thegns who had pressed tightly into the hall. Silence fell as everyone waited, the tension rising with every passing second.

"My council will discuss the matter." With these brief words the King signalled that the meeting was over. He swung a heavy deep red cloak round his shoulders and led the way off the dais. A clerk reached for the parchment before this piece of history was lost in the rushes while counsellors scrabbling for their own cloaks.

This terse reply did not satisfy the nobles. They left the meeting still unhappy with Ethelred's ruler-ship. "It seems that it would be up to individual shires to muster forces to defend their territory. We cannot rely on the King's own army." grumbled one man more vociferous than others. When the coastal guard rotas were firmly kept there was no trouble. Now we have Northmen seeking entry at the smallest port."

"Dorsetshire men were organised before under Lord Hugh. Let the old rota be resumed," suggested Alfred in a hoarse voice. "Ealdorman Aethelmaer is just over there. Why don't we ask him to prepare the list again?"

The ealdorman was young, hardly out of his teens. The gold chain of office seemed far too large for him, hanging droopily from his neck below a pronounced Adam's apple. "Well, I'm far too busy to look into the matter," he announced lisping through a wide gap between two front teeth. "Suggest it at the Hundred meetings. That is what they are for." Abruptly he marched out of the hall leaving the Dorset men stunned at his rudeness.

Alfred felt ill. He was alternately hot, then chilled, achy and sick. "Must be one of the King's cronies," he murmured under his breath. "No wonder he has not travelled round the shire, no-one would take him seriously."

Others nodded their agreement and hoped that when the King discussed the matter with his Council they would persuade him to reinstate the deterrent which had worked so well for his half brother.

Men left thoughtfully for their own homes, many hoping for the call to take their turn in a re-established coastal guard system.

Shortly afterwards instead of a call up came the news of the death of the East Anglian Earl at the hands of invading Vikings. Soon everyone knew of yet another raid about which their King had done little to defend the people of that shire.

"The fact that many of the inhabitants of the area were actually naturalised or third generation English Danes did not prevent a savage raid. You would not think they would attack their own people but no-one is exempt from their cruelty," stated Udric bluntly. "I have ordered a palisade to be built up around the house and closest cottages. You should do the same father, and all the men on the estate are to keep arms within reach at all times. There must be room for much of the stock, especially the horses, as well as every cottager who feels threatened. It seems that the choice of site for the house was a good one, being on the top of a rise. Even if the perimeter walls are raised to more than the height of a man, a guard could still see raiders approaching from the house."

Alfred already insisted that the men attend arms practice after church on Sundays on pain of his displeasure and a fine. Having introduced coin payments to his servants wherever possible, many now had money of their own. More and more landowners were turning to fines as punishment for infringement of rules on their estates. They followed the example of the King who often raised money for the exchequer by levying fines on people who displeased him. He frowned at the thought of further defence measures around Uddings but muttered that it might indeed be necessary. They had recently given some land for a chapel at Didlington to be built under the direction of the Cranburne Abbey monks. He followed its progress through the reports which were brought to him at Uddings. It would not have its own priest at first but he hoped to persuade the Wymburne priest to perform a Mass there from time to time.

Emma gave birth to a second child but it died within weeks, leaving her with milk fever from which it took months to recover her strength. She was listless, uncaring of her own appearance or that of young Aelfric who had quickly become a favourite with the woman who worked in the small kitchen. Her eyes were often red-rimmed from weeping, the slightest incident setting of streams of hot tears.

"There is little anyone can say to comfort you love. God must have thought that it was not perfect, even though you would have loved it," assured Brith holding the weeping girl's hand. "You have not been well. We took the poor little mite to the churchyard. It lies beside Udda."

This only resulted in another storm of weeping. Brith sat quietly until Emma fell asleep through sheer exhaustion.

"Poor, poor girl! To hold him, nurse him and name him, then to lose the child. There are no words to cure the pain, only time." Brith sighed and crept out of her son's solar; the private space used by the young couple and pulled the leather curtain across the doorway. Her heart felt so heavy, laden with sorrow. She smiled ruefully at Emma's mother who was fiddling with a distaff but obviously not in her usual dexterous way. Brith drew up a stool and gently took the knotted wool from the woman's hands, patting her arm sympathetically.

While Udric was away, Emma's mother who was staying with her, and together with the steward, ran the estate and mill between them. In a few short years of widowhood she was now respected for her skill and was no longer a hunched member of the work-worn class of humans. The Lady Elgiva no longer held her life in the palm of her hand, to give or take at a whim. Wain's so-called cottage had been little more than a damp hovel; badly build on waste ground beside the fields below the palace at Corfe. Now, she lived in her own wood-framed cottage with a roof which was re-thatched regularly and ate good food. She had bloomed so that premature ageing had been halted. Although her hair was grey, the curls were springy with health and cleanliness once she had been shown where she could wash in privacy in the river.

Soapworts, the broad-leafed plant which had such pretty pink flowers in the spring, had grown close to the stream for years and was regularly harvested. The crushed leaves produced the richest lather and left a fresh herbal smell on the skin or clothes. The comparative life of luxury into which she had been brought produced mixed feelings of happiness and great regret that Wain had never experienced a day without labour and the aches and pains of working in all weathers. Had she been able to clean his blistered hands and bandage them with healing salves, the dreadful fever which had taken him from her might never have been fatal. Absorbed in her thoughts she hardly noticed Brith's comforting gestures.

Now suffering from joint-ill as well as the cough, Alfred found it increasingly painful to walk or ride with ease. "I dread the next call to attend the King. One can only refuse if one is at death's door. I'm a long way from that God willing!"

He welcomed all interruptions to his quiet routine, being confined to his chair by the hearth for most of the time. His day was sometimes brightened by visits from Aethelflaed who brought her children to see their kinfolk. She told them of the work Hal had done at Woodcutts, ploughing up most of the fields so that the earth could renew itself. For the time being the two sheep ran on the common with the village flock while the ox was tethered beside the road to eat the rough grasses. As promised, she had calved, and there was now plenty of milk for cheeses or orphan lambs.

"He is building a new barn alongside the old byre to accommodate stores and animals. The house too needs a great deal of work, but this will be done when the barn is complete." She pushed a tendril of hair firmly under her headdress before filling her brother's mug.

"I miss the trees," she said wistfully as she described the more open aspect of Woodcutts and the village of Sexpenna.

"The soil drains quicker than here because of the flinty stones. Hal does not think the stock will suffer foot rot there. There is nothing to break the wind though, it whistles across the slopes. Mind you, there are few gnats or flies. The women do little except cook or tend vegetable beds. They grumble all the time at their lot, but none have the ability to do more than spin a little wool for another to weave on a narrow loom. The church demands the best animals or crops in tithe although we have not yet paid this year. Vannson apparently lost his best male beast last year and the priest now charges the villagers to use it for their ewes."

Alfred listened sympathetically knowing that it was common practice for the owner of the land to take a portion of the crop or flock. The annual tithe for the church also took their tenth and often, when the man of the house died, the best beast was paid in heriot, a sort of additional fine levied by the landlord.

"For the time being it is pointless to take more sheep from the Didlington flock as Hal already has the maximum allowed on the village common, but as soon as he has pasture close by perhaps he could take some of the surplus. Mind you I want the fleece first!" Seeing his sister's crestfallen face he hugged her affectionately, assuring her that with her husband's skill, it would not be long before new stock could be added to their small flock.

Brith joined them by the fire having sent the children to watch the horses. "Udric travels with the army," she proudly announced. "He has been as far north as Rochester. That was in the spring when the King ordered everything to be destroyed."

"I cannot think of an action more calculated to make enemies of the people up there," commented Alfred sourly. "Church-lands they may be, but also the livelihood of many cottagers. What does the King think they will do with no shelter and no crops to tend? What in God's name is the Council thinking of? I can't believe that he has the wit to order revenge like that."

They talked of many matters which concerned them all but as always conversation turned to the cloth which the women at Uddings continued to weave and yields from the farmlands. The children meanwhile, toured the farm with the steward's son who proudly showed them the new piglets which would soon harvest the acorns in the woods.

When Aethelflaed finally returned to her husband's farm, the panniers of the pony were again filled with food for the family at Woodcutts. Brith packed salted pork, game birds and a joint of mutton along with a pot of honey and saffron cakes which were freshly baked. Urging her to call again soon, Brith felt sorry for her sister by marriage, now living in a farmer's cottage without house servants, rather than a spacious hall.

"Hal is a hard worker. He will soon bring things to rights. The children are old enough to help now. Much as I enjoy seeing them, their place is at the farm working to improve it." Alfred softened his harsh words with a kiss as Brith lay beside him, warmly wrapped in furs.

During an extremely cold winter when even Uddings water was frozen over, Udric was kept away from home defending the King's northern borders. Despite advice to the contrary, King Ethelred had allowed the Mercian ealdorman who had been accused of treason, to return from abroad. He did however take some heed of his Counsel and posted a loyal garrison on the ealdorman's lands, at the young man's expense, to oversee his actions.

"The man's an idiot," murmured Alfred when he and Brith were alone in their small room. He uses soldiers from all over the country but does not ask advice from those who know a particular part of it. His army goes charging in regardless. Then he blames them for its failure."

These harsh words were his judgement on Ethelred after a soldier from Pamphill had returned badly scarred. Another would have to take his place but in the meantime his condemnation bordered on treasonous.

Choosing his words carefully, Alfred had spoken quietly to the wounded man after church the previous Sunday. He had advised him to measure his words a little more least someone report him to those in authority. "Don't forget the King's steward is forever telling tales. He has got more than one man into trouble for speaking out of turn. I am sure it is only a way of raising a fine but it has not made him popular.

I don't suppose you heard any talk of the coastal guards being reinstated did you? We asked Lord Aethelmaer over a year ago but absolutely nothing has been mentioned since. Many of us are nervous and the townspeople here, who live so close to the river fear a raid at any time."

The injured man was badly scarred. A deep red, puckered weal ran from the top of his head to his lip. The wound still looked angry; what was left of his eye now a pit of seeping rawness. It would be a brave woman to kiss or stroke the hideous face which now looked out on a frightened world. He mumbled a reply, suddenly calmed by the older man's wise advice. There had been no mention of any extra guards being appointed, only instructions to punish tenants of the Mercian leader so that they never rose against their King again.

When Udric finally returned he was warmly welcomed but refused to embrace anyone. He discarded the rust-tinted mail byrnie letting clatter to the ground. Lifting the hem of his tunic he showed them the sore patches. His skin was covered with rashes so that he itched constantly. Even his head was infected, hair coming out in dusty tufts. Bathing in hot water helped to clean the infected areas but it took all Emma's skill to finally cure the affliction. She plied him with fruit and the freshest foods, convinced that the salty stores he had lived on were partly to blame for his sickness.

His body had matured, his face showing sculpted planes. His eyes were bloodshot and glazed with fatigue or with the horrors he had witnessed. "Oh my love, we did indeed have poor rations and it was bitterly cold, especially at night. I feel as if I could sleep for a week!"

"Then I had better warm you! Come to bed, you will not be cold tonight!"

With gentle encouragement, stroking his chest and shoulder muscles, Udric relaxed and finally slept so that his mind and body started to heal.

He had seen such cruelty, baseness and sheer battle-madness during his time away. A noise or a smell was all it took to bring these scenes crowding back in his head until he doubted his own sanity. "I know for sure that my skills do not lie in fighting. Men became battle-maddened. Their eyes were sort of glassy and they just hacked even if the enemy was already dead. The screaming, yelling heathens with bare, hairy arms kept on coming as if they wanted to be killed. They used axes, swords and great round shields with metal points, swinging and punching with such force. The ground was awash with blood; the wounded lying among the dead. So much killing!

There was little planning for rations to reach us. No ale, no meat just hard bread. No fodder for the horses save what we could scavenge on the way.

Whatever the Council say, it appears that our Lord King does what he wants to do. Not once has he stood before us, not once has he led us. The Danes must be laughing at us; we are so ill prepared.

Arrows are bent, there are no sharpening stones and byrnies quickly rust without dry sand and oil. A rusted coat loses its flexibility so men discard them. Yes, the Danes must be laughing at us for we only get there when they have already stolen the riches from the churches and mens' homes." Udric's voice became more and more strained as each memory was visualised in all its horror.

The warmer weather completed Udric's cure but brought disease to the cattle. All but the strongest sickened, staggering until they dropped, lowing miserably. Alfred ordered the cowherd to slaughter the sick animals rather than let them suffer, and to burn the carcasses. "Let no man eat their meat," he decreed, "not even their horns or hooves should be taken in case any part of the animal could carry the sickness. Burn the carcases to ash."

The smell of scorching meat wafted all over the land, seeping into the houses, leaving its stench on skin and clothes alike. Fields could not be ploughed without oxen. Any beasts which had survived were suddenly worth a great deal. Brith lamented the loss of hide but agreed that it was too dangerous to keep any part of a beast which had died this way.

Until the chapel on the road to Chalbury was finished, the household continued to attend St. Mary's church at Wymburne each Sunday. There, the talk was all of the terrible disease which killed oxen overnight. Even at Kingston, the pampered beasts of the King had died. There was a glut of meat on the market but few wished to eat it so there were stinking piles of rotting flesh attracting flies until the elders ordered that fires be lit to burn the meat before scavenging pigs or wolves from the forest carried it away.

At the quarterly meeting on the slopes of Badberie the butcher came in for a great deal of criticism. Many of the townsmen accused him of trying to sell the meat from the diseased oxen. He was a very large man with a round face above at least two chins. Reddening under the tongue lashing he was being subjected to he reacted suddenly, spitting with fury and violent rage.

"Stop your wailing man! The beast was old and due for slaughter. How was I to know it might be diseased? It used to work the fields of Walford but William led it in that morning. There was no staggering or lurching or hopping or skipping! It was old but perfectly healthy for its age. It's you and your womenfolk who put the rumour round that it was sick." Blistering the air with a series of oaths, the big man stormed off muttering that he was not going to stand around and be insulted. "And don't bother coming to ask me to slaughter your beasts because I shall remember this!"

The King's steward had stood there with his mouth open, not making any attempt to calm either party. His report of the death of three of the estate's oxen had not been well received. The chancery department had sent a message to say that his care of them was probably the cause of their sickness. The fact that hundreds of beasts up and down the country had fallen sick of the same disease had obviously not filtered down to men who spent their entire day counting money in a gloomy room lit entirely by candles.

Further disasters struck Ethelred's kingdom when news of the terrible slaughter of people on the south western coast was carried by fleeing inhabitants making their way inland with anything they managed to rescue from their ravaged homes. The army had been concentrated in the north and on the eastern shores, ignoring the southern part of the Kingdom. The coastal guard had not been re-instated despite the King's advisors strongly recommending that a new rota be agreed. Rivers had given the marauders easy access, mooring for their dragon-ships and a quick retreat to the open sea.

"Lord Goda asked for help, having only his own fyrd men to defend the land. Apparently the King ordered the Earl of Devon to make peace with the Vikings but the Christ-less ones killed him and his men before plundering for miles inland," reported one wealthy trader who had been lucky to escape with his life and a few bags of coin.

"He led his men with blades sheathed. He hoped to trade with them and they struck him down," screamed another who had seen his family murdered. "Rape, desecration of our church, and the children taken. Why did we get no warning? There were no soldiers, just men with the odd blade or scythe. They were no match for Viking warriors armed to the teeth." He dropped to his knees weeping unashamedly.

Men stood around these victims uncertain how to comfort a grown man rocking to and fro in his distress. Bit by bit the reports of the savage attack could be pieced together.

More tales of pillage were circulated the following Sunday. Some queried the effectiveness of the King's army while others were openly fearful. "How shall we defend our town if they come here?" they asked. "Should we leave before they come?"

The young ealdorman of Dorset, Aethelmaer, called a meeting of all the landowners and thegns of the local hundreds. Criers in every village town and city passed messages and summonses so that no-one would have any excuse to absent himself from this vital gathering of the shire-men.

From the outlying areas bordering Holt Heath to the borders of Hampshire, the thegns, cnihts and freemen made their way to the moot on the western edge of the King's palace. The day was blustery and cold but the men crouched down, prepared to attend to the urgent matter in hand.

"It is time we met in a hall," muttered one man as he pulled his thick wool cloak tighter. Alfred coughed continually during the meeting, his flushed face causing alarm among the younger men. He complained too, of being cold, wrapping his woollen hat's trailing end round his neck. While sympathising with his condition, the meeting continued.

Elders stood up to give their advice or opinions. All were wrapped against the bitter wind which swept across the hills. There was a natural amphitheatre so that a man's voice could be heard by all, the grass close cropped by the sheep belonging to the palace.

The raid on the south coast of Devon, a few miles from Wareham, was confirmed. "The Danes either misunderstood the ealdorman's motives in riding towards them or far more likely in my opinion, decided that a small group of unarmed men aboard horses was a tempting target," explained the young ealdorman who had now filled out and gained the stature of a mature man. "The bastards wanted the horses and then laid waste to many of the fields and store houses. Several times pleas have been sent to King Ethelred asking for the coastal watch to be resumed but he is too busy dealing with Mercia or other matters. We have to take matters into our own hands now."

Everyone was nodding in agreement. Suddenly a man in authority was being decisive. It was decided to arm all men regardless of their occupation, the weapons to be carried when outside the home. It was not until they rose stiffly to return to their farms or business, that they realised that Alfred had not got to his feet. He was still partly hunkered down leaning on a grassy knob, his head falling to one side, his mouth slightly open as if about to speak.

Those closest to him crossed themselves. He had been among them for more years than they cared to remember. Grey haired, suffering from joint-ill and a cough he had always been a man of principle and generous. They made way for their leaders, men who stewarded huge land holdings for the King and those who had come across the river. They attempted to rouse him, calling his name and shaking his shoulders but to no avail. Alfred had died quietly during the last few minutes of their discussion.

"He's gone. Lord take his soul. He was a good man." The steward of Kingston crossed himself reverently. "Aye, the horses he bred and trained were good, really sound. We'd better take him back to Uddings."

Men gently lifted the body over the saddle of his own horse which snorted at the unaccustomed limpness of its rider.

They took Alfred's body slowly back to Uddings to be greeted by Brith who had expected her husband's return but not in this manner.

Startled, she cried out in shock before calming herself. She felt the blood drain from her face leaving her pale and shaken.

"Bring him in please. Lay him on the trestle. He said he had to attend the meeting even though he was coughing fit to burst his lungs. Oh, my love, you should never have gone." She stroked the rapidly paling face of her husband, placing his arms gently across his chest.

The elders, men from Canford and the King's estate, brushed aside her loss of dignity as understandable in the circumstances, calling for a restorative mug of strong ale for their comrade's widow. Thegn Alfred had been at Uddings long before they took up their own positions. As the King's steward had remarked earlier, he was a good man and had often calmed an ugly situation. The steward looked around him, admiring the stoutness of the walls and roof, noticing that the hall smelt fresh with only a hint of wood smoke. Even as they had crossed the little stream below the small hill with their sad duty still before them, his sharp eyes had noticed the signs of good husbandry at Uddings. Standing politely outside while women prepared Alfred's body, the Kingston steward and Cheneford's owner reminisced about him.

"He was ever one for fair play and practicality, rarely mentioned his dealings with princes and nobles. Many a man would have gossiped for weeks about going to court, even if it was only to see the King's horse-master." The steward screwed up his eyes to look into the distance where field-workers, unaware of the death of their lord, were scything grass or picking stones from the fallow ground.

"As you say, a practical man. I did not really know him well but he never offended me. Actually he gave me good advice on more than one occasion. Not a hero, and not unusually pious, but a good man all the same. Let's hope his son is of the same mind." The thegn of Canford, a tall, stringy man, had not held that manor long and was taming the land on the far side of the river Stour just as generations ago Udda had worked at Uddings. "There is hope for Cheneford if this is what can be done with heathland, not that much of my land is open. The trees grow almost to the river banks but the coastal side is more barren."

They talked quietly until a young woman came out to them. Her eyes were red and puffy from weeping, high spots of red upon her rounded cheeks.

They did not leave until they had paid their respects to the thegn's body which was now properly laid out in the hall, the diadem proudly placed on his forehead, his old seax in its leather scabbard across his body above folded hands.

Servants took up their tearful watch as the elders bowing solemnly to Brith, left the mourning household. A message was sent to Udric and Aethelflaed informing them of Alfred's death. The servant, a son of

Owenson's daughter, was practically incoherent with grief by the time he reached Didlington manor. Through sobs and many efforts to blow his nose the dreadful news of the death of Udric's father was conveyed. He needed almost as much comforting as his mistress at Uddings and rode back with Emma. Another messenger was sent on to seek out Udric and tell him the sad news.

Despite being pregnant Emma rode from Didlington clinging to the messenger's back. She understood the shock and grief that Brith was suffering.

"It would have taken far too long to get the ox in from the field, harness him up. Besides, your man was there with a stout horse. It was so much quicker this way." Her face expressed the concern she felt for her husband's mother, frown lines etched across her smooth forehead.

Mixing a calming drink, she sat with Brith until she slept, then knelt close to her in the dawn light to complete the watch over her father in law's body. The candles flickered as each servant came in, the news having spread quickly among the cottagers. The hall was filled with men and women sniffing noisily to hold back the ever ready tears. Snippets of conversation and sighs of regret and sadness competed with the old dog's occasional howl. No-one shooed the hound away from its self appointed position close to its master's head.

Soon after Udric's return the funeral was held in Wymburne, the body being laid to rest in the new cemetery. Quietly, Udric paid the priest for the burial mass and the grave digger for his services. Each man who attended did so freely, respecting the memory of a man who had given them leave to build shelters and had shared the profits of the wool crop with them. The steward from the King's palace and the thegn of Canford both attended the mass as a mark of respect as did many of the townsfolk so that the church of St Mary's was as full as on any Sunday. Candles were lit for Alfred's soul, the combined light forming a beacon of flame on the small altar in the side aisle.

"He was a good man" repeated Owenson's son. "My father's father was freed by Udda, his grandfather. I have been steward here for years and always found him wise and generous. Not like others I hear of in the alehouses. We will all miss him, young master, mistress. He has a place in heaven, but will always be in our prayers." Having made the longest and most emotional speech anyone had ever heard the rather taciturn man utter, the steward blushed furiously. He bowed to Brith and backed out of the hall, wiping tears from his eyes.

Udric stared after Owenson's departing back. His shoulders were still stooped with grief, his normally bright and alert eyes still slightly dazed as if they too had difficulty measuring the changes which had been forced upon him.

"I find myself faced with a dilemma. I need to find a replacement for myself in the King's army. In these troubled times I need to return to Uddings to manage the two estates. It would be best to see the King personally I think. To just walk away without a word of explanation might be taken as a lack of loyalty." He had stiffened automatically when talking of his army service. Emma would not be sorry if he stayed at home but he would no longer receive the two pennies a day for his service, a considerable drop in income which needed to be taken into account.

"Go carefully then son. By all accounts our Lord King is moody. Surely he will give you time to find someone to take your place."

Udric hugged his mother in her unaccustomed dark kirtle. Even her hair was covered with a homespun veil secured with pins. Her face showed the lines of suffering and there were purple shadows beneath her eyes. She had married for love not for position despite her father having once suggested a much wealthier husband. In private she rocked herself in her grief, ignoring the honeyed cakes and warm ale the servants brought to tempt her jaded appetite.

"Go with God. Good fortune in your dealings with Lord Ethelred."

The stable staff prepared the dead thegn's horse but removed the colours from the bridle at Udric's request. "Better not presume that I will be given his rank. The King will take it amiss if his colours are carelessly used. Look after the Lady Brith while I am gone. There are still homeless people seeking a place and for the time being she needs sheltering from demands."

The stableman nodded fiercely, assuring Udric that he would guard the Lady Brith and Uddings with his life. He pointed at his seax which was propped up beside the stable door. "An I know well how to use it!" he added gravely.

Carefully folded inside his jerkin was Alfred's diadem showing the royal colours woven in lozenge shapes of linen. By decree it had to be returned to the King. As he rode Udric fingered it, the soft fabric still a little wet from washing after it had been removed from his father's cold brow.

He had no trouble obtaining an audience with the King. Many of the soldiers who formed the royal body guard that month were former colleagues. They greeted him with friendly enquiries as to where he had recently been with the army before offering their condolences when he told them that his father had died.

After his suitably humble initial greeting accompanied by a small bow, Udric launched into his prepared speech.

"My Lord Ethelred, I am Udric, on leave from the army, son of Alfred, thegn of East Dorset. My father has recently died and been given a Christian burial. I bring you the colours you gave him with the plea that I may take over Didlington and Uddings from henceforth, on the same terms as my forebears." There was a moments silence as the two men studied each other. Udric felt rising tears but was determined to prevent them falling in the King's presence. For his part, Ethelred seemed to be considering the impact of Udric's statement, the eyelids over his slightly protuberant eyes falling so that they were half hidden. There were no counsellors to consult, no advice to be taken on this most personal matter.

The King sent his clerk to find the charters, inviting Udric to be seated while they waited for the documents. Not knowing the estate personally, he asked Udric about the produce from the farms. When Udric mentioned the mill supplying Cranburne hunting lodge, the King sighed.

"A favourite place of my brother! He loved to ride, to chase the beasts. My counsellors tell me that there is little time for that. Do you pay tithes?" For a moment Ethelred's face had brightened at the memory of his half brother.

"Yes Lord the tax is regularly paid to the church elders at Wymburne," Udric replied honestly. He then tried to bring the conversation round to the second reason he had come to court.

"My Lord, I elected to be the soldier required by you for every five hides a man owned. If I return to Uddings to oversee the work on the lands, then another man must take my place. At this moment I do not have such a man and would ask for time to find and train a suitable freeman. Many of my vassals and cottagers do not ride so my choice is limited. I can only send you a spearman to stand in the shield-line. Will you give me leave to send a soldier as soon as I can?"

The clerk returned with the charter setting out the terms under which Didlington and Uddings had belonged to Udric, son of Udda, then to Alfred, son of Udric. Reading it quietly to the King, the clerk emphasised the service and quality of milled flour which had to be delivered to the royal stores.

"Well, I think you should provide more flour in return for another charter in your favour. Make it for three more lives, clerk. How say you Udric?" The King was smiling; the corners of his mouth lifting with the pleasure of knowing that he had made a decision which would please his treasury officials. A crafty look passed quickly over his face before being hastily wiped away by a further thought.

"I also need a new horse," demanded Ethelred petulantly, already bored with the minutiae of business affairs. He had not even waited for Udric to nod his assent to the new lease. There had not been a word of praise for his father's long service to the King and his half brothers before him, not a word of comfort over Udric's loss.

Udric nodded silently, recalling briefly the beautiful grey stallion the King's brother had loved so much. He tactfully smothered a sigh of regret over its agonising death.

Ethelred dictated notes to the clerk on the new charter giving Udric title to the two estates on payment of the increased milled flour, provision of a horse at intervals and one soldier.

"Do you think you could find a man by Christmas?" demanded the King after dismissing the clerk. After some thought, Udric eventually agreed that a man from Uddings would report for duty by twelfth night. He laboriously wrote a note on the small tablet he carried and put it back in his scrip.

"Did my Lord wish to choose his own horse? I mean, visit the stables at Uddings, or shall we select two or three suitable ones and bring them to you? We have two five year old horses, of Norman cross parentage, presently un-gelded, or do you prefer a mare?"

A flash of irritation passed across the King's face. "I do not have the time to waste choosing a horse to ride," he snapped. "Just bring me an animal. A male horse if possible, but it must be sturdy and fully trained."

Udric nervously agreed to bring a horse to the King at the earliest opportunity. Not wishing to annoy him any further he was preparing to leave Ethelred's presence when he realised that he was still clutching the diadem belonging to his father. He held it out to the King, "My late father's, my Lord, he died at the moot discussing local defence against these Viking invaders." Udric was on one knee as he offered the token to Ethelred, his voice so tight with emotion that he had trouble drawing breath.

Udric was surprised when the King flinched away from the headband, even though it had been cleaned, refusing to take it. He was about to put it on the trestle when the King spoke. "Wear it my friend, as my thegn of Dorset. Take your father's place. You have served well in the army and shown your loyalty. I wish I did have the time to choose my own horse but the council are always pressing for my attention with one matter or another. The wretched Danes do not leave my land in peace bringing misery, even enslavement to my people. They despoil churches, steal stock and leave only bitterness, death and havoc behind."

Udric had heard tales of the Vikings taking the strongest people for slaves but was still shocked by the bitterness in the King's voice.

"My father ordered our men to carry arms at all times. Even when ploughing the fields the arms must be close by. I would return to Uddings as soon as the writ has been copied to select your horse and see to the defences of your lands in the South. With your leave Lord," he added, in case the King thought he had been discourteous.

On the point of leaving the King's presence a messenger barged in with a complete absence of respect or formality.

"My Lord King, news of great moment! Dunstan died last week at Glastonbury. I have brought the information straight to you without stopping for meat or drink on the way."

"By God's Holy Rood," swore Ethelred getting to his feet abruptly. He waved Udric away impatiently. "At last! His curse has come to nought. May he rest in peace of course, but he always favoured my saintly brother, born of the King's woman, not his wife as my lady mother. Well done young man! You shall be rewarded for your diligence. Go and eat, drink and celebrate as surely I shall." In a few short moments the King's irritation dealing with land grants had vanished. He was exultant, eyes flashing with joy at the thought of having bested the saintly churchman.

Riding home in the gathering storm, Udric recalled the quick flash of temper and rapid mood changes the King had shown. The late King Edward too had inherited his father's temper but had been equally quick to apologise for his rudeness. 'I'll choose a horse as different as possible to Edward's beloved stallion,' thought Udric as he approached Cranburne.

Dark clouds built up, piling one above the other but scudding quickly across the horizon. The promise of a deluge shortly to come charged the air with tension. Udric was glad of the white stones which marked the track. "We'll be home soon boy," he muttered to the horse who was becoming skittish as the atmosphere became almost threatening. Its tail swished in agitated circles, the haunches bunching in preparation for speed. In the distance a shaft of lightning came out of the heavens. "It looks like we could get very wet. Push on then and there will be a dry stable for you!"

The stunted bushes shaped by the prevailing winds shook and stirred as the gusts increased. Udric wrapped his hood tightly inside the shoulders of his cloak, lowering his head against the wind which now blew directly in his face.

While he was at court reports had come in of more raids by heathen Norsemen. King Ethelred had paid them a huge sum of money to leave his shores.

"No wonder he was so bitter and needs more tax," thought Udric. "What he does not need for the palaces or hunting lodges he sells to raise geld for the Danes."

The storm broke suddenly drenching man and beast. He took refuge at the nearby priory guest house where talk was mostly of the invading Danes, their ungodliness and legendary brutality towards the inhabitants. While the brothers had not approved of Ethelred using his army to turn the Bishop of Rochester off his lands, they were wholly in favour of using the army to repel the foreign hordes. There was no conciliatory talk of converting them to Christianity, of forgiveness or even sending an envoy to parley with them.

"But have you heard, the King has paid silver to the Norsemen?" stated one traveller who like Udric had been forced to take shelter. "The dragon ships sailed up the river Thames, as bold as you like. The citizens fled taking their households with them. There was some negotiation and a big sum of silver was paid to their leader. True the ships then set sail leaving locals undoubtedly grateful to the King, but where will the Danes attack next?"

"Surely once paid to leave they will come again. They have no need to even come ashore if the King is going to pay them to go away!" agreed another.

Udric mentioned that the King had expressed bitterness when talking about the Danes. He did not however, mention that the King had almost rejoiced to hear of the death of Dunstan, the Archbishop who had laid a curse on him at his coronation. There had been no mention of regret at either the Archbishop's death or that of his father. 'I don't suppose he grieved long at Edward's death. The man thinks only of himself, that he can pay to remove problems. Forgive me Lord, the King is your anointed but he does not have an ounce of compassion for others. To think that my lord Edward felt sorry for him! Ugh! Enough of that, I am sworn to him and will obey but as a man he does not inspire admiration.' With these deep thoughts Udric wrapped himself in his very damp cloak and lay down to sleep among the other travellers.

The storm blew itself out during the night leaving the travellers free to complete their journeys through newly washed fields and villages.

As the dour traveller had foretold, the Vikings landed totally without warning at Ipswich. The land was guarded by Earl Brithnoth, himself of Danish extraction long ago. Bearing in mind the disastrous attempt by Ealdorman Goda to parley with the invaders in Devon, Brithnoth had apparently advanced with all the forces he could muster to defend the King's realm. He was killed brutally and his son with him. The King's army never appeared, still being based in London. As usual the Danes ravaged the wealth and people of the area.

Udric fretted at the apparent lack of leadership. Even when a message had reached the army's base camp that help was badly needed, the soldiers had not left for two whole days, by which time the slaughter had already taken place. Not even the churches had been immune to plunder.

Archbishop Sigeric, having waited for years to succeed to the position, demanded that the King pay ten thousand pounds to the Danes to leave England. "It has to be a big enough sum to ensure they stay far from our shores," he thundered to the Council. Most of them were not soldiers, had no conception of the speed or ferocity of attacks by the Danes. "Why did it take two days for our soldiers to even leave their camp? They must be ready at a moments notice."

The archbishop only drew breath when the King walked out of the council chamber. His shoulders drooped, realising he had achieved absolutely nothing. The King would not change and the councillors had not got a spark of enthusiasm between them. People would be killed, taken as slaves and the churches desecrated. Whole villages were wiped out in a few hours, the people captured or killed, beasts slaughtered and the barns emptied of winter stores.

"Ten thousand pounds!" Brith's voice rose to a squeak so great was her astonishment at the size of the payment. "'Tis a King's ransom they ask for. We will all be forced to provide a share and the Lord only knows where it is to come from."

She had slowly come to terms with the death of her husband, living quietly at Uddings cultivating her vegetable garden with peas and beans and preparing herbs for winter remedies.

True to his word, Udric had sent a man from the estate to join the King's army. Related to Owenson, the man could use a spear and sword passably well. Being a younger son of a cottager on the Cranburne road, he was keen to make a name for himself. He had left Uddings on a crisp morning carrying his arms proudly, vowing to return with riches and glory.

Emma now had two healthy children, Aelfric, the elder by eighteen months and a daughter, Alfan. "I really do fear for the safety of our young children," she commented. "I am glad that Udric seldom goes to court for we need his strength here. He bought new seax from Winchester last time he was there. The blades have been sharpened and the men carry them, even in the fields."

Chatting with Aethelflaed on one of her visits, the two mothers had talked for hours about their offspring, their two heads close together as they worked. True, Gail and Udda were now of an age to help Hal on the farm but the fate of slaves taken by the Danes was too terrible to contemplate. "I would have them both married and safely established nearer the capital. They are better defended," stated Aethelflaed as she spun her spindle again.

"How long will they stay away with good English silver in their pockets? The army should fight them, send them running. Udric heard that the commanders despair of getting to grips with the invaders. By the time they are sent to support the local fyrd men the Norsemen have driven all the stock onto their ships and sailed away. He says they should not all be based in one place but should have camps in all quarters of the King's realm."

It was some time later that inland towns and villages heard that orders had been sent out to the coastal ports to sail all the ships which had been made in Lord Edgar's time, to the port of London. By now it was well known that King Ethelred wanted to fight the Danes at sea, before they could land. His army had enjoyed very little success on land, many soldiers becoming discontent at their continued impotence. The army boarded the ships under the command of four leaders with instructions to destroy the invaders ships, despite the known speed and skill of the Viking oarsmen.

Prayers were said in St Mary's church for the soldiers and the men who rowed the ships. Many families knew someone serving in the King's army or who sailed in the ships. "Surely if every village and town in the land prayed as fervently as we did today, God will look kindly on their mission," Emma commented. Her cloak hood was now lined with the fur from a wolf which had been killed. It had taken many washes to remove the musky stench from the pelt. Now its comfort was welcome as there was little warmth in the sun. Children played while their elders discussed the latest rumours.

"If warnings were available from beacons then the army could start off immediately," agreed the butcher folding his massive arms across his chest. "Now every fisherman is rowing his heart out to catch the dragon ships at sea. Of course, they know our shores and the seas well. As you say, lady, if prayers were the answer we would prevail. They are heathen men. Lord willing, we will defeat them." He crossed himself quickly, passing to another group to continue the discussion.

Stores had been collected again from everyone who owed food rents to the King, but this time they were willingly stacked on the aldermen's carts. Everyone believed the Danes would surely be defeated by a god fearing army of loyal men.

It was not until Owen, the cottager's son, returned that the details were known. He walked tall, now fully a man in the eyes of his family and those he represented. Some admitted to having heard gossip in the town. It had been too confused to understand the full impact of the treachery which had taken place. In the hall at Didlington he stood before the men and women who had crowded in to hear his tale. Taking a deep draught of ale he waited for silence.

"No battle has taken place. There was no glory or riches for anyone taking part. I for one was disappointed but I will tell you what occurred." As he related his adventures, he warmed to his audience and dramatised the events with gestures.

"Being under the command of the Bishop of York, we followed the ships of Thored, the Danish leader, out to sea. Some were ill with the rocking of the sea, but I was not," he added proudly stroking the small beard he had cultivated during his absence.

There was a titter of laughter from the older men when they heard the youngster deny that he had suffered from sea-sickness. Unperturbed by their disbelief, Owen continued.

"The ealdorman Aelfric stood high in the prow of his boat with his cloak blowing out behind him. He sent messages to tell us which way to steer. As the sun went down we spotted the enemy fleet, with great dragon's heads or strange beasts on the front of their ships. Their shields are clamped down the sides of the boat, the metal centres flashing in the light of the sun. They had already lowered their sails and had obviously not seen us. We did likewise quickly. The battle would be on the morrow so we ate pottage with fish and hard baked bread.

All night we rested even though there was not enough room to lie down all at once. We took turns to stand on the outside while those in the centre slept as best they could. After a few minutes I was drenched with spray, cold to my bones."

Owen beat his arms around him as he mimicked his attempts to keep warm, ducking to avoid imaginary waves or spray. Everyone in the hall was spellbound, cups poised half-way to lips.

"We sharpened our swords, polished the knives and arrowheads. The cord of the bows had been greased before we set sail but it had still got wet so all bows were re-strung by the light of a single lantern. It swung wildly, the flame blowing in the wind. At dawn we sighted the others and rowed to their flank but of the ealdorman there was no sign. Neither was there a single Danish ship to be seen. We set sail immediately heading for the open sea and eventually found one enemy ship. It was taken and every man slaughtered." There were approving nods from weatherworn men while women grimaced in distaste.

"We found out later that Lord Aelfric had sailed to the enemy at night, sneaking away from our fleet under cover of darkness, and warned the enemy of our numbers, advising them to flee. Our leader was condemned by his own actions, and we were cheated of victory."

Owen sat down, red faced with the effort of telling his dramatic story. Fists and cups banged on the trestles in appreciation before loud chatter broke out between groups of people crowded into the hall. He was the hero of the moment despite his lack of glory. He answered questions with a good grace accepting another mug of ale from outstretched hands.

When his orders arrived recalling him to serve again, he left quietly, taking his leave of Udric discreetly. "I was cheated of spoils and glory last time lord. This time, who knows?" He patted the new scabbard which shielded the Saxon sword with its bent blade. He had practiced using it either handed, cutting freshly grown turnips with ease. Had it been a man's neck, the head would have parted from the body with one sure stroke.

As head of the household and a thegn of the King's lands, Udric had been shocked to hear of Lord Aelfric's treason. "My lord King must have had his own reasons but I admit to being rather surprised when the ealdorman was re-instated. After all he had shown disloyalty before. The fact that he has disappeared only compounds his guilt."

"I agree with you, Udric. There should not have been a second chance. If there is a vote then I shall be for the man's death and not a quick one at that," finished his companion as they made their way to the King's hall. There was no sign of luxuries having been curtailed. No tapestries had been sold; no cheaper candles were being used unlike in most other houses where economies were being introduced in order to pay the silver demanded by the King.

At the Witan, the council unanimously approved the permanent forfeiture of all lands, chattels, stock and bondsmen of the traitor. "Furthermore, he is now as a wolf's-head, an enemy of the King. He has no rights, no rank. He should fear every decent man who is present here. A proclamation from the King will be sent to every market in the country," announced the Bishop from York whose churches had been desecrated. Standing before the assembled landholders of the King's realm he called on all of them to punish the traitor. He finished by enumerating the methods of killing he would employ if the ealdorman should come within his reach.

"Such language!" laughed Udric when he was once more in the fresh air. "I didn't know churchmen were so well informed."

"Where was the King today?" asked the man from Wareham who would ride back with him. "Mind you, more business is done if he is not present. Come let's get on our way. This place has a stink all of its own. I prefer the sea breeze any-day."

Udric looked about him as he led the horse out. His travelling companion was right. The yard was dirty, malodorous muck sticking to the leather of his boots. He wiped it off with difficulty, noticing how it did indeed smell of dirt, disease and the defecation of humans and animals. "Perhaps there are fewer servants to clean the place but it appears to me that while the whole country scrapes to afford the new taxes, the King makes no economies at all. We need to see that the burden is shared otherwise the discontent in the army will spread. In Wymburne there is muttering, people fined for the smallest offence and all to get silver to pay the Danes to go away. The last thing we need is a traitorous ealdorman. There should be no safe haven for the man, or any outlaw in this land. My man was in one of the boats, waiting all night only to find the Danes gone well before dawn. He was spitting with fury, not just because of the treachery involved but because he had no reward."

Only months later Ethelred's fury was further increased when hordes of Danes invaded the North eastern provinces. The army marched quickly to the Humber to contain the ravaging foreigners but the leaders had turned at the last minute, without explanation, apparently fearful of engaging in battle leaving the soldiers frustrated and angry.

"All three leaders of the army were sons of Danish forebears, apparently unwilling to slay or be slain by their own countrymen." reported the leader of the council. "How can we trust anyone who is not a pure Saxon?"

"Get out!" screamed Aethelred from his decorated chair. "I will have their heads. They have sworn loyalty to me, to me their King. It is not for them to choose who they will fight or not fight. I sent them to chase the God-damned heathens into the sea not to turn politely away in case they were kin." Ethelred ranted to an empty hall since even his guards had removed themselves to the far side of the double doors.

Aelfgin, the King's young wife, could not calm her husband's anger. A small lady, dressed modestly in a gown of soft blue wool, she nevertheless was prepared to stand up to her intemperate husband. By dint of a little flattery together with her innate common-sense, she persuaded the King to give thought before acting on some of his more outrageous schemes. Over the years of their marriage she had learnt to gauge just how much interference in state matters he would permit from a mere woman. Already tittle-tattle had circulated to the effect that the soubriquet of Redeless or unwise had been attached to his name. Often members of the Counsel had taken her into their confidence and hoped that she could persuade him to act as they advised.

She had given the King three healthy children which he adored, but while he allowed them to sit on his knee and play with his jewels he considered his revenge. It was not long in coming. Ethelred ordered that the son of the traitorous ealdorman Aelfric be bought before him to answer for his father's crimes.

As the court convened once again there were hushed whispers among the thegns and nobles. As they gathered in the hall, subdued greetings and conversation rose like the buzz of bees on a summer's afternoon. Every colour and hue was represented, especially by the wealthier men whose cloaks were thrown wide open to reveal tunics of even brighter colours.

Udric would have stayed close to Uddings as Brith was not well. His mother was thin, her eyes sunken into their sockets, her skin yellow. When the demand had arrived, she had insisted that he obey the King with all speed.

"There is a feeling of fear in the country. Fear of the Norsemen, fear of the King's anger. Of the first we can do nothing but do not bring the wrath of the King down on you needlessly. I shall be here when you return. Go with God son."

With a sinking feeling of dread, contrary to his mother's confident parting words, Udric had taken a mounted guard, young Udda, his nephew, and left for court wearing his thegn's diadem. His own son Aelfric had thrown a tantrum when he heard that his cousin was to ride to Winchester. The fact that he could only just ride his small pony did not deter the boy from wanting to act as body-servant to his father. Only the promise of being allowed to go when he was a little older had mollified the tearful child.

Inside and outside the hall the King's bodyguards were stony faced. They greeted Udric with a nod of recognition. Udda waited nervously outside with other attendants. Not having been to the capital before he had been full of questions as they approached the city. Now he was silent, the atmosphere of dread spreading like a contagious disease. He clutched Udric's knife in his belt while keeping watch on the door of the hall from a vantage point.

The counsellors entered solemnly, most wearing dark robes of the cleric. They were grimly determined to extract revenge for the ealdorman's treachery and the lack of loyalty displayed by the men who led the army.

The Bishop opened the meeting with a prayer, kissing his wooden cross as his eyes turned heavenwards as if seeking guidance from above. "God knows the anger we all feel but the sins of the fathers should not be visited upon the sons." He would have continued in this vein but was commanded to take his seat or leave the matter to men of this earthly court.

Aelfgar, son of outlawed Ealdorman Aelfric was brought before the assembly, held firmly between two burly, fully armed guards. Despite his unenviable position, the young man held his head up and faced the King bravely. His hair and clothes showed signs of neglect. A miasma of unhealthy odour spread from his body upon which the marks of fetters showed clearly. All heads turned to stare at the prisoner.

"What is the point of killing the youngster? He has taken no part in the actions of his father. I doubt if he is of age yet."

"Surely to get his father give himself up to the Sheriff all we have to do is to make it known that the boy's life will be forfeit if he does not."

There was a heated debate but many nobles attempted to dissuade King Ethelred from extracting the ultimate penalty of death. Their own children could be taken as hostage to ensure their own loyalty. This thought was not far from their minds as they argued to save the life of the former ealdorman's son.

Again the Bishop passionately recommended mercy, quoting the bible in support of his argument. His words must have affected the most vengeful men, for their shouts became less strident.

The best that the moderate minded could do for the young man was to agree to his further imprisonment pending the return of his father to face a court of justice. Many could not look Aelfgar in the eye as he was led roughly away chained like a criminal.

"Surely no man would see his son suffer for his own crimes," muttered a thegn from Hampshire who had just become a father and had received congratulatory remarks from everyone he had told.

"Normally I would agree with you but the boy's father has no honour. You would think that having been pardoned once he would have learnt a lesson but no, the man is treacherous and sly."

So the snatches of conversation continued until the meeting closed.

Explaining that his mother was gravely ill Udric left the hall as soon as he could do so. Outside he scanned the crowd of pages and servants but found no sign of Udda. With a flash of annoyance at the boy's disobedience he finally found him in the kennels where he had been admiring a litter of puppies.

"God's blood boy! I asked you to wait outside the hall. We have wasted time." He cuffed the boy round the ear, then felt annoyed that he had allowed his own fears for his mother's health to affect the way he treated a boy who still had a couple of years to grow before he became a man. Minutes later he accepted Udda's abject apology with good grace.

They collected the horses and left quietly for Uddings. Despite Udda's lively chatter, Udric remained thoughtful. He took little notice of the fields they passed, merely nodding to travellers going towards the King's court. The drizzle seemed to echo his mood. Udda's hair became plastered to his head, his hands chilled on the reins. There had not been the smallest glimpse of the sun all day. The horses walked steadily, rain drops falling from manes, heads down towards home. Udda rode the last mile to his father's farm on his own assuring Udric that he would go there directly. Waiting for a few moments to ensure that his nephew was safely on the right track, he squeezed his horse's sides gently and turned for home.

His arrival at dusk was greeted by a muted welcome. The fields were already deserted, the smoke of hearth fires mingling with the mist. Brith, the much loved lady of the Uddings household was apparently at death's door. The household servants were convinced that she was only waiting to give Udric her blessing before releasing her weak hold on life. A priest was already at her bedside when Udric pushed aside the heavy curtain of her private room.

Smiling weakly as Udric burst into her room she waved the priest away with her thin, blue veined hand.

"My son, thank God for your safe return. My time has come but I could not go without a proper farewell."

She beckoned him to come closer as her voice became weaker. Her thin chest rose spasmodically as she tried to gain enough strength to talk.

"My son, your father's treasure is now truly yours."

Udric tried to stop his mother talking to him, but she insisted, her voice a mere whisper.

"Grandfather Udda, when he was already an old man, told your father that he hid many valuables inside the old oak. Let no-one see you take it, but keep it safe for your children. Guard Uddings as best you can and love it as your father and his father before him. Bless you son, you have been good to your old mother."

She was silent, exhausted by the effort. Udric knelt beside the bed, holding his mother's hand, eyes already filling with tears, only stirring when he realised that the room was silent. The priest stood, his head bowed beside the door. He murmured the Latin dirge for those recently departed before closing Brith's eyes gently. There was a smile on her pale face, all signs of pain gone. The lines around her mouth and across her forehead seemed to melt away as the spirit left her body. He stood up and moved stiffly to open the shuttered window. "Go with God mother, there is a place in heaven waiting for you."

The priest smiled at the old tradition of allowing the spirit of the departed to leave the room through the open window. He crossed himself thoughtfully before bowing briefly to Udric and leaving the room.

Udric pulled the rug straight around his mother's body before calling for a female servant to attend her.

Tears were on the point of falling, balanced precariously on the lower lids of his eyes. He wiped his nose with his arm, a gesture he had not done since he was a child. Brith would have scolded him, telling him that there were leaves a plenty for the purpose.

His thoughts were whirling. "What 'treasure'? I have no time for hunting for trinkets. If only, oh God's Blood, why did the court have to meet just now? There would have been more time with her."

He sent a stable boy to ride for Emma who was supervising the stores at Didlington. Even in the darkness and drizzle the horses knew their way. The children too would miss their grandmother who had often spoiled them with treats. She had taught them the history of the family, of the lives and deaths of their forebears. Her comfortable hug had often comforted skinned knees, colds and childhood ailments.

The priest left to order a grave prepared adjacent to Udric's father in the new cemetery. Many of the house servants smeared ash on their foreheads, an old custom of which the church did not approve as it smacked of the old religion but could do little to prevent. Candles were placed around Brith's body as cottagers and servants came to pay their respect during the long night.

Even the weather went into mourning. Cold drizzle continued falling creating mud and discomfort for man and beast alike. Drips off the thatch puddled into the yard where miserable fowl shook their feathers before once more seeking sheltered roosts. The dogs brought mud into the hall and a unique smell as their fur dried before the cheerful fire.

Udric took advantage of the darkness to grope inside the old oak tree for Udda's treasure. As a boy he remembered being told of Udda's escape from Wymburne carrying treasure belonging to a prince but he thought it could have been part of the folk lore, the stories told during dark nights. His hands felt leaves, twigs and dust before he found a leather bundle amid leaves and rotted wood. Roughly pushing it inside his jerkin, he made his way to the midden as a genuine reason for leaving the relative comfort of his hall so late at night.

On returning he walked lightly between the drowsy servants preparing to sleep on the thickly strawed floor. In his late mother's private quarters where Emma had kept a light burning, the children did not even stir on their mattress alongside the bigger bed as he flung off his cloak.

Drawing out the hidebound bundle he laid it on the bed and cut the thongs which bound it tightly. The old leather cracked dryly as he peeled it away, pieces falling onto the bed covers between them.

"Looks like I need to make a new bag. Ugh, there are insects as well." Emma brushed the offending creepies off the coverlet.

"Jesu! A cup, a goblet! Of gold and gems!" Udric was so astonished that his words jerked. His mouth had gone dry. Emma was the first to recover from her surprise. Instead of helping to count her husband's inheritance as she had expected, she picked up the beautifully worked cup, turning it round carefully to examine the gems set into the thick base and bowl of the vessel.

"It is magnificent. Have you ever seen it before?" she asked quietly.

Udric shook his head rapidly confirming that he had never set eyes on it before, nor had it been mentioned to him with any certainty.

"Although I do remember stories told when I was a child of my great grandfather Udda, who founded this place. We know he was taken slave from Woodcutts farm and owned briefly by a relative of the King's father." "Let's see – Ethelred's father was King Edgar. Was he the son of Edmund or Edward?" In the flickering light of a single rush light Udric's eyes were already dark, the pupils widened. Now he frowned with concentration trying to work out when the treasure could have come to Uddings. His teeth bit gently into his bottom lip as in the gloom they both studied the gleaming surface.

"The cup has letters on it. Perhaps in daylight we can look again. It must be valuable, look at all the gems."

Between them they tried to work out the predecessors of the brothers before Ethelred and the late Edward, of blessed memory. Deciding that neither of them was sufficiently learned in the forebears preceding King Edgar, father of the King, Udric wrapped the cup in the remaining pieces of leather. "It could be buried in our mattress for safe keeping, until its owner could be traced," whispered Udric stroking the gleaming smoothness between the inset gems.

"It would be safer back in the tree husband, after we have studied it in a good light." said Emma practically. "After all it has lain hidden there for many years. Was there no silver at all then?"

"Now everyone is asleep I can have a proper look, well, not look but a feel. It was so dry in there that a flame might set the whole tree on fire. If it wasn't for the ivy a man could shelter there and be totally concealed. I'll leave King Edward's ring there. It's safe enough." He kissed the top of her head saying that he would not be long.

Putting his damp cloak around his shoulders once again, Udric left the hall heading towards the stables. He paused to stroke the nose of his horse which peered out curiously. Nothing stirred, none of the boys above in the loft awakened at the soft nicker of delight when Udric had given the horse a crust of bread. Padding quietly round the back of the stable block he made his way in the shadows back to the old oak. Even the creatures of the wood had decided not to call to each other. All that Udric heard was the steady drip of the rain all around.

'Thank God I know this wood well. To think that we played as children in this old trunk! We were so close to Udda's treasure and never knew of its existence. What a canny old man he must have been. God rest his soul!'

This time after feeling carefully along a natural ledge and disturbing only old nesting material he crouched down. Dust got up his nose and caused an enormous sneeze which he managed to stifle. Hesitantly he sifted the leaf mould of generations of summers. He jumped when a disturbed mouse or vole ran across the back of his hand its tiny claws scrabbling for a hold on his weather beaten skin. The leather bag clinked when he lifted it. Feeling guiltily relieved that there was indeed coin in the hiding place, he returned to the hall with the treasure weighing heavily inside the laces of his jerkin.

Taking off his shoes he tossed the bag to Emma and jumped into bed pulling the covers up. With a spare rug round their shoulders they counted the silver coins, noting that many were of different Kings and from a variety of mints.

"Ah wait! Here is a coin of Edgar and one of Aethelstan. Your mother must have added to the hoard when she could." Excitement was building as each coin was rubbed briefly before being examined.

They found others but Udric could not read the badly shaped letters. Putting all the different heads in a row, they gradually formed some sort of order with the minted marks but could not make out the same marks as those on the rim of the cup.

"It is the King in my great-grandfather's time we need to know," commented Udric now thoroughly irritated by the fruitless exercise with the coins.

"Who gave your ancestors Uddings?" Emma's new line of enquiry caused Udric's face to break into a wide grin.

"Clever girl! You're brilliant! Why didn't I think of the charters; I still have my father's charters in the chest." Clambering awkwardly down the bed to reach the wooden chest, Emma giggled at the sight of her husband. His tunic barely covered the cheeks of his bottom as he struggled to open the chest from the side with its stout hinge. She would have lightly smacked him but stayed her hand in case the children were woken.

Pulling the fragile pipes out with difficulty from beneath his spare clothes, Udric found the valuable documents and settled back into the poor light to read them as best he could. "Edward, son of Alfred, King of Wessex," he deciphered from one document, while another written in even smaller writing was from Eadwig and dated in the year of our Lord nine hundred and fifty six. It made reference to the one made ten summers before which set out the boundaries of the original gift.

"But my beloved, it is not Udda on that one but a different name."

Emma could read a little. Recently she had learned to write her own name and that of her husband, a skill of which she was justly proud. Udric re-read the first document. This one was indeed a gift of land to Udda in return for saving the life of the Aetheling Aethelstan from peril. "Udda must have been the slave of someone important, maybe even royal. Not even an ealdorman could pay for jewels like this," commented Udric patting the straw over the jewelled goblet's hiding place. "The second writ to Aelfred, grants Didlington and Uddings. He was the grandson of Udda, but why, what did he do?"

Neither slept well, excitement muted by grief over Brith's death. Her body lay on a trestle in the hall, four small rush-lights burning in case anyone woke to keep watch for a second night. There was still her faint smell in the bed despite all the covers being shaken. Both of them were restless throughout the dark hours, the lump in Udric's mattress a constant source of discomfort as well as a reminder of his discovery.

The funeral was performed with dignity after Mass. Wrapped in the finest woollen shroud the body was lowered into the ground close to Alfred's grave. Towns-people were complimentary about Lady Brith and offered their condolences with heartfelt sincerity.

The blessing of the priest, during a brief spell of watery sunshine, seemed to be particularly poignant causing tears to flow again. Almost the entire workforce from both Uddings and Didlington walked behind the empty ox cart on its slow and ponderous journey home.

Deciding to take the eldest Owen, who was now well into his sixties into his confidence, Udric learned more of his family's history. The old man still had the Celtic colouring of his ancestors although his face was deeply lined and tanned. He had few teeth now so dipped his food into ale to soften it. His eyes were clouded so that he peered to see the outline of the young master. Sitting together in the smoky atmosphere of his cottage Udric learnt the story of his great grandfather's enslavement by Aethelwold, kin of Alfred's son, King Edward. He heard of the subsequent return from banishment of Udda's father, and how he had died a sick, confused old man.

With some prompting Owen told him what had been passed down to him of Udda's escape from Wymburne late at night following the Prince and how the aetheling had later traitorously joined the East Anglian Danes and been killed in battle.

"My grandfather was made a free man by Udda," He mumbled proudly before aiming a large gobbet of phlegm into the small fire. "He gave a writ to my forebear as proof. We have served your family freely since then. A grandson of mine fights in the King's army for you."

Taking the old man by the shoulders, Udric thanked him sincerely for his service, friendship and loyalty. Owen returned to his stool beside the fire from where he continued to relate stories of the past to any who had time to listen.

Once more safely wrapped in the fur covers of their bed Emma and Udric shared the intimacy of married people. A candle guttered in the faintest draught which still entered through the smallest gap in the wooden walls. The shutter was firmly closed against the chill of the night. Comfortably relaxed and sweaty from their coupling, they lay closely wrapped under the bedcover.

Having solved the question of who might have owned the cup, what to do with such a valuable article was the next problem.

"It should be returned to the King," suggested Emma practically. "Udda must have put it there for safekeeping all those years ago, he could not return it to the Prince, so it has lain there ever since."

"What if we are accused of stealing such a valuable object?" countered Udric whose attention was not totally on the matter. "I can return it to the King's panterer. He looks after the King's plate and suchlike. Or should it be returned to the King personally so that he can hear how it was hidden?"

"Enough time has passed surely for your loyalty to be above doubt. Those who knew what happened to Lord Edward are gone or beyond spreading rumours that might harm you. Shouldn't you be totally honest with the King – tell him of Udda if necessary. After all, wasn't he brought to Wymburne by a prince later condemned as a traitor? It was no fault of his when only a boy. He brought the goblet away for safekeeping though he must have wrapped it in cloth or something to hide it. Surely no-one just walks away carrying a gold cup!"

"Aye, you're right, again, wife! Now sleep beckons," mumbled Udric whose eyelids were already beginning to droop.

Months later at the next meeting of the witan, Udric wrapped the cup carefully in fine cloth before packing it in his saddle pannier below pieces of manchet and fowl Emma had wrapped for him. Young Aelfric, now nine summers old, but tall for his age, was to attend for the first time, dressed in his best jerkin. Alfan had sulked, jealously wishing she had been the elder and born a boy of course. She complained bitterly as she watched her brother dress. The baby girl, still swaddled, continued to play happily even when no-one paid her any attention. "That's enough pouting young woman. Do as your mother tells you while we are gone. Just like my sister you are, pulling a long face when you cannot have your own way." He swung her up in the air hoping to bring a smile to her face as Emma watched benevolently from the doorway.

With young Owen, fully armed, to attend him, Udric led his party towards the capital. The boundary stones had been recently whitened so that all who passed would know of his ownership. They gleamed in the early morning light. The field workers waved cheerfully and the plough man nodded a greeting without pausing in his labours. He now used two native ponies to pull the plough.

Since the first glimmer of dawn light above the horizon there had been a flurry of activity. Having hidden the gold cup in the bottom of his saddle bag beneath food and a second tunic Udric had hardly paused for bread and cheese to break his fast before it was time to leave. Normally there would be no need of guards but carrying such a treasure made him nervous. Aelfric had not been told because children let all sorts of secrets slip when they get excited. Despite carrying his own sword, Udric was conscious of his eyes darting from one shadow to another in case they hid robbers. There were many who had left the army through discontent and lack of reward who now roamed the land preying on travellers or merchants.

Udric joined a party from Cheneford on the road as they splashed through a ford. They talked of their horses, of the threat from the Northern invaders, and of the King's ever increasing demands for taxes.

"He has twice paid the ungodly heathens to leave us in peace," grumbled one landowner.

"Baptising the King of Norway does seem to have kept him away though," commented another, "but Olaf's brother Sweyn, is made of sterner stuff. He refused to convert and swore by his own gods in front of the bishop. He will come back, mark my words."

With these words of prophetic doom, the riders checked in with the guards at the gates, left their arms with the captain, and made their way to the great hall.

It was there that the Dorset thegns learnt for the first time that the son of the traitorous Earl had been blinded by King Ethelred. Graphic descriptions of how the young man had been dragged from his prison and held down by the King's own bodyguard whilst hot irons had gouged out each eye in turn were told in muted tones. Many were appalled at such wanton cruelty, while some shrugged, saying that the King had the right to punish all subjects, high or low.

Udric was sickened at what he had heard. His resolve to return the cup to the King was considerably weakened, in case Ethelred jumped to the conclusion that an ancestor of his, or even he, had stolen the valuable object. He wondered how Ethelred felt after he had ordered the mutilation of a boy. Would he suffer nightmares and broken sleep?

The court opened formally when the leader of the council reported that the Danish fleet had once again left taking silver with them. "The King has shown them that we wish to live in peace." He announced unnecessarily.

There were mutterings from some about the cost of such action. Ignoring the interruptions the Archbishop continued.

"Now it is time to farm the land. With God's blessing, our stores must be filled again. Many hides of land have been despoiled by the invaders. The churches must be rebuilt and their riches restored as soon as possible. The King asks each of you to provide portions to assist in this work. According to your gifts shall you receive rewards in Heaven." Standing there on the dais, his hands raised in supplication, Archbishop Sigeric epitomised the saintly demeanour of a leading and well-fed churchman. Wearing ornate robes embroidered with costly pearls, his double chin wobbled as he prayed.

Reminding the assembly of heavenly approval in the future created heated debate among the earthly landowners. Ignoring the Bishop's pleas for silence, the Archbishop resumed his seat exasperated by the further interruption, his expression turning to annoyance when he over-heard angry comments.

"We have to provide stock, crops or silver, but the Welsh only give worthless wolves' heads as tribute!"

"What about the soldiers? We send armed men too, to serve in the King's army."

The discontented landowners ceased their grumbling abruptly when King Ethelred finally took his seat, demanding their attention for other matters of concern to the nation. He had grown a little stout over the last few years so that jowls now hung beneath his slack jaw. He slowly looked around the hall, his hooded eyes seemingly probing the thoughts of each man. Few caught his glance, especially not Udric who had deliberately placed himself inside a knot of other Dorset men.

Even when the meeting broke up there were still heated discussions about the increase in taxes required to raise money for the King's coffers.

"My wife grumbles that she cannot have a length of cloth this year. My son needs weapons but where am I to find the money for all this when the Commissioners have already taken it."

"Taxes for the King and to keep the army supplied is one thing but to give our silver to the Danes, pah!" The speaker's voice was tense with emotion. He spat in disgust leaving a trail of dribble on his chin.

Others grumbled that they could get no more stock on their grassland and no greater yield from their fields. They had no more money and if the commissioners thought they had hidden treasure then they were welcome to search. Udric gripped his saddlebag closely to his chest sure that everyone could see that he was carrying exactly that.

At the dinner served in the hall Udric reluctantly requested an audience with the King. He had tasted little of the delicacies provided, picking at the fowl leg he had selected. The clerk sighed deeply saying that everyone wanted to see the King to obtain some favour or another.

"It is on another matter," snapped Udric turning back to his companions at the table. He was not certain but thought the man had gestured that a 'gift' might help his request. Unable to relax, he was edgy all evening, retiring early after making sure that Aelfric was bedded down safely with the other youngsters. He did not sleep well, partly due to the saddlebag, with its valuable contents beneath his head, which was extremely uncomfortable. 'It would be cursed bad luck if the cup was stolen from me the night before it is returned to the King,' he thought during one of his many wakeful moments. The snoring of other men alongside also contributed to his restlessness. Without weapons, young Owen was little more use than any other man, purely an extra pair of watchful eyes. He lay next to Udric and had already fallen into a sound sleep.

It was not until late the following day when many had already left the capital, that Udric was called to see the King in his private quarters. He was quite sure the clerk had kept him waiting on purpose because of his irritable response, but gripping his saddle bag firmly and straightening his diadem yet again, Udric walked briskly up to the King to greet him, having been announced by the scowling servant. He went down on one knee and bowed his head.

"My lord, it is a matter of a private nature. May we talk alone?"

The King nodded, dismissing the bodyguard to the doorway where they attempted to look disinterested while trying to overhear the hushed discussion.

Udric drew out the bundle from the saddle bag and carefully unwrapped the old pieces of hide to expose the cup. He sheltered it from the gaze of the curious bodyguards in his hands.

The King stared at the gold and jewel encrusted goblet before looking up sharply, his mouth gaping with astonishment.

"Where did you get this sir cniht?"

"Lord King, it was discovered in an ancient old oak tree at Uddings. It was wrapped in hide to protect it ...from the weather," he added as an afterthought.

Seeing that the King appeared to be waiting for a further explanation, Udric went on to relate what he knew of the circumstances of his forebear's arrival at Uddings.

"He may have been a personal body servant, a slave, belonging to King Edward's cousin when he travelled to Wymburne. The Aetheling left in a hurry it is said, to avoid a battle with King Edward, but I do not have proof," he finished lamely. The King held out his be-ringed hands to take the goblet.

Turning it round so that the jewels caught in the light, he fingered the lettering embossed under the rim. "It is Aethelwold's cup. Look here it says 'Aethelwold me fecit'. I have my grandfather's cup and it is marked similarly."

"Guard," the King called abruptly, causing Udric to turn quickly, expecting to be arrested for theft. "Fetch my body servant. Tell him to bring my drinking cup immediately." Udric relaxed visibly when the King laughed at him.

"You thought I was going to have you thrown into prison in chains no doubt!" The King's eyes had narrowed slyly watching Udric's reaction.

Udric, sweating heavily, admitted he had been nervous. He pushed the old leather wrapping into his saddle bag to hide his blushing face, awaiting the arrival of the King's cup bearer. Moisture trickled uncomfortably down his spine. He only stopped himself wiping his forehead by a supreme effort of self control.

When the official arrived, stumbling in his haste with both wine and the cup, he passed the jewelled goblet to the King. Waving the man back a few paces Ethelred pointed out the similarities to Udric.

"This belonged to my father's father. It was given to him when he was crowned in the year of our lord nine hundred and ......, well two years before he died." The King's voice trailed off thoughtfully. "My brother used it before me of course."

Udric nodded, unsure if he should comment. The cup bearer now had both cups, which he filled with wine. He passed one to the King before offering Prince Aethelwold's goblet to Udric.

Seeing him hesitate, Ethelred nodded, encouraging Udric to drink from the royal goblet. "It tastes good, lord Udric, drink up!"

"My lord King, I am not used to wine and certainly not to drinking it from a golden goblet!"

Laughter lines crinkled about Udric's mouth as he sipped the wine delicately. Its initial taste was harsh, almost sour, but subsequent sips became more mellow as his palate adjusted. 'If this is the wine reserved for the King then the brewer could take lessons from the master brewers in Wymburne,' thought Udric trying to keep a pleasant smile on his face.

They talked for a while about the Danish invaders and the army. The King seemed to be convinced that having paid the King of Norway so much silver the problem was solved. "The army will remain, but need not be kept in such a state of readiness. More men can return to their homes to see their families. The Bishops can take up their pastoral work or return to the monasteries as they wish," explained Ethelred. "There seems little point in continuing the coastal watch. I have given orders to my captains to let the men go home."

Udric did not totally agree with the King's point of view but was reluctant to be too forceful with his own opinion, only commenting that the Danes were a greedy people and might return in the future. The recent evidence of Ethelred's cruelty and vindictiveness had made everyone wary of crossing him.

The body guard were by this time quite obviously staring at the King and Udric sharing a skin of best wine drunk from a pair of gold cups. The event would be recounted in the mess-room for many a night to come.

Their attention to duty was sharply jolted when they realised that a clerk had gained admittance through their ranks totally un-challenged. Udric took advantage of the man's arrival, bowing as he left. The interview with the King had gone surprisingly well. The goblet had been safely returned to the royal household without too many questions as to how Udda had come by it.

Despite the hour, Udric left for Uddings, immensely relieved that King Ethelred had accepted the return of his ancestor's cup without hesitation, and had actually honoured him with a drink from the vessel in question.

Aelfric, still excited by his first visit to the King's court, chattered all the way. "I want to be a soldier. I will beat the Danes with a big sword."

Owen humoured the boy chatting quietly, seeing that Udric was thoughtful. He was concerned about the reported ineffectiveness of the King's army, its apparent lack of leadership, and Ethelred's latest decision to stand the army down and relax the coastal guard.

"If the Danes have spies then they will know of all this lack of readiness and take advantage of it. The Dorset thegns can only protect their own coast if every one agrees and amongst one hundred and forty or so thegns there is little chance of that," muttered Udric to himself as they rode homewards.

That evening he told the diners in the hall of his visit to court. "My great grandfather hid Aethelwold's cup for safekeeping. It has now been returned to the King." He paused briefly considering how much of what he had discussed with Ethelred should be relayed. There was always the risk of provoking nervousness or even panic among those who had little knowledge of the King and his council. By and large it did not matter who was the ruler of the land, the fields still needed ploughing, sowing and harvesting, church tithes and taxes to be paid.

"We spoke at length of the Danes who have taken much silver from the King with promises to stay away from the shores of this land. I believe however, they will return for more. Uddings is a small estate with open boundaries which we cannot defend. Each man should continue to arm himself and constantly be vigilant. We will keep guard on the chapel roof at Didlington and set another man in the highest tree behind the hall here.

Torches will be prepared with tinder and a flint. Owenson will check that these are distributed to all cottagers or placed at communal places. We cannot hope to beat them off, but we can take our people to safety if warning is given. Pray for God's protection, keep your knives sharp. I would not ask this of you if there was any other way. Every man will take a turn and boys too if the parents agree."

Udric took his seat amid total silence as the field workers and house servants absorbed his advice and gloomy forecast. He glanced at Emma for her support and received a brief nod and a proud smile.

The very next day preparations to make the torches were put in hand. The children cut fresh hazel twigs and bound them into tight bundles with lengths of blackberry runners after their thorns had been removed by pulling the length through the narrow fork of a branch. An elderly cottager who made brooms from heather or hazel twigs had volunteered to finish the torches for both estates. He tied the twigs onto a thicker piece of wood before the tips were dipped in grease and hung up to dry. Not having any pitch, this was the only inflammable coating which was readily available all year round. Pig's lard was always rendered down for waterproofing of skins, the basis of ointments, small lights and also for cooking. The smell was pervasive causing Emma to move the huge melting pot to the furthest end of her kitchen. Smoke blew in all directions reminding everyone of Udric's fears regarding the Danish invaders. That night a bright shooting star sped across the heavens leaving a trail of sparks behind it. Those who saw it spread their terror among the townspeople and villagers.

Meeting after church it was obvious that many were convinced that the heavenly visitation foretold disaster in the near future.

Udric's cottagers often mentioned their precautions to their acquaintances. No-one laughed or thought the watch-keepers were unnecessary. Indeed other small communities determined to copy them and set up their own tree-top guards.

"We have a platform with wind-shield around it. Each man takes a turn. Even our master has spent a night up there," boasted one of Udric's cottagers.

"Arrows could also be fired from that height couldn't they," suggested another who was impressed that even a thegn had taken a turn with such an unpleasant duty. "The King's lands have little protection, except the actual palace of course. They renewed many of the uprights in the palisade last winter. I know for I helped cut them." He laughed at his own humour.

Udric was not called to the Easter witan at Amesbury. He heard afterwards that King Ethelred had appointed a new chancellor and Archbishop of Canterbury. The latter, Aelfric, was primarily a church man but he was acknowledged by many as also being practical in secular matters. A large contingent of the army was recalled to accompany the Wiltshire Bishop on his formal visit to the Pope.

Owenson's younger son was among those chosen to accompany the travellers. He had never been abroad but was proud to be chosen, although he admitted that he was unsure why the Pope could not pray for the Archbishop from a distance.

"What's a pallium anyway?" asked the youngster. "Can't he have the last Archbishop's?"

Udric gently explained that each Archbishop had to have a new cloak or cope. "The seamstresses in Rome embroider with gold and silver thread. As you say, it would be cheaper to use the old one but I understand that an Archbishop is buried in his robes. Anyway, it will be a new experience for you travelling abroad. Hopefully you will come back here and tell us all about the journey when the new man has been blessed. God go with you Owenson."

Udric backed out of the tiny cottage leaving the family to say their farewells in private.

Owenson bade his grandfather goodbye, receiving the old man's solemn blessing. No-one had travelled so far. If the young man returned he would be guaranteed respect for all time. His departure was witnessed with mixed emotions, many clutching charms to ward off evil. They stood and watched him walk proudly along the track. Sunshine reflected off the spear head. It had been sharpened and polished several times since the orders had been delivered. Bareheaded, the familiar jet black hair waved gently in the breeze.

The summer harvest was collected and stored safely. The annual Harvest supper was now totally Emma's responsibility. With small children around the preparations had taken longer than usual. "And this has to be done every year," she sniffed tearfully. "I'm sorry if I have been short with you but the children have not made it easy some days."

Udric held her tightly assuring her that next year would be easier. His face however betrayed the fact that his thoughts were not solely on comforting her. Beneath frown lines there was a glazed look to his normally caring eyes. Even though the harvest had been good and the weather continued fine and warm he was worried and had not shared his concerns with her. At the last moot he had suffered some ridicule from fellow freemen who were now convinced that the King's policy of paying off the heathen invaders had been the right move. He felt that his self esteem had been lessened by the arguments, that his fierce loyalty to the men who worked his land and those who lived close by had been cheapened by the snide remarks from those who had been his friends.

Some of the outlying cottagers were no longer convinced that the Danes would attack again and were reluctant to take a turn on the watch. Udric insisted that his orders be obeyed and for the first time in years ordered a man to be flogged for disobedience. It was to be carried out publicly as a warning to others that as landowner, his orders must be obeyed.

"I have been too easy going for too long so that my authority on my own land is questioned. I provide land, work, food and protection for all at Uddings and Didlington. In return I expect their loyalty and obedience," Udric grumbled to Emma in the privacy of their room when he had decided to confide in her. "God knows life is hard enough without having to call everyone in from work at mid-day. The mill is taking corn from the King's fields as well as ours; only two mares have foaled so far....." Emma smiled as Udric continued to list the ongoing tasks which remained to be carried out before New Year was celebrated and the autumn cull could begin.

The horn blew to signify that the estate workers were assembled in the courtyard. The offender, stripped to the waist had been lashed to the upright of the house servants' quarters. His kin stood beside him as they had been responsible for making sure that he turned up for his punishment. Udric addressed the gathering sternly.

"I ordered a guard to be positioned at each end of my lands, night and day so that we would all be warned of the approach of invaders. All adult males were asked to take a turn at either post. Many of you know that I have taken my turn. I have not shirked my responsibilities of guarding our homes, not just mine. This man here refused to fulfil his share of a night's watch leaving our defences wide open to a surprise attack. At our moot-court, he had no excuse; his kin and frankpledge were made responsible for his future good behaviour. Punishment of whipping is appropriate for such disobedience."

Udric stepped down off the stool and took up the whip. The man's kin stood back, heads lowered in shame as the first lash caught the man on the shoulder. He flinched but did not cry out. The steward called out the number of lashes, counting them on his fingers clasped tightly behind his back.

After ten strokes, Udric threw the whip on the ground at the offender's feet and strode off towards the stables, leaving the steward to oversee the return to work.

The man's relations released his bonds but showed little sympathy for the offender. They hustled him away from other fieldworkers who stared stonily. Children continued to watch wide-eyed. None of them had ever seen Lord Udric punish a man like this before. Everyone had seen offenders in the stocks or pillory in Wymburne and thrown their share of mud or dirt but to see a man they all knew beaten in total silence was a sobering sight.

"None of us like being up all night but if lord Udric thinks we need to set a guard then I for one trust him," spoke one of Owenson's sons stoutly. Others nodded before returning to their tasks.

"Mind you, that's the first time I have ever seen a punishment, in public I mean, or at Uddings for that matter," said the Miller, a vast, slow-moving man whose hands and arms were of legendary strength. So the experience stayed in the minds of men for many months.

The season continued with a fine, dry New Year, and the watch was continued without any further incidents, although other estates became more lax and discontinued the practice. At the quarter day moot, even the Bishop was surprised that Udric was so vehement about the importance of keeping armed guards alert at all times. Archery practice after church had become an unpopular ritual, especially when work on their Lord's harvest left little time for personal crops. A few grumbled in private, but carried out the regulation practice and guard duty with apparent good grace.

It was not until a few weeks later that news arrived from the eastern coast of Devon that a large Danish force had come ashore. The heathens had slaughtered all the local inhabitants, driven the animals onto their ships and plundered everything of value, including gold plate from the Abbey at Tavistock. The raiders had then calmly sailed their sharp prowed ships up the river Tamar, fired the riverside fishing villages and hacked every living soul to pieces. Even the babies had been cruelly slaughtered amid blood curdling shrieks.

Horrified at the reported butchery, the King marched the army to the area then   told the local fyrd leaders that there was no point in unnecessary loss of life. Many of them were disappointed that they had not been allowed to attack the Danes, having been ordered to withdraw to a safe distance.

"They have gone now, with much plunder. It is unlikely that they will return." stated the King emphatically. "The village can be rebuilt in time."

With this parting comment the King made his way back to the comforts of his inland court, and the captains had to appear to be content.

"The King's father would not have hesitated to attack invading forces, even if his army was out numbered." Some of the lower ranks muttered among themselves after they had buried the villagers.

"The slaughter is sickening. Why in God's name forbid us to prevent these raids or take revenge?" Instead of returning to families as proud fighting men or dying a hero's death in battle, the soldiers felt ashamed of their leaders. In alehouses in Wymburne returning men spoke in low voices of their disgust. Their tales spread around the town, including the graphic description of the bodies they had been forced to bury instead of taking the fight to the enemy as had been expected.

"It seems that my fears were well founded! The ditches around the King's palace at Wymburne are being repaired. Even villeins are pressed into service with the bonded men digging out the refuse and spoil. The gates of the town are now closed at dusk each day and the fords guarded by armed townspeople. The captain of the fyrd has positioned guards in the tower of St Mary's despite the Mother Superior's objections! She fears men will ogle her women from the tower. They pray constantly but all the saints' bones in the country will not help them if the Danes do attack."

Udric secreted all his treasure inside the ancient oak tree throwing leaves and dirt on top of the leather bags of silver coin. He spent much of each night prowling round the farm accompanied by the dogs, each slight noise in the darkness heightening his nervousness. Not daring to give her husband a calming potion, Emma could only watch in silence as her husband became haggard and irritable. When she suggested that the dogs just be let loose at night he had told her shortly to look after her own affairs. The hurt between them simmered for days.

In private she cried; partly at the break down of their loving relationship and partly because she could see how the worry was causing him to lose weight and his normal even temper. Cottagers and fieldworkers kept their distance when possible. They might silently agree with their master but had become devoted to Emma and hated to feel the atmosphere between them.

Owenson returned from Italy in the spring, full of the glories of the Pope's court and the sights he had seen. His stories of the wonders, the food and the riches made a welcome change to the diners in the hall who were already bored with tales of the Dane's brutality. At every telling the stories had become more exaggerated so that mother's threatened disobedient children with a Norseman if they did not behave.

The young man had grown a beard of rich blackness. He already looked older, his thin face with its dark eyebrows, more fearsome. "We crossed the water in a ship with oarsmen as well as sails. Many were ill with the motion. We were soaked with spray. It does not dry properly. I swear my cloak still has the stains of salt.

All day we rode in a grand procession. Villagers came out with flowers and threw them on the road before us. Apparently no one can touch a churchman riding to see the Pope. There was not much time to see what crops they grew but we have better and cleaner sheep than the French villagers.

The gates of Rome are golden, with massive uniformed guardsmen either side. They have pikes as well as small maces. Ugly looking weapon it is, being a spiked ball on a short chain. Make a nasty hole in a man's head I tell you." He was interrupted by men calling out that he should get on with his tale. Owenson raised his beaker of ale to them, emptied it and wiped the residue from his lips dramatically.

"Well, where was I? Oh yes, the golden gates. Well we entered the courtyard, all bunched up round the Archbishop. Dozens of stable-boys ran out to hold the horses. One fetched steps for the churchman to dismount. The only trouble was he placed them on the wrong side of the horse and the Archbishop had already got off on the other side! Anyway, we formed up round him then marched to the door of the Pope's palace. I tell you, the doors must be three times the height of a man. Gold and gems are set into the wood so that they sparkle. More guards appeared as if from nowhere. They escorted the Archbishop inside; we were left standing in the courtyard.

Later we went into a huge hall and saw our man flat on his face on the floor before the Pope." Owenson crossed himself rapidly while he drew breath. "Eventually he was raised to his feet and this robe put round his shoulders. It is all gold and silver, with precious pearls in rows. Archbishop Aelfric looked magnificent! We didn't know whether to applaud or bow to him. We were all blessed by the Pope himself and told to go to the quarters set aside for us. They had not even freshened the straw but the food was alright if you like olives and greasy things like that.

A week later and we started the homeward journey. The dryness there made the roads a dust-bath. The grit got everywhere, in your clothes, food and blanket. If we had a shower of rain the dampness was gone in hours of steamy heat. Oh, give me Dorsetshire any day," he finished with a flourish.

The diners applauded the telling, raising mugs of ale to the young man who returned to his place beside his blind grandfather.

Chapter Thirteen
AD997 – AD998

While Aelfric, now of age and newly elected to the tithing group, practiced with his spear and sword, Alfan, younger by two years, was already courting. Her young man was well travelled having visited Northern France to note the terms of trading agreements on behalf of his master. Edwin had been introduced to Udric's daughter at the King's palace in Wymburne when he had admired her skill at riding and the fine horse she rode.

"We have a line of stallions which has been kept as pure as possible. The original horses were imported from Normandy many generations ago. Why don't you come and see the horses at Uddings? After all, you have not been to my home. Surely you have time off from all your documents!"

As an invitation to a prospective suitor, a visit to see the family's horses might be a novel introduction but the young man had sufficient interest to act on her suggestion.

After the visit when Edwin had been more than impressed by the furnishings and facilities at Uddings he asked Udric for Alfan's hand in marriage. The young man had obviously been smitten with a sudden attack of nerves when it came to the important moment. His Adams apple bobbed nervously causing him to stammer.

"Fetch the men some ale then Alfan," ordered Emma in order to give Edwin time to regain his composure. She hurried to the kitchen to fetch her much praised honey cakes, laying them on a beautifully carved trencher.

Alfan smoothed a few tendrils of hair under the ornamented band keeping her hair off her face, then checked that the folds of her robe hung neatly below the decorated leather belt. The two women embraced fondly, whispering their thoughts about the young man currently talking to Alfan's father.

On Emma's return, followed shortly by Alfan carrying the precious jug of ale and two glasses, Edwin had obviously reached a satisfactory agreement with Udric. He was grinning from ear to ear. His dark hair surrounded an open, honest face. Alfan flew to his side and his embrace while her parents looked on fondly. "I have given my permission young maid," pronounced Udric. "I gather you two young people now plan to marry shortly."

"Aye lord! It should just be a formality but none of the King's staff can marry without his express permission. I will write to the head of his Chancery tonight."

Having tasted one of Emma's special cakes Edwin was full of praise, insisting that Alfan should bring the recipe with her when they were married.

The King absentmindedly consented to the Wymburne palace clerk marrying Udric's daughter, promising them a bridal gift when the event took place.

"That's if he remembers where Wymburne is! He has not been here to hunt for a year or more. Cottagers who live on the edge of his hunting forests complain daily that deer have spoiled their crops. It is time they were culled for this reason alone."

Fellow clerks wished Edwin well. Most were junior clerics who walked daily from the monastery in Wymburne. They often grumbled that they worked on letters, accounts and other notes in plain black ink while the ladies in the nunnery were reported to produce beautifully decorated copies of gospels and prayer books for the rich and powerful.

With the nuptials due to be performed by the senior priest at St Mary's, the cooks at Uddings were busy preparing. Fowl were fattened, vast quantities of berries and wood fruits were stewed with honey before being sealed into the finest clay pots with layers of wax or greased hide, while salted meats were washed to restore their flavours.

Edwin, a stout, dark haired youth, explained that he had lost both parents to the sweat.

"I was entered for the church then, taught to read, write and illustrate manuscripts. Some of my work came to the attention of the late King. He persuaded me to stay at the palace instead of returning to the monastery. Since then I have been entrusted with copying for the King. I keep accounts for my Lord at the palace and have my own room," he added modestly.

Udric and Emma were impressed by the young man's skills, described factually without boasting or exaggeration. He was at ease with everyone, admiring the quality of the horses in the stud and the colourful woven cloths which adorned the walls of the hall.

It was decided that Alfan would live with Edwin at his quarters in Wymburne until such time as he moved to another position in the King's service. She spent many hours dreaming of her future husband, Emma being forced to scold her daughter for inattention on several occasions. "You will have your own household to run one day and no doubt be given duties in the King's palace. Stand still while I fasten the clasp."

Standing back to admire her daughter, Emma praised her posture and choice of gown. Placing her own veil over Alfan's head and securing it with a deep blue headband, tears threatened to spill over as she recalled her own wedding.

"Go now daughter and be a good wife to Edwin. He is an honest young man and is in the King's favour. God bless you both."

They were married, their union being blessed in the porch of the church before a nuptial mass. The bridal procession accompanied by musicians, was noisy and light-hearted on the return to Uddings where feasting continued until late at night.

The hall was crowded with sleepers as dawn broke, many of whom nursed sore heads. Aethelflaed and Hal had made the journey, leaving a trusted servant in charge of Woodcutts.

While Aethelflaed, now somewhat broader but still dimple cheeked, chatted to Emma, cuddling her youngest child on her lap, Hal sought Udric out as soon as the bridal couple had left for the palace at Wymburne.

"I would discuss matters with you in private before returning to the farm. Can we walk over to the horses?"

Udric wrapped a woollen cloak about him to ward off the chilly wind before joining his aunt's husband in the yard.

"I have recently taken over the land of my former neighbour which was in a poor condition. You may remember he was the son of Guthrum. He had no kin so the land fell vacant when he died," he added by way of explanation. There were streaks of silver in Hal's hair but his face showed few signs of age, the skin still smooth and lightly tanned. He fiddled with the scrip which hung from his belt, nervously twisting the thongs.

"I let my flock graze all over the fields to rest my own lands. Then I put pigs in folds to give the land heart with their dung. The stream flows during the winter but will dry again come harvest time so we had a look at the well on the farm.

Udda went down on a rope to the bottom. He is a brave lad and strong too. It was deep and dark so he took a torch but it would not stay bright down there. He found these."

Hal passed a bag of coin to Udric. The bag was new, but the coins were of Alfred's time. There were thirty silver coins, some bright where Hal had cleaned them.

Udric gawped at the money, his mouth falling open with shock. He glanced at Hal questioningly; his eyebrows close to his hairline so great was his astonishment.

"This could be the messenger's money, the rent perhaps that he had collected in coin. It was with many other things belonging to Garth who was given Woodcutts by King Edward. He must have put the money in the oldest of the wells, dry for many summers, certain that no one would find it. There are only coins from King Alfred's time. If Garth's son had known of the money, he would surely have changed it for new coins. A knife was with the coin, also the metal binding of a staff, the kind you carry when on the King's business."

Hal took the knife from his belt and handed it to Udric who was reluctant to handle the weapon.

"You are sure it was with Garth's property?"

"It was with his amulet, I have been assured it was his," replied Hal confidently. "It is not the well where the suicide was done."

Udric hastily handed the bag back to Hal nodding. "It is just then, that you have his land. My forebears lost it by a falsehood and now it is back in the family. You have made it bigger, joining the community there. The money should be returned to the King's treasury for it is probably his by right. T'is passing strange that it is thirty pieces though. There is a story in the bible I think, about a betrayal for that amount. Well, as you say, had Garth's son known of it he would have changed it, perhaps only a few coins at a time, but it would have bought him labour, a bondservant even," suggested Udric remembering the story he had been told of the rape and murder.

They returned thoughtfully to the hall at Uddings, neither sure how to deal with the evidence which could clear the family of the stigma of being descended from an outlaw.

When all the guests had left, Udric was not only anxious to restore the previous routine to Uddings and Didlington, but to confide in Emma. Six days were taken up with work, followed by one day of rest, partly taken up by attendance at church. Afterwards, even if it was unpopular, the obligatory practice with weapons at the butts for men and boys while womenfolk wandered around the market. At church the priest continued to remind the congregation to trust in God and pray for deliverance from the invading Northerners. Udric paid little attention to the priest, preferring to put his faith in defence, watchfulness and alertness at all times.

Back in the privacy of their bed chamber Udric told Emma of the discoveries in Hal's well. After her initial astonishment she asked about Woodcutts farm and the man called Udda.

"As I understand it, and of course it is only as it has been passed down the family, Udda's father, the first Udric, found a King's messenger attacking his daughter who by all accounts was simple minded. He struck him and the man was later found dead without his money bag and staff of office. As you know Woodcutts is outside the village of Hanlega so there were no witnesses apart from Udda, a child at the time.

Udric's neighbour however, bore witness that Udda's father had killed the messenger and stolen the purse. There was no other evidence and Udric of Woodcutts was taken to the King after his trial. He ended up being banished and his family, a wife and the two children were dispossessed. A distant relative got the farm, an unpleasant man by all accounts. Anyway, to keep to the story, the wife died, the girl and boy were enslaved. Udda came to Wymburne with Prince Ae...., I forget who but he ran away when the new King marched down to Badberie. Udda escaped with the Prince's gold cup, the very one I have just returned to lord Ethelred, and lived wild here, at Uddings. He apparently rescued a prince and was given the land; hence as descendants, we own this land."

"But what about the girl? You said she was also a slave; did she die?" Emma had listened to Udric tell his story, holding her breath with each new revelation.

"Well that is where it gets really strange, in a nice way I mean. The girl was befriended by Owen, a welsh slave from the wars. After Udda had told his tale to a noble, I'm not quite sure how, this ealdorman who used to travel to palaces to tell the garrison that the King was coming and check that stores were sufficient, he sent Owen and his 'woman' to Udda as a gift!"

"Are you talking about Owenson's kin?"

"Yes, the first Owen did not even speak English very well. He came with his pregnant woman, as slaves, to work for Udda. The woman was Udda's sister which the noble had suspected was the case. Unfortunately the attempted rape by the messenger had weakened her mind and she died when the child was born. It died too, but Owen stayed and he was freed by Udda. You know, in church like the King's steward does once a year."

"So that is why you and your father before you do not like slaves at Uddings or Didlington."

"Mm, the first thing my father used to do was to strike off the collars or shackles. People either stayed and worked for him because they wanted to or went away I suppose. Not that I recall anyone moving away. There are at least two cottagers up on the Cranburne road that are descended from slaves."

Emma drew Udric down into their bed coverings at the same time as thanking him for trusting her with his family's past. She lay relaxed in his arms savouring the closeness and intimacy they shared. Their children shared a small bed on the further side of the room, subsequent pregnancies having ended in heartbreak and tears. A brief recollection of her grief just before sleep came reminded her to pray briefly for her family and for all those at Uddings.

On a bright morning when small clouds chased each other across a blue-white sky Emma raised the questions which had come to her during the night. Patiently Udric filled in the gaps in his tale.

"So you see, the man who caused the banishment of my namesake and the taking of his wife and family came to a bad end. Strange how it was exactly thirty pieces of silver though, exactly the amount Judas took for betrayal in the Bible.

It is said that the sins of the fathers are visited on the children but after all this time the farm is back in the family who owned it for generations. At one time I would have sought revenge on behalf of my grandfather but he died content with Uddings. It is not my right to open old wounds."

"Besides husband," interrupted Emma, "your sister's children will inherit Woodcutts, a strange twist of fate or the hand of God if you believe in such things."

Emma had been bitter about the death of her own father for years. "Not because he had hurt his hands on the rope, you understand, but because those responsible for leaving Udric in the well in which the murdered King Edward's body had been hidden, had never been punished. Queen Elfrida lived in some style as Abbess of her own nunnery, and none would be foolhardy enough to accuse the King of being involved in his half brother's murder.

"Thirty pieces of silver, t'is a common sum for betrayal I believe," reflected Emma as she pulled the weft thread through the warp of a new piece of cloth she was weaving.

Udric was surprised at the reference to Judas. "You were listening to the old priest's story then! I thought you were thinking about the Easter celebrations. And another thing, it is Aelfric's turn on watch tonight. He must take his turn like all the others or we will be accused of favouritism."

Several days later Udric took his son aside privately. Both openly wore swords with short knives tucked into their belts. The inhabitants of areas already plundered by the Danes were empty of people and animals. Those who had fled tried to find work inland or preyed on travellers despite the ultimate punishment which Ethelred had decreed would be handed out to those caught thieving.

"We have seen travelling bands on the road between Uddings and the mill. As long as they settle beside the road and do not forcefully take our people's land there can be no harm done. The land is not good but will support a man and his family if he has a trade. Make sure that there is no fighting or stealing. The land between the two estates is technically commonland, the King's, so I have no jurisdiction over settlers. King Ethelred has been asked repeatedly to rule on the rights of incomers or to give that power to our ealdorman. Which fyrd should they join? Who should be their lord?

People moving from the coasts have been requesting work regularly. At the recent moot I have heard other land owners complain that bands of Devon people are wandering round the area, fully armed, making a nuisance of themselves. Sheep, pigs, oxen and even horses have gone missing. Local people jealously guard their own land and the commons, chasing off intruders, sometimes with violence. Until the King sends writs instructing us, they are like strangers and as such are entitled to hospitality. We can use men at harvest time, but apart from replacing bondsmen or marrying into one of the families here, there is really no need for more workers on the land or with the animals, unless you have noticed a need for more hands?"

Aelfric had stood silently listening to his father list the problems surrounding Uddings and Didlington. For years the land between had been used for grazing the sheep. Suddenly this facility was about to be removed, if what Udric had suggested about the settlers was true.

Now in the first of the teenage years Aelfric's upper lip was covered with fine, dark hair. He fingered it self consciously while considering his reply.

"We should defend what is ours father. We have used that land since your grandfather's time. The King would give it to you if you asked him. The travellers could live on Holt Heath, or go on to the forests at Cranburne."

Realising that his attitude was less Christian than his father's, Aelfric hastened to make amends, adding that he would ride up to the mill and check that all was well. "I can see if anyone is building shelters on the common on the way. They may need help or food to see them through the winter. Our harvest was good, the stores are full. If the King allowed you to clear more land to the north, more cottagers would be needed to cultivate crops or tend the stock."

Udric agreed, his forehead still creased with a frown of concern. "I think that Uddings is a manageable size. It will be yours one day. You will be responsible for guarding the boundaries against bandits or thieves, for the safety of those who depend on you and acknowledge you as their lord. The time has come for you to know where my treasure is kept. Come with me tonight after the meal and I will show you your inheritance and your responsibility. Tell no-one why you are leaving the hall."

Aelfric spent the day wandering around his father's estates on the pretext of checking that all men were armed but in truth, noting all the places where there were signs of new huts, even if no-one was in sight or was actually erecting a dwelling when he rode past. Beneath his calm exterior excitement was building and occasionally bubbled to the surface so that his eyes glittered with expectation. The hours seemed to pass slowly as if a gigantic hand was holding back the passing of the daylight. All day the sun shone drying the soil, glinting off the cottagers tools. There was heaviness in the atmosphere so that a man sweated even if he was not working. Rain would be needed soon to freshen the air and provide badly needed new grass for the horses.

The majority of new arrivals, as his father had suggested, were on the edge of the track northwards where the commonland was to the east. Built of clods, thatched with heather and grass, they afforded meagre shelter to the occupants. Even though he called out in case anyone was within the hovels, no-one returned his greeting, being too frightened or perhaps having already fled from an armed rider.

Reporting back to Udric as dusk fell, Aelfric detailed the number of dwellings which had sprung up.

"There was not a man, woman or child in sight, father; no fowl, or crops. The cottages are built level with the earth, not raised to keep out the water. No ditch around either. There was no sign of smoke or fire. If anyone lives within these dwellings it is in utter misery."

Several men eating at the trestles that night commented that they had seen raggedly dressed strangers on the road, but had not noted where they went.

"They speak differently to us lord, but they were not armed or threatening us so we let them go in peace."

Emma suggested that food be left in front of the cottages with any old cooking pots. "At this time of the year the berries in the woods are in short supply. Hunger makes men desperate. They will steal to feed their families. If they are caught, they will be punished severely, regardless of having no lord."

Men nodded in agreement, for a man without a lord was almost an outcast and could be reprimanded by anyone whose status was above theirs. Udric's wife was well known for her compassion and wise counsel. Her humble start in life was also known to them and this endeared her to men and women alike for she had not adopted superior airs when

Udric married her.

Rain fell steadily all evening. Servants and bondsmen left for their beds as fires were damped down to conserve fuel, the merest glimmer remaining in the darkness. Emma left the shutters open so that the air inside the hall would be freshened. She lit rush lights because darkness only served to emphasise the noises of the night when owls hooted and the screams of their tiny prey sounded so much louder, frightening.

Leaving the hall quietly after silence had fallen in the night with a small dip light sheltered beneath their cloaks, father and son made their way past the midden to the old oak tree. The small wavering light caused huge shadows to dance wildly in the blackness. Both men felt tense as they pulled the twigs away from the opening in the ancient trunk. Pulling the fronds of ivy gently to one side, Aelfric squeezed into the hollow trunk. Udric whispered in the darkness imagining how scared the youngster could be in total blackness.

"There is a shelf above your head inside the trunk. Feel for it carefully so that nothing falls off. Bags of coin are locked in a wooden chest. Your mother greased it with fats to preserve it from water or droppings of fowl that may roost above! Rings given by the King to my forebears are also wrapped in leather pouches inside the chest. These could be sold if need be," he added thoughtfully.

Brushing the ground carefully to remove traces of their visit and pulling the ivy across the opening, they returned to the hall and replaced the light in its holder. Emma nodded, acknowledging their reappearance, before drifting back to sleep.

Udric and Aelfric shared a mug of ale talking quietly to avoid waking Emma. There were leaves clinging to the young man's tunic which Udric brushed off gently explaining that although he trusted everyone at Uddings, the things he had just been shown were for the family only and not to be shared. Nodding his understanding of the new responsibility which had just been passed to him, Aelfric embraced his father with affection, a love which was returned in great measure by Udric.

While most people slept, the dogs in the hall and stables maintained their half wakefulness. Before dawn they became restless. The eldest in his agitation pushed aside the heavy curtain of Udric's quarters, forbidden territory for even the most loved hounds.

Annoyed at being woken from a deep sleep Udric's first reaction was one of anger. The wet nose and hairy muzzle continued to push into his face followed by panting of canine breath. On the point of ordering the animal to return to its place in the hall, he paused to reconsider.

"It is not like you to invade my room. What has upset you? Show me what bothers you."

Udric pulled a heavy cloak about him and pushed his bare feet into his sandals. Not wearing a belt and unwilling to make a light and disturb the others, who still slept soundly, he found his short knife and stood up. Purely as a precaution he fastened the leather scabbard round his waist and slotted the old seax smoothly into the sheath.

The dog trotted out into the hall, glancing back to check that its master followed. It made its way steadily past the sleeping servants to the door. Udric let the dog out prepared to be slightly exasperated if the animal was merely suffering from a weakness of control. The hound sniffed, as if sensing Udric's borderline irritation. It led its master purposefully towards the woods, the fur on its back rising stiffly. The hound stopped abruptly, cocking its head. Udric too paused, listening.

In the stillness of the early morning, the false light of dawn just breaking, he felt more than heard slow hoof beats of walking horses. Putting his hand on the dog's head to calm it, Udric crept forwards, wishing he had chosen a darker cloak rather than his bright blue one of which he was so proud. Reluctant to remove it, for the air was chilly; he decided to use a fresh sprig of leaves to camouflage the colour of his clothes.

The young tree stem snapped loudly as he broke off a sizeable piece. The sound of the horses stopped just as suddenly. The dog's hackles rose, its tail lowered aggressively. Its lips drew back into a snarl and revealed sharp yellow canine teeth.

Suddenly shouts and hoof beats mingled loudly as riders burst out of the surrounding thicket.

Udric raised his dagger defensively. The helmeted leader of the riders laughed derisively as he raised a huge sword above Udric's defenceless head. Dodging the first blow, Udric spun round and stabbed the horse in the neck as it was pulled up on its haunches. It fell screaming, bloody foam blowing in jets from its nostrils and mouth. There was no time to ask God for forgiveness for killing an innocent animal; men on foot equally well armed now surged forward.

The warrior was thrown violently forward. Other riders now came in for the kill. Udric shouted loudly, screaming his own war cries. The dog barked excitedly nipping at the heels of the horses causing them to turn sharply when their riders were least expecting it.

Udric did not see the huge Dane approach him from behind. Struck with a blow that should have killed him, he fell to the ground, his fingers unable to hold the small weapon. The dog leapt at the warrior as he was about to strike a mortal blow, biting his unguarded arm to the bone. The blow meant to despatch Udric was deflected, catching the dog on its quarters causing it to scream in agony as bones broke.

It fled in terror barking wildly even while blood streamed from the wound.

Furious at the interruption to his death blow, the heathen warrior called coarsely to his comrades "Stick this Saxon pig to a tree. I will kill the impudent cur which bit my arm."

Until now he had ignored the deep wound so inflamed was his blood lust. Unwilling to appear weak before the rest of the band he had made no attempt to bind it or staunch the spurting blood which issued from it. Now he turned away following the spoor of the injured dog, winding a dirty bandeau around his arm with his sound hand and teeth.

His comrades meanwhile raised the limp body of Udric from the ground and held it against a tree trunk. They argued among themselves as to who should strike the mortal blow. Udric's eyes were opened but unfocused as they bound him to the tree with the thongs of their braided leather whips.

The man with a horned helmet finally lumbered across the glade his huge axe raised. It struck deep into Udric's body driving it firmly into the flesh of the tree so that his body was impaled. Udric's scream of pain was stilled as his spirit left his body, the once proud head falling forward over the bandit's mighty weapon. From a distance the unearthly howl of a dog was heard, followed by continuous barking and shouts of men alerted by the old hound's wounds. The look out man was screaming out directions to those below and waving his torch wildly trying to attract the attention of others.

The Vikings swore loudly, their efforts at stealth in the pre-dawn mist now totally undone. Mounting their stolen horses they galloped forward to Uddings screaming war cries, calling on their gods to witness valour as they spurred in to attack.

The old dog had limped back to the hall bloody and broken, setting all the other dogs into a frenzy of excited yipping, its fear being contagious.

"To arms men! Raiders!" shouted Aelfric fastening his armoured tunic, his call echoed by other early risers. Someone else blew the horn its clear notes carrying on the still air. Kitchen servants spilled out brandishing sharp cooking knives ready to defend their lord. "Defend yourself," shouted Aelfric to his mother who had appeared at the door to the hall in her under-dress. She fled indoors barring the door behind them.

Mounting his horse, despite the lack of a saddle, Aelfric galloped towards the enemy force, the fieldworkers running after him, armed with spears, seax, scythes or billhooks.

Appalled at the savagery he was witnessing, Aelfric raised his sword and struck out blindly at the Danish invaders.

There was no time to wonder at his father's absence as his own men were slaughtered mercilessly. The big man with the horned helmet was his target, apparently the leader, his shield decorated with the black raven, the feared omen of doom.

Kneeing the stallion firmly forward it gave its rider a height advantage. Using the weight of his sword, he swept his blade at one man's undefended neck, causing the Dane to fall from his horse. Not waiting to see if he was dead, Aelfric pressed on, inflicting considerable damage until he too was struck down as an axe caught him a buffeting blow on his mailed shirt. Pulled off the stallion, he hit the ground heavily. Momentarily winded, he feigned death as the riders moved away.

The Danes too suffered injuries from the defending force but such was their strength that most of Uddings men were now either dead or mortally injured. The raiders spared neither man nor beast, slaughtering every living thing that crossed their path as they forded the stream. The hall above them on the rise of the hill was almost undefended. Aelfric staggered to his feet before running along the edge of the wood to the outer buildings. One raider saw him escape.

"I will have that brat spitted," swore one fur clad soldier, nursing a deep cut to his leg. Following his comrades the raiders burst into the courtyard trampling fowl beneath their ponies' hooves. Blood spattered their clothes and dripped from swords onto their horses, so that their appearance at the heart of Uddings was terrifying to those within the hall.

Aelfric watched as the Danes attempted to break down the door. Having lost his own sword when he was unhorsed, he had found another belonging to a dying man. There was a red mist before his eyes but he was sufficiently sensible to realise that he could not attack the remaining Danes on his own. He reached for the horn hanging from the eaves of the cook house before creeping away to the rear of the new wing where he could get up on the roof. From there he blew three blasts before being spotted by the enemy force. They were not armed with bows and arrows but threw spears at him, angrily frustrated by their inability to engage him in close combat.

While all eyes were on Aelfric screaming abuse at the enemy below, reinforcements arrived on the scene. The swine herd had brought his herd, knowing that most horses have an aversion to pigs. The animals ran loose in the courtyard terrified by the noise causing many of the enemy's ponies to gallop off. Although many of the herd were butchered by the sharp blades, Aelfric took the opportunity to climb down from the roof and re-arm. It was not until he heard his mother's screams within the hall that he realised that some of the Danes had found an unguarded window and had forced an entry into the hall.

Frantic with worry, he urged a further attack on the Danes by those who remained in the courtyard. The stablemen threw spears at the enemy until the great door of the hall was opened to reveal several of the enemy. Many of the Uddings men now fled, intent on gathering their own belongings and family. Aelfric found himself almost alone while sounds of slaughter and wrecking could be heard from within the occupied hall. Once again he climbed onto the roof, scrambling up the thatch on hands and knees, intent on entering through the smoke hole. He was no longer thinking rationally. His head and shoulder hurt abominably. Under the mail of his jerkin there was a sticky wetness, ignored in his anger and grief. Puzzled by the absence of his father, he ordered the stableman to ride for reinforcements. No-one saw him fall from the roof. He landed on the sloping top of the storeroom and rolled down to the edge of the midden and lost his senses in a black mist amid the foul stench of human and animal manure.

Returning painfully to consciousness some while later Aelfric was alarmed by the silence. He crawled away from the foul smelling dung heap but was unable to stand. Reaching the comparative safety of the old oak tree he squeezed inside the opening and collapsed gratefully onto the dry leaf mould. He woke some time late to hear the enemy forces laughing and talking in heathen tongue. Peering out through the screen of twigs and ivy at the base of the tree, he saw them mounting his father's horses and leading others piled high with loot atop which bleating lambs were tied. No slaves were roped to the saddles but two youngsters were being dragged away. Aelfric felt tears of anger and defeat pricking behind his eyes. The best horses were being stolen and many men were dead. Those who were not had already fled from the slaughter and carnage. Fearing now for his own life, he stayed hidden until dusk fell, a prey to despair alternating with a depth of anger he had never experienced before. There had been no sound from either of his parents, not a single call from a cottager or servant.

Overcome with guilt and grief combined with a great weakness of body, Aelfric eased himself out of the cavity. The leaf mould and dried dung dropped away with every heavy step he took. As he rounded the end of the hall, he saw the hacked bodies of his friends and workers lying in unnatural postures, their blood thick on the ground. Even puppies had been slashed to death. A bitch whined as she slunk back, belly to the ground.

Overjoyed to see a familiar himan she approached him, only checking visibly when his unusual odours reached her.

"Hello lass," he murmured gently. "Are we all that remains this hellish day?" Even his voice was husky with the strain. "Where is the master?"

Since the raiders sudden attack Aelfric had not seen his father. Now he urgently needed to find out what had happened to his family. The door of the hall hung askew. A pig fled as he entered the hall nervously, a knife held firmly in his sound hand. The dog followed him closely, no doubt finding comfort from his presence, as he did from hers.

The fire was cold; the atmosphere was heavy with gloom and death. Most of the servants had been killed where they huddled in one corner, men, women and the children too.

Despite being empty he was violently sick. The smell of his bile rose, competing with the stench of his own body and clothes. The dog shivered fearfully but would not leave. In the private room, he found the most hideous death. His mother had been raped, probably until she died of the sickening abuse. Her unseeing eyes gazed upwards, a silent scream in the wide, bitten and bloody lips.

Aelfric fell to his knees utterly distraught. The bitch howled, sitting on her haunches, until her distress irritated him and he shouted at her to cease her keening. Closing his mother's eyes, he left the room, letting the curtain fall across the doorway. Numb with grief he sought the fresh air again, clutching the door post for support, unaware of how the time was passing. There was not a glimpse of the sun; under a grey sky the fields were empty, hurdles destroyed and stock dead or stolen.

The darkness was now complete, blotting out the brutal scene. The kitchen fire was also out but the bread had baked in the oven and been overlooked by the raiding party. Aelfric ate greedily washing the dry bread down with a pannikin of ale drawn from the jar. The dog too, accepted a crust.

"God knows we need our strength. Is there no one else in this God forsaken place?" Loneliness came upon him suddenly bringing tears and bitterness.

There were enemy corpses too, including that of the leader. Aelfric kicked the body viciously causing the head to fall sideways. The open eyes seemed to watch as he continued to search for survivors. Carrying a torch to light his way, he hoped it would also served to attract the attention of any who had escaped and were hiding nearby.

"It is Aelfric who summons," he shouted. His head rang with the effort. Part of him was terrified of attracting the attention of further raiders while the over-riding need to find a familiar face demanded that he call attention to himself and Uddings. In all his seventeen summers he had never encountered such isolation or anguish. There had always been a friendly voice, a comforting caress when he had hurt himself or suffered the aches and pains of childhood ailments. There was silence in the darkness. A pig shuffled into the edge of his circle of light eyeing him uncertainly as it searched for food.

Aelfric let it wander unchecked. He had no inclination to herd it back to a pen. 'Besides,' he thought, 'the pens have probably been destroyed, along with everything else.'

Momentarily full of self pity, Aelfric sat down to assess his circumstances unaware that he was talking aloud. "Mother raped and murdered, the sheepherd, the swineherd, the stablemen and the harness maker's lad all killed in defence of the hall, the cooks in the kitchen pole-axed in front of their ovens, the brewer dead by his ale vat. The horses stolen, the pigs scattered, and no doubt the oxen and sheep slaughtered, run down where they grazed," he thought bitterly mentally enumerating all the crimes which could be laid at the door of the heathens.

His misery was interrupted by the old dog which dragged itself painfully toward him, its back legs trailing behind, useless and bloody.

"Thank God for your warning old boy," he caressed its head gently. The dog looked at him, its eyes liquid with a mixture of admiration and pain. One back leg was obviously broken, the other gashed to the bone. Aelfric drew out his knife to put the dog out of its misery. He drew the blade quickly across its throat and held it tightly as it died, the eyes losing their focus as its body went limp in his arms.

Crying bitterly over the loss of a loyal companion, Aelfric wept for all the deaths, of his family and the people he had known since his earliest memories. He lowered the dog's body to the ground gently, muttering prayers for the departure of its spirit.

As he regained control of himself he paused to wonder if dog's joined their masters in heaven or hell. Convinced now that his father must also be dead, no other reason being conceivable for his continued absence from Uddings at such a time, Aelfric stood up shakily and looked about him for a last time before returning to what remained of the hall.

He slept restlessly in a corner, frequently waking to recall the horrors of the day. Every noise jerked him into wakefulness. The bitch brought in a half dead puppy in her mouth and licked it, determined to salvage one from her recent litter. She raised her head briefly when Aelfric spoke to her, but quickly resumed her rhythmic massage of the bloody bundle of fur which the Danes had made sport with in their orgy of wanton destruction.

By first light Aelfric was already awake, stiff and dirty. He found clothes in the chest almost by touch not wanting to look at the body of his mother which still lay sprawled on her bed. He flung the filthy jerkin and trews aside, dragging on the fresh garments as fast as he could ignoring the gash on his ribs which had now dried.

He found cold water and dowsed his face quickly before eating more bread. The silence and lack of activity was unnerving.

"I must get help to bury the bodies," he muttered to himself. "They cannot lie here unshriven. Thank God Alfan was not here or she would have been taken or suffered the same fate as mother."

Arming himself with his sword and two knives, Aelfric set off for the town, determined to bring back a priest and help to bury his dead. It did not occur to him that the invaders might have come from Wymburne so it was with purpose that he strode across the land and entered the trees. No birds sang amid the budding trees. He gripped the sword tightly, glancing over his shoulder nervously. The only sound was the wind among the few leaves on the trees. Entering a small clearing cautiously, it was with gut-wrenching horror that he saw Udric, his loved and much respected father, impaled against a tree by a huge weapon. Flies were already feasting on the thickened blood which had gushed from the tremendous wound. Aelfric uttered a wail of intense grief, careless of who heard his pain and sorrow.

Lifting his father's head gently he was shocked by the grimace of pain frozen on the familiar face. The stiffness of death prevented all but the smallest of movement as he stepped back filled with anger and disgust at the barbarity of such a death.

"God's blood! Ware the man who did this! No man deserves to die so, tied down and then stuck like a pig. Fighting against outlaws is more decently done than this, and numbers more equal," he added between gritted teeth

Looking around he saw signs of battle and bloody spoors. "I hope you took some of them with you father. Maybe it was you that struck the heathen warrior who is dead at Uddings. His body shall be tossed out to the carrion crows to rot in hell."

Aelfric could not shift the huge axe which impaled his father's body and reluctantly left the clearing as he had found it, his thoughts full of unchristian ideas.

Wiping his nose on his arm, he muttered to himself as he strode over the top of Colhill, calling on the old gods of his ancestors as well as God in heaven to witness his grief and anger.

At the top of the hill he paused, shocked instantly out of his self pitying mood. The town had been destroyed. The stones of the church tower stood, but fires burnt all around it. Not a house was left standing. Even the monastery and its forbidding entrance had been reduced to rubble. Timbers rose in the air, flames licking at the edges like greedy tongues determined to finish what the invaders had started. He could see some movement, but who still lived among such destruction he could not tell from a distance. Of the Danes and the stolen horses there was no sign.

Aelfric ran down the hill, splashing through the ford regardless of the spray he caused and entered the place where the gates had stood. They lay battered and broken upon the ground, flung aside brutally just like the door of the hall at Uddings.

Brought up sharply by the incredible sight of bodies strewn round the small church, even of women and children, he passed from one to another recognising some while others were too mutilated to even guess at their identity. "Sweet Jesus, is no-one alive in this hell hole?" A small voice called out to him. A young girl crept out from beneath the skirts of her dead mother. He lifted her up gently, cradling her in his arms as he searched through the ruins for further survivors. Two monks approached warily from the smoking ruins of the main church. Both looked scared, white faced and nervous.

"We hid in the tower," they explained. "The heathens came from the south. What they could not carry off they destroyed. We raised the fyrd but they were overwhelmed by the Norsemen's battle axes. Even the women took up arms to defend their homes but to no avail. We were trapped in the church by the fires but barred the door from inside until the enemy forces left."

"Did anyone flee?" questioned Aelfric putting the girl down although she scrabbled wildly to retain a hold on his hand.

"Some left for the fort beyond the King's palace. They went along the road then across the fields instead of the river path in case the Danes were keeping watch. They have ravaged the farms, driven the deer out of the forest and laughed as they killed, calling on their gods to witness their deeds."

The monks muttered prayers hastily at the mention of the heathenish idols. They described how the savage hordes had descended on the town without warning, screaming and waving their battle axes. The thick doors of the monastery had been beaten down, the occupants slaughtered, even those in the chapel.

"No-one was spared. They came out carrying stores, precious plate and even the ornaments from the altar table itself. Some the nuns fled but others were taken or hacked down as they ran. I saw one man picking the jewels from the cover of a missal with his knife, then throw the book in the dirt."

Aelfric had overcome his initial revulsion at the sight of so much death. He took charge of the gabbling monks who alternately described the scenes they had witnessed and called on God to punish the wicked.

"We must give the souls of the dead what comfort we can and bury them decently. Take the bodies beyond the gates; there must be a cart somewhere. We cannot possibly give each a place, but on the side of the hill we can dig the earth away and then drag more down to cover them decently."

Sending the monks to find a cart, Aelfric searched for spades in the abandoned blacksmiths store.

Working in grim silence, the three men laid the bodies across the cart. At first each body was handled with reverence but it became impossible to take such care as the pile grew higher. While all three were absorbed in the task other men approached. Aelfric faced up to them with his sword drawn, crouching to attack if their identities did not match their Saxon appearance. Each had a tale of horror to tell as they took turns digging. A couple of women and children had also survived. They were sent back to the town to scavenge for food for everyone.

"We must stay together until the job is done. The church has a bit of roof; we must live there for the time being. Gather bedding, clothes, tools, weapons and animals, anything useful. Has anyone a flint?"

It took three days work from first light to beyond dusk to cover the dead of Wymburne. Out of nearly two hundred souls, no more than a score had survived. A few could not be accounted for but as the priests checked the laboriously scratched lists on hardened parchment found in the church, there was not a single family which was untouched by the massacre.

When the gruesome task had been completed, a few prayers were intoned over the mass grave, before the church men left for Sherburne to report the loss of the nunnery to the Bishop.

"Tell him also that thegn Udric was killed at Uddings," added Aelfric as he bade them a safe journey. They had armed themselves as best they could with discarded weapons, but it would be several days before they reached the safety of the Bishop's house. They set off nervously repeating prayers knowing that not even their dark clerical robes would save them if they met the Danish raiders.

"If you see Wymburne people tell them to return. The town will be rebuilt but it will take time," one of the men shouted at their departing backs.

Without the sounds of people bustling about their business the silence of the town was depressing. Two of them had gone into the nunnery in the hopes of finding women who had escaped the butchery. Passing through rooms where no man had been allowed for centuries was a weird experience. Clothes were scattered on floors and stools, tables were upturned and crucifixes desecrated. There was not a living thing within the walls. A tiled floor bore testament to the bloodshed which had occurred, splattered spots of dark blood, some smeared, attracted the flies which rose sluggishly from their feasting.

Aelfric persuaded some of the survivors to come back to Uddings with him to bury his father's tenants and servants. There, they once again elected to lay the bodies on the side of the hill among the trampled crop. Aelfric wrote a list naming each person and their occupation. He shuddered as he wrote his mother's name, tears falling unashamedly as her name was recorded on his father's wax tablet. He had shrouded her so that men might not see the evidence of rape. A few cottagers were unaccounted for and he prayed that they had escaped unharmed.

"It will take years to restore the farm," he commented as they scraped the soil down onto the corpses.

"Places have been wiped out before by the sweating sickness, but have grown again," retorted one burly man as he threw the dirt to the furthest edge of the grave. "No Dane is going to move me from my land and your father would not be pleased to think that Uddings was finished. Where is thegn Udric?"

With a gasp Aelfric remembered his father's body in the wooded glade. Every muscle screamed in protest as he stood up abruptly.

"I would like to bury him here with the others. He would prefer that to a grave in Wymburne."

The two strode off to the wood leaving the others to search for food. The children were sent to look for any livestock which might have escaped into the woods so that they had little time to dwell on the death of their families. "You must stay together. You boy, blow this horn if you have need of us." The tallest boy with a snotty nose clutched the horn to his chest. Tear stains running down his dirty face showed that he too had recently suffered a loss. For the moment Udric could not remember whose son he was but felt that there was ample time in the weeks to come to establish everyone's name.

Aelfric was glad of the strength of his companion. Grunting with the effort, the hugely powerful arms of the blacksmith removed the Danish axe impaling his father's corpse to the tree. The body collapsed slowly, watched in silence by the two men.

Together they rolled Udric onto a cloak and still without speaking picked up the corners of the fabric.

They buried Udric facing his beloved hall, Aelfric swearing that he would work the farm to his own dying day and revenge his family's slaughter at the hands of the Danes.

"I shall have to see the King, to report my father's death, but once that is done, Uddings will be worked again. Any who wish to stay here are welcome. I shall be their lord as my father and his father before him on this land." With hands on hips he faced the small crowd of tired men and women who had buried so many on the slope of the small hill at Uddings.

Some agreed to stay and work to restore the farm. The little girl who had survived the massacre outside the church was taken in by a grieving mother while men cheerfully chose the small cottages they would rebuild.

"God knows how the Danegeld will be paid this year," grumbled Aelfric as he sought to restore some order in the remains of his father's hall. "Perhaps the King will not charge it now that it is so obvious that the Danes do not keep their word. This time the invaders have affected the King's own lands. Perhaps now he will take notice of those who wanted to keep the guards on the coast. Without the Norman blood horses there is little enough to spare on this estate. There have already been rumours of unjust treatment when King Ethelred imposed the tax of twelve pence per hide of land. But when the land can no longer produce saleable crops or stock because of destruction, how then shall men pay the tax?"

'The sooner I see the King, the quicker matters will be put to rights,' decided Aelfric that evening as once again a communal fire gave heat and warmth to the men, women and children who sheltered in the hall. Even without a door, the hall had stoutly withstood the attempt to fire it.

One elderly horse had been found peacefully cropping the common land. The miller's son had found him when making his way to Uddings to report the terrible events which had overtaken the mill and the newly completed chapel at Didlington.

"They smashed everything they could not carry away. Father was killed trying to prevent the heathens from stealing the corn. All we have left is the winter corn for the animals, they took the rest or...... spoiled it," he added miming the action. Because there were women present he did not describe how foully the Danes had spoilt the bags of flour, forcing the miller to watch as one after another the marauders had urinated into the middle of each sack, causing maximum damage and distress to the miller before they killed him.

Those who were not killed had fled, reported the miller's son who admitted hiding in terror until the attack was over.

Even those who had newly settled beside the road, having escaped from the previous coastal attack, had not stood their ground, but run at the first sign of trouble.

Aelfric went to take stock at Didlington, riding the old horse slowly as he saw the destruction around him. Hardly a hurdle was still standing; the fields empty of sheep, goats, oxen and horses. The children had found two piglets in the woods and these were now living in the old ox stall beside the hall, their own pen having been destroyed.

So far not a single ox had been recovered although no-one remembered having seen oxen being driven away by the Danes. At least one had been slaughtered for meat, and several sheep had met the same fate for the bones had been left to rot. The rest of the flock had scattered. Men would be sent out with any remaining dogs to round up any animals which could be found while the fences were being repaired.

Aelfric left for court accompanied by one man. Both wore armour but with only one horse, the journey took two full days. They passed the Cranburne Abbey which from its outward appearance had apparently not been harmed, but as there was no sign of life as they approached, Aelfric decided not to delay his arrival at court by investigating the apparent desertion of the church.

"No doubt having raided Wymburne, the King's palace and Uddings together with anything else to hand as they came up Colhill, they were eager to get back to their boats. How they get all the stock on board I don't know. Perhaps we should look for the horses over towards Hame. Surely the boats could not have come up-stream beyond there could they?"

His silent companion grunted some sort of reply about mist rising from the river as he trudged alongside the elderly horse. Unable to ride properly he had found taking his turn in the saddle to be a very painful experience after the novelty wore off. He was glad to see the walls of the capital in the distance. There he would have time to come to grips with his new situation. Grief had numbed his mind so that talking had become difficult. All he wanted was revenge for the deaths of his whole family in Wymburne, for the loss of his livelihood and to keep himself alive until his wits returned.

Aelfric was astonished to find court life apparently unperturbed by the Danish raids into the neighbouring county. Conscious of his appearance, still dressed in bloodstained clothes, even the clerks seemed unwilling to take his request to see the King seriously.

It was not until another surviving landowner, Wulfwen from Cheneford arrived at court in a similar distressed state that the King's servants suddenly changed their attitude.

Wulfwen's estate was several times bigger than Uddings and had been attacked from the river. He too had lost many of his family and the cottagers had fled in terror. "It may be unmanly to cry but I screamed to heaven that night. My wife; daughters; all gone or killed brutally. The useless carnage, the blood; oh as God is my witness, so much blood," confided Wulfwen as they picked at a fowl on the trencher before them.

"At Uddings too, almost everyone was killed and all the stock taken. They even killed pups not yet weaned, raped my mother and pinned my father, lord Udric, to a tree with one of their filthy axes. No doubt you saw the state of Wymburne on your way?"

Both men were kept waiting for two days, fretting at the inactivity and unconcern of the courtiers, before they were grudgingly admitted to the King's quarters. The men had decided not to change their clothes, nor to offer excuses if they were to get the King's aid.

Bowing low to Ethelred and offering their apologies for the state of their dress, both men described the horrors of the slaughter and destruction inflicted on their estates.

"Wymburne is destroyed my lord. The churches are desecrated, the monastery raised to the ground, the plate stolen even from your own manor; only a score or so townspeople have escaped. We buried the rest as best we could."

Wulfwen gave a similar harrowing report of the destruction of Cheneford, his emotion causing him to falter in his account of the cruel deaths suffered by all but a few women.

The King nodded understandingly as the two men asked for relief from the Danegeld until the farms had been restored and were productive again. He appeared to have difficulty focusing on them, drawing his head as far back as he could, but had not uttered one word of comfort or offered condolence at their great losses.

"My father, thegn Udric was killed hideously but apparently mortally wounded the leader of the raiders before he died," reported Aelfric with something approaching pride in his father's achievement. "I regret that his headband is damaged beyond repair."

The remains of the bandeau were passed to the King, The fabric was bloody and almost ripped in two. He dropped it in disgust when he realised what had caused the stains, hastily calling for a servant to pick it up and remove it.

"Fetch a new band for this man," he commanded abruptly. "You will take your father's place, Aelfric of Uddings. You are excused Danegeld for the period of one year. I will send a captain of the guard and a garrison of men to rebuild the palace.

Everyone must help rebuild the town, the church and the defences. No doubt the Bishop will send new churchmen to care for your sick, and to say prayers for those who have perished. We will take revenge on the Danes for this outrage. It is the fault of the Norman court which gives them shelter and even buys the goods from the pirate raiders."

The king was working himself up into a rage, his face reddening as he sought to blame anyone but himself for the lack of defences. The two men shifted uneasily, glancing at each other as the king paced the floor in agitation.

"They take our horses, even the beasts which toil in the field, our treasure and stores. I will have revenge I tell you. Go now thegn Aelfric, son of Udric of Uddings. Lead your people back to prosperity and you too thegn Wulfwen of Cheneford. God go with you both." Dismissed from the King's presence, Aelfric passed the new diadem from hand to hand before tying it round his forehead, smoothing his hair as best he could.

"I too would revenge the deaths of my family. If the King has plans to mount an attack I would be part of it. Other men can see to Uddings while I am away. I have no son or wife to tie me to the land."

The man from Cheneford turned slowly, tears in his eyes. "They spitted my sons like sucking pigs, raped my wife so that she died of her hurts and grief. If there is a just God, those who did this will rot in hell."

"There are two or three rotting on my dung heap at the very moment," interrupted Aelfric rudely. "I have buried our dead, and many of those at Wymburne, but none would be persuaded to give the heathens a decent burial."

They journeyed back to Dorset together; Aelfric's bodyguard now more willingly mounted on the elderly horse and trying to copy the lord of Uddings' gentle swaying movement rather than holding himself so stiffly as he had on the way up. Aelfric himself rode a stallion from the King's stable. True, it too was aged, but it had been bred out of an Uddings stallion and might be the saving of the bloodline if suitable mares could be found. He stroked its neck gently as the small party left the capital where so many had obviously never experienced such a catastrophic change in their lives. The lack of concern and pity had upset all of them. There had been criticism at the state of their clothes, their unshaven appearance and uncombed hair. They had all found it difficult not to be irritated by the snide remarks and haughty looks they had been subjected to by nobles and servants alike. Smug in their relative comfort they had no idea of the terror and cruelty inflicted by a Danish raid. Wulfwen and Aelfric shared this knowledge, their hearts harder for it.

For a brief moment Aelfric regretted that his father had been so honest and returned the jewelled cup to the King. The re-building of his palace at Pamphill was of more importance than the lives lost in Wymburne; restoration of the church more vital than sharing the grief of the survivors at Uddings.

The young man was well known to the King's stablemaster having visited and shown a genuine interest when he had accompanied his father to court. Having wasted two days waiting to see King Ethelred, he had emotionally related the raid on Uddings to the headman. Eyes wide with shock the stablemaster had hastily taken him to the stall where the dapple grey stallion munched contentedly on hay.

Calling to it gently, Aelfric ducked beneath the chain and went into the stable. It smelt his face, breathing hay and horsey odours at him before bending its huge head in recognition.

"Aye he'll know you alright! The King took him back from some lord or other in fines. He would hardly notice if ....."

"You mean take him with me? I have no mares but others may still have one or two and be glad of his colts. It's a big risk but yes, when I leave the stallion will return to Uddings with me. After all that has happened my senses are shocked. It is hard to accept that some people are willing to help and for that you have my thanks. Can you leave harness then if questioned you will know nothing."

"For all the notice my lord takes it's little risk. I would not see his line lost. Have you feed? No, well there will be some in a sack by the harness when you go."

The two men embraced, united in their conspiracy.

The two Dorset men compared their experiences of the raid and commented on the King's apparent lack of concern over the massacre of the Dorset people. "He was more worried about his own palace than all the homes which have been burnt, the stock and crops stolen. The army was never even mobilised to defend us! He says he will take revenge for us and I would join any force that he sends, but in the meantime there is much work to be done rebuilding our farms."

They parted company on the boundary of Uddings, promising to meet again soon. Aelfric rode on thoughtfully. Having surveyed the damage at Didlington he was thoroughly depressed. The fields were empty of sheep which Hal of Woodcutts had been so proud of.

A few carcasses lay pathetically on the ground where they had been struck down. Crows squabbled noisily over the beasts' heads. They flapped away heavily as Aelfric approached, settling saucily a few paces away. "Get them butchered, the meat should be alright and will keep us from starving. Better we store it than let it rot as waste," ordered Aelfric, his face stony as he remounted the restless stallion. They returned to the hall at Uddings to a cheerful welcome. The children had found many of the piglets in the woods together with two oxen and some goats.

They had already been returned to the courtyard where temporary pens had been built. Two colts and a filly had also been recovered, obviously unable to keep up with the stolen mares; they had wandered back to the place they were born. Hastily patching up the hurdles the horses were returned to their paddock.

Making a fuss of the children lessened the depression into which he had fallen since riding through his lands. The enormity of the task ahead was daunting and with few to help, it would take time despite the land being in good heart.

Calling all the men to council that evening he emphasised the need to produce food again.

"Any grain that can be saved will be milled as we need it but there is not a great deal, certainly not enough for the oxen during the winter. They will have to be grazed during the night or have grass cut for them. The soiled grain can be used as seed for the fields. I don't think even the wetting that it has suffered will stop it growing."

The miller's son grinned at Aelfric's description of how the grain had been despoiled by the raiders. He outlined his plans for restoring the prosperity of the estates, promising each tenant shares in the profit as his father had done before. At first many of the new-comers were sceptical of such a pledge, but the miller's son confirmed his new lord's words.

"Oh yes, my lord Udric gave each man a share of the wool money. We had coins of our own. Whatever a man's trade, and we had skills here to work leather, potting, weaving and well,... no matter where we worked we shared the Harvest feast, Christmas and so on. I for one will take lord Aelfric as my lord. Be my witnesses!"

The faith shown by one youth in Aelfric's ability to renew the profitability and viability of Uddings persuaded many others to follow suit.

Over the next few months many women were married to men who had lost their wives so that children would be born in wedlock. Alfan and her husband Edwin returned from the King's service to take over the running of Didlington. They had been living above the storehouses of the King's hunting lodge in Cranburne when the Danes had destroyed the palace in Wymburne. All their possessions were either stolen or wantonly smashed in the raid, causing Alfan to rail at their destructiveness. She was pleased to be back on familiar land, greeting those she knew with affection and sympathy. Having spent some time on the fringes of court life at the palace her gown was too highly decorated for practical work at Uddings. Reluctantly she took Emma's spare robe off the peg in her mother's room. With a wide belt she lifted the hem off the ground and covered the front with a linen apron.

Having lost her first baby, she was taking great care of herself during the early months of another pregnancy, but quickly agreed to supervise the preparation of meals for all those who remained. She sent a message to her cousin Udda who had recently taken over his father's farm at Woodcutts requesting a dozen in-lamb sheep to restock the pastures of the estate. Gail, now blossoming into a pretty woman, accompanied the wagon bringing surplus supplies to supplement the winter stores at her cousin's halls.

"Udric of Uddings helped my father in his time of need. Now it is our turn to repay that generosity. Many of the villagers have offered shelter. Hanlega was not touched by the raiders being only a poor village but the news of Wymburne's destruction has reached them and they pray for the townspeople."

Appalled by the conditions which greeted her arrival with the bawling sheep, she set to work with a will, baking and brewing ale to fill the store shelves again.

Traps were set to catch the eels in the stream and when an angry sow accidentally trampled a piglet, she supervised the cooking of every morsel of the tiny carcass.

Aelfric sent trusted men to Shaftesbury to buy cheeses, salt and milled flour to replenish the larders while others picked the autumn fruits, made new hurdles to fold the stock on the fields or hunted wildfowl. He silently thanked God for keeping his father's small store of silver pennies safe in the old oak tree.

Repairing the mill at Didlington would have to wait until he had the labour and the time. Until then bread would have to be made from bought flour, an expense he could well do without.

While the immediate grief was blunted, the underlying need for revenge simmered just beneath the surface. Even though the graves of those who died grassed over, no ox or sheep would graze there, constantly reminding all of the dreadful slaughter.

In the town the few survivors toiled to build themselves shelters taking any timbers which remained useable regardless of former ownership. They scavenged among the nunnery stores ignoring the guilt which pricked at consciences quickly hardened to permit such wanton behaviour.

The destruction of Wymburne by armed berserkers intent on terror, rape, killing and plunder left the living with little but embittered fury and their determination to re-build their houses, their church and their tight knit community. Above all, it left them with a deep-seated wish for revenge, a desire to take an eye for an eye at the very least and if God in his Mercy would look the other way for a few moments then the life of a Danish raider would make much better recompense.

No-one ever thought that the saintly Dunstan's curse when King Ethelred was crowned would fall so devastatingly upon the people.

Author's Note

The history of East Dorset has few charters but, of those still in existence, two of the oldest are for the small Saxon estate of Uddings on the outskirts of Wimborne, an area I know well. Only the King making the grant, the land involved and the name of the recipient are provided. Bear in mind that the name is spelled as the clerk heard it and a place name can be written in two different ways within the same document!

The characters have of necessity been shaped and moulded by what is known about the people at the time. Slaves were common and most land used for agriculture was between tranches of common or inhospitable waste-land. Towns and churches developed in easily defendable places.

Many historical facts recorded by monks or by chroniclers who wrote after the event and from the point of view of the victors, are woven into the story of ordinary people affected by the friendships, oaths of loyalty, brutality, diseases and other trials of the short life in Saxon times. The treatment of hostages, the deaths of shire leaders and churchmen are all true and can be studied for yourselves.

Names of many real characters are known and these have played their part in the forty years covered by this part of The King's Chalice trilogy. Again, history merely records their names and sometimes their positions. Their human traits and mannerisms as well as how they looked is all imaginary, the 'fleshing out' of the barest bones from dry and dusty sources.

Young King Edwy the Fair really did absent himself from his coronation feast to visit his mistress and the involvement of Dunstan of Abbotsbury, and his later miraculous escape when the council chamber floor collapsed have been recorded in myths and legends ever since.

Celestial events were recorded because the church was the centre of people's lives but knowledge of the old gods had not yet faded from consciousness. Seeing bright lights with tails searing across the night sky brought terror of the unknown. Curses were something to be feared, words spoken prophetically, which they believed would come true. Rain which arrived just in time to douse a raging fire was a gift from God.

Edward the Martyr has become a saint in the ancient history of this land but only reigned for three years and far preferred the company of hunting companions to those of his clerks and councillors. It is his untimely death for which he is remembered rather than any laws or deeds. The recovery of his body is down to speculation but the mystery of its apparent preservation and who actually struck the fatal blows has never been solved.

There was little accurate medical knowledge and no veterinary science at the time. With the benefit of hindsight, taking the few clues and descriptions recorded at the time, men of great knowledge think that King Alfred may have passed Crohne's Disease on to his descendants. Left untreated it would have been extremely unpleasant. Herbal remedies and those based on the four humours were the extent of the monastery Infirmarian's experience, the seeds of the opium poppy for pain relief a rare and expensive import. Water drawn from rivers was often downstream of places where noxious substances leached into tributary streams or fleeces were washed leading to frequent water-borne ailments in addition to the frequent visitations of the plague.

The murrains of cattle, goats, pigs and sheep might nowadays be classed as foot and mouth or a similar area-wide infectious disease.

I have tried to keep fact-tampering to a minimum. The date of the first Danish raid on Wimborne is not definitive and as many of the records would have been kept at the nunnery which was destroyed the facts are never likely to be discovered. Their raids were brutal massacres of villagers and townsfolk, women and girls raped, the churches stripped of any gold and silver ornaments, the stock either stolen or killed indiscriminately and virgin slaves were highly prized! That they were for the most part heathen endowed them with all the evil traits of character that the Saxon people could muster. Prayers were said in churches to preserve them from the Northern raiders.

History has not been kind to King Ethelred. Was he the mummy's boy so often portrayed or was he just young and totally inexperienced? He had never fought in battle, and knew that many thought him ineffective and naïve. His singular attempt to take the fight to the Danes at sea was foiled by the ongoing treachery of Aelfric.

Old terms for trades, foods, positions and animals have been used to add a flavour of the time when they were in common usage. Greetings and farewells often invoked the name of God, a strange notion perhaps for modern readers in this age of technology and theism. The fathers was omniscient, owning everything and everybody in his family. Women had little power except domestically, and had no influence over the events in their lives. They asked for permission to court or marry, for money to buy new cloth or trinkets. They were kept out of council meetings, the moots for the Hundred, inquests unless directly involved, and held no positions of authority. Any respect they gained was from doing good deeds and caring for those in the household or on their husband's estate or being particularly skilled in baking and brewing.

I hope I have brought the reader a better understanding of Saxon times, the founding of the kingdom melded from the tribal lands of the Britons and early settlers. Writing the trilogy of The King's Chalice has involved research into so many aspects of life in the 10th Century, the people, the food, the crops, animals, beliefs and so much more. It has been a genuine voyage of discovery which the reader is invited to share as we move towards the momentous events of the Norman invasion.

Janet K L Seal
December 2014